Echoes of Forgotten Places

Echoes of Forgotten Places

HELEN F. WAND

Author of *Where Eagles Nest*

LUMINARE PRESS
WWW.LUMINAREPRESS.COM

Echoes of Forgotten Places

Printed in the United States of America

Luminare Press
442 Charnelton St.
Eugene, OR 97401
www.luminarepress.com

LCCN: 2021909156
ISBN: 978-1-64388-594-0

To our sisters,
Ruthie and Dorothy

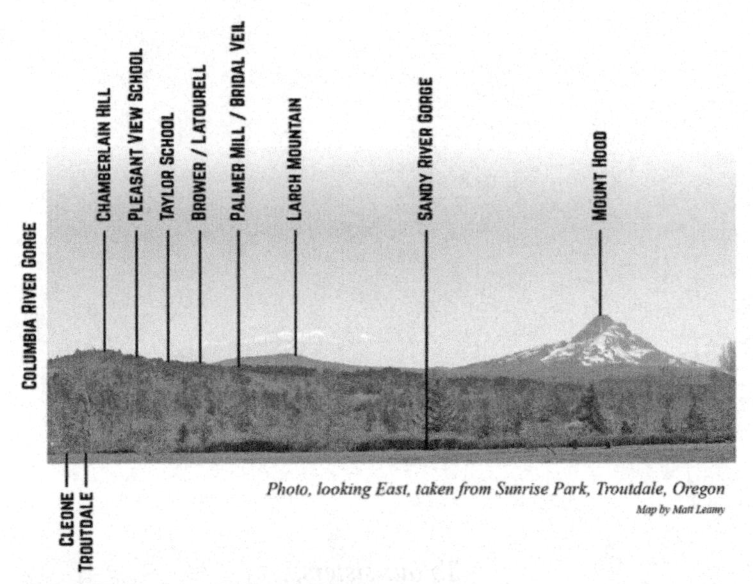

Photo, looking East, taken from Sunrise Park, Troutdale, Oregon

Map by Matt Leamy

About the Title: Echoes of Forgotten Places

On the bluff overlooking the confluence of the Sandy and Columbia Rivers is a 900-foot volcanic mountain identified on late nineteenth century maps as Chamberlain Hill. Named after a family of early settlers Chamberlain Road is snugged into the eastern edge of the hillside where it winds its way down to a landing on the banks of the Columbia.

Pleasant View School stood on the southern ridge of Chamberlain Hill overlooking the deep cleft of the Sandy River Gorge. A small contingent of area settlers constructed the school in 1887 and it soon became the focal point of their community. Nothing is left of the school and many of the families are gone, but their names live on in area roads: Siedl, Lampert, Marok, Mershon, Ogden, Nielson, Wand, and Woodard.

Unincorporated East Multnomah County ranges from the Sandy River to the west, east passed Larch Mountain to the county line, south as far as Ames, and north to the Columbia River. At one time this region contained Pleasant View as well as ten other schools covering approximately 134 square miles; *the area Corbett School District #39 incorporated in the early 1920's. Informally called Staggerweed Mountain by area locals, people who lived there were glued together by the schools, small hamlets, and mill towns. Many settlements no longer exist and this area is again marked primarily by roads named for families: Brower, Hurlbert, Knieriem, Evans, Ellis, Benfield, Louden, Palmer Mill, and others.

The once vibrant mill town of Bridal Veil has shrunk to a cemetery and a post office operating in the former mill tool shed. A few families live in Latourell today and the now privately-owned school building still stands. Ames is a neighborhood near the Clackamas County line. These places, along with Hurlbert, were once thriving settlements; while Pleasant View, Mountain, and Egypt had only their schools. Springdale won the "coin toss" over its former name Gage. Taylor, rumored to have changed owners due to a gambling debt, was renamed Corbett and is now the largest of the remaining Staggerweed Mountain villages.

In the 21st century, five generations later, new families have moved into the area where pastures and fields were cleared of forest 150 years ago by pioneers and farmers. Echoes of Forgotten Places brings the reader into the lives of these early settlers who raised their families and survived in the remote, rural area between the Gorges of the Sandy and Columbia Rivers.

* 1. Corbett School District #39, General Obligation Refunding Bonds, Series 2008, Section265(b)(3)(B)of the Internal Revenue Code of 1986, as amended. 2008

2. Klock, Dorothy, Crown Point Country Schools, 1874 – 1974, 1st Edition, copyright, 1973

ABOUT THE TITLE

Echoes of Forgotten Places

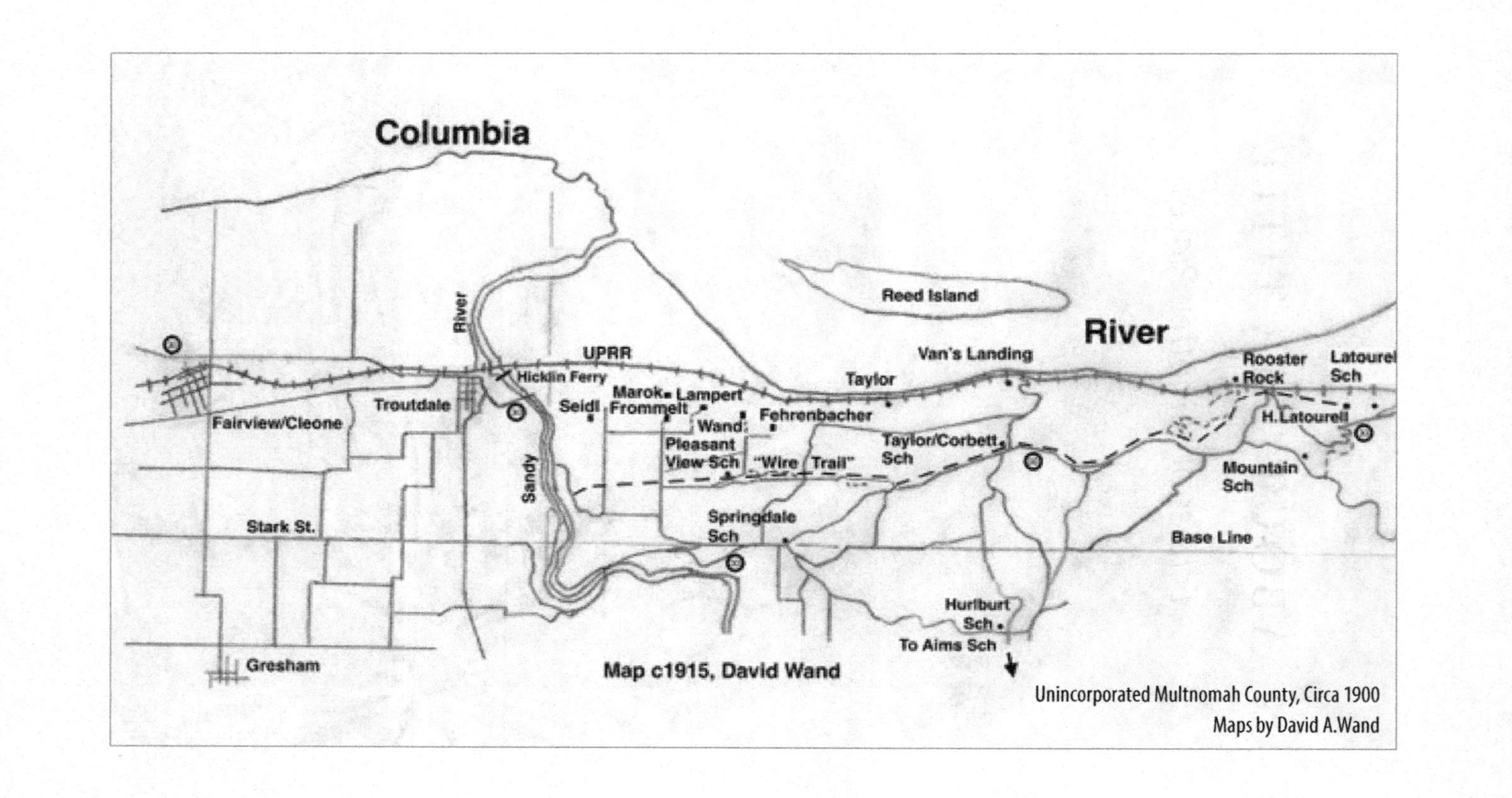

Unincorporated Multnomah County, Circa 1900

Maps by David A.Wand

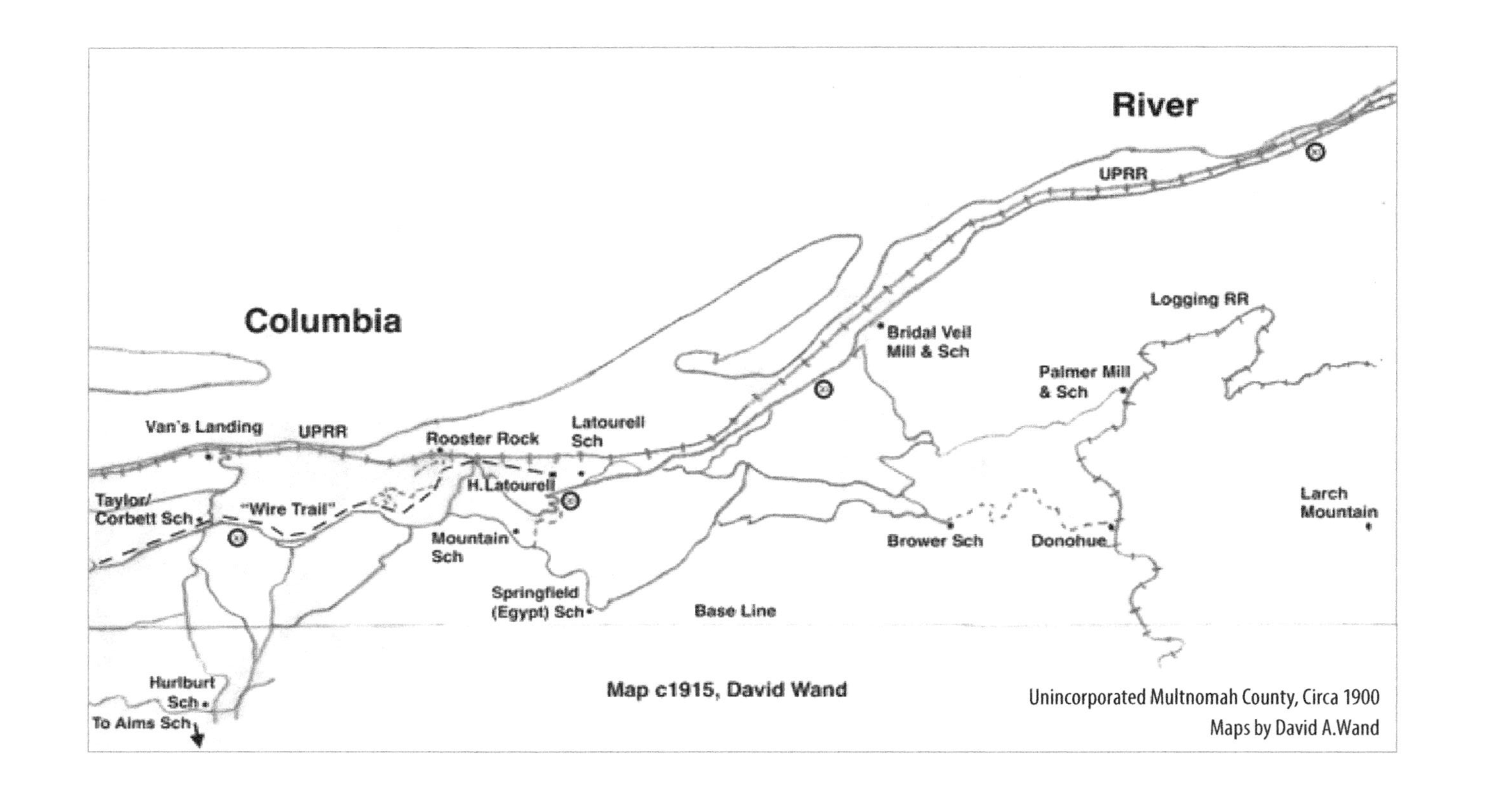

Unincorporated Multnomah County, Circa 1900
Maps by David A.Wand

PROLOGUE

Late Winter 1897

On the trail by the corner where the Frommelts' and Lamperts' properties met, Katherine Frommelt approached the cross marking the spot where they had buried Julianna Lampert's husband, Alex, last September.

Julianna, Katherine's best friend and confidante, had been young and lighthearted when they first met in Illinois back in '82. Julianna roomed with her and Franz while making wedding arrangements with Alex . Thrilled then to be the bridesmaid for her new friend, Katherine shuddered now at the thought of how life changed Julianna—her eyes dark and hollow and ladened with a strange combination of fear and sorrow.

Two Lampert crosses now stood at the corner, the second for the Lamperts' youngest child, Bernard. Julianna's baby had died on Christmas Eve. Consumption, the doctor called it, the same as his father. Now her friend faced a life of loneliness while raising her eight remaining children. Close to penniless, Julianna's only possession was the homestead land, deep in the wilderness of the Columbia Gorge.

Katherine turned her gaze toward heaven, *"How could you be so unfair?"* The cold east wind burned her lips and seared her eyes.

She stopped at the graves as her thoughts drifted back to that fateful week before Christmas when the baby's illness had become more severe. The weather had turned ugly with rain and high winds.

"Julianna's baby's very sick," Franz had said, as he came in from the barn, water dripping from his hat. She remembered the two older Lampert boys, Ferd, age nine, and Arnold, age seven, standing soaked and shivering behind him. Katherine wasn't sure if there were tears running down the children's cheeks or rivulets of rain.

"She needs us right away."

Katherine gave her oldest daughter, Mary, a few quick instructions, grabbed what rain clothes she owned, and immediately left with Franz, who carried the lantern. The boys followed close behind as they hurried down the muddy path.

When they arrived, Julianna's eldest child, Tracy, stone-faced, asked Katherine for help making hot mustard compresses for the two-year-old, and Franz took over supervision of the other children. Katherine remembered feeling useless. Nothing she or the girl did seemed to help the toddler's wheezing.

After a short while, Julianna asked Franz to please hurry to Troutdale and fetch the doctor. Katherine had agreed, grateful that the storm had passed.

Franz gathered the lantern once again and headed out into the darkness. It was close to daylight when he returned with Doctor Volp. The kindly doctor brought a bottle of medicine that smelled rank and musty, but seemed to quiet the wheezing child, and for a while the small group felt some hope for the toddler.

Katherine, Franz, and the three older Lampert sisters toiled, helping where they could, for the rest of that day and all the next night, but the baby's cry went from a whimper to an inaudible gurgle. Julianna worked even more frantically, but the baby's soul seemed to slip from their hands. Just after dark the third day, the toddler breathed his last, and the house was still except for the occasional sniffle of an older brother or sister.

Julianna sat quietly in the rocking chair that Alex had so lovingly made. In her lap lay the small still child. All night, she stared at some unseen thing on the ceiling. In the morning Franz went home to build a coffin and a cross, and on his way back, he dug a small grave beside the child's father.

Katherine stayed on, helping with the burial preparations and household chores, but more for emotional support, as she realized Julianna's inability to carry out even the most insignificant duties.

The following day, the four Catholic families who lived in the small community attended the service, which Franz officiated. He promised to get to Portland as soon as possible to bring a priest out to say Mass and bless the final resting place.

Now, Katherine shuddered again as she remembered what a tragic Christmas that had been for everyone. Tracy, at thirteen, seemed to be frozen in a stupor, unable to comprehend even the simplest commands. For a moment, Katherine had been as worried about her as she was for Julianna, but soon after the service, the young girl regained her senses. She put her grief in a drawer somewhere in her mind, and slid it closed. Tracy's recovery was as visible as it was immediate, and she took charge of her mourning family.

Only Julianna seemed unable to recover. As the dreary winter days turned into weeks, each of the neighbor women took turns checking in on the family. A late January snowstorm kept the women at home for several days and after the thaw, Katherine went to the Lamperts. When she returned home, she said that Julianna had brightened up somewhat during the visit.

"I can see a bit of her old self now," she had told Franz.

But in recent weeks when she visited Julianna, she was unable to find it. When she looked at Julianna and listened to her voice, Katherine sensed something inside her friend had died with her husband and child. As time passed, she became more sure of it, but kept her counsel and smiled as enthusiastically as possible when people marveled at the widow's recovery.

PART I

Children of the Hill

Chapter 1

EARLY SPRING 1897

Pleasant View School
Tracy Lampert

Tracy felt eyes on the back of her head and turned to peek. He was staring again. Why did he keep doing that? Flustered, she lost her place.

"Theresa, please continue," the teacher, Mr. Allard, said, his voice stern.

"Yes, sir," Tracy said, wishing the floor would swallow her. *"And the voice of that wayward song is singing and saying still: 'A boy's will is the wind's will, and the thoughts of youth are long, long thoughts.'"*

"That will do, Theresa," Mr. Allard commanded. "You don't do much for Longfellow's work." He paused and looked around the room. "Logan, you seem to be somewhere else; let's bring you back to school. Come to the front of the room and read the next passage."

She heard Logan get up from his seat, his footsteps moving up the aisle, and then he was beside her. When he reached for the book, he mouthed, "Will you?"

"Maybe," she murmured, her eyes avoiding his.

Logan began reading, but Tracy's thoughts were elsewhere. *Mother probably has something else for us to do*, she thought. *She would never let me see Logan.* She argued with herself. *But it's only a picnic; he just wants me to share my basket with him. What could be wrong with that?*

Logan's voice droned on. The oppressive humidity in the room added to her already sweaty palms and sticky petticoat. And what about Lucy?

A few days before, her best friend, Lucy Mershon, had confided to Tracy and her sister Emma that she thought Logan was the nicest-looking boy in school. *I'm not telling her that I think so too,* she remembered thinking at the time.

"I want to marry him," Lucy had said, and Tracy had agreed that Lucy was pretty enough. Any boy would want to marry her.

If the truth be known, Logan Chamberlain, with his dark curly hair and laughing eyes—one of the older boys attending Pleasant View School—had most of the girls' attention, and certainly Mr. Allard's. The stern teacher's eyes were usually focused on him, his friends, and their antics. Rumor had it that Mr. Ogden, the school clerk, had recruited a male teacher to deal with the bigger boys, who at times could be unruly and disruptive. In Tracy's view, they were often downright disgusting.

But Logan's attitude seemed to have changed this year. Tracy wondered if she were imagining things. He seemed nicer to her since Papa died. He told her once how sorry he was and asked if he could do something. She had lowered her eyes and murmured, "Thank you, no," and wished she had said more before he turned and left her standing by the schoolroom door. That was several weeks ago, and since then his eyes softened when he looked at her. That is when she finally mustered up the courage to look him in the eye.

For heaven's sake, she scolded herself, I'm acting like

a silly goose.

"Logan likes you," her sister Bertie said later on the way home from school.

"Of course, he likes all the girls." Tracy said, tossing her hair, indignant that Bertie had brought up the subject.

"Yeah, but he likes you best," Emma said, guiding their seven-year-old brother, Arnold, around a protruding tree root in the trail. "Isn't that right, Mary?"

Mary Frommelt at thirteen was close to Tracy's age and a year older than Emma, and had been their playmate since they could remember. Tracy loved her happy disposition and wished her hair was as curly as Mary's.

"Maybe, but I think Leroy Mershon is much handsomer, anyway."

"I think so too," Bertie piped up. "He's so manly."

"What do you know about 'manly,' Bertie?" Emma said. "You're only ten years old."

"I'll be eleven in September," Bertie retorted.

"Don't quarrel, girls," Mary said. "You know how I hate it."

Tracy chose to ignore the conversation and turned to see their brother Ferd and the Frommelt boys engrossed in a long-dead rabbit they'd found at the trail's edge. "Ferd, come on! Get away from that nasty thing," she urged. "You know Mother wants us to walk straight home. Besides, we might get wet if we don't hurry."

The rain started slowly, a drop here and there, spurring them on down the trail to the back stoop of the Lampert home. The Frommelt children waited in the kitchen for the shower to pass before continuing on their way home.

"Mama, can we go to the picnic next Saturday?" Bertie

asked amid the lively chatter. "It's going to be so fun. The older girls are supposed to bring a picnic basket to share with a boy."

"You're not an older girl," Emma said, with a sniff.

"Well, you're not either; you're only twelve." Bertie wasn't one to let something go. "Besides, Logan Chamberlain wants Tracy to share a basket with him."

"You don't know that," Tracy said, stealing a glance at her mother. She noticed her mother's lips tighten, but she remained silent.

Tracy's stomach churned.

Later in the evening, when the younger children were tucked in bed and the older girls were finishing their homework at the table, Julianna came and sat down.

"The lamp is getting low, girls," she said, her voice quiet and kind. "Are you almost done with your papers?"

"Yes, Mama." Tracy feared what was coming next.

"Good, I'm proud of you. You've worked hard and have learned English very well." Their mother spoke in German when they conversed, having never mastered the strange and difficult new language. It seemed to Tracy that she quit trying after Papa died. After all, the neighbors were German, so there was little need of her to put forth the effort.

Inwardly, Tracy sighed with relief. Maybe Mama would let them go to the picnic.

"But you must remember," their Mother continued, "school is for one thing only. You must learn to read and write. The picnics are fun, and I wish we could go more often, but we have planting to do, and that needs to be done as soon as Joseph can get the ground ready."

The girls nodded sadly.

Julianna paused, looked at her oldest daughter, and

continued, "And Tracy, remember that Logan comes from a Protestant family. He's a nice young man, but your Papa would never have let you see a non-Catholic boy."

As Tracy walked into the schoolyard the following Monday, Logan came around the corner near the steps and beckoned to her.

"Where were you on Saturday?" he asked, walking toward her. When he reached her, he laid his hand on her shoulder.

"We had chores to do, Logan," she said. "We all had to help." She paused and made herself look at him. "I am sorry. I wanted to come," she said touching his hand.

"Next week will be my last week of school this year. Papa wants me to help him on the tie drive down the Sandy River."

"That's such dangerous work." Tracy felt a lump in her throat, picturing him jumping from railroad tie to railroad tie as he guided the log raft down the river from the saw mill to the railroad yard in Troutdale. "Are you sure you want to do that?"

"Yes, I'm excited about it. I'll make good money, but it means I won't see you every day."

Tracy caught her breath, and her heart sank.

"May I come to call?" he continued softly.

Tracy hesitated. "I want you to, but Mother is very strict." Her heart raced as she looked into his pleading eyes. "Maybe you could come over and ask her."

He nodded. "I'll do that." He took his hand away but seemed reluctant to end the conversation as they made their way toward the schoolhouse.

When they arrived inside, Tracy was surprised to see

a stranger: a young woman greeting the students. She had dark auburn hair with lots of large curls and a kindness that seemed to surround her and settle in her green eyes. The lady smiled cordially and nodded to her. Tracy couldn't help but smile back.

"Good morning, students," the new teacher said when everyone had taken their seats. "My name is Miss Block, and I am your substitute teacher until the end of the year."

"Good morning, Miss Block," the students spoke in unison.

"As you know, Mr. Allard likes to take some time off during the spring salmon run to help with the seining at Rooster Rock," she continued, her voice pleasant.

Tracy could hear the boys in the back snickering like they always did around pretty young teachers. She wanted to say something. Instead, she turned and gave them a stern look, which silenced them for the moment.

As the morning droned on, and the younger children recited, the boys became louder and more unruly.

"Oh Lord, what a racket," Miss Block suddenly shouted. "I expect quiet in this room while these youngsters read." Her eyes flared.

"Please continue, Josie," she said as she glared at the back wall where the older boys sat. Eight-year-old Josie, Tracy's youngest sister, began her recitation again, her soft voice barely audible to the students sitting behind her.

After Josie finished reciting, Miss Block, her curls shimmering in the late morning sun streaming through the window said, "It's stuffy in here. You, the tall boy in the dark shirt," she pointed to Logan, "please open the door and prop it."

Logan did as he was told, his heavy boots clomping on

the log hewn floor. As he reached the door, a paper wad went flying over the younger children and landed on the teacher's desk.

Miss Block ignored it and went on with her work. It seemed strange to Tracy that she didn't acknowledge the defiant act. Mr. Allard would never have let that go.

Tracy noticed after Logan returned to his seat, he lowered his head as if concentrating on his assignment. She couldn't tell if he was actually reading, but it appeared he was. She had noticed that he paid more attention to his studies lately and, anyway, she knew he would never do something as stupid as throwing a paper wad.

Tracy went back to studying her spelling words while trying not to listen to the younger children stumble over their lessons.

"Who the devil closed the door?" The teacher's voice startled Tracy. The gracious lady who seemed so polite had just cursed!

Logan dutifully got up, opened it again, and climbed back in his seat, trying not to get his long legs tangled in the small space beneath his desk. He went back to his studies, but not before he glanced at Tracy and smiled. She smiled back and tried hard not to let her cheeks burn, but they did.

"MISS BLOCK USES BAD WORDS," BERTIE SAID AS SHE AND Emma sat eating their lunch in the play shed later.

"Mother wouldn't like it," Emma agreed, picking up on some of the older girl's use of the word "mother." At age twelve, it was evident that she was trying to sound grown-up.

"Let's not tell, girls," Tracy said, overhearing the conversation. She, Lucy, Mary, Sue Chamberlain, and Hattie and Alma Graham were off by themselves, a treat the older girls rarely enjoyed. "Miss Block's a nice lady. I'd use bad words, too, if I had to deal with the likes of those boys."

As the days passed, Miss Block became more and more agitated. Tracy couldn't blame her. She wished Mr. Allard didn't want to fish and was back in the classroom. He had kept the boys in line, and everyone learned more.

One day, the following week, when lunch period was almost over and everyone was still outside playing, Alowis Frommelt, standing next to the window, whistled quietly and motioned for everyone to come over. They took turns looking in the windows and came away with shocked expressions.

When Tracy's turn came, she saw Miss Block seated at her desk, her head completely bald, and her hair in her hands.

"Oh, my goodness," Mary said, standing next to Tracy.

"How can that be?" Hattie murmured, looking over Tracy's shoulder.

Stunned, Tracy couldn't stop staring.

"What happened to her hair?" Bertie asked, her eyes wide.

Tracy shook her head. "I don't know," she murmured. "I've never seen anything like it." Bewildered, she gazed at the strange scene.

Some of the smaller children ran into the school to get a closer look. Miss Block, startled, quickly placed the wad of now tumbled hair back on her head. Without a mirror and in her haste, it perched cock-eyed, covering one eye with a curl. Hastily, she wrestled with it until it looked better, but not before some of the big boys saw it and their snickers turned to outright laughter.

"What's the matter? Haven't you children ever seen a wig before?" she asked, red-faced.

The children circled her desk, wide-eyed, unable to believe their eyes. They gathered in small groups until Miss Block called for order, but the children could not settle down. Whispers and giggles could be heard throughout the room. Flustered, Miss Block dismissed school early.

"MAMA! MAMA! SHE WAS—" JOSIE AND FERD RUSHED into the kitchen eager to tell their mother about the bald-headed teacher. In their haste they tripped over each other and almost knocked little Arnold onto the floor.

"She didn't have any hair on her head," Bertie said, coming in the kitchen right behind them.

"What do you mean, no hair?" Julianna looked puzzled.

"She is bald, Mother. She has a wig," Tracy explained. "And she took it off when the classroom was empty. Alowis saw her through the window and called us over to see."

"A wig?"

"Yes, it's false hair. We didn't know what it was either," Emma interjected, "but Miss Block told us. She got all red in the face. She told us a runaway team of horses scared her so bad she lost her hair."

"Then she told us all to go home," said Bertie, sitting on the kitchen bench, her legs swinging.

"Yes, and she says bad words," Josie piped up.

"What are bad words?" Julianna asked appearing puzzled at the thought; English was still almost indecipherable to her.

"She said '*devil*' and '*Lord*,'" said Ferd, who laughed and bounced the ball he had received for Christmas. "And she even called us *foolish*. That's probably the worst one."

Tracy, silent, wondered what her mother would say and was surprised when Julianna only shook her head.

The next morning, Mr. Allard was back at school.

Chapter 2

APRIL 1897

Julianna

Julianna set her pen into the inkwell and glanced through the window at her good-hearted neighbor and Katherine's brother, Joseph Marok. She watched the mud fly from the horses' hooves as he made the last turn in the field.

Rain traveling down the glass blurred her vision and reminded her of the tragedies of the past year. She wished the pouring water could wash them away. If only she could bundle up her children and whisk them home to her family in Baden. Run away from all the heartache and worry flooding over her, leaving her with a feeling of helplessness that she did her best to hide from the children.

This morning she had been surprised to see Joseph walking down the lane, leading his horse. A five-gallon bucket was carelessly slung over his arm.

"Joseph, what brings you here today?" she had asked. Standing on the front porch, her arms were wrapped in her apron to stave off the early chill. "I thought you weren't going to get to our field until next week."

"I just got a feelin', Julianna." He stood, his eyes fixed on the southwestern sky. "I just got to thinkin' this looks like rain. I've been in this country long enough to know we can get some healthy storms in April. I finished my field early, so today's your turn."

Julianna smiled her thanks.

"You know how hard it is this time of year to get the crops in the ground. I couldn't pass up the chance," he continued, handing her the lidded metal bucket. "Here's your seed. It's all there: carrot, corn, and bean." He paused, adjusting the reins as he spoke. "I picked it up for you when I went to Troutdale to get mine."

"I truly don't know what I'd do without you," Julianna said. "And the other neighbors," she hastened to add.

"We help each other," he said, shrugging his shoulders. "Remember, Elma's baby will come next month." He smiled, showing his gleaming white teeth through his mustache. He had let it grow over the winter, and Elma liked it so well, she asked him not to shave until the summer got too warm.

It was true; Julianna had attended most births in the community. If she needed help, her neighbor, Katherine, was always there, either to watch her children or to help with the birthing. She always thought the two of them made a good team.

As she turned to go back into the house, she nodded to him and thought about all the springtime work and how it helped to take her mind away, but not her heavy heart.

Joseph's prediction came true. It started raining just as he was finishing. Now the field was drenched. She would have to wait to plant until the earth dried. She smiled ruefully and wondered how fate had brought her as a young woman all the way to America from the village of Malch in Germany's state of Baden and finally to Oregon and this farm above the Columbia River.

She hurriedly finished the letter to her mother, carefully addressed the envelope, and ran to catch Joseph before he left.

"Mail this, please," she said, pulling it from her skirt pocket, trying to keep it dry. "Why don't you put the horse in the barn? We have plenty of hay. I'll see the children feed him."

Joseph nodded. "I'd be grateful to do that," he said. "I've been working him pretty hard the last couple of days. He will have more rest if he stays here, and I'll have to disk this one more time anyway." He headed toward the small barn to unhook the disk and rub down the wet horse.

When she went back into the house, Julianna glanced at the clock on the shelf at the foot of the stairs. Near two-thirty, she thought. The children should be home in an hour or so and would be wet and cold.

She could hear the two younger boys stirring in the bedroom as they woke from their naps. Smiling, she thought of how Jackie, who'd just turned five, was indignant about a rest, protesting that he was too old and that he went to school in good weather. Once again she'd had to remind him that when he was home, a short rest in the afternoon was good for him. She was far too protective of her two younger sons. He and little Alex, who was about to turn four, were not going to follow the path of her husband and baby boy. Determined not to lose anyone else, she shivered and went into the kitchen to stir the fire.

Tracy would turn fourteen in June and loved school. *I don't know how to tell her,* Julianna thought, wishing there were some other way. She doubted the forty-five dollars she received from the sale of the eastern twenty acres of the homestead would last until fall.

"I'll give it until midsummer, and if things look bad, then I'll talk to her," she said out loud, with much resolve.

Chapter 3

JUNE 1897

Julianna

"Mama, please come," Emma begged Julianna. "Everyone will be there."

Julianna sat with her chin in her hands, half listening to the children's chatter around the table.

"Yes, Mama," Ferd chimed in. "I'm supposed to recite 'Beat, Beat the Drums.' Walt Whitman wrote it, and it's about war. I know the first two verses." A shadow crossed his face but quickly disappeared. "I still have trouble with the third one. Please Mama, come hear me," he said, his eyes shining.

Julianna's heart warmed to see her nine-year-old son looking happy for the first time since they lost their father. "Since it will make you happy, we'll go to the end-of-the-year school picnic," she said. *Alex would have insisted that we go.*

The children's father had never missed a chance to visit with his neighbors. Julianna's English, never strong, did not seem to be a problem for the small community of Pleasant View. Most were northern European and could speak enough German to converse with one another. She always enjoyed herself when visiting with her neighbors. The truth be told, she loved the people of the area dearly; she recalled how they helped her through her darkest days.

It's just that sometimes it was all she could do to get out of bed in the morning, let alone get ready for a picnic. *Come, come, this will never do,* she chided, pulling herself out of the familiar slump. *We are all going, and we're going to enjoy it.*

She found herself remembering the excitement in the air when Alex and Franz had helped John Smith, the clerk, finish building the school. She and Katherine were there when Smith's daughter, Blanche, named it.

"I think the view from this ridge is so beautiful. Look, you can see Mount Hood over there," Blanche had said, pointing to the east. "It's such a pleasant place. And look, the Sandy River Gorge is down there." She pointed to the rolling forested hills to the south where the Sandy River, a greenish brown ribbon, peeked through the trees as it wound its way toward its two mouths, each dumping its flow into the Columbia. She had paused, and her face had lit up. "I know, let's call it Pleasant View School!"

Julianna remembered how everyone had agreed that it was the perfect name, and how over the years, it had become more than a school. It served as a community center and a meeting place. The men had a barn raising a year after it opened and built a large play shed behind the school where, even on rainy days, the children could go out for a breath of fresh air and to spend some of their energy. The thought suddenly made her want to go and bathe in the warmth of her kindly neighbors.

"Mama! Tracy, Emma, and I are going to be in the spelling bee," Bertie said, her voice an octave higher in her excitement. "I'm going to win this year."

Yes, Julianna thought. *I must make the effort. We'll all be better off.*

Aloud she said, "Tracy, why don't you take Ferd and run to Katherine's? Tell her we plan on walking with them to the picnic tomorrow. Ask her what she's going to bring, and find out if Joseph and Elma can join us."

"Yes, Mama! We'll go right now." Tracy jumped up from the breakfast table and snatched her sweater from the back of her chair.

"Be careful, now!" Julianna called to them as the door closed, but they were already running down the lane toward the gate.

Bertie rose from her chair, smiled the smile that reminded Julianna of Alex, and began to clear the table. Josie followed close behind, her feet fairly dancing with glee.

"The first readers are going to sing, 'America,'" Arnold proudly told his mother. "It starts with 'My Country 'Tis of Thee.'"

"That's wonderful! I can hardly wait to hear it," Julianna said as she wiped the milk off Little Alex's mouth. She winced at the nickname. Alex had given most of the children shorter versions of their names, and she had learned to live with that. But Alex, his namesake, he had insisted on calling *Little Alex*—"so people won't get us mixed up," he had told her with a laugh.

"Next year I go to school every day," Jackie said, patting his mother's arm.

"Yes, dear, next year," his mother said absently as she smoothed his silky hair back from his eyes, wondering again what would happen to them all and where they would be a year from now.

Everyone had fun at the picnic, and to Julianna's surprise, she even forgot her heartache for a moment. Until she looked up from where she was sitting and searched the group of men, wondering if Alex was getting hungry. Tears came when she realized he wasn't there, but she blinked them back before anyone could see.

"Can I get you a plate?" Katherine murmured softly, her hand on Julianna's arm. Somehow, Katherine always knew. *Perhaps it's the way I hold my head?* Julianna wondered. It puzzled her, the way Katherine owned the uncanny ability to see things that weren't obvious to most people.

Julianna remembered the time that Katherine had hurried up the trail to meet her and the children. Her friend was frantic, knowing that something had happened to them—and she had been right. Julianna and the children had come upon a rabid wolf-like beast in the middle of the path. Probably a hybrid dog, Alex later guessed. She had sent the children running back to fetch their father and he killed it. Katherine had come running upon the scene and held Julianna as Alex buried the beast and Julianna finally quit shaking. "I just knew you were in trouble," she said over and over again. "I was afraid something terrible had happened to you."

"I don't know," Katherine said and shook her head when Julianna asked her how she'd known about her peril.

She asked again later, when they sat over a cup of coffee, and Katherine told her that her grandmother also could tell when certain things were going to happen. She added, "My mother said it had bypassed her and she was glad."

"Glad? Why was she happy about that?"

"Because Grandmother told her it was a big responsibility, knowing things about people and whether to tell them or not." That puzzled Julianna, and she wondered if Katherine had known about Alex and Bernard's impending deaths. She never discussed it with her, though, and doubted she ever would.

"I'm going to get you a plate of food," Katherine said again, jarring Julianna back to the present. "You're just too thin. It's my job to put some meat back on those bones."

Julianna laughed at that. She had been plump all of her life and knew that under different circumstances she would love to be her present size.

Katherine and Anna Graham, another neighbor, wandered off to the picnic table, and Julianna found herself visiting with Maria Seidl. She liked the tall raw-boned Bavarian woman. They had become fast friends since Maria and her husband, Jacob, had bought the farm near the Bluff Trail to Troutdale seven years ago. The Lamperts and Frommelts had celebrated the Seidls' arrival, which meant there was a third Catholic family on the hill.

Later, when Joseph arrived and brought his wife, Elma, it added a fourth, all clustered together within a mile. Now they hoped a traveling priest from Mount Angel Seminary might come to them someday and celebrate Mass in one of the homes.

"Jacob stopped at St. Joseph Church in Portland on his way home the other day," Maria said, hoisting Elizabeth, her toddler, onto her lap.

"Oh, I do miss that little church. All of the children were baptized there except Tracy," Julianna said, remembering the happy times they'd had taking each baby into the city and staying with Matt and Sophie Foeller. The baptisms were happy celebrations, with good company and good food. She loved the Foellers, but had been unable to write to them about the deaths. Thank goodness Katherine had done it.

"Yes, it is so nice to be among people who speak German, isn't it?" Maria agreed.

Julianna nodded and was surprised to find herself smiling.

"Jacob says he talked to Father Schwartzman," Maria continued as she rocked her child. "He says we should be able to have a priest out here soon, especially to consecrate the graves. Father said that was the excuse they needed to get us on the circuit."

"I would like that. We need his blessing. We're miles from nowhere up here." Missing her little German village, Julianna tried to keep the bitterness from her voice. She knew she should not blame the rugged country for taking her loves, but sometimes the thought snuck in. Each time she stomped it into the ground or flung it away, but here it was, rearing its head again.

"It's too bad we need an excuse, but when Jacob questioned Father about it, he said that the graves indicate a community and stability."

"Well, thank God we have community even if it took two deaths to do it," Julianna heard herself saying, with a hint of bitterness. She thought about the happy community before the graves were in place and wondered at the sanity of the statement. She knew that Franz's earlier request for a priest probably helped confirm the need, so she was happy that he had petitioned.

"Here's your dinner," Katherine said, interrupting the conversation and handing Julianna one of the two plates she carried.

Alice Ogden and Sarah Mershon came to join the group of friends, and they ate and chatted until the program began.

Tracy once again won the spelling bee. Julianna could tell Bertie's dismay by the look on her face. Emma looked like she didn't care and told her mother she was glad that awful Freddy Dunn lost because "he was mean," and she didn't like him. Emma had more distinct opinions than her sisters. It made Julianna think of her own sister, Theresa, and how solid her beliefs were at such a young age. Emma doesn't care much if she is liked or disliked by her classmates, Julianna thought. It is more important for her to be comfortable with her convictions.

The first reader class sang their hearts out, and only a couple of the children were off-key. The audience didn't care. They were hungry for music and enjoyed anything remotely resembling a choir. The families had a special treat when young Bert Chamberlain played "Turkey in the Straw" on his harmonica, accompanied by his father, Lige, playing a lively fiddle. When they were done, the crowd whooped and hollered and stomped their feet until the pair commenced playing "Sweet Genevieve."

Julianna would have been happy just to listen to them for the rest of the afternoon. The music made her feet itch to dance and reminded her of the lively German tunes that she and Alex had danced to that summer in Baden when they fell in love.

The pair played two more songs, bowed, and promised to practice Christmas carols for the December holiday party. Then the children were back to reciting their presentations, and all too soon the afternoon waned into evening. People gathered their things and their tired children and headed for home in the twilight, traveling different directions over the paths leading away from the school.

In spite of herself, Julianna had had a pleasant time. The children had not been this lively since before that awful day in September when they realized they were losing their father. With the passing of their baby brother, Christmas was almost more than any of them could bear. Consumption is a terrible disease, she thought; it stole my husband, my child, and part of my soul.

Her memories made her realize, once again, how very much all the children depended on her now. She must go on leading the way, to raise these young people: an overwhelming responsibility. At that moment she realized this was a feat she didn't know exactly how to accomplish.

Chapter 4

LATE MAY 1897

Logan and Julianna

Tracy spotted Logan coming out of the woods from the school trail. She resisted the urge to run to him and instead calmly stood up and smoothed her skirt. She wanted to pat her hair, but her hands were dirty from crawling on the ground weeding carrots. She knew she would never get to the house without him seeing her, so she pushed the hair out of her eyes with the back of her hand and waved.

He was close enough for her to see his face light up as he waved back and picked up his pace.

"Hello!" he called as he came closer.

"Hello, yourself," Tracy replied.

"I'm telling Mother," Emma said as she got up from her hands and knees.

"No, you are not," Tracy hissed through clenched teeth as she continued to smile. "You're kneeling right back down there." She struggled to keep her anger in check. "I'm taking him to Mother myself, and you, my dear sister, will not interfere." She pronounced the last three words definitively. Emma, approaching womanhood, was sometimes beginning to be more of an annoyance than a friend.

Emma surprised her by doing as she was told, while the other children watched with eager interest. Emma's compliance, along with Logan's presence, shocked them into silence. No one ever believed that Logan would really come to see Tracy. Mama was much too against it, but here he was almost running down the path toward Tracy, his long curly black hair bouncing on top of his head, and the curls on his forehead moist with sweat.

My goodness, he is handsome. The thought ran through Tracy's head, just before she was overcome with mortification, remembering her dirt-smeared clothes and hands. I hope my face is clean.

"Hello to all of you," Logan said, grinning widely at the children, who stared in awe. Bertie let out a barely discernable sigh.

"How come you're here?" Ferd was the first to find his voice. "You're supposed to be floating down the Sandy River on railroad ties."

"We just finished the first drive," Logan answered while looking at Tracy.

"Oh my, was it fun?" Bertie said breathlessly, gazing at him with wide-eyed admiration. "I think you are very brave."

How dare she look at him like that? Tracy caught herself and felt silly for feeling jealous of her younger sister.

"It's nice to see you, Logan." Tracy wished the others were anywhere but here.

"Thank you," he replied. "I came as soon as I got off the river."

"That's nice." Flattered, Tracy felt at a loss for words.

She took a deep breath and, finding courage she thought she didn't have, said, "Let's go to the house. I can clean up, and we can talk to Mother." Julianna had gone into the house earlier to tend to Little Alex, who had awoken with a fever and sore throat that morning.

"You don't need to clean up," Logan said. "You look cute with that dirt smudge on your nose," he teased her.

Her cheeks burned. If he thinks I look cute now, he must really like me.

"You've been gone from school two weeks. Does it take that long to bring the ties down river?"

"Oh no, I had to help in the mill first. There weren't many ties in the pond when I got there."

"Pond?" Ferd's face shone with admiration.

"It belongs to Lloyd Lowe. He owns the tie and lumber mill up on Walker Creek, near Aims," Logan said without taking his eyes off Tracy. "I get to ride a log raft all the way down the Sandy River to Troutdale." He grinned at her, his eyes twinkling.

"Was it fun?" Arnold asked.

"I'd bet you'd like it. You have a lot of courage, just like your sister."

"How do you know that?" Tracy asked with surprise.

He studied her a moment and said, "Because look at all you do. You're in charge of your brothers and sisters. You are always either working in the fields, cooking, or going to school." He stopped and looked up in the sky as if searching for the right words. "It seems to me riding that raft is the easiest, simplest job in the world."

She pondered his words. He really does appreciate what I do. No one has ever admired me like that, except maybe Papa. Courage? I just do what needs to be done. Out loud she said, "I think you're talking about a different kind of courage, Logan."

"Well, maybe, but whatever it is, I have the easier job." His gaze was unrelenting.

"It's kind of you to say so, and I appreciate your thoughts, but please, you must be careful." She looked up at him square in the eyes and caught her breath. She had to look away then because it made her neck hurt. When she looked at him straight on all she saw was his shirt buttons. He bent a little as if to reach for her. She hesitated, wanting him to come closer, and then remembered Mother might be looking out of the window, so she ducked out of his reach.

He laughed and said, "Don't worry; I know your mother can see us."

The thought of Mama ran a stab of fear through her. She knew how her mother felt about this wonderful young man.

They walked to the back door, but Tracy didn't feel right about asking him in that way, so they went around and entered by the front door into what passed for a parlor. She invited him to sit down, called to her mother, and hurried to the back to wash her hands and face. Looking in the small cracked mirror, she patted her hair down and tried to tie it back with a blue ribbon she had left on the bench earlier. *It always does this,* she thought, looking at the strands sticking out every which way in a precarious manner.

She came back to find her mother sitting across the room from Logan. They seemed deep in conversation, Logan saying, "After the ties are milled to size, we lash them into rafts and flume them out of the pond into the river. Then we float them down to Troutdale to the railroad." He spoke slowly, with a word of German here and there in an effort to communicate with her mother.

Logan clearly loved his job; his large hands and broad arm-span showed them the dimensions of the finished product, his face animated.

"Me and my father and two other men ride the raft downriver. There are a couple of places where the rapids are pretty bad, even in the spring. There's no way we could do this when the river gets low in the fall."

Tracy smiled at his enthusiasm, secretly glad that it was a seasonal job yet still worried at the danger, especially the rapids. She was somewhat amazed that Mother seemed engrossed in what Logan was saying, nodding her head at the appropriate places.

My goodness, Tracy thought. *Maybe she will let me see him after all.*

Chapter 5

MID-AUGUST 1897

Tracy

"We have enough vegetables to keep us through the winter," Julianna said, her voice flat. "But the chickens will stop laying when it gets cold, so we won't have egg money to rely on."

Silence hung in the air. Since Papa and Bernard had been gone, Mama wasn't the same. Long periods of quiet often marked the children's time with her, followed by terse, clipped conversations. Once in a while, Jackie or Little Alex could coax a smile and a quick hug, but mostly they were met with only hushed lulls and sounds of tears from her room.

"Mama, we lost two more hens last night," Ferd hesitated as he spoke. Tracy knew how hard it was for him to tell their mother.

"*Ja*, there was feathers all over the place." Arnold was braver now that Ferd had broken the news.

Julianna sighed and shook her head. "What are we to do?"

"I have an idea on how we can keep the fox and skunks out," Ferd said, scrambling to sit while reaching for the oatmeal. "Arnold and I will fix a place in the barn for the hens. We can't leave them in the pen overnight, and no one can patch that fence."

"I think putting them in the barn overnight would be a good idea," Tracy said in an effort to be optimistic. "We still have a rooster. Let's set up a nest in the barn, too. Maybe a hen will set."

Julianna nodded.

Her mother brightened a bit, but Tracy worried about her mother and her siblings. She herself made extra efforts to be available for them and encouraged Emma and Bertie to do the same.

She remembered the overcast June day when Arnold had caught her crying while she thought the rest of the family were out picking strawberries.

"Tracy! Why are you crying?" He'd looked like he was close to tears himself.

"Oh, Arnold, please don't cry." She held him close and reached for her handkerchief. "Don't tell the others. It'll only upset them."

Blinking back the tears, he nodded.

She squeezed the seven-year-old and added, "This is our little secret. No one else has to know. When you feel really sad, you come find me, and I will do the same."

"*Ja, meine Schwester.*" He sniffed and ran his nose over his sleeve.

"Now take the bucket on the back stairs to Mama, and when you are done picking berries, you can bring me back a nice ripe one."

Now the family sat quietly eating at the breakfast table as Tracy's mind wandered, escaping the difficulties of their life as her mother's voice droned on about the family struggles.

Tracy, tuning out the conversation, remembered the dream she'd had again the night before. The dream, always the same, started when she was walking to Troutdale on the Seidl trail. A young man suddenly came around a bend on the path, toward her. He was tall and good-looking with thick, curly brown hair and a pleasant smile. While his image was familiar, Tracy could never put her finger on who he was.

When she awoke, she could not get his picture out of her mind. He wasn't Logan, and why would she dream about anyone else? His smiling face continued to haunt her.

"Ferd Harlow came to Fox's store last week when Ferd and I were delivering eggs." Julianna's words startled Tracy out of her reverie. Her mother continued her conversation, her voice resolved. "He suggested that one of you girls come down to Troutdale and work for his wife. She needs a nanny and housekeeper."

It took Tracy a moment to understand that her mother was talking about her. The shock caused panic to rise in her throat.

She pushed back from the table. "The children need me here," she managed to say. She couldn't bring herself to think about how much she needed them.

"I can't see any other way," Julianna continued. "Tracy, you can spend the workdays in Troutdale and come home on Sunday as often as possible."

"No! Tracy can't leave us," Jackie protested, shaking his blond head.

The other children also shook their heads. "Who'll help us? Who'll take care of us?" cried Josie, tears welling in her eyes.

"Mother, how can you ask me to leave the family?" Tracy, close to tears, spoke more firmly this time.

"To me, you are almost indispensable, but we have to make sacrifices if we are to save the farm. Emma will take charge of the younger children, and Bertie will tend to the meals. The other children will help me in the fields." Her mother sat with her hands in her lap. Tracy noticed her mother hadn't touched her breakfast, but her anger didn't let her care.

Julianna continued, her voice quavering but determined. "I promise we'll spend as many Sundays together as possible. Mr. Harlow said he'd pay eight dollars a month for someone to help his wife." Julianna paused, letting the conversation sink in. "That money along with our garden will feed us." She shook her head. "You must leave on Monday."

Tracy gagged and, rising silently, fled out the door into the moist chill of the morning. The children's voices followed her. Not heeding them, she felt nothing but her pain. First Papa, then Bernard, and now this.

She made her way up the lane to the corner where Papa and the baby lay buried. She knelt to pray but instead threw herself over Father's grave, and with a soft south wind blowing her hair, she sobbed. All the tears she had not shed since her father's passing, came now in a torrent, rolling down her cheeks and falling to the earth. In all of her fourteen years, she never remembered feeling so lost and lonely.

Her thoughts turned to Logan. *How can I even get word to him?*

A few moments passed before Tracy felt a soft touch on her shoulder. "Tracy, please don't cry." Josie's voice was soft. "We'll see you on Sundays, and Mama said Emma can bring us down to visit you when she and Ferd make deliveries to the store."

Her beloved Josie, the happy, carefree little girl who so took her heart. Tracy smiled through the tears and gave her sister a hug.

"My dear little *Fraulein,*" she said with more bravery than she felt, "that will be wonderful." She brushed the child's hair out of her eyes and, pulling determination from her soul, managed to say, "Yes, I'll be home as many Sundays as possible and every chance I get. We'll just make the best of it."

Josie nodded silently and would not let go of her. Tracy had never seen her youngest sister cry so bitterly.

Tracy smiled weakly and gathered herself in an effort to sound more courageous than she felt. "We probably should go back to the house. I'm sure the chores are waiting."

"I am sorry you have to go," Emma said when Tracy entered the kitchen. "I would go in your place if I could." Emma and Bertie gathered their big sister in an embrace, with Josie refusing to let go of her hand.

"No, Emma, Mother wants you to stay here. I'll go, but I'll miss you all so much. I'm homesick already." She kept silent her concern about the sadness that wracked the house. "But you must promise me you will hug the children often," she added.

THE FOLLOWING MONDAY MORNING, THE CHILDREN walked Tracy up the lane that led past the Frommelts' place, onto the Seidl trail and down the bluff to Troutdale. From the crest of the hill they stopped and watched her walk until she was out of sight.

Chapter 6

MID-AUGUST 1897

Harlows of Troutdale

Tracy walked slowly, inspired by the pungent smell of the woods in the days of the early August rains. The trail, still damp, had long easy slopes with switchbacks along the steep bluff to the Sandy River. There she continued on the path beside the river to the Hicklin Ferry. Once she crossed the river, it didn't take long for her to reach the Harlow family's home. She hesitated only slightly before knocking on the door.

A beautiful twenty-three-year-old woman with large brown eyes and delicate features opened the door and smiled at her.

"Hello," she said, her voice ringing with friendliness. "You must be Tracy."

"Yes, yes, I am," Tracy sputtered, surprised by the pleasant, youthful lady.

"I'm Minnie Harlow, Ferd's wife." Her smile warmed Tracy's heart. "I'm glad you are here. Come in, please, and meet the children."

"This is Harriet," she said, motioning to a three-year-old who jumped with glee, happy for company. The child had light red curly hair and her mother's soft beauty.

"And this is Lucile." She pointed to a crib by the window. "She is just three months old."

Tracy smiled at the children and caught her breath as she gazed into the fine living room. On one end of the room was a rounded garden window with a reading bench. The wall beside it held two small shelves containing books with intriguing-looking titles. Beside the door stood a dark blue soft, shiny couch with a small table placed in front of it. Across the room was a large stone fireplace that took up almost the whole wall. Above the mantel was a picture of an unsmiling bearded man with a kindly face.

Noticing Tracy looking at the picture, Minnie said, "That gentleman is my husband's father, Captain John Harlow." Then after a pause, "He started Troutdale, you know?"

"I guess I did," Tracy responded although not quite sure where she had heard the story.

Mrs. Harlow nodded. "Come, let me take your bag and show you to your room. You can get settled in. We'll talk over dinner." She smiled again. "Ferd usually comes home for the midday meal. You will meet him then."

Tracy followed her up the steps to a room at the head of the stairs.

"I want you to sleep in this room because you will hear Harriet in the night if she needs something. I hope you'll be comfortable here." She opened the door to a freshly painted room with a window that looked east across the Sandy River to the trail that Tracy had just walked.

Speechless, Tracy put down her bag and sat on the red-and-white log-cabin quilt that covered the bed. She slowly ran her hand over the perfectly seamed cover.

"Isn't that gorgeous?" Minnie asked, as if reading Tracy's mind. "My grandmother made that quilt when she was a young woman. She told me this part is an old apron of her mother's." Minnie pointed to the red print square. "I just treasure it."

"It's lovely," Tracy stammered, wondering why in the world she would put something so beautiful on the hired help's bed.

The room was furnished with a nightstand and a chest of drawers with a pitcher and bowl. A plain mirror hung on the wall. Tracy had never seen such luxury. All her life she had shared a room and a bed with her sisters.

"Where's Harriet's bed?" she asked.

"Harriet sleeps in the next room. You will have to sleep with your door open to hear her, but she has her own room for now. When Lucile is older we'll put her in there as well." Minnie turned to go. "Please feel free to arrange the furniture and put things where you feel comfortable."

Tracy didn't know how long she sat on the bed looking out the window. She didn't hear Harriet's tiny footsteps on the stairs and was startled when she turned around and spied the child.

"Your room." Harriet pointed to the next room and added, "My room is there."

"Yes, that seems to be the case."

"We play?"

"Yes, we can play. What is your dolly's name?" Tracy pointed to the blonde rag doll that Harriet clutched in her arms.

"Dolly," was the answer.

"That's a pretty name. Does she have another name?"

Harriet shook her head no. "Then maybe we can give her another name," suggested Tracy. "Would you like that?"

"Yes."

"Would you like to call her Mary?" Tracy said, thinking of her friend Mary. "I've always liked that name."

"Yes, yes, that's a pretty name," the child said gleefully. "I am going to tell Mama about Mary."

The rest of the morning Tracy and the child worked together to unpack her few clothes and move the bed around so the first thing she saw when she got up every morning would be the Sandy River and the trail to her home up the hill in Pleasant View.

Mr. Harlow came midday as Mrs. Harlow had promised. He was a young man with a mustache and dark hair parted down the middle. He had to stoop to come in the kitchen door. His blue eyes smiled as he greeted Tracy.

"I'm glad you're here to help Minnie. She has her hands full with the girls, and I need her to do my books. I still have some obligations in the circuit court in Portland, so I'll be gone some of the time. I feel much better leaving, knowing she has you here with her." He shook her hand.

Tracy nodded, hoping she didn't show her nervousness. No one had ever shaken her hand before.

He went on to say, "Your mother said you were good with children and could cook. This is a rare combination for someone so young."

Tracy nodded again, not knowing what to say to someone as learned as a lawyer, although she wasn't quite sure what a lawyer did.

"Come, sit down. We can visit while we eat," Minnie said as she put Harriet in her high chair.

Tracy had never considered herself shy, but for some reason she felt at a loss for words. The table was set with beautiful rose-patterned plates with the middle of a table laden with bread, cheeses, and pears, along with a platter of fried chicken. It reminded her of Thanksgiving instead of just a day in August. She began to see the poverty of her own family. *No wonder Mama needs me to work.*

"This looks delicious, Mrs. Harlow," she finally managed to say.

Minnie laughed. "No, Tracy, I'm Minnie, and this is Ferd. We don't stand on ceremony in this house. As long as you live here, you are part of the family."

Ferd nodded. "Absolutely, you are to be like kin to us. We insist that you treat this just like home."

"Thank you, sir," Tracy murmured as she thought about the bare-board home on the hill where she and her family lived, with three bedrooms for nine people. "I will consider it a privilege." She was beginning to feel more relaxed.

"Now let's speak of your duties," he continued. "You will help Minnie with the children and meal preparation, particularly breakfast. She'll take care of the children's needs at that time. The rest of the meals you and she will decide. Is that all you want her to do, Minnie?"

"She can help me with the laundry and the cleaning," Minnie said, smiling at Tracy. "We'll figure it out as we go."

"I'll do whatever you wish, Minnie." Tracy felt her skin crawl, calling such a sophisticated woman by her first name.

HER FIRST DAYS ON THE JOB WERE FILLED WITH LEARNING new skills. Tracy appreciated the older woman's patience and was gratified when Minnie told her that she was a "truly remarkable young woman with many talents." Swelling with pride at the compliment, she couldn't help but recall the nice things Logan had told her. She felt a twinge of angst and uttered a silent prayer he would find her.

True to her word, Minnie allowed Tracy to go home every Saturday afternoon and come back on Monday morning, so just about the time Tracy felt her heart would break with loneliness from not seeing her brothers and sisters, Saturday would come and she would climb the trail to home. When the weather was nice, often Josie and some of the other children would walk down the path past Frommelts to meet her.

In November, the weather turned ugly, and Tracy missed going home for two Sundays. The week of Thanksgiving made up for it. The Harlows planned to take the train to Portland to spend the holiday with Ferd's sister and her family.

"Mr. Frommelt was at the store this morning," Ferd said as he walked in the door for his midday meal. "He received a letter from Mount Angel. They're sending Father Milton up to say Mass at the Frommelt home the Sunday before Thanksgiving. The trail is too muddy and dangerous to ride on, so the priest will leave his horse here in the corral, and you and he can walk up the hill together. You just plan on spending the whole week at home with your family.

Chapter 7

HOLIDAYS 1897

Though the weather was blustery, Thanksgiving week with her family felt warm and comfortable. Tracy enjoyed her family with the gusto that only comes after a long absence. The two sacks that Tracy and the priest had carried up the hill contained wonderful surprises. The Harlows sent two pounds of cheese, a dressed-out turkey, a large bag of walnuts, and cranberries. The family had never tried the round hard little berries, but before Tracy left Troutdale, Minnie told her how to prepare them. They were a big hit with the children. After Thanksgiving dinner, Emma passed around a piece of paper, and each child wrote a thank-you in appreciation of the Harlows' gifts.

Mama seemed more content now than she had for a long time. Tracy thought it might have something to do with having a priest come and say Mass. It occurred to her, too, that the graves were now consecrated, and perhaps that had brought her mother some peace.

Once during the week, she came to Tracy and slipped her arm around her waist. "Tracy, dear, you must know how we have missed you," she confided, "but you've saved us with your wages. Thank you, *mein* dear."

"I've missed you and the children," Tracy replied, "but the Harlows are a wonderful family, and I can see the Pleasant View hill from my bedroom window, so that helps." She blinked back tears. She'd had no idea her mother was so grateful.

WHEN TRACY LEFT TO GO BACK TO WORK THE FOLLOWING Monday, she felt less dread than before. She had two families now.

Mama told her she could keep a dollar of her pay to buy the Harlows a Christmas present. She thanked her, thinking how happy she was that her mother let her regularly keep two-bits a month, which mostly she saved for presents for her family.

One day about a week after Thanksgiving, Minnie, hunched over her desk, said, "Tracy, you'll have to walk down to the store today. We need some flour for holiday baking, and I just don't have time to go. Ferd wants these accounts done when he gets back from Portland. Do you mind terribly?"

"Oh no," said Tracy, thinking it was the perfect chance for her to buy their gift. "The walk will do me good, and it's not raining."

She bundled up against the bitter east wind, wearing the blue stocking cap that Emma had knit for her birthday.

It was a quarter mile walk to Aaron Fox's General Mercantile store. She walked north along the lane. When Tracy turned west on Main Street, she wrinkled her face and felt her nostrils burn as the stench of the Union Meat Packing company arrived on a gust of wind.

Seeing the north side of town made her smile. "A 'one-sided town,'" Papa used to say. "The railroad owns the whole north side, so no one can build there," he had told her, which explained why only the depot, one house, and the water tower were down by the tracks. He'd told her only the train station masters were allowed to live there.

Tracy walked by the Troutdale Hotel and the livery stable, and by the time she arrived at Fox's store a chill had come over her. Stamping her feet and blowing on her hands, she stood by the stove and surveyed the wondrous wares.

She hadn't been in the store often; usually she had stayed home with the children while others went, so this was a special treat.

Tracy looked around, wandering through each aisle, appraising the array of merchandise in search of the perfect gift for the Harlows before settling on a pretty lead crystal candy dish that cost forty-five cents. *Good,* she thought. *I have money left over to buy candy for Harriet and my brothers and sisters. We'll think of Papa and Bernard, but we'll make them happy memories.*

"Will you wrap the dish carefully, please?" she asked Mr. Fox. "This is my present to the Harlows. I wouldn't want to break it." Then remembering why she came, she said, "Oh, I almost forgot, I need five pounds of flour, too. I can't carry a hundred-pound sack. Minnie said you wouldn't mind weighing it out for me and asked if you would please deliver the rest."

He nodded and picked up the scoop. Tracy watched him as he worked and decided she liked the roly-poly man with the friendly smile.

Wind out of the east had picked up while she was in the

store. When she turned toward the Harlows', little flecks of sleet burned her cheeks. Sometimes a gust of wind sucked the breath out of her. She couldn't cover her mouth and carry the sack, so she turned and carefully walked backward until she reached the protection of the trees. By the time she arrived at the Harlow farm, it was sleeting hard, and she was out of breath and chilled through.

The storm intensified, and for several days it snowed intermittently until the drifts around the house and barn were higher than the fence. It made it difficult to feed the stock, even though they were secure in the barn. Ferd was stuck in Portland, so Minnie insisted on doing the chores, leaving Tracy to stay with the children while she took hot water out twice a day to thaw the trough so the animals could drink.

Wearing Ferd's knee boots, Minnie faithfully cleaned the stalls. Obviously this was something she'd never done before and held in great disdain. Only once, however, did Tracy hear her complain about the barn's odor. She had wrinkled her nose and said, "I wish I didn't have to bring 'the smell of horse manure' into the kitchen." She and Tracy laughed about it, but Tracy knew she meant it.

Still Ferd did not come home. Minnie's look of concern turned to one of desperation.

Mr. Fox and his son stopped by the house later in the week and said the trains were not coming through from the east at all, so rail-traffic dare not leave Portland for fear of being snowbound. His son split some more wood for them, as the pile had shrunk. When the east wind blew hard, the wood burned much faster, sucking the heat up the chimney. Tracy could see the worry on Minnie's face, but at least they were warm.

Tracy wasn't worried about her family on the hill. The neighbors had split plenty of wood for them, and over Thanksgiving, she'd helped them chink the cracks in the house with pages from old issues of her mother's German newspapers. They had lots of canned vegetables in the cellar, but didn't have much meat. Some bacon carefully stored in the lard-filled crock was all they had, but she knew that at least they wouldn't go hungry.

As the storm continued, Christmas grew closer, and Tracy began to worry that she wouldn't get home for the holiday. Then suddenly, ten days after the freeze started, a warm south wind came, and the air felt balmy.

"Well, well, it looks like Ferd will get home for Christmas after all," Mr. Fox said as he stepped in the door. "This Chinook wind will thaw everything quickly. My bet is the train will get at least to Cleone within a couple of days. Ferd can walk from there. Not to fear, Minnie, you'll see him by Christmas."

"He certainly will be a welcome sight," she replied. "I'm so tired of barn chores, I don't care if I ever see another horse." She laughed gently, surprising Tracy. She'd only heard Minnie complain once during the entire storm.

"I'll tell him, if I see him first, that he may have to sleep in the barn for a few nights." Mr. Fox laughed and then looked sheepish as if perhaps he should not have made that comment.

"Tracy wants to go home for the holiday, too," Minnie said, ignoring Mr. Fox's attempt at humor. "If someone comes off the bluff in the next few days, have them stop over here to fetch her on their return trip, please. I want someone to walk with her during this nasty weather."

He agreed, saying he would ask the first person down the bluff to stop at the Harlows on their way back. He laughed and said, "It'll be easy, you're right on the main trail."

True to Mr. Fox's word, Ferd walked the five miles from Cleone two days later. Evidence of drifts were still everywhere, but the temperature stayed in the high forties. The ground was rapidly losing the ice, making a sticky mess of the lane. Ferd's boots were covered with mud up to the top, and his pants were wet to the knees.

He said, "Tracy, it's just as well you don't try to get up to the home place until this dries out a little. That bluff trail will be slippery. I doubt if anyone will be down for a few days."

She knew it was true, but she worried that there was only a week until Christmas Eve. *I don't know if I could bear to be away from my family at Christmas,* she thought to herself. *What will they do without me—and worse—what will I do without them?*

Taking a deep breath, she changed her mind. *I will get home,* she insisted to herself. That evening she prayed the rosary especially fervently, begging God to help her get up the hill for the holiday. She wondered if she would see Logan if only she could make it home.

The weather continued to moderate, and within a few days the mud began to firm up. Just about the time Tracy was giving up on going home, Mr. Seidl stopped by. It was about noon the day before Christmas Eve when he knocked at the door.

"Can I speak to Tracy, Mrs. Harlow?" he asked in broken English. "I've stopped to take her up the hill."

"She'll be so happy." Minnie wiped the cookie dough off her hands with her apron. "I'll call her."

Tracy grabbed her coat and the package she had for the children, along with a few belongings that she had packed earlier just in case. The pair headed to the ferry and up the bluff.

Mr. Seidl was a tall, quiet man so they walked mostly in silence. He carried a large pack on his back laden with supplies from the store. About halfway up he offered to help Tracy carry her packages so she let him carry the bag with her clothes, but she hung tightly onto the sack with the candy for the children. There was still mud on the trail, but according to Mr. Seidl it was not as slick as it had been earlier.

They made good time and were at the Seidls' by half-past one. Mrs. Seidl, a sweet woman with a kind face, asked her to come in and warm herself. As Tracy clapped her hands to get the feeling back, the neighbor handed her a freshly baked cookie and a cup of warm cider.

"As soon as Jacob puts away the supplies, he'll walk you home. I want him to find a nice Christmas tree for your family on the way. Emma and Ferd were over here day before yesterday and said they didn't have one. I promised them they would have one by the holiday." She talked as she busied herself between the stove and the drain board in an effort to finish the holiday baking. "I'll get a Christmas package ready for you to take as well."

Her small daughter, Aggie, was underfoot, smiling shyly at Tracy. Tracy smiled back and quietly reached into her sack and gave her a licorice stick.

Tracy and Mr. Seidl arrived at the Lampert home just before dark with a small tree. The screams of joy and the hugs of the children at the surprise of having both Tracy and a tree for Christmas went on for what seemed like several minutes with Jackie and Little Alex clutching her legs, unwilling to let go. Amid the mayhem, suddenly Julianna appeared, put her arms around Tracy, and without a word pulled her close.

That evening and the next day were spent in holiday preparation. The children strung popcorn to hang on the tree as the older girls helped Mama in the kitchen. For a Christmas surprise, Mama baked her special treat, *Schnitzbrot,* a bread with little pieces of dried prunes, apples, pears, and a few hazelnuts.

"It's just something I dreamed up as a Christmas surprise for my family," she said with a rare smile.

On Christmas morning Tracy's package was under the tree when everyone came downstairs. There was a large decorated package from Emma, with mittens she had knitted for each family member. Bertie and Josie had made popcorn balls with the children's names made from pieces of popcorn dyed with grape juice. The popcorn balls weren't very big, so they had to abbreviate some of the names, but the children loved every bite.

The younger boys' eyes lit up when they opened Mrs. Seidl's Christmas package to find three dozen oatmeal raisin cookies and a plate of fudge. When they opened the large package from Ferd and Minnie, they found large orange aromatic fruit.

"What are these, Tracy? They smell good."

"They're called 'oranges.' They come from California and are very expensive. Here, let me show you. You have to peel them."

"No, Alex, don't eat the peeling." She caught him too late, just as he was spitting out the bitter outer coating. "Here, eat this." She split off a section. "See, isn't that better?" she asked as she hugged him.

Later that afternoon, the family gathered by the woodstove in the living room and said the Joyful Mysteries of the Rosary for Papa and baby Bernard. It made it almost seem like they were all together again.

At Christmas dinner Mama announced her present to the family. "In the spring, when the weather is no longer a threat, I want to take all of you to town. We'll catch the train and visit the Foellers. I'll write a letter and tell them about when we will be there. Tracy, I want you to come as well, so find out from the Harlows when a good time is for them to have you gone for a few days. You take the letter and have Mr. Harlow mail it. We all deserve a few days on holiday, and Franz promised to take care of the stock."

"Remember, Tracy," Emma said later while drying a plate, "when we all went to town? Ferd was a baby. Mama had us girls and Ferd's picture taken. She sent one back to Germany to Grandma Gross and one to Grandma Lampert in Liechtenstein."

"Yes, I do believe that was the last time we were in Portland. I think I was about eight then, so that would've made you six years old." As they chatted, Tracy noticed a quiet calm about the house. It seemed like years since she'd felt this kind of peace at home.

"I bet Papa's here," she said to her sisters. They all agreed, he wouldn't miss a Christmas with his family.

Chapter 8

APRIL 1898

"Will Mama ever be happy again?" Josie asked, following Tracy as she carefully wound her way through the woods in search of wild Miners Lettuce, the succulent spring prize. Every year, after months of potatoes, carrots, and cabbage, these early native plants were a treat for the whole family. All, that is, except for Little Alex, who often complained when served green vegetables.

"I'm not sure, *Liebe*," Tracy answered, absently. She was enjoying the sweet pungent smell of the lush forest undergrowth on this bright spring Saturday. "Maybe we can tell her a funny story. Let's think of one." Tracy didn't have much hope it would help, but thought it at least might cheer up her and her younger sister. *If we are really lucky, it may even erase some of the gloom that seemed to return after Christmas.*

And if the truth be told, Tracy had fervently hoped that somehow Logan might magically appear during the holiday season. When she didn't hear from him, it cast a shadow over her and seemed to follow her.

Josie, quiet for a moment, stared into space. She was rarely silent. She had inherited their father's joyful nature and his subtle good looks. Tracy turned and waited for her sister, who once again began climbing through the dense undergrowth in an effort to catch up.

"There was one funny thing that happened in school last week," Josie said, climbing around an extraordinarily large lush sword fern.

"What was that?"

"Everyone thought it was funny, but we probably can't tell Mama."

"Why?" Tracy asked, half-listening.

There was silence for a moment. "Because Arnold put a frog in Miss Emily's desk and when she opened the drawer, the frog jumped out and scared her."

"Yes, I think we'd better not mention that." Tracy hesitated. "Did he get into trouble?"

"Yes, he had to stand in front of the class with his nose to the blackboard for thirty minutes."

"That would be a difficult punishment for him," Tracy said, thinking how her little brother's energy often had to be directed to something worthwhile.

"Not only that, but Miss Emily made us all write a paragraph on discipline and read it out loud in front of the whole school." Josie made a face. "I didn't know what it meant, so I had to raise my hand and ask. She said it meant different forms of punishing bad behavior."

"So what did you write?"

"I said that I thought making a little boy stand with his nose to the blackboard for thirty minutes was too hard for just putting a frog in a drawer."

Tracy, suppressing a laugh, said as solemnly as she could that she thought that it was too harsh as well, but she bet that Arnold would not ever do it again.

"On the way home, he told me he wouldn't, if I didn't tell Mother." Josie caught up with her then and added, "I promised him I wouldn't."

"Your secret is safe with me, unless Arnold's behavior becomes a problem. I agree it is a funny story, but I doubt Mother would think so. I'll speak to him, though. He needs to know school is a place to learn letters and numbers, not to misbehave."

Just then she spotted some of the zesty greens. "Look here, Josie. Here's our dinner tonight. Won't that be good with potatoes and bacon?" she asked as she cut the greenish-blue, juicy leaves and put them in her basket. "There's some more over there." Tracy pointed to a large clump by an alder tree. "You go get those."

Josie obediently did as she was told. Tracy watched her for a moment, amazed at her compliant personality, and suddenly she was overcome with affection for the small eight-year-old.

She walked over to her sister, bent down, and gave her a gigantic hug. "If anyone can make Mama laugh, you can." Tracy kissed her blond curls. "But we'll keep this story to ourselves."

"YEAH! IT WAS A BIG FROG, TOO," ARNOLD SAID LATER when Tracy spoke to him. "Frank Frommelt and I found him down by the spring."

"Frogs, snakes, and other small animals belong by the spring, and little boys belong in school to learn their letters and numbers," Tracy said firmly. "Do you have any idea how lucky you are to have a mother who thinks school is important?" She hesitated, trying to think of something to say that would leave an impression on his active brain. "There are many young boys your age who aren't able to go to school and will never learn to read. Remember you told me once how you were looking forward to learning?"

He nodded silently, looking sheepish, but staying to listen to his older sister.

"Promise me you won't do anything like that again," she commanded.

"I promise," he said. "Besides, I already promised Josie."

"Good, two promises are better than one." She patted him on the shoulder and sent him off to help Ferd feed the goats.

The conversation about school had flooded back memories of Logan. She wondered how he was and if he was still working with his father. She had loved school and had tried to wring every drop of learning possible in her time spent there.

Now she knew her place was to help her mother, and that meant working away from home most of the time. Today she was home for the end of the week, and besides the greens for supper and her conversation with Josie, she felt her presence was needed to help channel Arnold's energy in a positive way.

Their mother's grief over the loss of her husband and child sometimes left her unable to handle the most basic of household and child-rearing chores. This pulled the children closer together, like the stones in the arch of the church pictured in Tracy's school reader. The stones connected and stayed strong through earthquakes and storms and other forms of adversity. Likewise, each of the children depended on and supported one another, and for that she was grateful.

Tracy knew the children missed her, which brought her home as often as possible. She also knew her mother had all she could do to see that there was enough food on the table, that the children's clothes were mostly mended, and that the crops were tended and harvested. Tracy's job was to see that she and the other two older sisters helped nurture the younger children.

With that thought, she sighed and wished Logan would stop by to see her, and wondered if he even knew she lived with the Harlows.

JULIANNA COULDN'T SEEM TO SHAKE THE SADNESS AND fear. It wasn't just about the loss of her love and her baby, but also now what was she to do? Her choice was to sell or work the land.

At times, she wanted to pack up the children, take them into Portland, and have her friend Sophie help her get settled. She felt sure that the parishioners at St. Joseph Church uptown by the cathedral would hire her as a midwife. She'd helped those women when she and Alex first moved to Oregon. Things at the parish could not have changed that much in twelve years.

She did promise the children a few days' trip to Portland but now wondered if she could afford to take the time or the money to do it. She secretly thought that if they got to Portland she would inquire as to the possibility of moving there and getting away from the hill.

But the land was Alex's fondest wish. *I followed him all the way from Germany chasing his dream, and now he can't even enjoy it.* She clenched her fists in anger. "How can you take him away from us, Lord," she cried, wondering if He could hear her or if He even cared.

She had taken this moment, when the younger children were down for their nap, to wander into the garden on this first sunny day in April, trying to make sense of her life. She needed to come to important decisions, but it was so hard to do it alone. Her emotions were still too ragged and raw. Whenever she tried to sort out past events, more tears came. She could not let the children see her cry one more time. They tried so hard to make her happy, telling stories of Papa and begging her to tell them how they met so long ago in Baden.

The thought brought more tears. Alex, so young when they fell in love, was an earnest fellow who wanted to leave his mark on the world. She thought of their first kiss in the park in Baden, and the memories flooded back, washing over her and bathing her with bittersweet joy.

Her stomach knotted. She fought a sudden urge to vomit, swallowing back bile, until finally the gagging bent her over and she retched in the grass.

When she finished, she buried her face in her hands. The image of her mother came to her, and she cried harder. She wished she could curl up in her mother's lap, feeling the comfort of her hand stroking her hair and listening to her heartbeat through her apron. Suddenly, for a moment she could smell the *Apfelkuchen* baking in the oven.

She walked over and sat on her favorite stump, the mosses dry in the afternoon sun, and wept bitter tears. When her sobs finally ceased, fatigue swept over her. She sat in silence for a few minutes, freeing her mind, now trying to rest and to make peace with the overwhelming uncertainty she faced.

Finally she wiped her eyes and straightened her shoulders. *This will never do. I have too many responsibilities.* She scanned the field with the urgent thought of how time flies and that now it was time to prepare the field for planting once again.

I wish we had a horse, she thought, then laughed because she had no idea what she would do with one. She could barely feed her children and felt lucky the goats pretty much fed themselves. She hadn't seen Joseph for several weeks and wondered if he would have time to disk her fields again this spring.

The following Tuesday while the family sat at the breakfast table, Julianna glanced out the window and noticed Joseph leading his horse through the gate. She grabbed her shawl and rushed outside to meet him.

"Elma sent me over to check on you folks," he said in his kind voice. "She told me to bring this to you." He untied a basket from the harness and handed it to her. The smell of freshly baked cake, wrapped in one of Elma's embroidered tea cloths, made her mouth water. "And there is a batch of cookies from Katherine in there, too." He continued, "The women send their love, and Katherine told me to tell you she will be over for a visit in a day or two."

"Please thank them for me. That was very kind." Julianna managed a smile and cheered up at the thought of seeing her old friend. "Tell Katherine I'll look forward to the visit."

"I wanted to check with you." Joseph paused and looked over the field he had worked for her last year. "What are your plans for the farm this year?"

Relief washed over her. "If I can get someone to plow and disk for me, the children and I can plant and weed."

"I can do that for you. I'll let Ferd help so when he gets a little bigger, he'll know what to do," Joseph said, looking off toward the fields. "I planted a lot of cabbage seed in February, so I can share the seedlings with you. That is, if you want to plant cabbage."

"Yes, thank you. It sold well last year. I'll gladly pay you for the plants as soon as I get the cash from the sale of the east twenty acres."

"I'm not worried about that. I have plenty of plants comin' up. I'm far more uneasy about you folks managing the farm," Joseph said. The furrows in his forehead indicated genuine care and deep concern. "Now what else do you think you should grow as cash crops? Potatoes were in demand up at the logging camps last season."

"Yes, I thought potatoes, and before he passed, Alex told me that he'd like to try some Danish squash. We had a bit in our garden last year, and it grew well." Julianna's spirits continued to brighten. "Alex spoke about curing it once, and when I asked him how to do it, he told me to pick it when there is a yellow spot on its belly. He said that's how you tell it is ripe, and then you put it in a warm, dry place to cure. Last summer we picked it in mid-September and put it back in the corners of the attic. It's a good keeper. We ate the last of it in early March."

"I do remember you speaking of that." He patted the horse as he spoke. "Let's not worry about raising enough to sell yet, but planting plenty for our families to eat through the winter makes good sense."

"It was very difficult, time-consuming work. Perhaps just raising it for the families is best."

"Write down what kinds of vegetables you plan on planting this year, and Katherine can give the list to Franz after her visit. He's expecting to buy our seed the next time he goes to Portland." He led the horse to the trough by the spring. "Be sure and put Danish squash on your list," he hollered over his shoulder.

"I told the children we'd take a trip to Portland this spring," Julianna said to Katherine as they visited over the mending. As promised, Katherine and her children had walked the path in the rain that morning so she could check on everyone and help wherever she could.

"This would be a good time to do it. You can't get a lot done outside with this kind of weather."

"That's what I was thinking, too," Julianna said as she looked through the pile of clothes for another pair of pants to patch. The boys wore out more knees than anything else. "I'll write a letter to Sophie before you leave. You can have Franz mail it." Julianna's mind went in several directions trying to fit things together and make the puzzle work. "I'll send a note to Tracy, too. We'll go next week and only stay a few days. It'll be nice to go to Mass in a church. It's been such a long time."

"Yes, hasn't it, though. If my children were older, I'd go with you." She laughed, and soon Julianna joined in. They spent the next hour trading news and family anecdotes with the time passing all too quickly.

"Oh, I must go," Katherine said, looking at the clock. She fled out the door, her family duties pulling her away, but her short visit helped Julianna face the day.

The following Thursday, the little group, each carrying a small bag with a change of clothes, hiked down the muddy trail, caught the ferry, and met Tracy at the train depot for the ride into Portland and Sophie's house.

THE SHINY RED TROLLEYS WERE THE FIRST THING THAT caught the children's attention as they stepped off the train and into the multitude of well-dressed people milling around the station. The smell of popcorn from a nearby vendor prompted Tracy to take the two bits Mama let her keep from her last week's salary and spend a nickel on a bag to share as they walked to the Foellers.

After the noon meal, the boys and Josie went to play outside, while Sophie and Julianna exchanged news; the older girls listened.

"I'm so anxious to go to Mass," Julianna murmured. "It's been such a long time." She paused in apparent reflection and continued, "You know Alex was thinking of moving somewhere closer to a church before his illness."

Sophie seemed surprised, and a discussion about the lack of spiritual facilities for Catholics in the remote area of the gorge followed.

"So what does everyone want to do while you are in town?" Sophie asked in a lull in the conversation.

In the next thirty minutes they formed a plan to visit the Portland Zoo and see the exotic animals. The next day found them at the gate of the new facility reading a plaque about Richard Knight, who had founded the Portland zoo in 1888 with two bears. All morning they walked around the enclave and laughed at the antics of the monkeys, stared in dismay at the immenseness of the grizzly bear, and gazed in awe at the iridescence of the parakeets' plumage.

To say nothing about their surprise when a zookeeper in striped overalls and a square white-billed cap came out with a small can of seeds and asked, "Joey eat?"

To which a surprisingly stunning blue, green, and yellow bird answered, "Joey eat." He was immediately treated with a snack, as were the other birds in the cage.

They all agreed that they could do nothing as fun as the zoo. So on Saturday they stayed at the Foellers', where the children played outside, Tracy and Bertha tried a new recipe in the kitchen, and Emma found a book in which she immediately became absorbed.

On Sunday they attended Mass at St. Joseph's and came home to a Sunday dinner complete with all the chicken they could eat and the dessert the girls had made the day before, then spent the rest of the day visiting with the Foellers.

After nearly four days of city life, they piled back onto the train on Monday morning to return to Troutdale.

"Mama, this city life is too busy," Arnold said, looking out the window as the train started up. "Besides, I didn't see any animals except horses and mules. Where are all the rest of the animals?"

"You're right, Arnold. I missed them too," Bertie said, her voice reflecting the amazement of the difference in living in the city.

"There's way too much light and noise at night. I could hardly get to sleep," Ferd looked out the window as the train crossed the Willamette River.

"But the bridges are fun," Jackie exclaimed, his nose pressed against the window as he watched the steel struts fly by. "And so were the monkeys and the talking birds." They all agreed that was the zoo was the best part of the trip.

As the train continued east out of town toward Troutdale, the conversation continued with the general consensus being that no matter how hard life was on the farm, not one of the children would trade it for the city life they had witnessed.

It rained off and on for the next two weeks, keeping the ground too wet to plow. The vegetable seeds and seed potatoes came, but it was too muddy to plant. April quietly slid into May, and still the rains persisted. By the second week of the month, the sun finally showed itself enough for Joseph to come and work the ground. "At least if I turn it once, it'll dry out faster," he said, his voice discouraged.

The rains held off for three days, and Joseph came once again with his horse hooked to the disk. "We'll get this field ready for planting. It'll be as smooth as glass when Sam and I get done with it." He patted his horse, appraised the worked ground, and continued, "I've never seen soil like this. It dries out fast in the spring, but in the summer, just a small bit of dry mulch on top will hold the moisture in during the dry spells." He shook his head. "With darned few rocks to boot. Alex and Franz knew good land when they saw it."

Julianna kept the children home from school to help with planting. Despite a couple of showery days, the early potatoes, cabbage, carrots, and squash, along with the kitchen garden, were finally in the ground.

"We'll put in another planting of potatoes and cabbage in a month or six weeks," she explained, remembering what Alex had told her. "Then we'll have some produce to sell up to the beginning of the fall rainy season. Maybe we should put in more carrots," she mused. "They store well, and I'll bet they'd sell up at Palmer. I'm going to ask Joseph to have Franz buy us some more seed next time he goes to town."

"That's a good idea, Mama," Ferd said, mounding up the last of the potato rows. He and Emma seemed to be the most ardent gardeners, while Bertie would rather be in the kitchen. The rest of the children were always eager to get the farm chores finished so they could play.

Chapter 9

JULY 1898

Tracy

Today's the day, Tracy thought, as she breathed in the cool morning air. A hint of the peppermint she watered filled her nostrils as it thanked her with its pungent aroma.

Yesterday, when she'd gone to the store for supplies for Minnie, she had overheard Mr. Fox telling a customer that the boys from the mill were bringing down another raft of ties today. It seemed like the longest three weeks in history since the last drive when Logan had come to visit her. He had surprised her and when she asked how he found her, he'd laughed and told her he asked Mr. Fox.

Logan's face flashed across her mind's eye, and she flushed, though there wasn't anyone close by, and she had no reason to be embarrassed. *My goodness, I'm doing too much daydreaming,* she chided herself.

The last time the drive came through it was just past noon, so she knew now was too early, but she couldn't help staring at the Sandy River in anticipation. She was unable to remember when happiness had so completely surrounded her—certainly not since before Papa and Bernard died.

Back in the house, she busied herself with the children, while trying to not get too far from the window. Even though the house was quite a distance from the river, she still had a good view of floating objects—such as men riding on logs.

"Tracy, will you read to us?" Harriet pleaded.

"Read!" Lucile echoed, clapping her hands in glee.

Tracy tried to be patient, but their pleas were impossible to ignore. "It's such a pretty day," she finally answered. "Why don't we go outside for our story?"

Harriet eagerly grabbed *The Five Little Peppers* and handed it to Tracy. Tracy sighed, picked up Lucile, and followed the eager child to the lawn's edge, where she settled herself and the toddler on the ground and sat Harriet beside them. Leaning against the fence, she opened the book.

The bookmark reminded her she was on chapter VII. She didn't mind the story, in fact she had actually enjoyed it the first couple of times, but it was getting a bit old. She often wondered how someone as young as Harriet could absorb the story, but the child listened intently, and it kept her quiet.

With a child snuggled on each side, she began to read, all the while keeping one eye on the river. Although there had been some brief showers earlier in the week, the air was now bright and clear, with a promise of warm temperatures later in the day.

Afterward, Ferd mentioned that that small amount of moisture hadn't brought near enough rain for the farmers, and he wondered if the logging would have to shut down because of fire danger.

When Minnie called them in for lunch, Tracy reluctantly left her post. As soon as the children were down for their nap, she took one of Ferd's copies of the *Morning Oregonian* newspaper back down to the fence to read while she watched for Logan.

Just about the time she was ready to give up and go up to the house to check on the girls, she saw the first of the ties floating down the river behind the island where Beaver Creek meets the Sandy. Soon the river was filled with rough cut tie rafts destined for the railroad. The men riding them looked tiny as they hopped from one end to the other like fleas on a dog's back, skillfully maneuvering the slick rafts.

"Oh my God," she muttered under her breath. She lowered her head, unsure she could even stand to watch, but unable to resist. She slowly opened one eye and peeked. It took several minutes for the logs to move down the river, riding the swift current. Watching the men pull in the ties with their peaveys, attempting to keep them in a tight bundle, reminded her of the cattle drive she'd seen from the train window during the family holiday up the Columbia on the way to Celilo Falls before Papa died.

And then the men on the rafts disappeared behind the trees, as quickly as they had appeared. She could hear them shouting to each other over the roar of the river as they threw ropes to the shore when they neared the railroad bridge, just a short way downstream. A boom on the bridge caught the ties and hoisted them onto waiting railcars.

Reluctantly, she rose to check on the children, but not without skipping a step or two, knowing Logan would soon arrive. *Would he make a nice husband?* She blushed at the thought.

After what seemed like a long wait, he finally appeared walking down the lane. She could spot him easily now, recognizing the way he walked and held his head. His hair was slicked back, and he wore a lopsided grin. *He looks happy,* she thought with a smile. *I'm just glad that he survived another drive.* The thought blazed through her with a shudder, and she promised herself to encourage him to get a safer job.

She ran to the gate to meet him, and he took her hands in his large calloused ones and said shyly, "I'm surely glad to see you."

She smiled back, feeling his calm strength. The children, awake now, rushed out to greet him. Minnie came to welcome him with an invitation to dinner before she hustled the children back inside, seeming to understand that he was important to Tracy.

"I guess this will be my last drive for a while," Logan said later when they were settled into the porch swing.

A flood of relief came over Tracy. "I can't say that I'm sorry," she answered.

"I know, but I make six bits a day at the mill and five dollars for each tie drive. I've got almost forty-five dollars saved. At this rate, I'll be able to go into Portland to school soon." He glowed as he talked, and when he reached to take her hand, her heart, suddenly out of control, leapt to her throat.

"The river is too low for any more drives, and the woods are too dry to log. There's a big fire danger. They don't dare use any equipment that might cause a spark. The boss said they probably won't be able to start up again until the beginning of November, and then we'll work until the snow gets too deep for the horses."

"That makes sense," Tracy said, secretly thanking God that her dear friend would be out of the woods at least for a short time. "So what will you do now?"

"Jum' Mershon tells me the early Chinook should be runnin' any time. He and I are going to try to get on with Papa at the seining grounds at Rooster Rock. I'll make almost as much money with them." He stared out toward the road with a distant look in his eye. "If that doesn't happen, I'll get a job at the fish cannery down there."

A silence settled itself between them. Logan began to say her name, then hesitated.

"What?"

After what seemed like a long pause, he quietly said, "I'd like it if I could officially come to court you."

"I'd like that very much, Logan."

His eyes lit up, and then he said, "I doubt your mother would approve."

"If I'm grown-up enough to help earn money for the family, I'm old enough to see who I please." Tracy set her jaw, but not for long as he squeezed her hand. She found herself wondering what it would be like if he kissed her, then blushed again.

She excused herself to help with meal preparation, but Minnie would have none of it. "You go right back out there and enjoy your company. You get very little time off; besides he's such a nice young man. Go now!"

Tracy scurried back to the porch swing where the two of them sat and chatted until they saw Ferd coming down the lane.

She thought she saw a worried furrow on his face, but ignored it. Nothing could mar her joy at this moment. When Logan rose to welcome him with an outstretched hand, Tracy nearly burst with pride at the handsome young man who conducted himself with such good manners. She made a mental note to help her brothers become more like him.

After dinner, Tracy and Logan washed and dried the dishes. Tracy had never seen a man do dishes. When she mentioned it to him, he said, "This is where you are, so that's where I want to be."

Later, when he left, he leaned over and brushed his lips to her cheek and promised to return soon.

The next morning, Minnie invited Tracy to sit with her at the breakfast table. Her usual smile was absent and in its place was a worried frown.

"Tracy, Ferd tells me that we're going to have to board up the house for a few months. He is being called to work in Portland and has no idea how soon he will be able to come home," she said quietly. "Naturally, he wants us to come with him. He's going in today to find us a suitable place to live. I have pondered whether I should have you come with us, but have decided against taking you so far from your family."

Tracy gasped at the sudden news.

"I heard Mr. Fox say they needed some help at the store," Minnie continued. "I think you should go down there right away today and ask him. I don't want you to be out of a job now, but when we come back I would like you to work for us again if at all possible."

"Oh yes, Minnie. I'll be waiting. I'll miss you and the children," she said, grateful that the change would still allow her to be close to Logan. "Do you think I could actually work in the store?"

"Of course. Mr. Fox is a fine man and most helpful. You'll learn so much, and I know how you love to learn new things."

Tracy nodded. "I'll surely miss the girls," she told Minnie. But Tracy knew Minnie was right. She couldn't bear to be any farther away from home.

Chapter 10

1898

The General Store
Tracy

"Be sure to dust the shelves before you stock them, Tracy," Mr. Fox reminded her on his way back to the meat counter, a customer in tow. Tracy had been working in the general store and post office for two weeks and had come to realize that when he instructed her to do something it was not an admonishment, but a helpful suggestion.

Like Minnie, he smiled a lot and seemed to be happy all the time. He was a short, slightly rotund, balding man with a moustache, and a dimple on his left cheek that moved when he talked. Fascinated, she tried not to watch it when they conversed.

Someone told her he could be a bit risqué, but she didn't know what that meant. She wondered if it was slang for a Jewish tradition. She knew that was his religion because he spoke of it often and seemed very proud of the fact.

"Be sure the new socks and shirts are out," Mr. Fox added as he hurried back past her toward the till.

"I will," she assured him.

"Those Eastern Oregon cowboys will be in this afternoon, and they will want clean clothes, a bath, and a measure of whiskey after they get the cows to the slaughterhouse." He always sounded as though he were in a hurry.

Tracy nodded. "I can't blame them wanting a bath," she murmured, the memory of their look and smell when first off the trail was fresh, powerful, and difficult to forget.

She glanced at the clock. *Oh my, it's almost twelve o'clock.* Turning, she ran out the door and the four blocks up the hill to the house to fetch Mr. Fox's noon meal. After her quick meal, she delivered his food and finished stocking the shelves. After that she returned with the dirty dishes to the house and spent the rest of the day helping Mrs. Fox with whatever chores she needed doing.

The Foxes paid her two dollars a week, and Mama said she could keep twenty-five cents. She felt positively rich. She slept in the tiny attic, which had a small square window that looked north where shimmering patches of blue or gray among the trees let her know the Columbia River was still in the right place.

It comforted her to know that and to know, too, that Logan was just a few miles east working with the fishermen. After the spring tie drive down the Sandy, he and his father joined the seining fishermen on the beach at Rooster Rock. They used their team of horses to help bring in the fishing nets full of salmon, steelhead, and an occasional sturgeon.

"When did you come to Troutdale?" Tracy asked Mrs. Fox, trying to pry her mind away from Logan. She carefully ironed the collar of Mr. Fox's white shirt and then went to a sleeve. Mrs. Fox had told her that Mr. Fox was very particular about his shirts.

"We moved here seven years ago, in '91 from Baker City," Frances Fox said, looking up from her needlework.

"That wasn't that long ago."

"No, quite the contrary, it seems like only yesterday."

"What made you come to Troutdale?" Tracy wondered why anyone of Mrs. Fox's refinement would want to settle in such a remote place. She thought of her mother, remembering the time Julianna had almost died in childbirth up on the hill and there was no one near enough for a five-year-old to run to for help. It was clear that Mrs. Fox was soon to have another child, and Tracy wondered if she would go into Portland when it was her time.

"My brother, Emanuel, was a partner in the Union Meat Packing Company here," Mrs. Fox replied. "He wrote us, telling of the need for a store. He said all the laborers from his company, not to mention the distillery and the mill, needed supplies. They didn't have time to go into Portland or even into Cleone for that matter." Frances paused for a moment and glanced out of the window. "I have to admit, I wasn't enthusiastic about the idea, but I've come to love the area, and it seems to be building up even faster than Aaron expected."

"All those men living in tents will bring their families out here one day," Tracy agreed. She glanced out the window at the sea of makeshift houses on the hillside starting at the edge of the Foxes' garden as she placed the cool iron she had been using onto the stove. Exchanging it for a hot one, she reached into the laundry basket for another shirt. She loved visiting with Mrs. Fox and enjoyed her small boys, although they did seem to get much dirtier than Harriet and Lucille.

Time passed quickly as Tracy's new job demanded more time and energy than her previous one, but she enjoyed it all the same. Her first Sunday to go home, she gave Mr. Fox ten cents for penny candy, and he gave her twenty pieces. When she protested, he shooed her away, muttering something about her being a "top hand" and deserving a bit extra. He was that way, though. She had seen him slip an extra handkerchief or an extra scoop of sugar into a customer's sack, especially if the person appeared to be down on their luck.

She caught the Hicklin Ferry, then climbed the long sloping trail up the bluff. When she arrived at the top, she waved to Mrs. Seidl, who was in the orchard harvesting Gravenstein apples. She would have stopped to chat ordinarily, but today she couldn't wait to see the children and give them their special treat.

They saw her when she rounded the bend, and by the time she opened the gate, the family had descended on her with Josie leading the pack. Even Ferd left his post in the garden harvesting the early corn to greet her. He was quieter and more formal as if to remind everyone that he was, after all, the head of the house now. At least until he and Mama clashed.

"Tracy, I knew you'd be coming home today," Josie said, mostly out of breath.

"How did you know?" Tracy put her pack down and gave them each a hug.

"Mama said you might, but I knew you would."

"I did, too," Arnold stated flatly.

Jackie and Little Alex's heads bobbed up and down.

Their faces smeared with dirt and grime were not all that appealing, but Tracy squeezed them anyway, purely happy to see them.

When they got to the house, Mama was busy in the kitchen, carefully placing corn on the thin wooden slats of Papa's racks. Each pair of slats held a row of shucked corn. When it was full with several rows, Arnold took the rack out and placed it on the shed roof to dry. The dried kernels would be removed from the cobs to be used for soups and stews in the winter. Mama claimed it was very nourishing.

When she saw Tracy, she wrapped her arms around her and held her for a long time.

"It's lonely around here without you, *Liebe,*" she said simply. Then in typical Mama fashion she said, "Tracy, you can relieve Bertie and shuck corn so she can go out and help Ferd finish."

"Don't say anything until I get back," Bertie begged as she headed out the door. "I don't want to miss a thing."

Tracy tried waiting for Bertie and not visiting, but the children kept asking questions about her new job. Although she was disappointed to have Minnie leave, she found herself enthusiastic about the Foxes and their children, who were rambunctious but very dear.

"The house is beautiful and close to town on Fourth Street," Tracy said, answering Josie's question about where she lived now. "Mrs. Fox has beautiful roses and a big garden. I have a little room upstairs where I can look out and see the Columbia River."

"Oh, it sounds lovely," Emma said. "When I get married, I'm moving to Portland where there's people and stores and excitement."

"No, Emma, you can't leave us," Jackie complained.

"Not for a long time, dearie," she said. "Not for a long time."

But Tracy wasn't sure. She had peeked at her mother's accounting figures the last time she was home, and the family did not have enough money to get them through the winter. Her mother was too busy in the fields for her to continue her midwifery. Tracy had even offered to give Julianna all of her money, but her mother was firm that she should keep a bit of her salary to buy dress material and other necessities.

Later, when the younger children were in bed, Tracy approached Julianna once more about the family predicament.

"Yes, we need money," Julianna said. "But I have a buyer for the twenty acres, the part with the nice spring that comes rushing out of the rocks. They'll pay us $350. If this sale happens, it will get us through the winter and put some crops in the ground. Say a prayer, *Tochter.* If that happens, then you can come home and be with us this winter."

"That would be a dream come true, Mama," she said, before she realized that Logan would want to come to court, and she hadn't mentioned that to her mother.

Chapter 11

LATE SEPTEMBER 1898

Julianna

"Thank you, Jacob," Julianna said, taking the long-awaited letter.

Jacob smiled warmly, his rugged Slovakian face lit up at her gratitude.

Such a kind man, she thought. *I'm grateful for neighbors as good-hearted as the Seidls.* Placing the bag of supplies on the counter by the sink, he turned to leave and bid her goodbye.

Tearing the letter open, she saw it was written in English. Dismayed, she handed it to Emma, "Please, what does this tell us?"

Emma translated:

My Dear Madam,

Please know it is my regret to inform you that my wife and I are unable to purchase your 20 acres at this time. Our bean and tomato crop failed this year. The potato crop came in, but there is only enough money to see us through the winter.

We are very disappointed, but as farmers we have

learned well enough to take what comes. We very much wanted to move to your area. We will not give up and will contact you when we have the money in hand. In the meantime if you can sell it, please do so with no hesitation.

Sincerely,
H.R. Lewis

Julianna caught her breath. Joseph and Jacob had taken her vegetables with their own on the deliveries to Palmer, but she only had slightly more than thirty dollars to see the family through the winter.

Emma swiftly gathered the children and left the room as Julianna sat down at her desk and gazed out the front window. *I have no choice,* she thought, and picked up her pen.

My dear Sophie,

It has been many months since I have written. I hope this letter finds you all well and happy.

We have spent the summer planting and harvesting. We have almost everything put up except the late planting of cabbage. Joseph will be taking a load of it to Palmer to sell tomorrow. I will make sauerkraut with what is left.

We have a good crop of apples, but there is no market, as everyone's trees are full. We are drying many bushels for applesauce and pies when we can get the flour.

I just got word from a potential land buyer that he will not be able to follow through with his hope to purchase the east twenty acres. I don't know how I will get the family through the winter, even with Tracy working in Troutdale.

Would you please ask your neighbors and friends at St. Joseph if they could use a strong healthy young lady to work for them? I will be sending Emma in, as Bertie is too young at twelve to go by herself to the big city. Just that one year makes such a difference at their age. The children out here in the country are much less sophisticated than those in town.

I can hardly bear to send another child away, but I have very little choice now that the sale has not gone through. Please know we are surviving, but it has been a difficult couple of years. I can hardly believe that Alex has been gone for a little over two years and the baby for two years on Christmas Eve.

Please let me know what you find out and thank you for all you do.

With love,
Julianna

Julianna sighed as she put down her pen. *How will I tell them?* she wondered. The littlest ones still hadn't gotten over Tracy's absence, and now Julianna was faced with separating them even further. *I wonder what Mama would say? And Papa? He'd probably tell me that he told me so. It wasn't Alex's fault that he died. He was so sick, but how I miss him. I so wish he were here.*

In three weeks a letter came from Sophie Foeller stating that Matt wanted Emma to stay with them and keep house, as she was very busy with church work. There would be short jobs for other St. Joseph parishioners, but they would be just a few hours apiece as "*Matt does not want her to stay with anyone but us.*"

"Don't leave yet, children, I have something to tell you," Julianna announced after they had finished supper. Her heart filled with dread at seeing their joyless faces. All of them worked hard, and they were so young.

"As you know, the letter a few weeks ago told us that the sale of the east twenty acres did not go through." She hesitated, not quite sure what to say next. "Emma, you are old enough now to go to work." She paused again, waiting for an angry response.

Emma nodded. "Yes, Mama." Her face was solemn. "I have been thinking about that."

"No, no, we already don't have Tracy," Josie cried. "No, Mama."

"No, I need Emma." Little Alex sniffed, rubbing his fist in his eye.

"I'm sorry, children, but we have no choice. Tracy can't bring in enough money. I just hope we can sell the land next year, so I can bring you both home," Julianna said, relieved that Emma understood.

Emma got up and took the two little boys in her arms. "I'll be back as soon as I can," she murmured. "Josie, we have to be brave. Papa would want that."

Josie nodded but did not look convinced.

"It's so lonely here without Tracy. I don't know how we'll stand it with both of you gone," Bertie pouted. Katherine had once told Julianna that Bertie "had a touch of the dramatic."

Two days later, the children escorted Emma to the Seidls so she could walk with Jacob to Troutdale. He had promised to see her safely aboard the train.

"Tracy, you have a visitor," Mr. Fox called to her from up front.

Tracy rose from stocking the extra supplies on the shelves of the storeroom. She pushed her hair back out of her eyes and brushed the soot off her sleeves. *Who could it be?* Logan was working. He had told her he wouldn't be back until the end of the month.

"I'll be right there," she answered, smoothing her apron.

Just then Emma rushed through the door, a whirlwind of energy. "Tracy, I'm so glad to see you." Her eyes glowed, but Tracy thought she saw a hint of sadness.

"Emma, what are you doing here?"

"Mama doesn't have any money; she got me a job with the Foellers." Words tumbled out between gulps of air.

"Oh Emma, I'm so very sorry I'm not a man, so I could make better money," Tracy said. "Logan makes in a day what I make in a week." She hesitated, thinking maybe she'd said too much.

Emma laughed and smiled slyly. "How do you know that?"

"Never you mind," Tracy said after a moment's pause. "Just tell me what happened. I assume the land didn't sell?" It had been nearly a month since Tracy had gotten time off to go home.

"No, it didn't. Mama sent a letter to the Foellers. She didn't tell me, but I knew what it said. The truth is that she would have to send someone to work in town and Bertie's too young," Emma said with a hint of pride. Tracy noticed her straightening her shoulders and standing a bit taller.

Tracy felt a surge of admiration for her younger sister. "Well, that's grown-up of you. I think you are very brave to go into Portland like this."

Emma and she had had their differences over the years, but her sister was very dear to her, and she knew her to be much braver than she herself had been.

"When I saw how much courage it took for you to leave, I couldn't say no." Emma hesitated, and then added, "All of us admire you, Tracy, and the children miss you, but you did what you had to do, and so will I."

Chapter 12

ROOSTER ROCK SEINING BEACH

October 1898
Logan

Rain came in torrents for short periods, then eased. A cold gray westerly wind whipped the horses and beat the men who worked to control them.

Logan, waist-deep in the battering river, struggled to rein his father's team as the tired animals, hitched to a net laden with fish, strained to make their way toward the beach. Out of the corner of his eye, he saw his friend Leroy upstream working frantically to drive the Mershons' team toward shore.

As the weather got uglier, the men grew tense watching the seining turn darker and more dangerous. Everyone moved at a frantic pace, laboring to keep the horses and men from drowning while focusing on bringing in the nets writhing with the catch. Wind whipped the waves, slapping the horses who struggled with their load while the men strained to keep their footing and avoid falling into one of the many holes on the river bottom.

This week the weather had steadily grown worse as the fish run waned. Now they mostly caught the oceangoing trout known as steelhead and a few Chinook salmon. The coho, sockeye, and chum had stopped running a few days before.

Just this morning, Logan had heard the fishermen who oversaw the operation speak in hushed tones among themselves, wondering if they should quit fishing for the season or stay with it, trying to squeeze in one more week before finishing.

Their decision had been to finish the week, much to Logan and his father's dismay. They had been on the job over a month, and the farm needed them. Logan missed Tracy. Now at the end of the day, he could see his horses were exhausted. He was sure their other team was as tired as this one, so a substitution was not possible.

The Percherons were up past their bellies as he urged them on, hoping they could land the net one more time. Then he would beseech his father to quit. As strong and courageous as they were, the horses could do no more. A week ago the water had been much lower. Now with the rain, it had expanded the distance they had to struggle to deposit the load onto the long sandy beach. And the tide had come in. Even at a hundred or so miles upstream from the Pacific Ocean, the river was affected by its rise and fall.

Logan saw his father waiting on the beach, but was too far away to see the concern on his face. He knew it was there though, because both of them knew their teams well and could tell when Job and especially Jake were in trouble. He wondered if he should cut the net loose and save the horses. No, he thought, as he watched them strain and slowly move forward. The team is strong.

But the wind blew with greater ferocity, and now the rain beat down on his face, blinding him. Making his way to the front of the horses, he grabbed onto Jake's bridle with one hand while still holding the reins with the other. Jake was the older of the two animals and Logan's favorite.

"C'mon, boy!" he hollered above the gale. "We have to get you out of this deep water." Logan was standing in water almost up to his chest, with waves lapping higher. Even with his high rubber boots and waterproof suit, the storm's chill crept in. *Dad-gum, this is cold,* he thought as a shiver ran through him.

One foot and then the next, the three of them continued moving toward the last seventy-five yards to the beach. Without warning, Jake stepped into a hole and sank down with only his head above water. He struggled in a panic, bringing Logan down with him as they both fought to stay afloat. Logan, with great effort, pulled his face above the water, and grabbed a breath of air before he and Jake went under again. He popped up again, gasping for air, still holding on to the team with the reins and Jake's bridle.

He struggled, keeping his head free while pulling the horses up as best he could, but the weight of the net and the depth of the hole made it impossible for the team to push forward.

He let go of the bridle and reached for his knife to cut the horses loose just as his head sank once again. Groping for the handle with his free hand, he searched wildly, knowing he'd put it on his belt this morning. Just like he did every morning, but where was it?

Holding his breath, he frantically felt again. Nothing! He continued groping until finally his hand closed around it. As he pulled the knife out of the sheath, he fought to get back to the surface. Finally after an eternity, he felt his face break free of the water. Spitting and coughing, he gasped for as much air as his lungs could hold and dove toward the back of the horses.

Still holding the reins, he wildly searched for the tresses that hitched the animals to the bulky net. He opened his eyes, intent on cutting the horses free, but he was met with the inky blackness of the raging water.

Fighting down panic, he felt his way along the side still feeling for the lines. His lungs bursting, he managed to work his way to the surface once again and gulp another breath. He noticed someone walking toward him, arms waving and water splashing. It must be Papa. Yes, it was his father yelling something, but the wind took the words away.

He dove again and, grabbing the traces, he followed them back to the hitch. He clutched the rope that held the net and sawed as hard as he could. His lungs bursting, he surfaced for another breath, dove again, and continued cutting.

Finally the net slid loose from the harness. He felt the horses moving forward as they broke free of the net. Pulling himself again toward the surface, something tugged at his leg, holding him immobile. His foot caught in the netting, jerking him under. He tried to reach down and cut it loose, but could not reach it. He kicked as hard as he could, but it remained tightly wrapped around his foot.

He kicked once again, his lungs bursting. Panic came instantly. He knew he was trapped. Again he wildly reached to try to cut himself free. His hands, numb with cold, were beyond command. Desperately, he tried to work them.

"Jesus, help me!" he prayed. Darkness closed in around him.

Chapter 13

LATE OCTOBER 1898

Julianna

"My God, will it ever stop?" Julianna sank heavily into the chair, her eyes on Franz, who had brought her the supplies she ordered from the Fox's store and with them the news of the Chamberlain boy.

"How in the world did it happen?" she asked when she could find her voice.

"Aaron Fox told me the poor boy got caught in the horses' traces and was pulled under before anyone could get to him," Franz said as he emptied his packboard on the kitchen table.

What will Tracy do? Julianna had done her best to discourage her, but she knew how it was when you find that certain young man. The thought took her instantly back to the park on that summer day in Baden and the time when she first noticed Alex talking to Papa. What a long time ago—a lifetime now.

There are times when I'm sorry I didn't try to talk Alex out of coming to America, though. I still don't understand this horrid language, she thought ruefully. *And it will soon be twenty years since I have laid eyes on my family.*

"Mr. Fox told me that Tracy is taking this very hard."

Franz's voice abruptly brought her out of her trance. "She hasn't been to work the last two days. She hasn't even been out of her room. I guess they are pretty worried about her."

"I wondered about that when you told me," she said quietly.

"I guess I must have missed that romance. Josie confided in me not a month ago that Tracy cared for him."

"I tried to dissuade her. The family isn't Catholic, you know, and it's difficult to be married to someone who doesn't share the same beliefs." Julianna sighed.

Franz smiled and shook his head. "No one her age is going to listen to anything that practical, especially from a parent."

Julianna reluctantly agreed, remembering Papa's discontent over Alex, and suddenly she had even greater worry about her eldest daughter. "I need to go to her," she murmured.

"I think that's a good idea." He paused and said, "It would be good for both of you. You've only been off this place a few times since Alex passed away."

Julianna fought back tears. *What's the matter with me? I couldn't cry at my own husband's funeral.* But now try as she might, the tears could not be stopped. She turned her head, hoping Franz wouldn't notice and he, being an understanding gentleman and a dear friend, didn't say anything.

"So silly of me," she said as she dabbed her eyes and blew her nose. "I'll go in the morning after the children are off to school. I'll drop Little Alex off to play with Jennie, if that's all right?"

"Of course. I know Katherine will be glad to help. She was complaining this morning that she hadn't had a good visit with you for a long time. Be prepared to stay awhile, so leave early," he said as he patted her shoulder and walked out into the misty afternoon.

TRACY TRIED TO IGNORE THE GENTLE TAP AT HER DOOR. She was not fit to see anyone. She knew she didn't want to talk just yet. But the knock persisted, and she reluctantly answered, "Yes?"

"You have a visitor."

"Who is it?"

"I'll send her up." She heard Mrs. Fox's footsteps on the stairs.

In a moment, the door opened, and Tracy looked up to see her mother standing hesitantly near the threshold. Before she knew it, she was in her in mother's arms.

"I'm so very sorry, child," Tracy heard her say through her tears.

EMMA, SITTING ON HER BED, TORE OPEN THE LETTER. It had been a long time, over two months, since she had had a word from home. Hoping Mama had sent her permission to come visit for Christmas, she eagerly began to read:

November 1898
My dear Emma,

I've been meaning to write for some time, and have put it off long enough. I hope this letter finds you well and happy. We are fine here, thanks to our neighbors and our ability to raise a good garden. We have enough food put in to last the winter and Franz and Joseph bring supplies up the hill when they go to Troutdale. Remember, some of these supplies come from money you and Tracy bring in. I want you to know how much we appreciate your working.

My plans are that, come spring, we will buy some baby chicks from Mr. Graham and sell eggs, probably to Fox's in Troutdale and later in the season to the folks in the logging communities. Franz convinced me last week to get a couple more nannies because there seems to be quite a demand for goat cheese. He says it's easy to make and he will teach me. This should help bring in more money and will be easier with the children getting older and more able to help out.

We have some sad news. The Chamberlain boy drowned three weeks ago while helping the seining crew at Rooster Rock. Tracy has been quite upset, as you can imagine. I'm sad for the family, as he was a nice young man. The whole community turned out for the funeral.

A pain grabbed Emma's chest, and she felt a few tears slide down her cheek. The letter fell to the floor as she pressed her hand to her mouth to stifle a cry. "Oh, my God, not Logan!" She slumped over, her tears dropping onto the letter.

Not a soul knew how she felt about the young man with the laughing eyes and the curly dark hair. Certainly not Tracy, whom she had purposely tortured, half in jest, over him, and not her mother, who firmly believed that her children should avoid marriage with a non-Catholic.

She had secretly hoped that one day Logan would notice her and decide she was the prettiest Lampert daughter. Maybe then he would change his mind about Tracy and ask to marry her instead. In fact, she had decided that was exactly what would happen. She just hadn't yet come up with a plan to let him know how she felt.

A bang on the door announced that Bobbie and little Sophie were up from their nap and ready for play. She hastily wiped her eyes and smoothed her hair. "I'll be right there," she called.

Later that evening when the kitchen chores were done and the children were down for the night, Emma found the courage to pick up Mama's letter again.

I hope you can come home for Christmas. Tracy will be here. She will be coming on December 22 and the Foxes have generously given her until the first part of January before she must return to work. If you come out on the train on the 21st, then you can walk up the trail with her. This, of course, all hinges on the weather. If we have a bad storm, I have already told Tracy that I want you girls to stay where you are. You mustn't worry about us. We have plenty of wood and kerosene and will be just fine.

I have enclosed a note to Sophie as well, so please see that she gets it. The children say hello and they hope to see you soon.

Mit Liebe,
Mutter

Emma dried her eyes, carefully folded the letter, and slipped it back into the envelope. She tucked the note for Sophie into her apron pocket so she would remember to give it to her.

EMMA GAZED OUT THE TRAIN WINDOW AS IT PULLED into the Troutdale Depot. The rosary she had said daily since receiving her mother's letter had worked well, she thought. No snow—in fact, mild temperatures for this time of year.

She gathered her grip and coat, clambered off the train, and followed Harlow Street up the hill to Troutdale's main street. Her new modern, brown high-button shoes protected her feet from the wet and mud. *Thank goodness Sophie insisted on me going shopping and spending some of my money on them. I hope Mama doesn't mind.* She shuddered. *What if she does?* She shook her head and lifted her chin. *Well, they are stylish and I love them, so I guess I'll just take my medicine if Mother disapproves. I am, after all, 13 years old.*

She stopped at Fox's store just long enough to find out that Tracy was waiting for her up at the Fox house, so she trudged the short distance up the hill and rang the doorbell.

She found Tracy solemn, but much better than she thought she would be. "I'm glad to see you, little sister," she said before Emma could say anything.

"I'm happy to see you, too." Emma paused and said, "I'm so sorry for your loss."

Tracy nodded. "Thank you." After a moment, she continued, "Mama came down to see me."

"She did? What did she say?"

"She said she was sorry for me and sorry for Logan, too."

"My goodness. She never ceases to surprise me."

"I know," Tracy said. "Somehow, it made me feel much better."

Tracy led Emma to the workroom in back of the house. Sitting on a wooden crate, she waved for Emma to sit in the old chair beside her and then stared at her hands. Emma squirmed and waited, wondering what she could say to help her sister.

"I wanted to marry him, you know," Tracy softly said.

"I'm not surprised. I saw it on your face when you looked at him."

Emma put her arm around her sister, and they sat a long while in silence.

THE RAIN HAD STOPPED BY THE TIME THEY REACHED the top of the hill, but the trail up the bluff was slippery, and climbing it was not easy. "It's a good thing Papa taught us how to use a packboard," Emma had said earlier as she clung to a tree to keep from slipping back down to the bottom of the cliff. "It keeps my hands free. It would be a long way to fall."

Tracy laughed then, the first she had been able to muster, but she knew they could never have made it up the steep embankment carrying satchels and bags. That's why she had insisted on unpacking everything and repacking it on the packboards. It annoyed Emma, who had to wait and was impatient to start for home.

It was almost dark by the time they reached the home gate. Ferd's collie, Max, greeted them with barks and kisses, alerting the children, and soon siblings began to gather on the porch to greet their sisters.

Bertie came out of the house, wiping her hands on her apron. It seemed strange to Tracy to see her younger sister, now twelve, taking on the role of the cook. She looked older than Tracy remembered, though it had not been but a couple of months since she'd last seen her.

Ferd and Arnold ran from the barn carrying half-full pails, with milk splashing and sloshing all the way. It was hard to believe that Arnold was already eight, and old enough to help Ferd with the chores. *Well, I guess that's when Ferd started,* the thought ran through Tracy's mind. *The children have to help or we would all perish.*

Josie came up and slid her arms around her big sister. Tracy smiled down at her and again was stunned how grown-up she looked.

"How's Mama?" she asked.

"She's been sad about Logan, but more talkative lately," Josie replied. "She even sang Christmas carols with us when we put up the tree, and she went to the Christmas play at school." Josie was the sibling who saw goodness in everything. *Oh my, how I've missed her,* Tracy thought.

Mama came out and hustled everyone into the living room where a warm fire radiated from the stove. They hung their wet coats, handed their packboards to the boys to haul upstairs, and headed for the kitchen to assist Bertie as she finished cooking the evening meal. Meanwhile Mama helped Jackie and Little Alex remove their muddy boots and overalls.

The family spent the next three days getting ready for the big holiday and catching up on the news, most especially the loss of Logan. Tracy was surprised that Emma seemed so sad when she spoke of him. She had always been the first person to taunt her when the opportunity arose. She shook her head and decided that she would never figure out her sister and might as well not even try.

Christmas morning there were presents under the tree for everyone from Mama who, according to Bertie, had spent many weeks sewing something special for each child. Tracy and Emma each brought treats as well, and Josie and Bertie—who was becoming quite the chef—made special Christmas cookies that they hid in a lidded tin in the cellar until the family finished the morning meal. Then they were doled out: one apiece.

After breakfast, everyone bundled up and walked over to Joseph and Elma's to celebrate Christmas with them and the Frommelts. Joseph built a makeshift table and set it up in the living room and fixed a play area for the younger children in the woodshed.

The men spent some time out there, telling their wives it was to watch over the children, but Tracy knew it was to get away from the hubbub of meal preparation.

She suspected they had a bottle of wine stowed somewhere.

It was good to be home. Coming back, she realized how badly she had missed everyone. Katherine in particular seemed most eager to visit with her.

"Tell me, Tracy, about life in the Foxes' store. What are your duties?" she asked while stirring the gravy, with baby Joe on her hip.

Tracy answered the best she could; although that was the last thing she wanted to talk about. She sensed that Katherine was hungry for news of life away from the hill.

Tracy couldn't understand that. All she wanted was to be home and to have Logan with her. Now neither of those dreams was remotely possible. She shook her head and tried to banish the thought. *I'm going to enjoy the day, no matter what.*

PART II

Frank Wand

Chapter 14

NORTHWEST ILLINOIS 1893

Frank Wand

Frank squinted away from the evening sun toward the barn and the whinnies of Manny and Mel, the matched pair of Belgians that were old man Wehrenberg's pride and joy. *I can't blame him,* he thought; *I'd be proud of those chestnut beauties if they were mine.*

He wondered if Cecilia Libby would find him attractive enough to take a wagon ride with him if he owned those two magnificent creatures. *No, probably not,* he decided. Not as long as Lenard Lentz lived across the road from her. Besides, if that weren't enough, Lenard had a promising career in the banking business with his father, something that would turn any girl's head. Frank sighed. *I'm just a farmer who likes to build things.*

The eighteen-year-old had been happy Papa had sent him over to Mr. Wehrenberg's to work on his farm this summer. "I need you to make some money for us," Papa had told him. "Uncle Phillip and I will work our two farms together. Mr. Wehrenberg will pay you a fair wage, and we can use the extra cash."

The Wands, like most everyone, were feeling the depression. Steep hillsides and a wide creek made much of the

Derinda Road farm unproductive. This meant that when farm prices were low, the family suffered.

"I wish we wouldn't have had to leave the Woodbine place," his father had confided in him one day. He had not replied, but he felt the same way.

Now Frank walked slowly to the barn with carrots for the horses. His hip still hurt from the fall, especially after a hard day's work. He wearily patted the horses and remembered the first month on the job. He had been so tired he could barely finish supper before falling into bed. Not even second helpings could tempt him to linger at the table.

"I have to make sure our hired men have plenty to eat," Mrs. Wehrenberg would say, as she slapped another helping of mashed potatoes on his half-emptied plate. *I have to admit,* he'd thought, *she's a darn good cook.*

Frank loved the long days in the field, the smell of fresh-cut hay, and the dry feel of it under his feet when putting it up in the barn. He enjoyed each step of the haying process, from working with the horses to curing the hay with rock salt, broadcasting and scattering it about from a large coffee can over each load of loose fodder forked in the barn. Papa often seemed to be too busy to discuss modern farming practices, so Frank appreciated his employer's farming conversations, especially the discussions about the new block and tackle fork that Mr. Wehrenberg had just installed.

He never stopped being fascinated by the large black two-pronged fork hanging on a heavy rope, high up near the ceiling of the barn. The rope ran through two pulleys, each in a block—one in front by the door and one in back where the hay was stored in the loft.

When the wagon, piled high with loose hay, pulled into

the barn, it was Frank's job to get on the top of the load, carefully place the two-pronged fork into the hay pile, and stomp it down to set it. If it wasn't set properly, it could trip halfway across the barn.

Mr. Wehrenberg had been firm when explaining this part. "It would take valuable time and cost a lot of money to clean up the mess all that hay would make if it's dropped in the wrong place." Frank remembered the old man smacking his lips and shaking his head, so he knew he'd better get it right.

Once the fork was anchored in place, Frank scrambled out of harm's way to the back of the wagon and signaled Hank, the main farmhand, who'd already unhitched the horses, brought them around to the back of the wagon, and hooked the rope holding the fork to their rigging. When Hank caught the signal and saw that Frank was safely away, he slapped the reins and whistled to the horses. If the fork was placed correctly, half the wagonload started to move, like some giant lumbering behemoth rising ever so slowly toward the ceiling.

They had gotten better at signaling after Frank was knocked off the wagon one day when the rope from the fork had gotten twisted. He had fallen off the loaded wagon onto his behind and had sat for a minute, wondering if he could even stand up.

"Whoa, young fellow, that's not the way to get back to the ground." Mr. Wehrenberg helped Frank to his feet.

Frank rubbed his hip now, remembering how bad it had hurt. He'd just about not made it through the rest of the day, and had had trouble getting out of bed the following morning. Over time it gradually felt better, but it was still sore to the touch.

He thought about the wagonload and the mechanized process that took the hay off the wagon. Sometimes Frank had to guide the fork load a bit, but mostly he just watched from a safe place. When the load reached the first pulley, the fork snapped into place and flung itself and the hay toward the back of the barn, while the horses continued to move ahead. When the fork load came to the back pulley, again it snapped into place, and the load of hay leisurely descended. As soon as Mr. Wehrenberg could reach it to guide the drop, he moved it where he wanted it to fall and signaled Frank to pull the smaller trip rope. About the same time, Frank motioned to Hank to stop the horses.

It usually took only two of the huge fork loads to empty the wagon, which had initially surprised Frank because the wagon held twenty or so field shocks that took two men with pitchforks a couple of hours to load.

Just thinking about standing under the hay as it moved off the wagon made Frank's back itch. The younger men hayed in their sleeveless undershirts to try to keep the seeds from sticking to their clothes. Since that was nearly an impossible task, they leaned under the water pump at mealtime in a futile attempt to wash off the barbs.

Frank many times wished Papa had a setup like this at their farm. It would make things so much easier for them. It might have been "newfangled," as Papa would say, but Frank had found that it was a big time-saver.

Thinking of Papa and their new farm on Derinda Road reminded Frank of the farm they'd sold when he was thirteen. His family fled the land in Woodbine, a few miles east of Derinda, in 1885. It was a wonderfully sprawling acreage, with rolling hills and a spring-fed pond. Papa said the windmill out by the barn was already on the place when he bought the land, and he had carried water from it to the house until the family could hire a well digger to dig into the well and install a hand pump outside the kitchen.

I wonder if Uncle Phillip is having the same trouble we had, now that the buildings are all torn down. I haven't heard him speak of it lately, Frank mused, absently rubbing his hip.

Chapter 15

WOODBINE FARM REMEMBERED

Stroking Manny's neck, Frank marveled at the large horse with the huge hooves. Wishing he could afford a team like this, his mind wandered back to the night at the Woodbine farm when a team of horses had changed his family's life; a team they heard arrive, but never saw!

"Wonder who's comin' this time of the evening?" Papa had mused as he shoved his empty plate aside.

"Maybe it's Phillip. You never know what he'll do," Ma answered. They heard the horses and wagon pass the house and the brake on the wagon wheel squeal as the rig came to a halt in front of the barn.

"I'm in no hurry to go find out, Frances. It's been a long day, and anyone that would come over after dark can just find their own way to the house," he huffed and reached for his bowl of applesauce.

The harness clanged and rattled as the horses were being unhooked, and they heard the barn door slide open.

"Must be Phillip. He's the only one who would unhook the horses at this hour." Ma's voice sounded puzzled. She took another sip of coffee and got up to clear the table for company.

They finished dessert in silence, trying to hurry for visitors. Frank, now fourteen, hoped his pretty twelve-year-old cousin, Anna, would be with her father. They were good friends. Anna had even told him once, a month ago, that she planned on marrying him. He liked the idea, but wondered if he could get permission, since she was his uncle's daughter. He decided he had some time to persuade his father.

Frances came back and sat down to finish her dessert. They heard the porch screen door open and footsteps tromp on the stoop.

Frank, eager to see Anna, jumped up to greet the visitors. He dashed into the kitchen to find the door closed and the kitchen empty. His heart sank. Not again, he thought, and yelled, "Pa! Ma! There's no one here."

"*So ein Mist,*" Papa spat out the words as he came into the kitchen, grabbed the lantern off the wall, and hurried to the barn with Frank and his younger brothers Leo and George close at his heels. When the four of them reached the barn, there was no wagon, no horses, no open barn door, nothing, and nobody.

"*Hallo!*" Papa called, but only a deafening silence answered him. "*Verdammt,*" he swore. "I'm sick of this! This is the worst yet!"

The hair on the back of Frank's neck stood up as he wondered what Papa would do. He suddenly became aware of his brothers looking wide-eyed and clutching his pant legs tightly. In an effort to calm them he patted their heads, but it was difficult because he was as frightened as they appeared.

He remembered one day last spring, just before dark, his older sister Lizzie had called to Papa from the kitchen, hollering that she saw someone in the barn throwing hay down to the stock.

It was just after Papa and Frank had finished feeding and milking and were back in the house, cleaning up for supper.

"Ignatz," Ma had called to Papa, "I see it, too."

"All right, Frances."

"Come, Frank, let's go see what this is all about," Papa hollered over his shoulder.

They hurried down the path toward the barn, looked up, and saw hay falling past the upstairs window near the loft. When they opened the door, there was no hay by the stanchions, and no one was anywhere around.

Frank remembered how Papa had grumbled about being alarmed at this kind of activity, but tonight, hearing the team and wagon was the first time he saw the anger and helplessness in his father's eyes.

"I DON'T KNOW WHAT TO TELL YOU, IGNATZ," PHILLIP said thoughtfully. "It sure wasn't me that come over the other night. I must say it's mighty unsettling."

"*Ja,* strange things are happening more often these days." Ignatz removed his wide-brimmed hat and wiped his forehead with his dark blue handkerchief. "Mama says she often hears the pump squeaking out back just before daylight. When she goes to investigate, there's no one around, but sometimes the ground is wet."

"Well, you know that fellow was shot here back in the early '60s. Do you think that has anything to do with it?" Phillip squinted his eyes in thought.

"I just don't know. It's hard to put up with, and it's just darn spooky." Ignatz spoke quietly. "I doubt it helps that the Woodbine Cemetery is on the property line." He shoved a thumb toward the graveyard and continued, “I’ll speak to Father Schmidt next Sunday. Maybe he can help.”

After a moment he shook his head. “Although I have my doubts. Even if Father could do something to help us, my wife is ready to leave. She’s tired and scared of it, and I can’t say as I blame her.”

“Well, this is prime property, and I’m right next door.” Phillip brought his fist down with a smack on the tailgate of his wagon. “If the priest can’t help us and it gets too bad, I’ll buy the place, tear the buildings down, and farm it.”

“This is choice land,” Ignatz said, despair in his voice. “I hate to get rid of it, but my family is about at their wits’ end. Lizzie told her mother the other day that there was something that looked like a cloud above little Annie’s crib. Frances went to check the baby, who was crying her eyes out, and didn’t see anything. Like she says, Lizzie’s not likely to make up a story.”

Now Mel nuzzled Frank’s shoulder, asking for attention, bringing Frank back to the present and Mr. Wehrenberg’s place. He absentmindedly reached over and scratched the big Belgian’s neck, wondering if things might have been better for Mama and Papa if they’d not had to flee the Woodbine farm.

Chapter 16

FALL 1893

World's Columbian Exposition
Chicago

"I'll bet that thing's 400 feet tall," Frank said, shading his eyes and looking up at the big wheel. The metal plaque on the side read "Invented by George Ferris."

"Probably so. Taller than a barn anyway," Johnny answered, his fists jammed into his overall pockets. "Never seen anything like it. Are you gonna ride on it?"

"You bet your life. I'm not gonna pass up a chance like this. Why, they say you can see Indiana and Michigan from up there." Excitement surged, and Frank couldn't keep it out of his voice. "I wonder if you can see all the way back to Woodbine."

"I doubt it; it's a long way." Johnny laughed.

"Maybe so, but it's a long way to Indiana, too," Frank responded with disdain. Sometimes Johnny annoyed him. Frank had always been taken aback by his cousin and could never figure out why. Maybe it was because Johnny was older and often reminded Frank of it. *At least I wear fashionable clothes*, Frank thought, hooking his thumbs in his suspenders and glancing down at his brand-new brown trousers.

Frank knew that Papa was happy when he learned Johnny would be going with him to Chicago. "You've worked hard for your money this summer, son, and I think you should take some of it and go." Frank nodded, agreeing with his father's advice. He had given most of his earnings to the family anyway.

That was all it took, and here they were standing in line to pay ten cents for a ticket to ride the "Wonder of the Mid-way." Frank heard someone behind him commenting about how this was the "Eiffel Tower" of the Chicago fair.

Soon they were scrambling into a brightly painted car with plush seats and a smooth grab bar. They stopped several times to load and unload passengers and were almost to the top by the time the last car was full.

Sure enough, they saw a large ship on the horizon of Lake Michigan and a smaller boat unloading fairgoers at the park entrance. Below them spread the immense city of Chicago, bigger than any town they had ever seen. The horses on the city streets beneath them looked like the toys that Grandmother Goldhagen had given him one long-ago Christmas. He remembered that he had played with them until most of the paint had worn off and one of them had a broken leg that he was unable to patch.

He glanced at Johnny and saw the wonder in his eyes. He knew then that his cousin felt the same excitement. *I guess he must be a fine fellow most of the time.*

"I wonder if that's Indiana." Johnny let go of the bar just long enough to point to the small land mass barely seen to the east.

"Probably," Frank said. *I'm not lettin' go,* he thought. *Just goes to show you; Johnny ain't got any sense.*

Frank looked at the tiny people in line for the next ride. It reminded him of a small snake winding itself around one of the fence posts on the farm. With the wind in his hair and the tight grip on the bar, he felt like he was on top of the world. He sucked in air. Never had he felt this kind of exhilaration. *Ma and Papa will never believe this.*

When the ride was over and his knees less wobbly, he steered Johnny to a stand where he bought a penny flyer with pictures of the amazing machine.

"I want my family to believe me when I tell them what I've seen," he told Johnny.

"*Ja*, they'll never believe us if we don't take 'em some proof," Johnny agreed, and handed the vendor a penny for his own copy.

"We'd better go over to White City and see something educational," Frank said as he carefully folded a brightly colored flyer and put it in his back pocket. "Papa was pretty firm on that."

"Let's get another one of those carbonated sodas to drink on our walk over," Johnny replied. "I'm really thirsty."

"That's a great idea. I'm gonna try a cherry-flavored one this time," Frank said as they turned toward the food stands. "That lemon soda I had last time was really good."

Now that their excursion was almost over, he was looking forward to returning home. He was wondering if the shotgun he bought the first day would beat him home like the Sears & Roebuck salesman had promised. Brothers Leo and George would be excited too with the double-barreled, 12-gauge "Quality Machine Gun," as it said on its side, because they had owned only single-barrel shotguns.

Chapter 17

ILLINOIS

March 1899

"I think you should reconsider, Johnny," Frank said. "The opportunities are out west." He took off his cap and rubbed his forehead, thinking about his father wanting to sell the Derinda Road farm. He did not want Papa to give up the farm, but it just didn't have enough productive land to ward off the effects of the last decade's depression. Besides, he could tell that Papa hadn't been feeling well the last few months. Frank was beginning to think that getting away from the work and worry of the farm and buying a business in Elizabeth would be a good change for him.

"I don't know, Frank. It just doesn't appeal to me," Johnny answered, slowly as if searching for words. "It's a long way from Illinois and the family, and besides, it's a long way from Anna Artman."

"Anna is your cousin, Johnny," Frank said, fighting down his impatience.

"My third cousin, *um Himmels willen!* Father Wagner said he would marry us when she says yes." Johnny sounded exasperated. "We've been over this before."

"I know. It's just that there's so many of our relations

around here, it's tough to know who to court." *One more reason to get on that train,* Frank thought, and said, "I'm going! Think it over. I'm not leaving for a couple of weeks, so you have a few more days to decide." He grabbed the saddle horn, threw a leg over Ol' Bessie, and scooted comfortably into the seat.

Sitting tall, he patted his horse and said, "She's the only girl I'll miss."

Johnny laughed. "Well ol' friend, you will be missed, not only by me, but by many girls in Jo Daviess County."

Frank threw back his head and laughed heartily. It felt good to laugh with Johnny. *I'll miss this old fool,* he thought.

On the way home his head grew lighter, and he could feel himself getting weaker. *Oh no,* he thought, *is that doggone ague coming back? I thought I had gotten rid of that for good last time.*

By the time he got to the barn, his body was shaking so badly he couldn't undo the bridle and had to call Leo to help unsaddle the horse. Sweat poured into his eyes as the fever worsened. He made his way into the house. Stubbing his toe on a loose stone poking up from the path, he somehow managed to maintain his balance.

"Frank, what is it?" Ma asked, her voice alarmed as she noticed his unsteadiness. "Oh no, the fever's back, isn't it?" She grabbed his arm in an effort to keep him steady. Even through the veil of malaria, it seemed strange to him that his short mother could brace his five-foot-ten frame and keep him from falling into the boiling pot on the stove.

He could feel her, though, as she steered him to his bed out on the screened back porch. "I'll get some of that tea that Dr. Murray sent home last time you had the fever. I still have some in the cupboard." She hurried back toward the kitchen.

He grabbed his covers and pulled them up under his chin. By now the chills shook him so badly the bed bounced like an outfield baseball grounder in the back pasture.

He knew he couldn't hold the cup still enough to sip the tea without spilling the hot liquid, so he brushed her hand slightly and shook his head when she tried to hand it him. She held it and his head as he sipped small hot swallows, slowly emptying the flowered teacup. He didn't know what was in the concoction, but he knew it made him sleepy and eased the severity, for at least a little while.

He was a bit better by the second day and was able to drink the rich broth his youngest sister, Annie, brought him, but it wasn't until day three that he could get out of bed without help. He hated these spells. They left him weak and wobbly as a newborn calf. He wouldn't let himself think about what would happen when he went out West.

He remembered a railroad advertisement he had seen downtown a few weeks ago. It held information about a mineral hot springs in a remote town in the eastern part of Oregon that claimed a cure for malaria. As soon as he was able, he wanted more information.

Chapter 18

SPRING 1899

Tracy

"I can't remember what he looked like sometimes," Tracy mused. She wished she could say more, but she didn't know how much her sister understood. Josie was so young, and Logan had been gone over a year.

"Don't worry, Tracy," she replied. "He's still in your heart, even if his face isn't in your memory."

"What a nice thing to say." Tracy gave Josie an affectionate hug. They were enjoying the brief carefree moment away from the drudgery of the farm while Tracy was home on a short holiday from the Foxes' store.

Josie nodded, smiled, and stopped to examine a clump of trilliums alongside the path. "Aren't they pretty?"

She always sees the beauty. I wish I could be more like her, Tracy thought to herself. Out loud, she said, "Yes they are."

Continuing on the wooded lane that led down to the path into the Frommelts' front yard, they stopped again to admire the three-petaled white flower.

They were on a mission for Mama, carrying some letters for Franz to mail and to find out when he or Joseph could come and work the field for planting. Most of all, they were excited to see Katherine. She was as close as they would ever come to knowing an aunt, since all of their relatives were either in Illinois or in the old country.

"Katherine'll be glad to see you," Mama said. "She's still grieving over Mary." Tracy had nodded, understanding. She too, missed Mary and had been devastated by her death. They were good friends, and so close to losing Logan made it doubly difficult.

Late last summer, Mary had gone into Portland on a holiday. She visited with Emma, and they made a trip downtown for lunch. The next day a group of young girls from St. Joseph Church went swimming in a creek that ran through Portland, past the tannery, and into the Willamette River. Emma was unable to accompany them because of her duties, which turned out to be a blessing for her.

According to her mother's account, when Mary arrived home she'd had a high fever. Later, Emma said that two other girls had gotten sick as well, but neither died.

After a week, Mary developed a flat blotchy rash. By then, both Mama and Katherine had known that it was typhoid fever. "I'd seen it before in Illinois," Mama said, shaking her head.

After week of severe fever, abdominal cramps, and exhaustion, Mary died. Tracy had known she was ill, but did not know about her death until Mr. Seidl brought the news on his next trip to Troutdale. By that time, the service was over, and Mary had been buried on the hill beside Papa and Bernard. One of Mr. Seidl's chores that day was to mail a letter to Mount Angel Abby and ask for a priest to come as soon as possible to say Mass and bless the grave.

Earlier in the day, Tracy and Josie had stopped on the way to the Frommelts' and visited the three small crosses just off the path and up a small hill. They stood silently, each deep in her own thoughts. Tracy said an Our Father and a Hail Mary, which made her feel better. Her thoughts turned to Logan, and she wished she could visit his grave. *Maybe I will one day. Right now these prayers are for him too.*

"Tell me about the funeral, Josie?" Tracy broke the silence.

"It was really sad." Josie paused, and after a long while, she said, "Katherine leaned on Franz, and they both cried."

"Oh my, we must keep them in our prayers."

Tracy knew it would take a long time for Katherine to accept Mary's death, but she hadn't thought about how it affected Franz.

Look at Mama. She still isn't well after losing her husband and baby. I hope Franz and Katherine will be able to recover from their grief faster. Tracy had watched her mother struggle with the losses for years, and she knew she could never wish that kind of grief on anyone, especially a friend. Logan came to her mind again, along with the ghastly realization that she, too, must learn to live with the loss or would end up suffering like her mother. The thought startled her—much like a blacksmith's hammer slamming down on the anvil. She reached for a nearby tree for support and, sucking in her breath, she closed her eyes until she regained her senses.

"What's the matter, Tracy?"

"I'm so, so sorry for our dear friends." Tracy shook her head as she started down the trail.

"Me, too," she heard Josie mutter, but she could not acknowledge her sister.

"How good you look," Katherine exclaimed when

she answered the knock on the door. "I was hoping to get a chance to visit with you during your holiday." She looked weary and worn, but was happy to see them.

Katherine's kind voice and welcome hug soothed Tracy as much as Josie's words, and she marveled at what good medicine they both were.

"I'm glad to see you, too, Katherine. It's been far too long," Tracy smiled fondly at her dear friend and felt a hollow spot in her heart where Mary was supposed to be.

"Josie! Come look at the baby calf!" Lena ran in from the backyard, out of breath and excited, as her words tumbled out. "Papa said I could raise her." Her dark eyes shone. Lena Frommelt was close to Josie's age, and they were fast friends.

"Where is Bertie?" she asked, looking around.

"Mama needed Bertie and Emma to help her today, so they had to stay home," Josie said as they pulled the back door closed and hurried out to see Lena's new treasure.

"So how are you, dear?" Katherine asked as she handed Tracy a cup of coffee and sat down across the table, wrapping her fingers around her own mug.

"I'm much better, I think," Tracy said, contemplating her answer. *Yes, I think I am,* she thought, impressed that Katherine cared about her while immersed in her own grief.

"What about you?" Tracy asked, "Are you all right?"

"It's been terrible," Katherine said, pausing a moment. "But we must carry on, you know. I have to be strong for Franz and the children. They are having such a hard time of it. That's why when one of the cows died, Franz gave Lena the calf. She was beside herself with grief, and Franz thought perhaps having something to be responsible for would be good medicine. I'm happy to say that it looks like his plan is working."

Tracy sipped her coffee. It had been several days since she had a cup, and she found it comforting. Mama didn't have the money for coffee right now and really didn't like it that much anyway, preferring herbal teas. The herbs she foraged for with her Chinook friend, Mae. Under Mae's tutelage she had learned several healing recipes, many of which used the lush nettles gathered and dried in the spring.

For the next hour, Tracy and Katherine chatted, catching up on the happenings on the hill with Tracy carefully taking mental notes so she could relay the news to her mother.

Chapter 19

SPRING 1899

Family Time

"Bertie told me that Hattie told her that she saw Alma dancing with Charlie Bramhall at the Valentine's dance at school," Josie said in an excited tone.

"That's what Hattie told me," Bertie reiterated, chin out.

"Isn't that just like Alma to go clear up to Aims to meet a fellow," Emma joined in, "and a logger at that."

"Well, good for her," Tracy replied. "I hope he's handsome." The family gathered around the kitchen table eating supper and catching up on news.

"Hattie thinks he's good-looking," Bertie answered. "And she has a keen eye for the gentlemen."

"Girls, let's not discuss our neighbors in that tone." Julianna shot Bertie a stony look.

"All right, Mama," Bertie responded with a sheepish voice, and hung her head. "Lucy Mershon said it, too." Tracy heard her say, her voice barely audible.

"Lena likes her new teacher. What do you boys think of her?" Tracy said, hurrying to change the conversation.

"I like her lots," Jackie said enthusiastically. "She's really smart."

"Yeah, and sometimes she lets us have long play periods," Little Alex chimed in.

"What do you think of her, Arnold?" Tracy asked her nine-year-old brother.

"I like her. She lets me do more numbers than reading, and I like that." Arnold barely looked up from his plate of potatoes and eggs. "I have to quit school now though, 'cause I gotta help Ferd in the field." He sounded dejected.

Tracy looked at her Mother and saw a hint of pain in her dark eyes. *Poor Mama,* she thought. *I forget how terrible this must be for her. She, so proper, with such a love of books, is forced to have her children quit school at such a young age.*

"Franz won't be able to come over until week after next, so you might be able to go for another week or so," Tracy said, trying in a small way to comfort him.

"Yes, I won't need any help until after the fields get plowed. I think Arnold could go for a few more days, Mama," Ferd squeaked between bites. At 11, his voice was beginning to change.

Tracy thought about teasing him, but immediately dismissed it. *He doesn't need anything else at this moment.*

Julianna nodded. "Perhaps that would work. I would like it if you and Josie could get in a bit more school. I doubt you'll be able to go much next year."

The family sat together, finishing their meal and discussing Tracy and Josie's afternoon outing at the Frommelts'. They had come home brimming with news and excitement.

"Your mother rarely gets off the place," Katherine had told her. "I worry so about her. I try to get over to see her as often as I can."

"I'm so sorry I can't be there to help her," Tracy had confided.

"I can assure you, you are helping more than you know." Katherine had reached over and patted her hand.

Tracy nodded thoughtfully. She had brought Mother ten dollars and that small sack of flour that Mr. Fox had fixed to carry on the packboard. The load probably didn't weigh much more than thirty pounds, but the bluff was steep and it had exhausted her. Mr. Seidl and Franz could haul those hundred-pound sacks up the hill with such ease. She wondered how they could do it, and how such a small amount of flour could possibly help her family.

"I am not excited about leaving tomorrow." Emma's voice brought her back to the present.

"I hate to have the both of you go," Julianna said, reaching to refill her tea cup. "I've so enjoyed you girls this week."

Tracy felt her eyes fill with tears. She quickly blinked them away and ducked her head so no one would see. She glanced at Emma, and unspoken words bounced between them. She knew her sister felt the same. Having to leave home, the hill, and her siblings was the hardest thing she had to do, even if she dearly loved the Fox family.

Early the next morning just as daylight broke, Emma and Tracy quietly shut the door and made their way up the path to the gate, where they paused, turned for a last peek at the house and were surprised to see Mama standing in the doorway waving goodbye. Waving back, they turned and walked down the hill, out of sight.

Chapter 20

SPRING 1899

Julianna

Julianna closed the door and turned, ready to build a fire in the kitchen stove and heat water for her morning tea. The children were still asleep and the house quiet, interrupted only by the occasional creaking of its wooden frame and the crackling of the fire as it softly lapped at the kindling.

She sat at the table in the silence of the morning and thought about her mother. It had been many years since she had seen her family in Baden. Her father, who had not wanted her to leave, was gone now, and her sisters both had married and were living close to their mother. The last she had heard, Greta wanted to take her mother in to live with her family but was getting resistance. *Not surprising,* she thought. *Mother and I are so alike.*

After she poured her tea, she sat down with her pen and tablet and began a letter.

April 6, 1899
Dearest Mutter,

It's springtime in northwestern Oregon and it reminds

me of home. The daffodils that Alex planted for me a few years ago have multiplied and come up every year. They are finished blooming now, promising me that another spring is here.

Franz is coming next week to work the ground, so we can get the early crops in. Ferd is eleven now and growing, so he and I will be able to raise more vegetables. Franz says he will take all we can raise. He and Joseph have a nice route up to Palmer and Brower selling produce to the stores and the logger families.

I've accumulated enough Burbank seed potatoes for about a quarter of an acre. It's taken me over two years to save that many, but it's been worth it. They are a large, smooth-skinned potato and have a delightful flavor. They have become a staple for the family as they are delicious and keep well over winter.

Tracy and Emma just left to go back to their jobs. I do hate to have them so far away, but the family depends on the money they provide. Tracy hauled a small sack of flour up the bluff trail, along with other supplies. Grateful to have it, I worried about all that weight for such a slight-built girl to carry in a packboard. We had been out of flour and sugar for close to a month. The children were excited to have a loaf of bread. I have quite a bit of jam left, and the family is hungry for it.

I'm hoping that Franz or Joseph will get a salmon for us. Meat is such a luxury. I only kill a chicken when it stops laying, as the children need the eggs and we can sell what we don't eat.

I can tell you that with Emma and Tracy both working, things have been some better this winter. By the end of next summer, Bertie will be almost fourteen, and old enough to go into town and help the Foellers. Emma has already been asked by a family at St. Joseph's in Portland to help with their household chores and see to their children. Sophie said she needs her until Bertie is old enough to come in and work for her. Unlike Emma, Bertie is excited to get away from the drudgery of the farm. She's a bit too curious, and I worry about that.

I miss you so, Mutter. Please know my love and thoughts are with you.

Deine liebende Tochter,
Julianna

As she sealed the envelope, a movement out the kitchen window caught her eye. A second glance didn't reveal anything. *I must have been dreaming*, she thought. A third time, she caught the top of the ears of what seemed to be a large cat creeping slowly toward some unseen prey. The hair stood up on the nape of her neck, and her palms dampened. *Maybe that cougar is the one I keep hearing at night.* Just then it stood, stretched, and cocked its head as if to mock her fear.

Oh my God, I hope the girls are far down the trail by now. Her thoughts raced as she ran to the front window, looked out, and breathed a sigh of relief, seeing the gate closed and no one in sight.

Back at the kitchen window, she stood frozen as she watched the animal pounce and come up with a large rat writhing in its mouth. She cringed and wished Alex were here. *This Godforsaken place.* Thoughts raced through her head as her hands gripped the window sash.

What was I thinking when I agreed to live out here? She felt her face flush as her anger surged. She let it carry her past her fear. *You better not hurt one of the children or any of the livestock*, she thought, *or I'll take care of you with Alex's gun.*

Living out here had been Alex's dream, and she had known it was a wife's duty to follow her husband. She remembered Father Middendorf preaching that in the homily as a teenager, and she had resented it. Nevertheless, after some thought, she had come to believe it. Now she doubted it once again. *I'm the one paying the price, and I don't know if I can do it.* She put her hands to her face, weeping bitter tears.

After a few moments, Julianna sat on the bench by the table and wiped her eyes with her apron. She quietly pondered the moment, studying the paint on the kitchen wall against the curtain. Finally, grudgingly, she admitted that it had been her dream as well.

JULIANNA WAS JERKED AWAKE IN THE NIGHT BY A CURdling scream. "Oh my God," she exclaimed. *It's that cougar again*, she thought and listened to hear if the children were stirring.

Hearing nothing, she arose, lit the lantern, and walked softly to the bedroom closet where Alex stored his guns. He had bought the lever-action Winchester and brought it home a year or so before he died and had carefully stood it in the closet next to his prized double-barreled shotgun.

She remembered how pleased he was when he'd carefully placed the ammunition high on the top shelf. "We don't want the children to reach them," he said as he looked at her and smiled. With that memory, she leaned against the doorjamb and let the tears flow again, thinking how tired she was of hiding her grief from her children and how difficult it was.

"Come, I want to teach you how to use this," Alex had said a few days later as he pulled the rifle out of the closet. "I've worried about you being here alone so much with only that old shotgun. That thing kicks so hard when you shoot, it will knock you on your fanny."

Reluctant at first, she knew he was right and wondered why it had taken him so long to realize how dreadfully alone she felt. Neither of them had even a hint of how genuinely alone she would become.

He had taken her and Ferd into the woods down by the bluff and had taught them to load and sight the rifle. Once he was satisfied they understood, he asked them to shoot off several rounds apiece.

Later, he had brought home another box of ammunition, and they had a second lesson. They had not touched the rifle since. Truthfully, just knowing guns were available these past couple of years had taken away much of her fear.

If that big cat leaves us alone, I'll not harm him, she thought through gritted teeth. Closing the closet door, she blew out the lantern and climbed back into bed.

"I heard a terrible ruckus last night, Ma," Ferd said over eggs the next morning. "Must've been that cougar I saw up by the shop last week."

Julianna stiffened. "Why didn't you tell me?" she demanded.

"He seemed more afraid of me than I of him," he said with a shrug.

“You must keep me informed. We’ve too many animals and little children around not to know of this.”

“I’m sorry, Ma! I forgot. It didn’t seem important at the time.”

“Important? My goodness, Ferd, it’s our responsibility to take care of every living thing on this farm.”

“Yes, Ma.” He hung his head.

“You boys take more pains than usual to see that the chickens are locked securely in the shed. We can’t take a chance on losing any of them.”

“Yes, Ma,” Ferd and Arnold murmured in unison.

When the Frommelt children arrived on their way to school the next morning, Julianna gathered them together and told them what they heard in the night. “Now, I want you to make a lot of noise on your way. I’m sending Josie and Ferd with you for the next few days.”

Frightened to send them without some protection, she worried that Ferd was too young and inexperienced to carry the rifle to school, so in the end, she took the gun herself and walked the half-mile up to the top of the hill with the children and watched them on the trail until they disappeared around the bend toward school. That afternoon, she was there to meet them and walked the Frommelt children most of the way home.

Franz came the next morning, a worried look in his eyes. “I’ll walk with them today. I want to see if I can find signs of him. I heard him last night. It sounded like he was down over the bluff.” Shaking his head, after a pause he said, “That’s the first time I’ve heard him.”

He brought the horse over the next day and plowed the two acres for spring planting, but quit when it was time to go meet the children.

He walked the children to and from school for the next several days, but said he only saw fresh signs of the cat twice. Julianna heard the screams two more nights. Then only stillness with an occasional coyote call.

"Bert Chamberlain said his father heard the cougar," Arnold announced one evening.

"So did Rod Bates," Josie chimed in, not wanting to be left out.

Julianna shuddered but didn't join in. *I don't want scare them too badly. But the children need to know to be careful,* she argued with herself while attempting to keep a stoic expression.

"I'm on my way to Taylors' after I drop the children by school," Franz told her the next morning. "I'm going to find out if anyone's sighted this cougar. We have got to do something about him."

"Yes, it's far too dangerous to have that beast around." She shuddered, remembering the rabid wolf-like creature that had attacked her when Bertie was a baby. That time Alex had rescued her with an axe. Now he was gone. Thank God for the neighbors!

"The cougar has been sighted at Van's Landing and even farther east near Latourell," Franz told her that evening. "Taylor said they figured he was a young cat and probably looking for territory. He said the younger animal might have to fight an older cougar for the land. That's the way of the wild."

"I haven't heard him for several days. Maybe he's moving on," Julianna said, hoping against hope she was right.

"*Ja*, that's what I'm thinking," Franz agreed. "I'm still going to walk the children to school for a few more days. And I think you folks need to be vigilant while working outside. Just keep the trusty rifle handy in case he gives you trouble."

He handed her several German newspapers. "Taylor said he's been saving these for you."

Julianna thanked him, glad for his thoughtfulness.

"He said to tell you that the cougar hasn't made the paper yet." Franz laughed.

Franz's jovial spirit and the stack of fresh reading material cheered her. Later that evening she read that someone named Bell had invented a machine that would enable you to talk to people down the road or even across town. She thought about how much better her life would be if she could have a machine that would allow her to ask Franz or Joseph for help, or even talk to Katherine about mundane fun things.

At the end of May, when the school board dismissed the children to help in the fields in the summer, everyone gathered at the school play shed for the year-end picnic.

There was a general feeling that the cougar had indeed moved to another area, probably farther east up the Columbia Gorge. No one had heard or seen signs of him for more than a month, to Julianna's great relief.

Chapter 21

JUNE 1899

Tracy

Tracy said goodbye to Emma at the depot, all the while wishing she could go with her sister to Portland. *It seems like forever since I've traveled anywhere just for fun. Logan's been gone a long time. Maybe I could forget him if I could get away awhile*, she thought.

"Your birthday is Friday. We should have celebrated," Emma yelled back at her, almost as if it were a second thought.

"I'm sorry we didn't," Tracy shouted over the sound of the engine as she waved.

And then the train disappeared in a cloud of steam and with a roar headed off down the tracks for its next stop at Cleone.

Even Cleone would be fun, Tracy thought ruefully and trudged back up the hill to the Foxes' store. When she arrived, Mr. Fox greeted her warmly and handed her a list of tasks that he'd saved for her.

She went about her duties with a heavy heart. She couldn't keep her mind off Logan's death. When she wasn't thinking about him and Mary, she thought about Mama and the family's predicament.

The week dragged by. As each day passed, Tracy's loneliness grew. Some of her sadness, she realized was not being able to celebrate her sixteenth birthday with her brothers and sisters.

Joseph Marok stopped by to get supplies for his wife and Tracy's family. She was never so glad to see anyone in her life.

"Your Ma's doing better, I think. She looks more like her old self these days," he replied to her questions.

She hung on his every word from home, even though she tried not to show her feelings. It would never do for word to get back to Mama that she was homesick.

"That's good," Tracy acknowledged, but secretly doubted his words. Mama's brow was continually furrowed, and she rarely smiled. Even the neighbors had taken to covering up the truth about her mother to spare the children's feelings.

She went about helping him fill the lists he brought in. When he left, she felt worse. A tear snuck down her cheek before she could wipe it away. She hoped no one noticed. She spent more time than necessary in the back room inventorying the supplies and making lists of what items the store needed.

Mr. Fox peeked in a few times but didn't say anything. Tracy, glad for the quiet, prayed he didn't notice her unhappiness. The past few days of cloudy, rainy skies had not helped her mood.

Friday morning, however, dawned sunny and warm, the change of weather a welcome delight. *What a nice birthday present,* Tracy thought as she looked out the window and saw her usual morning scene of shimmering velvet green trees and glimpses of the sparkling blue Columbia. Seeing the river was still there was a comfort, no matter how bad things seemed.

She walked down to the store with a lighter spring in her step. No matter, her birthday was a special day even if she had to celebrate it by herself. When Mr. Fox bid her good morning, she smiled—something that lately had been difficult to do. Shortly after she arrived, he left, saying he'd be back shortly.

Busying herself with morning chores, she didn't hear the bell ring as the door opened, but hearing the shuffle of feet, she looked up to see Josie running toward her.

"My goodness," she exclaimed. "Where did you come from?"

"Mama said we could walk down and see you on your birthday," Bertie cried out, running behind Josie as Ferd and Arnold brought up the rear.

"What a wonderful surprise." Tracy tried to gather them all in her arms at once. "It seems forever, but it's only been a week."

They were all talking at once, loudly and over each other, when Mr. Fox walked back in with a cup of coffee.

"What have we here?" he asked in his usual jovial manner.

"It's Tracy's birthday." Josie bounced up and down, her blond curls following suit.

"*Ja*," Arnold confirmed. "Mama let us come to see her."

Ferd, quieter than the others and a bit more dignified as the man of the family, said, "It's her sixteenth birthday. She needs her brothers and sisters."

"Indeed she does." Mr. Fox's head bobbed and a smile curled under his bushy mustache. "Indeed she does." After a second he continued, "Tracy, take your family up to the house, and tell Frances that I said you could have the day off."

The gaggle of children trooped toward the door and just as Tracy reached for the knob, he called out, "You boys come down here at noon, and I'll have a food basket ready. You children can have a birthday picnic up in the yard under the apple tree."

Chapter 22

LATE JUNE 1899

Frank

Frank enjoyed his stay with the William Wascher family and met some nice people at St. Joseph Church on Sunday. He had stepped down from the train onto Portland turf several days before and went immediately to find Wascher, a friend of his father's from Freeport, Ill., and now a fireman in Portland. He didn't realize until he found him in Station Number Two on Oak Street that he was the fire chief.

Frank easily found a short-term carpenter job shingling a roof on a new building on Third Street, but it was soon finished. Then on Sunday morning he heard of the wheat harvest in a small town outside Pendleton—a place called Helix—and it piqued his interest.

He had enjoyed working with the threshing crews at home—the exhilaration at the sight of the golden grain berries as they poured from the chute. He loved the dusty smell of the straw mounds coughed out of the monster machine like procedural afterthoughts.

The map showed that Helix was close to the hot springs in the Grand Ronde Valley. After the harvest, he figured he'd have plenty of money to get the treatment for his malaria.

But a lovely young lady caught his eye, and his plan wavered. She walked by the building where he was working several times. One morning the foreman sent him out to get more shingle nails. As he turned the corner on his way back, his arms piled high with boxes, someone slammed into him. He dropped the top box, but nothing spilled.

"What the—?" Frank sputtered, and with a slight gasp he saw the young woman sprawled on the boardwalk in front of him.

"Why don't you watch where you're going?" she demanded.

"I'm truly sorry." He dropped the other boxes and reached to help her to her feet. "Please forgive me," he said, while thinking, *Verdammt. This is a hell of a way to make a first impression.*

She hurriedly brushed herself off and looked him straight in the eye. "Next time perhaps you should use a wheelbarrow."

"*Ja*, I think that would be a good idea." He could see a bit of a smile on her face, so, not wanting to miss an opportunity, he stuck his hand out and said, "My name is Frank Wand."

"From now on kindly watch where you are going, sir." Ignoring his hand, she tossed her hair and continued on her way. A fellow on the crew told him her name was Sally Pehl, the daughter of a downtown clothing merchant.

"A spoiled daughter," Otto the blacksmith told him later. Frank had walked down to the Grand Stable on Sunday afternoon after dinner to see what was going on, and Otto happened to be working.

"What are you doing down here on Sunday? Wanna rent a horse?" he greeted him, not warmly, but as Frank would soon find out, in typical Otto fashion.

"No, but I will say hello to a couple of 'em, especially that fine Morgan." Frank walked over and patted the black horse. "Got anything I can feed him?"

"Yeh, there's a few carrots in that barrel. It's out of season, and they have been stored, so they aren't the best, but the horses like 'em."

Frank nodded and fed the horse a couple. The gelding in the next stall whinnied, and Frank gave the third one to him. He's a nice animal, he thought. I wouldn't mind taking him out for a ride.

He mentioned it to Otto.

"*Ja*, he belongs to Mr. Pehl, too."

"He must be a rich man," Frank said, hoping to get more information.

"You bet, he's well enough off." Otto shrugged his shoulders and sounded a bit bored. "We stable three horses, a carriage, and a buggy for him."

Otto didn't appear very busy, so Frank hung around. "I think I might go to Eastern Oregon and help with the harvest for a while this summer," he said, sliding some tack over and hoisting himself up on the top rail of an empty stall.

"Yeh, you're a good strapping young fellow," Otto agreed. "I've heard they work the hired hands hard, but they treat them right and feed 'em good."

"Do you know anyone who might be interested in hiring me?"

"I'm thinking up around the Umatilla country near Pendleton might be a good place to look. There are lots of ranchers of all kinds up in that country, and it's easy to get there by rail."

"*Ja*, a fellow at church this morning told me about a town just outside of Pendleton that is pretty much the heart of grain country. Maybe I'll just hop the train in a day or two."

He stayed awhile longer, visiting and watching Otto shoe a hefty Belgian draft horse. He admired his deft ability in hammering out a shoe that fit the large foot perfectly in what Frank thought was record time.

That horse must be at least seventeen hands high, he thought, as he admired the blacksmith's ease of handling the large animal. He knew that even though the breed had a reputation for being gentle creatures, their immensity made some people fearful. *I'm going to have a pair of those beauties one day,* he promised himself as he patted his money belt, ruefully thought about how little money he had left, and once again was thankful for the roofing job.

Later that evening at the Waschers' he brought up the subject of going east to work. William nodded his head and said, "I doubt you would be happy in the city for very long anyway."

Frank agreed, thinking about Portland's flurry of activity and noise. He hated all the clatter. That was the hardest part, trying to sleep with horses and wagons going by at all hours and people shouting to and at each other. To say nothing of the lights all night. Yes, William was right. *Big cities are not for me, but for a few days they are fun,* he thought grudgingly.

The next day he went in search of Pehl's Suit and Dress shop and found it downtown on Fourth and Main. He walked in like he had money to spend and was greeted by a portly middle-aged gentleman with a pencil mustache and a bald head. A fringe of graying hair stuck out above each ear. "May I help you, young man?"

"I was just looking," Frank mumbled, suddenly unable to come up with a good reason to be in the store. He couldn't say he wanted to say hello to the fellow's daughter.

"Well, let me know if I can help you find something," the clothier said and headed back to the counter.

Frank looked at the trouser rack, admiring the new styles and wishing he had enough money to buy a pair. He liked nice clothes. Even if he spent a lot of time in the fields, he liked looking scrubbed and spiffy at the end of the day. He remembered how his mother bragged on his appearance many times.

"Father, I stopped at the bank like you asked," he heard a familiar voice come in the door behind him, and when he turned he saw her. The same dark hair and the large blue eyes, but this time she was dressed nicely and even had a ribbon tied around her curls.

"What—what are you doing here?" she stammered, her eyes wide.

"I—I was looking for a new suit," he lied. Taking a breath, he recovered enough to say, "It's nice to see you again, Miss Pehl."

"It's nice to see you as well, Mr. Wand. I hope you are finding everything you need." Her cheeks flushed with embarrassment.

It occurred to him that perhaps she hadn't told her father about the mishap when he ran into her the other day, so in the interest of seeing her again, he decided it might be wise to not mention it. He doubted her father would take to kindly to a fellow who had knocked his daughter to the sidewalk.

"This store has fine quality merchandise," he said quietly and, because he had spent most of his money on the trip west, felt it prudent to change the subject. "I'm on my way up to Pendleton in the next day or two on business," thinking that sounded better than seeking work as a field hand.

She sighed, obviously relieved that he didn't discuss their earlier disastrous meeting. "How long will you be gone?"

"I should be back by the end of summer." He saw her father throwing inquiring looks at the two of them, so he moved toward the door.

She followed him outside and when he turned to look at her, he was again attracted by the tilt of her head and the curve of her mouth.

"Did you come here looking for me?" The directness of the question took him by surprise. Most girls he knew never took the lead, and something about it appealed to him.

He grinned at her. "What makes you think that?"

"I don't know." She paused.

"As a matter of fact, I *was* looking for you." He took a deep breath and, working up his courage, blurted, "Tomorrow is the Fourth of July. Would you like to go to the parade with me?" His palms turned damp. He hated that. It never happened when he talked to the girls back home.

He could swear her smile held a hint of rebellion. He wasn't sure, but he did find it alluring.

"I'll meet you on the corner of First and Stark." Her voice reflected her defiance.

"I'll see you at 10:00 in the morning, then."

Frank couldn't remember when he'd enjoyed himself more. The parade was as good as any he had seen at home. He reveled in Sally's good company and began to wonder if he should go to Eastern Oregon.

Sally ran into an old school chum, Maggie, and her beau, James, and before he knew it they were joining her friends for a picnic on a patch of grass they found on the banks of the Willamette. They laughed and visited over Maggie's roast beef sandwiches and Frank's bottle of Italian red wine.

"Let's go to the Odd Fellows' dance tonight," James said, as they basked in the warm sunshine.

"Oh yes," Sally answered before Frank could ask her.

"Sounds like fun," Frank agreed, thinking, *What a nice idea, dancing with a pretty girl.*

"They don't have a hall yet, so it'll be on the second floor over the Mosby's Tobacco shop downtown," James droned on.

Frank nodded absently and glanced at his pocket watch. Half past three. The dance wouldn't start for another four hours.

Turning to Sally, he asked, "Would you like to walk a bit?"

She nodded, and they all started off west on Stark Street, the three Portlanders pointing out the sights to Frank.

Later they danced until almost midnight to the music of a fiddle and an accordion, reminding him of the Midwest dances he had so often attended back home.

"I think we'd better go," Sally had said, and now he walked her down the dark street to her home on Eleventh. He reached to take her hand, and she gave it willingly.

"What church do you attend?" Their conversation halted. Her question abrupt.

"Catholic. Why?"

She didn't answer immediately. "Papa won't like that."

Frank didn't comment, waiting for an explanation. He had seen his share of prejudice against Catholics back home and had heard tales of the Ku Klux Klan in the Southern states after the war. He even heard some stories of their activities here in Oregon.

"Papa said he doesn't want me to have anything to do with Catholic boys." She paused again. "Only Jewish boys."

"How do you feel about that?" he asked.

"I didn't care until now."

They walked in silence, her hand comfortably nestled in his. "What would you like me to do?" he asked, not sure he wanted to hear the answer.

"When are you leaving for Eastern Oregon?"

"I was thinking of taking the train tomorrow." He wasn't sure he wanted to go now, but he needed the money and was eager to see how they farmed in that part of the country. Besides, he was fearful of the ague and wanted to get to the hot springs for the cure.

"I'll tell my parents that I met a nice young man. Maybe they will let me bring you to dinner when you get back." She smiled at him. "They can't help but like you."

"Pretty country, isn't it?" offered a stately gentleman accompanied by a lady dressed in finery. "I've lived in Pendleton all my life, and I never get tired of the scenery."

Frank nodded, looking out the train window at the patchwork of amber and beige fields sprinkled here and there with rich brown quadrants stretching as far as the hills permitted. It reminded him of the quilt on his parents' bed.

"Why do they leave such large fields lying fallow?" he asked.

"We only get about twelve inches of rain a year here," the stranger answered. "Those brown fields are reservoirs for next year's wheat crop. The ranchers work up the top couple of inches of soil just a bit so it acts as a mulch to save what moisture is there."

Frank thought that was a good idea and said so. They had just crested the brim of the hill and were headed down a steep grade toward the Umatilla River. He caught his breath at the breathtaking vista unfolding before them. The steep fields covered with wheat, their seed heads turning light umber, surrounded them. A ribbon of water glistened at the bottom of the ravine.

The train hissed and clanged to a stop at the Pendleton depot signaling they had arrived in the small town nestled in the hollow by the river. A sign boldly stated: "Oregon's Fourth Largest City, Population 4,400."

Frank scrambled off the train carrying his coat and a grip containing all his possessions. The conductor told him it was ninety-seven degrees, but the arid heat felt different than the kind of oppressive, almost unbearable summer temperatures he was used to back in Illinois.

After inquiring as to the whereabouts of a boarding house, he headed in the direction of the newly built Woolen Mills.

"You workin' in the mill?" the slightly built, gray-haired landlady questioned.

"No, I don't have a job yet," Frank replied. "But I'm going to be finding one right soon." He hesitated and realized her question and answered, "I got enough money for a few days rent, though." He pulled six bits out of his money belt and offered it to her.

"Fine, young fellow, but just remember, lights out at 10:00 p.m. and no women in your room."

Frank nodded and assured her that he would abide by the rules. Besides, he was sure that Sally wouldn't like him fraternizing with other women. He also felt quite sure that she wouldn't think being lonesome was a good enough reason.

Chapter 23

LATE JUNE 1899

Julianna

"All ready for plantin', Miz Lampert." Robert Graham smiled and gestured toward the smooth, freshly disked field. He called her by the more respectful title ever since Alex died. At first it annoyed her, but over the past few months, she became more comfortable with the formality of it. He was, after all, a married man. He and his wife, Ann, were good friends, and the children loved their daughters, Alma and Hattie.

As Joseph became busier with his and Franz's places, Mr. Graham had taken to spending more time helping her on her farm. She was sure he didn't want neighbors' tongues to wag. However, she knew her family could not survive without the neighbors' help. If the more formal title made him more comfortable, then she was fine with it.

She also knew there would never be another man in her life, if for no other reason than she had promised herself she would not have any more children.

"Yes, thank you. It looks very nice."

"Joseph said to tell you he would be over day after tomorrow with seed for your late planting. He wasn't sure if you planned to put in more potatoes, but I told him to bring some planting stock because those people up at Palmer eat way more spuds than most anything else. It's a good cash crop for all of us."

Julianna couldn't agree more; besides, putting in a late crop after the major spring rains lessened the weed problem. She nodded, as she noticed Arnold running toward her. "Mama, Bertie told me to tell you that Jackie won't finish his row," he called as he stubbed his toe and almost fell.

She sighed, thinking how sad that her children were forced to work like adults. Jackie, only seven, had more energy than any of the other children, save perhaps Josie, but channeling it had become a problem, not only here but at school as well.

Just a month ago, he had come home with a note from his teacher, Miss Huddleston, asking Julianna to please come in and discuss the youngster's behavior. *I'm half afraid to go back and see her again, in case he hasn't improved*, she thought, making a mental note to walk the children to school the next day.

"Well, I gotta be going," Mr. Graham said, tipping his battered black cap. "I have to go up loggin' tomorrow."

Julianna smiled and, thanking him again, she turned toward the field where the children were working. The early onions were now six inches high, but the weeds were higher and needed pulling if the crop was to reach maturity by the end of summer. She prayed that she and the children could get the job finished before the weeds became too big to control. After that her prayer would be for a good warm east wind to spur their growth.

If the weeds overtook the crop, she would likely lose most of it. Like last year, when rain fell every day for two weeks. By the time she could work in the fields, the weeds had completely buried the onions. When they pulled the weeds, the onions came with them, and the crop was almost a total loss. She wanted to replant, but it was the end of April and too late to seed them by then.

"Arnold, now tell me what happened," she said, trying to keep the impatience out of her voice.

"Jackie just wants to play, Ma." Arnold sounded like he didn't blame his little brother one bit.

"Jackie, come here now," she said, her voice as hard and authoritative as her heart was sympathetic.

The brown-haired youngster came to her side, looking reluctant and a little sheepish. "I'm tired, Mama," he whined.

Julianna had to turn her head to hide a smile when she noticed a cowlick spraying from behind one ear and one precariously perched on the top of his head. He had a smudge of dirt on his cheek, which told her that he had a runny nose and no handkerchief.

"I know you're tired, son," she said, wanting to put her arms around him. Realizing that would not get the job done, she continued, "I understand. Everyone else is tired too, but this crop is dangerously close to being too weedy to save."

Julianna had decided long ago not to spare the children the truth. Her philosophy had been to tell them the dangers with the hope they would be more willing to help. She was pleasantly surprised at how the older children had responded, but Jackie and Little Alex still were inclined to wander off in the woods under the pretext of getting a drink of water or taking care of toilet needs.

"Come, Jackie, that row must be finished. You can play for a few minutes when it's done," she said, reasoning that he might respond to a bargain. He wasn't one to take orders well.

To her surprise, he came back, dropped to his knees, and started to carefully pull the weeds, leaving the onions. *Maybe he is growing up*, she thought, her mind flashing back to Alex with a flare of anger, resenting that her children were forced to work so hard. *He left us. How could he have done that?*

Her mind wandered back to Baden and her *Mutter's* kitchen garden. How she hated having to put on her bonnet and go out and pull weeds. *How little I knew back then*, she thought. *Here I am the sole owner of a farm an ocean away where pulling weeds could mean the difference between eating or not.*

"Mama, who's that?" Josie's voice interrupted her thoughts.

Julianna looked up to see two figures step out of the woods above the bluff and walk toward them. She eyed them, suspicious because they weren't on the trail.

As they came closer she could see their unkempt clothes. The hair on the back of her neck stood up. Her heart turned over, crashing into her stomach.

"Ferd, run and get Papa's shotgun. Be sure it's loaded." Stooping over, she picked up a hoe that one of the children had left lying in the row, the closest thing she could find for a weapon. *I hope it's good and sharp.*

"Be careful!" she shouted to Ferd as he raced across the field.

"Bertie, see if you can catch Robert."

She looked up to find the men close enough to see their scruffy beards, one with what looked like long dark streaks of tobacco running its full length. She shivered. "Hurry," she hissed.

The strangers stopped at the upper end of the field, and

stood eyeing the group. The older of the two walked toward Julianna, tobacco stains fully evident now. She caught her breath and gripped the hoe harder. *If they want my children, they'll have to go through me,* she thought. Catching his gaze, she took a step forward.

"What do you what?" she growled, her eyes holding his, her heart pounding.

He stopped and she noticed he swayed a trifle. He looked around as if to find something to steady himself. She waited for an answer, her eyes never leaving him. Determined not to let him know how frightened she was, she ever so slightly brandished her hoe.

"Have you been drinking?" she asked, her voice hard.

"No, ma'am, nothing like that." He took a step backward and almost fell. "We ain't had a bite to eat since day before yesterday and before that it was several days. Just a mite weak, ma'am."

"You got money enough to buy tobacco," she snapped back trying her best to speak in perfect English and frustrated that it came out with a thick Alemannic German accent. Her heart beat so fast she was afraid it might show through her bedraggled shirtwaist.

"No, ma'am, no more money for food and none for tobacco neither."

Julianna, still suspicious, debated with herself. *If I relent and let my guard down, they may turn on us. On the other hand, they look pretty pathetic and down on their luck. Where is Ferd with that gun?* Her eyes were still locked on the strangers.

The man took another step backward. Julianna, wondering why, turned to see Ferd racing toward her, shotgun swinging wildly with each step, the barrel pointing into the air. *My God, I don't know which one to be more frightened of,* she thought catching her breath.

She turned to see the man's eyes wide with fright, and took comfort in the look.

"You were saying?"

"I…I, ma'am, we need some food. Please, lady?"

"Here, Mama," Ferd said, handing her the gun. "Be careful. Both barrels are loaded."

"We're pretty short on most food," she finally replied, the weapon in a ready position. "We do have some potatoes and carrots, though. Maybe I could find a meal for you, if you help us weed the rest of these onions." She went from fear to relief.

What an answer to prayers. This may be the way to save her crop and her family. A shiver went through her. Not one to let her guard down despite the hope in her chest, she leveled her gaze at him.

Bertie ran up out of breath. "Robert… Mr. Graham has gone," she managed to say.

"No mind, now. These gentlemen would like a meal." Julianna tried to remain confident and appear unafraid for the children's sake. "Go get two bowls of soup from the kettle and bring them out with a piece of bread each."

"Yes, ma'am. This here's my son. His name is Sonny. We'll do 'er! If you'll feed us tonight and tomorrow, we'll help. Looks like we might finish up by then." Appearing grateful, he apologized for his appearance as he and his son gobbled down the food, and set to work beside her and the children.

Later when the sun was low, Julianna invited the two to take the big boiler tub and a bar of her homemade soap, and go out back of the house and clean up. She showed them the pit where fires were built in the warmer months when the children bathed outside.

"Wait one minute before you start." She turned and went back into the house. "Here," she said, returning shortly, handing them a pair of Alex's clean shirts. "Please burn the ones you have on." She wished she had clean trousers for them, too.

Shorty, the older man, had been right. They finished weeding the onions the following afternoon, and Julianna asked them to stay on to help for a few more days. They had a warm, dry place to sleep in the barn and seemed to be happy with the endless pot of soup.

They readily agreed.

Two days later when Joseph delivered four sacks of potatoes for planting, the two men and the family had the early carrots almost cleaned out. The cabbage was easier to weed because the plants were eight inches apart in the row and could be hoed.

Three days later they finished the weeding late enough in the day that Julianna invited them to stay one more night. The next morning she fed them breakfast, and they went on their way, their clean shirts already stained.

Julianna pushed her hair back from her eyes and straightened up, looking for the sack that held the seed potatoes. While the rest of the family finished the weeding, Josie and Arnold sat on the porch and carefully cut the potatoes into small pieces, each with an eye of its own.

She spotted the larger seed sack at the end of Ferd's row. She and the children each carried small tote sacks filled with the cut-up Burbank planting stock and a short-handled hoe borrowed from Franz. Each bent over a row marked off by Alex's two-and-a-half-foot row marker and systematically dug a small hole, dropping in one piece of potato. Covering it by pushing the dirt into a mound, they moved up the row a few inches to plant the next hill.

Julianna rubbed her back and looked fondly at the children so diligently helping. She dreaded having to send Bertie to town next year. *I want her here with me and the family*, she thought bitterly, once again realizing how she treasured her children. Her mind wandered to Emma and Tracy and wondered how they were and what they were doing. She was grateful that Emma was beginning to enjoy city life at least a little bit.

Near dark, they ran out of seed and counted twenty-four long rows planted.

"If we are blessed with a good season, we should harvest at least sixty bushels off this field," she told the children. "We'll store forty bushels for our own use."

The rest, along with the earlier plantings, should bring a nice profit if all goes well. She sighed and rubbed her back again, trying not to worry about how they would harvest this large crop yet relieved and hopeful that it would be more bountiful than last year's.

Chapter 24

EARLY AUGUST 1899

Onions

"I don't understand it," Julianna said, shaking her head in dismay. "They were growing so fast a few weeks ago; now they look parched." She turned to look at Joseph, putting her hand up to shade her eyes. "How can they be dry? It's been raining for days."

"When did this start?" he asked.

"I came out to the field day before yesterday and noticed some large areas of onions whose tops had started to flop over. I knew it was too early for that. They aren't even close to being ready." She paused and looked over the small field one more time to make sure what she was seeing was indeed true. "I pulled up some of those onions just to see, and they're way too small for the tops to start dying off."

Joseph shook his head. "It's too bad."

Julianna held back her frustration, trying to block the anxiety that had become part of her life since she lost Alex. Not only had the onions always been a good cash crop, but she'd been hearing that their price had gone up. The best crop of onions she'd ever had was in danger of dying, and they couldn't even figure out the cause. They fought to save them from the weeds and won. And now this.

"Look Mama, the onions are lying down in round circles," Josie said, pointing to the largest ring, down in the swale.

"By golly, whatever it is, it's killing them in rings," Joseph said. "And they're worse down in the swale where they're protected from the wind."

Julianna nodded in agreement, wondering what that had to do with anything.

"Well, we won't plant the onions down there again," Ferd stated, his fist clenched and eyes flashing.

"That's using your heads, children," Joseph agreed. He removed his cap and rubbed his forehead. "I think they might need to be at least up on the hillsides, if not on the brow of the hill. It appears as though for some reason they aren't getting enough circulation of air."

They walked slowly back to the house in quiet thought. Julianna spent the time trying to pull herself from her overwhelming hopelessness. All that money for seed and all that time breaking their backs getting the weeds out.

"I wonder if we pull up all the dead and dying ones and throw them over the bluff, maybe we can save the rest of them," Julianna said more to herself than anyone.

"That might not be a bad thing to do," Joseph agreed in a tone that said he was still pondering the situation. "At this point you've got nothing to lose."

"I have some flour sacks," Julianna said after another silence. "What if we drag the sacks along the rows and put the dead onions in them."

"That's a great idea, but I think you ought to carry them. I'm afraid they might spread whatever is causing the problem if you pull them along the ground." Joseph stopped to scratch his chin. "I'll be over tomorrow. Get all the sacks you can find, and I'll bring some of Elma's. We won't throw them away; we'll just dump the onions, and then you wash the empty bags. They'll be as good as new."

"Oh Joseph! How kind of you." Julianna couldn't contain the tears. "How can I ever repay you?"

"Never you mind about that," he said gruffly. "We have a crop to save here. I don't want to drive up to Palmer this fall with a half a load of produce." He patted her shoulder.

Julianna rarely cried in front of anyone now, and she tried to hide her embarrassment. She remembered the day that Josie had surprised her standing at the kitchen sink in tears, her arms up to her elbows in soapy dishwater.

She'd put her hand over her eyes and, with tears running down her cheeks, heard Josie say, "Mama, what's wrong?"

Startled, it had taken her a moment to come up with an answer.

"I think I have something in my eye."

Josie, being Josie, insisted that Julianna sit on the bench at the table so she could find the culprit that hurt her mother's eye.

JULIANNA STRAIGHTENED HER BACK AND SURVEYED THE field. The strong odor of onions stung her nostrils. Big patches of the pungent bulbs were gone, replaced by the dark, moist soil where they had once grown. The children finished the job, carrying sacks of the dead onions out of the field and then dragging them to the bluff where Arnold and Ferd deftly picked them up and emptied the bags over the steep embankment.

With the three-day project completed, Julianna was grateful Bertie was preparing supper. Her back and shoulders hurt so badly she wondered if she could make it to the house.

She stretched again and let her eyes drift north over the river. The Columbia, wide at this point, had started its midsummer withdrawal. But with the late, unseasonably heavy August rains, the Washougal land strip protruding into the river had shrunk almost to spring freshet levels.

Her hand traveled instinctively to her shoulder, and she began an attempt to rub the pain away. She had missed Joseph's help today. He had noticed dead circles of onions on the lower part of his field, so he had taken sacks home with him yesterday in hopes of cleaning them out too.

"I'll send some of the children over as soon as we get done here. The more people working, the sooner you can get the job done," Julianna had told him. She wished that she could go as well, but her laundry had piled up the last few days and the children were running out of underwear and socks. Still, she owed Joseph so much. Nothing she could do for the Maroks or the other neighbors could ever repay them for their many kindnesses.

"Come, children, we're done here for now," she said, still rubbing her shoulder.

THE NEXT MORNING SHE SENT ALL THE CHILDREN BUT Jackie and Little Alex to help Joseph. *I wish I could go and help and maybe even visit with Katherine or Elma,* she thought, but quickly dismissed the idea as she gazed at her pile of dirty clothes.

"Boys, gather some wood for the fire," she commanded, then winced as she began to pump water into the big boiler tub she used for laundry. The pain in her shoulder reminded her of the last few days of brutally hard work. *I hope it was worth it*, she thought, and whispered a silent prayer that the rest of the onion crop would thrive.

The little boys scurried around, gathering kindling and splitting pieces of wood. Soon they had a good fire going in the kitchen stove.

"Thank you, boys," Julianna said, throwing the first batch of clothes into the hot water. Stirring them around in the bluing she'd added, she picked the dirty laundry out piece by piece and rubbed the bar of soap on each article, then carefully rinsed it in the hot, now sudsy water.

She handed the clean item to the boys, who, as soon as it cooled, carefully wrung out the water as best they could with their small hands and placed it on a pile on the table. Julianna periodically came over to the pile to give each article of clothing an extra twist or two over the sink until she was satisfied that they were dry enough to hang on the line.

When the basket was full, the three of them carried it out to the side of the house where Alex had made a clothes-line for her. She smiled at the thought of him and how he had been so exacting as to get the line taut and not too high.

"I have to make it easy for my *kurze Frau* to reach," he had said with a grin. He had often teased her about her four-foot-eleven-inch frame and then kissed her and told her how he always liked the shortest girl in the class anyway.

Thinking about Alex brought familiar nausea and her hands shook, but hastily she swallowed back the bile knowing she dare not permit herself the luxury of escape.

By the time the older children came home, they had finished the washing and folded the clothes that were dry enough to take down from the line.

Julianna dug deep into her soul and, with the help of Bertie and Josie, found the strength to get supper on the table. By the time Ferd and Arnold were done feeding the chickens and milking the goats, they were ready to sit down.

The house took on an uncommon silence as the family ate the simple fare—potatoes and beans that had simmered on the stove beside the wash tub for most of the day. The two youngest boys fell asleep at the table before they finished their meal and were helped to bed by their older brothers and sisters.

Julianna sighed and slowly rose from her chair and cleared the table, setting the dishes in the sink. She pumped water and rinsed them off, setting them on the drain board that Alex had fashioned when he built the house.

Making her way to the bedroom, she shut the door firmly, wishing she it could shut out the brutal life that burdened her. Culpability raised its ugly head as it often did when she thought about her babies. The memories of her idyllic, golden childhood in Baden brought the taste of guilt to her throat for the savage life she had inadvertently brought to her children.

Reaching for her rosary and caressing the familiar smooth beads, she murmured prayers for her family and for the crops that fed them.

Chapter 25

SEPTEMBER 1899

"Tracy!" Bertie's voice rang through the store.

Tracy ran to her sister, carrying the work shirts she was pricing.

"What are you doing here? Is someone sick?"

"Oh no, everyone is fine." She paused. "Except for Mama. She's worried about the onion crop," Bertie replied, out of breath.

"What's the matter with the crop?"

"A lot of it died. Joseph and Mama think it's from all the rain in early August. I told her that at least half of it still looks good." Bertie shook her head. "But she didn't hear me."

"What brings you here, and so early in the day?"

"Mama says it's time for me to go in to Portland and work for the Foellers." Tears filled her eyes. "Oh, Tracy, I don't want to go. I'll miss everyone so bad. I used to envy Emma, but now I'm afraid."

Tracy put her arms around her tearful sister and led her to the back room for some privacy.

"You'll be just fine. Emma's there, and that will help," Tracy told her as they sat down on the workroom bench. "And don't forget how cute the Foeller children are, especially little Vic. The last time I saw him, I thought he was adorable. Remember how much he laughed and teased?"

Bertie sniffed, wiped her eyes with the back of her hand, and nodded. "I remember, but that was a long time ago."

"Yes it was, but Emma says he is just getting cuter since he's gotten older."

They sat in silence, Tracy absorbing the angst, wondering how she could help. With her usually busy hands folded in her lap, she pondered the situation and remembered how she had felt when Mama sent her away on her own. *Maybe I could take her into Portland*, she thought, her mood brightening as the answer flitted through her mind. *Yes*. If Mr. Fox could give her a day or two off. She had over five dollars saved, and would never turn down a chance to see Emma.

"Bertie, what if I took you in on the train?"

"Oh, Tracy, could you do that?"

"I don't know, but I'm going to find out. Stay here; I'll be right back."

She went in search of Mr. Fox and found him at his favorite place by the cash register, talking to "Mother" Hubbard, who ran the boardinghouse for the Union Meat Packing Company. She always brought her weekly supply list in on Mondays for her renters. Tracy thought it funny that they actually called her their mother.

"Mr. Fox, I need a favor," Tracy said as soon Mrs. Hubbard walked out the front door. "May I have two or three days off to take Bertie into Portland for her new job? She's frightened, and I don't want her to go alone."

"Of course, Tracy," he said without hesitation. "It's been a long time since you've had a holiday, and I don't remember you ever going into Portland. Stay a week if you'd like."

"Oh, thank you, sir."

"Here, take this," he said, handing her a silver dollar. "You'll need it for train fare."

"Thank you, but I have some money saved," she said proudly. But he insisted.

AFTER SHE PACKED A SMALL GRIP, THEY MAILED A LETTER that Mama had written to Grandmother Gross in Germany and headed for the depot, where Tracy paid the train fare with Mr. Fox's silver dollar and received four bits in change.

"Oh Tracy! I'm so happy you are going with me," Bertie said after they boarded the train and settled in.

"I am too! It's been ever so long since I've been to Portland."

They giggled and gazed out the window. After they left Cleone, the sights along the way were mostly of cattle grazing near the tracks.

Cleone used to be called Fairview, but a post office in Coos County already had that name so the city fathers had to choose a different name. Tracy smiled, remembering overhearing some plaid-shirted logger with muddy boots tell Mr. Fox the story one day.

"Where in the world did they get a name like Cleone?" Mr. Fox had asked.

"Hell," the logger said and then looked sheepish as he glanced toward Tracy. "Sorry Miss." Then with a laugh he said, "It's Oregon Export Lumber Company spelled backwards."

"Well, can you believe that?"

"*Ja*, they voted to keep all 'likker' out, too." The logger frowned when he said it. "A lot of people aren't one bit happy about that either."

"Tell 'em to come to Troutdale," Mr. Fox said with a grin. "We got three saloons."

Tracy giggled at the thought and shared it with Bertie. A man sitting in the seat in front of them turned and gave them a knowing smile.

The girls spotted a threshing machine out of the window. It stood at the edge of the field near the tracks, as horses and wagons hauled the bundled sheaves of grain to it for the separation process. Tracy watched, riveted by the scene, the smoke bellowing out of its steam-powered engine while the thresher spit out the kernels of wheat. It looked like a yellow waterfall spilling into a waiting burlap bag held by one man. When full, it would be sewn shut by a different man and pushed to the ground. The chaff blew out in the other direction of the billowing monster onto an already enormous pile of lemon-colored straw.

She and Bertie shot wide-eyed looks at each other, and Tracy wondered what it would have been like if her Papa had lived. Maybe they would have had one of those machines. She vaguely remembered him telling Mama that he would like to raise their own grain one day.

When the train stopped at the Clarnie depot, the conductor came through to remind them this was the last stop before they arrived in Portland.

"This is a funny place for a depot; there's only one store." Bertie looked confused. "It looks like we're still in the middle of the country."

Tracy nodded, thinking the same thing, but noticed many people getting on and the train filling up.

"They must've needed a place for more people to board. It would still be a long walk into Portland." She remembered Mrs. Fox telling her that Mr. Fox thought people were in too much of a hurry these days.

Surprised at the lack of houses and businesses after their last stop, it seemed like no time at all when they arrived at the newly built Union Station. The tall brick structure dwarfed the buildings around it. Tracy gasped as they entered the magnificent interior with its marble floors, bench-filled waiting area, and long ticket counter. The high ceilings in the immense room caused voices to reverberate from wall to wall, echoing with hollow tones. It put the old tenth street depot to absolute shame.

"I've never seen so many people in one place," said Bertie, eyes wide with wonder.

Tracy laughed and agreed.

They inquired where Twelfth and Couch Street was located from the station. A friendly man in a blue uniform and billed cap pointed out the front door onto the street and said, "It's quite a walk. You might want to take the Flanders Street Trolley."

"What's a trolley?" Bertie asked with an inquisitive look.

The man laughed. "It's a car that runs on tracks and is powered by electricity."

"Electricity?"

"Yes, electricity is made at the falls at Oregon City and is brought here by wire. Then it's channeled onto the wires above the trolley lines. The cars have poles on the roof that touch the wire." He paused and added, "That's what makes them go." It seemed to Tracy he had a great deal of patience to take time to explain something so complicated to a couple of young girls.

"My goodness! You mean it doesn't need a horse to move down the street?"

"No, the electricity makes the trolley move from place to place." Bertie's face showed the puzzled look that Tracy felt.

"How much does it cost?" Tracy worried about money and would rather walk if it was too expensive.

"A nickel apiece."

"Good," Tracy murmured, thinking they could afford that luxury. "Thank you," she said, glad that she wouldn't have to find her way.

Bertie grabbed her arm as they left the immense brick structure and headed for Flanders Street.

After a short wait, they heard the clanging of warning bells as the bright, shiny trolley with the numbers 1042 painted in yellow on its side, whirred around the corner and came to a stop in front of the small group of people.

Several passengers disembarked before the girls could climb aboard and find a seat. Tracy wondered how they would know when to get off and worried that they'd miss their stop. There was more to coming to Portland now than just catching the train in Troutdale.

I wonder how Papa would feel about the city now, she thought, remembering his carpentry days in the city and his tales of the underground tunnels. She shivered but knew she felt safer than he had probably felt. *Maybe I just don't know any better*, she thought ruefully.

Once they'd caught the trolley, Tracy realized the street numbers were obvious, and the bells rang out a warning at every intersection, so when the streetcar stopped to let passengers off at Tenth Street, she and Bertie got off and walked the last two blocks, in awe of the wonders of the big city.

Francis, Vic's brother, and two playmates were playing with marbles on the Foellers' small front lawn when the girls approached. The boys looked up quizzically when Tracy greeted them. They smiled and went back to their game as the two Troutdale girls walked up the steps and rang the bell. In a moment the door opened and Emma, holding a small baby, squealed with delight when she saw her sisters standing in the sunshine.

HEARING THE COMMOTION AT THE DOOR, SOPHIE rounded the corner from the kitchen, her face brightening when she saw the two girls. "My goodness, what brings you two to town to bless our home?"

"Mama said it's time for Bertie to come to Portland to work. I haven't been in the city for so long that Mr. Fox gave me a week to visit." The words tumbled out in Tracy's excitement.

"Yes, I didn't want to come by myself," Bertie confessed.

"Well, I had to come in alone," Emma said, shooting them an indignant glance.

Tracy smiled and nodded, "Yes, but if she'd have come by herself, then I wouldn't have gotten to see you," she said, hugging her sister tightly. "I've missed you so much."

"And I've missed you," Emma replied then turned to give Bertie a hug.

"And you too, little sister."

"Me, too."

"Now you girls must come in to the kitchen," Sophie said. "I have some coffee made, and you can tell me all about what's happening in Troutdale." She led the way and motioned for them to sit at the table, then took the baby from Emma and asked her to please pour the coffee.

"You girls must meet Catherine," Sophie said, pointing to the wide-eyed, blond curly-haired baby. "She's not quite four months old."

"Can I hold her?" Bertie wanted to know.

"Of course." Sophie handed her the baby.

"Now, please tell me, how is your dear mother and her friend Katherine?" Sophie asked, her face soft with concern. "What a sacrifice your Mama made to send all three of her oldest girls to work away from the farm," she added. Her care surprised Tracy, who had rarely thought of it that way.

"Mama's upset," Bertie said and told them about the onion crop. "She still has half the crop left, but it'll be an awful lot of work to harvest with just her and the younger children."

Tracy listened to her sister, amazed at her insight at such a young age. *The farm and Papa's death made us grow up fast*, she thought, smiling as she tasted her coffee. She rarely drank it, so it was a treat.

"Mama rarely sees Katherine, now," Bertie continued her report, seeming proud to be able to relay the news. "I saw tears in her eyes one day when Franz came over to help her. He was telling her how much Katherine missed seeing her. She told him that she had to keep the farm going and had no time for visiting. She was not happy about it, I could tell."

"Your poor mother. She's had nothing but sadness, it seems," Sophie said, shaking her head. "And poor Katherine losing Mary like that."

They chatted the rest of the afternoon as they cooked dinner, and reaffirmed the plan that Bertie would stay with and help the Foellers.

Emma would go work for the Scherhausers, who were friends from St. Joseph. Mrs. Scherhauser was about to have her third baby and had no one to look after the two little ones. Mr. Scherhauser was a postman, according to Sophie.

"That's good," Emma said. "I know she needs me and her children are darling, but I'll miss you and the children."

"We'll miss you too, dear, but we'll see each other often. The Scherhausers don't live far from here."

The next day they chatted some more, catching up and enjoying sisterly bonds. Sophie encouraged them to walk downtown to sightsee. "I think Bertie needs to learn her way around," she said. "I'll need her to do errands for me occasionally."

"Emma, what should we see first?" Tracy asked as they walked down the sidewalk.

"Oh, the Blagen building for sure. It has four floors and an elevator."

"Elevator?" Bertie exclaimed, "What's an elevator?"

"Come, I'll show you." Emma picked up her pace.

They nearly ran down Twelfth, turning on Ash Street, and soon Tracy found herself looking at the tallest building she had ever seen. It had four rows of columns stacked on top of each other.

"Someone told me that the columns are made out of cast iron," Emma said breathlessly. "Whatever that is."

"It reminds me of one of Katherine's layer cakes," Tracy said. Emma laughed.

A uniformed man opened the door for them.

"What can I do for you, ladies?"

They giggled at the title. "We'd like to see the elevator, sir," Emma said, standing as tall as she could.

He frowned, but signaled for them to come in. "You must not be noisy," he said. "This is an office building and is very busy. You can ride the elevator, but you only have twenty minutes, then you must leave."

They followed him to the elevator door and watched him push a small button on the wall beside it. When the outside doors opened, a man inside pulled on a handle opening the inner metal gate and signaled for them to come in.

Tracy felt a little reluctant, but her curiosity got the best of her and she entered the small space. The others followed.

The ride started slowly with a thunk and a belch. The car trembled and with a grinding sound it began to move. Tracy glanced at Bertie and noticed her wide eyes as she clutched the railing around the car. At each floor there was a bump and a hesitation, and then the ride continued upward until they reached the top floor. When the door opened, which Tracy felt took far too long, the man pulled on the gate lever and they walked out, their knees wobbly, onto a corridor with windows at the end.

Mount Hood stood sentinel in the east, naked except for patches of white where the snow never melted. Looking down to the street below, they watched the tiny horse-drawn carriages and buggies, streetcars, and pedestrians going about their business.

Even in the highest tree she had climbed, Tracy had never been this far off the ground. Dizzy, she stepped back from the window. Then curiosity got the upper hand, and she cautiously peered again in awe of the miniature scene below.

The elevator came back and when they rode it down, she was sure she had left her stomach on the top floor. Bertie's face turned slightly ashen.

"My stomach feels funny," Emma said.

"I thought you'd ridden this before," a surprised Tracy muttered softly.

"Oh no, I wasn't brave enough to ride it. I needed you two to give me courage."

"Well, if I'd have known that, I'd never have ridden it." Bertie paused. Her face, the color of dirty underwear, with beads of sweat bubbling up across the bridge of her nose. "I think I'm going to throw up," she declared.

"Don't you dare," Tracy growled. "Don't you dare."

They got to the street without mishap, much to Tracy's relief. She was glad to be back in the fresh air, but she wasn't about to admit it to the two younger girls.

They wandered back up Ash to Second Street and turned south, looking in shop windows and commenting on the new dress fashions.

"Look at how small they make your waist," Bertie said, peering in the window at a blue velvety dress on a headless mannequin.

"It's not the dress that makes that small waist—it's the corset, and they are really uncomfortable," Emma replied.

"I sure wouldn't want to wear one of those, even if it is stylish," Tracy joined in.

They continued down Second and came upon a store where the sign said *Fashionable Ladies Millinery Shop.*

"Did you bring a hat with you?" Tracy looked at Bertie.

"I don't have a hat."

"You'll be going to Mass with the Foellers. It would never do for you not to have a hat. It's the proper thing." Tracy continued to gaze into the shop, admiring the lace and velvet that made up the array of dresses and hats. She tried not to think of the coin purse tucked safely in the waistband of her skirt.

The bell rang as they opened the door and trooped into the shop with its array of colorful, modern ladies wear, hinting of elegance and smelling of lavender.

"Oh my," Bertie exclaimed under her breath.

"Look at all these lovely bonnets!" Emma's face glowed.

"May I help you ladies?" A friendly clerk came out of the back room, leaving her sewing machine.

"Yes, please!" said Tracy, who as the oldest felt it was her responsibility to take charge. "We need a hat for my sister. She needs it to wear to Mass."

"I have some lovely small but fashionable hats back here in this corner."

Tracy expected old unattractive merchandise, but the bonnets and hats looked wonderful. *I'll never be able to afford this*, she thought, but went ahead and asked how much they cost anyway, just in case.

"I have this one for sale at just $1.29," the woman said as she picked up a light brown, small-brimmed hat with a wide white bow and a flower on the side.

"Oh my," Bertie said again. "That is lovely." She paused as the clerk handed it to her, and she tried it on, "But I only have the dollar that Mama gave me for the train." She looked in the mirror.

"You keep your dollar, Bertie," Tracy said. "Do you like the hat?"

"Oh yes!" Bertie smiled broadly. "I think it's very pretty. What do you think, Emma?"

"Yes, I like it."

"Then we'd like to buy it, ma'am."

"Oh, thank you, Tracy." Bertie glowed.

In the end, Emma bought a lighter-colored one with no flower, but a small white feather. Tracy splurged on herself as well, spending a dollar and six bits on a black Bollman with a narrow red ribbon and a wide red feather. She was sure it was the most splendid hat in the entire store.

On Sunday, the day before Tracy had to leave for Troutdale, the three Lampert girls, all sporting their new millinery, sat in the front row at St. Joseph Church and reveled in the admiring glances of the other parishioners.

Chapter 26

SEPTEMBER 1899

Frank

Round Post Office stamp:
Hood River Oreg., Sep 3

Addressed to:
Mr. Ignatz Wand
Elizabeth Ill
Jodavis Co.
Box 89
Hood River, Ore

Sept the 2nd
Dear Elizabeth

I came here Thursday and feel as happie as ever and I hope you are the same. two weeks ago I went up to hot lake and used the water cure and now I feel like a new man. the water has a fine taste almost like chicken soup, only more sulpher. it is so hot they can boil eggs in four minutes it is 184 degrees. I saw this myself. and it is true. that is a good country it's the grand ronde valey. its over 20 miles long and 14 wide and almost round. It is rite in the mountains on the south side of hot lake is a mountain over 2300 feet high. I went up and could see all over the valey. in back of me was a lake that was about three acres of land. there I found a few pretty rocks. now I am here and don't know a sole. and get work the same yesterday I worked in a sawmill but it is to much like work. tomorrow I will go up the valey and pick prunes. this is a fine country it is only 26 miles from Mt. hood and 48. to Troutdale. why don't you write last letter I got on 4 July or did write and sent it to Helix? then it is gone. are you don thrashing and how did it give out. where I was the wheat went 34 bus. to acer. Now I expect a letter in two weeks and be sure and tell me all the news.

Frank Wand
Hood River Ore
Wasco Co[1]

1 Frank's Letter from Hood River. Dated September 3, 1899. Addressed to his father, Ignatz Wand. Greeting to his sister, Elizabeth (Lizzie).
Copy of the letter is in the possession of David Wand, Damascus, Oregon.
Patricia Wand transcribed the letter above and stayed as close as possible to the original spelling, grammar, and punctuation.
Letter transcribed at the residence of Jerry Wand in Sisters, Oregon. July 21, 2019.

Chapter 27

EARLY OCTOBER 1899

Frank

Frank blinked his eyes in the bright sunlight. Stepping from the train, he limped slightly as he walked out of Union Station and onto Seventh Street. *If these new boots don't get broke in soon, I'm gonna give them away*, he thought.

He caught a whiff of perfume, making him think of Sally, and his heart gave a little thump. His mind took over again when he realized the sweet scent came from a well-dressed, portly, middle-aged woman who hurried beside him as they both rushed toward the Flanders Street Trolley.

He grabbed the handle on the side of the arriving trolley with one tan hand and flung himself up the stairs onto the platform. Then he turned and helped the woman and her friends up the stairs. They smiled in appreciation and found their seats.

The Waschers lived in a modest but lovely home on Sixteenth and Lovejoy, not far from the sprawling brick St. Vincent Hospital that reigned over Portland from high in the West Hills. He remembered how shocked he'd been to see it when he first came to Portland: he had never seen a hospital so large. Studying it now, as he made the short walk to William's place, he once again was overwhelmed by the immensity of the seven-story building.

His room at the Waschers' was closest to Lovejoy Street, and he was awakened more than once that night by the sound of the ambulance wagon blowing its horn as it raced up the hill, hauling some poor unfortunate soul with undetermined injuries. When he awoke in the morning, he stretched long and hard, reflecting on his night of little sleep. He frowned at the thought of the noisy, chaotic place that he found the city and couldn't help but compare it with how peaceful it always was out on the Eastern Oregon ranch.

The following morning was Sunday, and Frank scrubbed as best he could from the water in the pitcher. He put on his only white shirt after he shaved. *A bit wrinkled*, he thought, *but at least it's clean.*

He planned on going to see Sally after Mass. *I hate to surprise her*, he thought, *but I don't know how else to do it. Even if they have a telephone, I know her father would frown on using it for frivolous reasons.* He wondered if he would ever have a telephone. He knew only the rich people had them. *Maybe someday.*

After church, several congregants gathered by the front steps to visit and catch up. Sophie Foeller, the friendly young woman he recognized from the last time he'd attended the church, moved toward him and waved a greeting. Her small son, Vic, hovered close by his mother.

"How are you, Frank?" she asked, her voice welcoming.

"Fine, fine," Frank assured her. "I've been up on a wheat ranch near Helix most of the summer."

"Matt and I wondered whatever became of you."

"Well, I enjoyed the harvest and learned a lot, but now I'm back looking for work."

"I may have something for you," Sophie said, with some hesitation. "Mrs. Lampert, a widow woman out in Troutdale, needs help on her farm. If you don't mind more country life, you could make a trip out there and talk to her."

"Well, thank you, ma'am. I'll take that into consideration."

That may be something worth looking into, he thought as he walked to Sally's house. *Too bad it's so far from Portland.*

He rang Sally's doorbell and, after no one answered, sat on the bench beside the front entrance to wait for her return. He wasn't sure when Jewish people attended church. Someone told him once they attended on Saturday. Thoughts raced and angst rose with the combination of surprising her and the possibility of meeting her family. He found himself up and pacing, then sitting once again.

As time dragged by, it warmed considerably. Frank was beginning to perspire, so he moved to the shade, his shirt already wet. He looked at his pocket watch once again, but the hand had barely moved from the last glance.

His mouth dry, he searched for a water pump, but there was none in front of the house, and he wasn't comfortable going to the back yard. Instead he pursed his lips and, spying a tree with shiny ripe apples in the neighbor's yard, he walked over, reached across the fence and snatched one. Closing his eyes, he bit into it, snapping the bite and savoring the crisp tart flesh.

"Frank, what are you doing here?" Sally's surprised voice jerked open his eyes.

"H...hello, Sally," he stammered. "I...I was thirsty. While I waited for you I...er, borrowed one of your neighbor's apples." *This is not going at all like I hoped it would*, he thought. He swallowed, thought about tossing the apple into a lavender bush growing on the sunny side of the house, but decided against it and waited for her to say something.

"I haven't heard from you for weeks." She sounded upset.

"I...I couldn't write often. I was up quite a ways out of Pendleton." He paused. "It was a long ways to the post office." *Why do I feel like I have to apologize?* He squirmed, feeling like a worm on a hook.

"I talked to Father and Mother about you."

"Oh, what did they say?" He wondered if he really wanted to know.

"They don't want me involved with a Catholic man."

"How do you feel about that?"

"I thought you weren't coming back."

"I told you I would."

"Sally, what's going on here?" A man, who looked slightly younger than Frank, walked up and took Sally's hand. Wearing a brown Chadwick vest and a fashionable straw hat, he made Frank feel underdressed with his wrinkled, sweaty shirt and his tight boots. Instinctively, he ran his fingers under his collar.

"Nothing, Ralph, this man has the wrong house." Turning to Frank, she said, "I think the people you are looking for live on the next block." She pointed to the next street over. "I'm sorry."

He turned and walked out the gate and down the sidewalk. In a fit of anger, he pitched the apple and watched it explode on the brick wall of the carriage house next door.

FRANK ROSE EARLY AND HEADED DOWNTOWN AFTER A sleepless night. *Maybe I can get on as a carpenter somewhere,* he thought. *I've done plenty of that kind of work.*

But he knew his heart wasn't in it. Besides, he didn't want to run into anyone in Sally's crowd. Thinking of her brought a mix of anger and hurt to his throat. He swallowed but it wouldn't go away. He had known that any relationship with her would have problems, but somehow he hadn't seen this coming. Maybe he hadn't wanted to.

Frank spent most of the day wandering the streets. While he was impressed with the bustling city, the more he saw of it the less he wanted to live in it. Especially now, after Sally's unkind, ruthless attitude.

After a weak moment thinking maybe she didn't really mean it and that he should try to find her and talk to her, he reconsidered. *The last thing I want to do is see her again and let her kick me when I'm already down.* He knew he wasn't good with words anyway, often having to search for the right one as people waited patiently. His ma always said, "My Frank is the quiet one. Always thinking up new ideas, but does not readily share them."

Frank glanced in a shoe shop window as he walked past and saw a handsome pair of black stovepipe boots. The sign read: *Boots, Many Sizes and Heights, Low Prices.* He turned on his heel and found himself inside the store bargaining with the owner. He came out wearing a new pair of ten-inch-high boots and carrying two dollars in his wallet in trade for the ones that had pinched his feet.

As he walked down Stark Street, he noticed some construction east of Fifth Street and decided to see if they needed a hand. He was a bit hesitant because William had told him the North End was a seedy part of Portland and suggested he avoid it, but that only piqued his curiosity.

"Need any help?" he asked a bearded older man, who appeared to be the foreman.

"You have to ask Jonathan Bourne. He's the boss," he growled and turned back to the job at hand.

The hair stood up on the back of Frank's neck. Bourne? He was the fellow that William said was notorious. "Yeh, it's pretty common knowledge that he's mixed up in everything from sailors' boardinghouses to houses of ill repute," he had told Frank.

The information hadn't surprised Frank much, having been to Chicago, but then William added, "The worst part is that he's a politician and has been accused by many of stuffing the ballot box and other shenanigans to throw the election in favor of Joseph Simon." That hadn't sat well with Frank. He took his politics seriously and wanted fair elections when he voted.

Dismissing the carpentry idea, he continued his explorations. Late afternoon found him down at the waterfront, watching a large vessel tie up. He noticed another steamship and a four-masted sailing ship anchored nearby. In mid-river a small sternwheeler pushed a log raft downriver toward a sawmill in the distance.

Behind him, close to the water, stood a grain silo with the name *B.G. & Co.* painted in bold letters on the side facing the Willamette. Several crew members were hooking up a large round chute from the granary and coupling it to an opening in the steamship's hold, preparing to fill it with wheat.

He had to duck under the two-foot round metal pipe as he walked toward the sailing ship to watch the crew load the four-mast barques with milled lumber of all sizes. A crowd had gathered, and he heard someone say the vessel was headed for San Francisco and then on to Asia. The ship was the largest on the waterfront, but it still seemed small to Frank as he watched it bob up and down. He decided he had no desire to go to sea in any vessel, no matter how brokenhearted he was.

He heard a gentleman who looked like a wealthy businessman or perhaps a city father telling his friend standing beside him that Portland was the biggest city in the Northwest. That didn't surprise Frank: he knew a bustling city when he saw one.

When Frank returned to William's, he had decided to head out to Troutdale. Maybe he could find the widow woman. To him the city was a lonesome place and ranked up there with going to sea; neither appealed to him. Besides, he missed the horses.

AT DAWN THE NEXT MORNING, HE CAUGHT THE TROLLEY to the boundary of East Portland where he stopped and had breakfast at the Last Chance Saloon on the corner of Twelfth Street and Sandy Road. As he was in no particular hurry, he decided to walk the rest of the way to Troutdale. Since he had traded in his grip for a packboard, he could carry his few belongings on his back.

His stomach growled and rumbled by noon when he reached Cleone, but he couldn't find much of a place to eat in the tidy little village. When he inquired, he was told the Methodists did not allow taverns in their town, but about two miles down the road, Troutdale had three saloons and they all served acceptable food.

He bought a stick of jerky and had a long drink of water and continued on with his journey, grinning at the thought that Troutdale might just be his kind of town. Half an hour later, he arrived at the Larsson Bros. Saloon on Troutdale's main street.

Chapter 28

MID-OCTOBER 1899

The Homestead

"I'm sorry, young man. I do need a hired hand," Julianna said after they had introduced themselves, "but I have no money to pay you." She paused. Carefully choosing her words, she continued in a voice weighted with disappointment, "We lost half our onion crop this year."

Frank stood in the doorway, studying the short, middle-aged woman with unhappy green eyes and rough calloused hands. He knew she had once been young and pretty. He wondered what had brought her here to the rugged remote wilderness of the Columbia Gorge; an area so empty that he had passed only three houses in the timber on the trail between here and the Sandy River bluff.

As Julianna talked, she tucked her arms under her apron as if to stave off a frosty morning, although Frank didn't think it was one bit cold. The two small boys who peered out from behind their mother looked freshly scrubbed. He suspected they might have played in the mud earlier, as the ground was still wet from the downpour during the night.

Although it had not been raining when he left Portland, it was evident it had rained out here. The trail was steep and muddy, and it had taken longer than he thought it should have for him to climb up the side of the bluff. The bartender pointed out the trail to him when he had inquired about the Lampert home's location.

"I understand, ma'am," Frank said. Pausing in thought, he finally asked, "Do you mind if I take a look around?"

She shook her head and told him he was welcome. A hint of dejection sounded in her voice and hung in the air between them.

He thanked her and walked around to the back of the house and down a hill that was too steep to farm and served as pastureland. Several goats greeted him with bleats and nuzzles. He instinctively petted those that came to him.

He crawled through the fence and walked across a field of onions; half of them were dug, and he wondered what they did with the harvested ones.

In an adjoining field, he stepped over rows of cabbage and nodded to two young boys with knives, cutting and trimming the heads and leaving them in the row. A pretty young girl picked them up and carefully packed them in the empty crates spread out around the field.

"What do you do with the produce?" Frank asked.

"Joseph, one of the neighbors will come over tonight to pick it up. He sells it to the customers in Brower and Palmer," the older boy answered. He appeared to be about ten or eleven years old with blond hair and piercing eyes that flickered between sadness and a maturity beyond his years.

"Brower and Palmer?"

"They're loggin' towns up toward Larch Mountain," the younger boy piped up, pointing to the southeast. He resembled his older brother, but his eyes were gentler.

Frank nodded and studied them in silence. The girl, blond and round-faced, had a smudge of dirt across one cheek and a welcoming smile. He found that he instantly liked them, feeling drawn to them as if some invisible hand had opened his heart to these hardworking children and their unfortunate mother. He couldn't help but contrast them to Sally's privileged life.

"Where's your horses?" he inquired.

"Got none." The older boy sat back on his heels and met Frank's eyes. "Papa kept saying we were gonna get one, but he never did." He paused and said, "He died before he could buy one."

"I see he built a barn."

The children nodded.

"My name's Frank. What's yours?"

"I'm Ferd, and this here's my sister Josie and my little brother Arnold," the boy said, his face solemn. "Why are you here?"

"How do you do," Frank said, extending his hand down to the lad who answered with a firm shake. "I heard you folks needed a hand."

Arnold rose and shook his hand, and Josie copied her brothers, making Frank smile. "Do you mind if I look around?" he asked, and the children shook their heads.

He headed east up another steep hill that was only partially cleared and down the other side, where he saw many charred trees in a wide swath, evidence of a fairly recent fire. Following the burned area northeast, he came upon a flat bench about halfway down the hill. The burn had mostly cleared a good two to three acres, and at the bottom of the canyon a trickle of water indicated a winter spring.

Walking south up another hill, he came upon a large rock pile and wondered what had happened. Many of the rocks were too large to be dragged there even by horses.

But it opened up a wide clear area from which he could see Mount Hood to the southeast and the Columbia River to the north. Frank shook his head in wonder at the beauty as his eyes followed the river upstream until it got lost in the wrinkled, steep blueness of the ridges in the Gorge.

He sat on a rock for a long time, enjoying the peace, as it slowly dawned on him that he wanted to live here. *This place must be close to heaven*, he thought as his bruised heart drank in the autumn beauty. A house and barn would fit well on that bench down there. Frank heard the bees and the grasshoppers and thought of the noisy buzz of the cicada back home in Illinois. He drank in the freshness of the recent rains and the sweet perfume of the nearby woods.

Reluctantly, he finally rose and headed back down to the widow's home. When he got there, he inspected the barn, happy to see tools in the shop just inside the door. Back behind the shop, the rest of the barn was one big open room, with a wooden fence containing a large haymow almost completely full, ready for wintering the goats.

He walked to the house, rapped gently on the front door and waited for Julianna to answer.

"I don't want money, ma'am," he said, politely when the door opened. "I'll work for land."

MY GOODNESS, SHE THOUGHT, *NOT INTERESTED IN MONEY? Lord knows I have plenty of land.*

"What kind of farm experience do you have?" she inquired, trying not to sound suspicious, but she couldn't help being curious and a bit dubious. Mostly, though, she was scarcely able to believe the possibility of this good fortune.

"I grew up on a farm in Illinois, ma'am." He spoke in

German with quiet deliberation, a slightly different dialect, but easy enough to understand.

"Illinois? Where in Illinois?"

"My father's first farm was in Woodbine Township, but that didn't work out so well, and we moved to a hundred and sixty-two acres on Derinda Road outside of Elizabeth."

She liked him, in spite of the wariness she felt from the long isolation. How could she know if he was honest? Was he experienced? The handsome young man looked healthy and strong.

"We lived near Freeport for a short time," she said.

"That must be how you know the Foellers. Sophie told me about you at St. Joseph last Sunday."

"Sophie's a dear friend of mine. How is she these days?" she said. He was Catholic, and he knew the Foellers.

"Everyone appears fine, ma'am. She has a new baby they call Catherine." He seemed to realize her thirst for news. He paused and tried to sound reassuring. "I just got back from Eastern Oregon. I worked on a threshing crew near Pendleton most of the summer and picked prunes in Hood River on my way home."

Julianna remembered the area from her own trip out west and knew what a threshing job and fruit harvest entailed. She took a deep breath and decided to chance it. *Lord knows I need him*, she thought.

"You can help with the rest of the harvest. We'll see how that works out." She hesitated, thinking about the logistics. "If we agree on terms, in late winter we can go see Mr. Fox in Troutdale and have papers drawn up. He'll help us, I'm sure."

Frank nodded.

"In the meantime, I'll get you a blanket. I'm sorry, but you'll have to sleep in the barn."

Chapter 29

MID-OCTOBER 1899

Frank

Frank threw his blanket on the straw and put his packboard in the shop. It was sparse accommodations—but after a summer roughing it, any accommodations did not seem all that bad, especially with the prospect of earning a farm.

He heard a wagon and walked out to meet it. A pair of matched chestnut Suffolks pulled the rig. It stopped, and a stocky muscular man leaned over to shake his hand when Frank introduced himself.

"Nice to meet you. I'm Joseph Marok."

Impressed with the cordial man, Frank explained that he had come from Portland, knew the Foellers, and was here to help in any way he could. He patted the horse nearest him as he talked, and it nickered in response.

"Good-looking pair of horses you have here."

"Yes, I'm proud of them. I bought them a year ago from a fellow in Troutdale. They're strong and have a lot of endurance for the deliveries. The one you're pettin' is named Matty, and the other one's Sam."

They visited while loading Julianna's vegetables and, with her permission, Frank rode back with Joseph to his place and helped load his and Franz's produce. He felt like he had already made a friend.

"Would you mind if I ride along tomorrow?" he asked as they unhitched the horses and tossed them some hay.

"No, it'd be nice to have some company."

"I'll ask Julianna if she has something for me to do. If not, I'll be here before dawn."

Frank walked home in the dark, wishing the moon was full to help him find his way. A light in the living room window indicated that Julianna had not gone to bed. He tapped lightly on the door.

"If you don't have anything urgent for me to do tomorrow, I'd like to ride with Joseph on the route," he asked.

"I think that would be a good idea," Julianna answered after some hesitation. "I think you need to get to know our customers. My father taught me that."

Frank nodded, happy to know she understood what he wanted to do.

"My father was a successful businessman in Baden when I was a little girl," she added. "I often went with him when he called on his customers." They visited as he ate the bread and cheese she gave him.

"Thank you, ma'am." He turned to leave.

"Wait," she called to him. "You'll need this." She handed him a small lantern and a handful of matches.

He took them and gave her a grateful nod. Lighting the lamp, he walked to the barn. It wasn't long before he climbed into his blanket, blew out the lantern, and settled down for a little sleep.

THE NEXT MORNING THEY LEFT BEFORE DAWN FOR THE

twenty-mile-or-so round trip. Frank took note of the wagon road and the trails running from it. He wasn't quite comfortable with so much brushy, wooded country, and knew it would take some getting used to.

It had rained during the night and parts of the road were muddy, but the horses could see where to step, and they moved right along. Joseph's wagon had a cover over the seat so they would stay reasonably dry if there was more rain along the way.

They stopped at several homes in Brower and then at the general store to rest the horses. Frank put a feedbag on each of them and went in for a cup of hot coffee. Joseph's wife, Elma, had made them each a sandwich of cold meat on thick slices of bread. He couldn't remember when anything tasted so good.

They chatted while they ate, Frank trying to orient himself; he knew they couldn't be too far from the Columbia River. They had after all, followed it for a good share of the way.

"*Ja*," Joseph said between mouthfuls. "Brower is just two or three miles south of the town of Latourell."

Frank nodded; he remembered seeing Latourell built close to the Columbia. In fact, the train stopped there on his way to Portland.

"Yes," he said. "I remember that town. I swear the wharf was one of the biggest on the river."

"You may be right. It's probably the oldest town west of The Dalles."

They climbed aboard the wagon and headed east toward Palmer. It was late afternoon before they sold the last of their vegetables and headed down the mountain for home. There was a light rain falling and a chill in the air. They stopped to light the wagon lanterns, and Frank led the horses through some of the muddiest areas. It felt good to be close to animals again.

"How much money do you take for the trip?" he asked, climbing back on board.

"I take six bits for the horses and six bits for myself from everyone I sell for. Sometimes there's produce from four of us when Robert Graham has vegetables to sell."

Frank rode in silence for a ways, thinking things out. He could make three or four dollars a week, if Joseph would let him use the horses. Joseph would get some money for their use and be freed up to work his farm. *I wonder if Julianna would mind*, he thought. *I'll ask her tomorrow.*

"I'd like to take the route for you with Julianna's permission," he finally said.

"You know your horses, that's for sure," the older man replied after a pause. "Do you think you could remember the places we stopped?"

"I'm pretty sure I can," he said quietly, "and I could use the money."

"I'll tell you what," Joseph finally said, "if it works out with Julianna, you and I'll go one more time together, so you can get the route in your mind, and then I'll take you up on your offer."

Frank had the opportunity to make two trips by himself, happy to add a couple more dollars to his savings before the weather turned ugly in the middle of November. Most of the produce was sold by that time anyway, and the roads turned to mud.

After a discussion with Julianna at supper one evening, Frank built a small room in the barn next to the shop. He insulated it with some extra burlap bags that he bought from Joseph and filled with straw, and he built a log floor, covering it with a foot of hay, where he laid his blanket.

"You're a good carpenter," Julianna said, standing in the doorway of his new bedroom. "Alex was a joiner, you know."

"Yes, ma'am. I could tell by his tools."

"It's nice to have someone on the place again who is capable of fixing things." She pointed toward the house and the roof he had just finished patching. "And thank you for being so kind to the children. They have been through a lot, with losing their father and baby brother, not to mention having to work like adults." She paused and looked out over the field. "And besides, Alex was only able to clear about twelve acres. I'd be happy to have a bit more cultivated land."

Frank nodded and murmured, "Yes, ma'am, I can do that."

"Don't forget, the girls always have coffee or hot water for tea on the stove. When you need to warm your hands, please come in and help yourself." She turned and walked out of the barn.

"Yes ma'am, and thank you for the meals, too."

When I go to Troutdale for supplies for her, I'll get some Christmas gifts, he thought as he shook out his blanket, *and I'll get me another blanket. Joseph thinks we're in for a cold winter.*

Chapter 30

DECEMBER 1899

Tracy

When the entrance bell rang, Tracy looked up from the counter where she was helping Joey and his little brother. Each of them had a penny clenched in their small, grimy fists and were taking their time picking out hard candy. Joey had just pointed to a large dark piece of horehound.

"Ferd! My goodness, where did you come from? Is everything all right?" she asked, surprised to see her two brothers bundled up against the cold, faces red from the outdoors.

"We come to get supplies," Arnold said before Ferd could answer.

"We're fine," Ferd said, ignoring his younger brother.

Tracy couldn't help but smile. Some things remained the same no matter the length of time. She ran around the corner of the counter and gathered the scruffy boys in her arms, then hurried back to her position to assist the waiting young customers.

"Now, tell me all about the family," she said after the little boys paid for their candy and left.

"We got a hired man," Arnold said, "and he's nice."

"How can we ever pay him?" Tracy asked, happy for the news but wondering, as always, about money.

"Don't worry," Ferd said, "he don't want no money."

"*Ja*, he wants land," Arnold piped up.

"Oh my goodness, that is wonderful news."

"Mama says he's a good worker, real steady. He started delivering the produce too, but that's done 'til next year. Joseph says he's happy to have someone else do it, and Frank says it's a good way he can earn some cash."

They chattered until the next customer came in and then began to gather the supplies on Julianna's list.

"But you can't carry all these things up the bluff. What about this fifty-pound sack of flour?" Tracy worried that her mother's requests were unrealistic.

"Oh, no." Arnold shook his head. "Frank'll be here in a minute to help carry it. He stopped at the post office. He wanted to mail a letter to his family."

Presently, the door opened and a tall, slender, clean-shaven young man with curly, dark brown hair parted in the middle ambled in with a rush of cold air as the east wind sneaked past him. His clothes were old but clean with brown suspenders visible under his coat. His gray-green eyes crinkled at the edges when he smiled at her.

Her heart did a tiny flip—something that hadn't happened for a long time. Not since her school days with Logan. Embarrassed, Tracy felt a hot blush move from the back of her neck up to her cheeks. He looked familiar, but she couldn't quite place him.

"This is our sister, Tracy," Ferd said, relieving her of having to speak for the moment.

Frank walked over, pulled off his glove, and stuck his hand out. "Tracy, these boys told me all about you."

"Oh my, I hope it wasn't all bad," she mumbled as she returned the handshake. Although his hand was cold, she admired the strength and his quiet gentleness.

"Yeh, she's a good sister," Arnold said. "She doesn't scold us."

"I'm not home enough to be grouchy." She laughed.

Frank bought a blanket and asked for a sack of candy. "For the children for Christmas," he murmured as he laid the rest of his supplies on the counter.

Her heart warmed at that, and when he brought over a shawl that she had had her eye on for several days, her interest was piqued.

"Do you think your *Mutter* would use something like this?" he asked in a quiet, hesitating voice.

"*Mutter*? You want to give this to Mama?"

"Yes, she's been very good to me. I can have coffee whenever I want, and she feeds me well." He paused, and after a moment said simply, "I think she needs something for herself."

Tracy couldn't believe what she was hearing. Either this was a very good-hearted young fellow or he was a crooked, smooth-talking confidence man. She guessed time would tell.

"I couldn't agree more," she said, but even as wariness reared its head, she couldn't help but be attracted to him. *I'm going to watch this one carefully*, she thought, wondering why in the world he looked so familiar.

Tracy helped the boys arrange the supplies in their packboards. She watched Frank as he put the sack of flour in the middle of the board and carefully packed the many other supplies and gifts around it. *That backpack must weigh over a hundred pounds*, she thought. *And the bluff is so steep.* As much as she worried and wondered if he was what he seemed, she had to admire him.

When they were done, she gave all of them a slice of bread and jam and a cup of coffee from the back. Then she hugged her two brothers, and they said their goodbyes. *Thank God, Christmas is only a few days away,* she thought. She missed her family more than ever.

"When will you be coming home for the holidays?" Frank asked as they were ready to leave.

"Emma and Bertie are supposed to come out from Portland on the train day after tomorrow. We'll all come home then."

Frank nodded and followed the boys to the door, then turned and said, "I'll come to the other side of the river and help you carry your things up the bluff if you like."

In spite of herself, Tracy's heart raced. She managed to say thank you and tell him the approximate time they'd be there, and then the door shut and they were gone.

The loneliness and the homesickness that she had shoved so deep inside bubbled up and flowed, the tears caused small rivulets down her cheeks, lifting away her burdens.

After her tears stopped, she sat alone. Much to her relief, no customers entered the store. Her thoughts went back to Frank. She knew she had seen him somewhere, but where? Then she remembered the nights she had dreamt of meeting a smiling young man on the trail.

"That's him!" With a shiver, she murmured, "Frank. My dream. The man I met on the trail on his way up to Pleasant View."

"Oh my, it's good to see you!" Tracy exclaimed as

Bertie and Emma walked down the steps of the train and into her arms.

"We're glad to be here," Emma said. She grabbed her hat as a gust of east wind caught it and almost sent it back down the tracks to Portland.

"Oh, Bertie, I swear you're half a foot taller. You're all grown-up," Tracy said as she led the way into the depot and out of the weather.

"Yes, she's already got a beau," Emma said, clinging firmly to her hat as she ducked in the door.

"No, do you really?" Now Tracy was surprised.

"No," Bertie spoke, in what was a more adult voice than Tracy remembered. "Donald Heintzman danced with me at the Young People's Harvest Frolic down at the church, and now everyone thinks he's my beau." With a wave of her hand, she said, "It's nothing, really."

But Tracy noticed she held her chin a bit higher. *She's finding some adventure away from us,* she thought and smiled.

"You should've seen Emma," Bertie continued.

"What about Emma?" Tracy asked as a black cap caught her eye, the wind bouncing it along the depot platform. A young boy, arms outstretched, chased after it. A bare-headed man followed close behind him.

"Yes, what about me?" Emma asked.

"All the boys flirt with her."

"No, they don't."

They laughed and chatted, gathering themselves together for the walk from the tracks to the store. They bid the depot master good day and found themselves struggling against the wind as they made their way up the hill to Troutdale's main street and the shelter of Fox's mercantile.

Each carried a grip, and Tracy lugged the blue polka-dot bag the girls had brought with them. They informed her that she could not look in it, because it held all the family Christmas presents, including something that Sophie had made just for her.

By the time they reached the store, tiny pellets of snow had started to spit, and the sky had gone from light to gloomy hues of blue-gray. Tracy shivered and looked southwest where the sky was the darkest.

"I'm thinking we're in for a good storm, Tracy," Mr. Fox said in a voice that raised her concern.

"I hope we can beat it home," Emma said. "I'm so eager to see everybody."

"Me, too," Tracy agreed. "Frank said he would come down the bluff and help us carry things up."

"Frank? Who's Frank?" Emma looked puzzled.

"I'll bet I know him," Bertie said. "He's that handsome man from Illinois who came to St. Joseph. Sophie said she was going to tell him about Mama."

"Yes, that's him. He came down with the boys day before yesterday. I told him about what time we'd be there." Tracy felt excitement run through her as she talked about him. A corner of guilt popped into her mind, wondering if she was being unfaithful to Logan.

"It's against my better judgment for you girls to go out in this weather, but I can see you're determined, so I'm going to loan you each a pair of these heavy wool pants to wear," Mr. Fox said, pulling them from the shelf. "They'll be too big, but they'll keep you warm." He handed them to Tracy, and said, "And here, take these mittens, Bertie. You can keep them. It's far too cold for anyone to be out without a good pair of gloves, like your sisters have."

"And besides," Mr. Fox added. "The footbridge is washed out. You'll have to take the ferry."

They thanked Mr. Fox, hurriedly bundled up, and packed the polka dot bag and Tracy's family Christmas packages onto Papa's packboard. Tracy had brought her grip with her to the store, and as soon as Mr. Fox helped her strap it on the board, they were ready to go.

They left the store with hasty goodbyes and rushed headlong into the wind on their way to the Hicklin Ferry, hoping it was, by some miracle, on their side of the Sandy River. The wind howled through the trees and burrowed under their clothes. When their scarves slid down from their faces, the strong breezes caught them trying to inhale and whisked the air away, leaving them breathless and icy cold.

When they arrived at the riverbank, the ferry was halfway across, bringing a traveler to their side of the river. They stood in the lean-to shelter and waited, happy to be out of the wind.

Tracy prayed Frank would be there to help. The snow seemed to be falling faster, swirling in odd patterns, piling up in some places and leaving bare spots in others.

She wondered if they were doing the right thing. A shiver ran through her, thinking Mr. Fox might have been right about venturing out in a blizzard.

Chapter 31

DECEMBER 1899

The Trail and the Blizzard

Once aboard the ferry, the girls paid their nickels and sought shelter in the operator's booth. The ferry's cable tied onto and slid along another cable that stretched across the river, but even with that set-up, the wooden craft had to be guided by Hicklin or his hired man. Tracy strained to see the other bank but could only see blurs of trees through gusts of wind.

"You girls going to try to make it up the hill?" Hicklin asked. His usually gruff voice had more concern than question.

Tracy nodded. "Yes, but *Mutter*'s hired man will be down to help us," she said, trying to sound confident.

"Good, because this storm is gearing up to be a whopper." He nodded toward the open doorway as the east-side dock suddenly loomed in front of them. His eyes widened as he ran out of the cabin to stop the boat and tie up.

Tracy peered into the snow but saw nothing except a white lace curtain swirling in front of her eyes. *Maybe we should go back to Foxes' while we still can.* Sheer panic thrust through her for an instant. *No, Frank will come to help us.*

"I'll wait here for twenty minutes or so and see if you come back," Mr. Hicklin said and patted Tracy on the shoulder.

"Thank you, sir."

The girls walked off the ferry onto the solid feel of the dock. They turned and followed the trail south along the shelter of the bluff, protecting them from the strong winds, and making it easier to search for Frank.

When they got to the place where the trail veered up the hill there he was, coming down. Tracy went weak with relief. He carried a coil of rope over his shoulder and a walking stick in his hand.

Pulling the scarf from his face, he mumbled hello and set to work quickly. They took the town girls' grips and uncoiled the rope, tied them together, and placed them on his back as if they were a packboard secured tightly around his shoulders.

Finished, he motioned for the girls to go ahead of him, warning that some places were slick. As they started up the hill among the trees, he found each of them a sturdy stick to help with their balance. Tracy led the way up the now-frozen dirt path. The snow had stopped falling, and it felt warmer in the protection of the bluff.

They came to a frozen winter spring, which turned the path into a treacherous sheet of ice. All the times Tracy had walked up the trail, she had never seen the spring so large. Most of the time it was easy to navigate. She hesitated and waited for Frank to make his way to the front. He got down on his hands and knees and crawled over the frozen ground, then signaled for each girl to do the same, one at a time.

Relieved, the little group with their heavy loads made their way up the grade. About halfway they found the usually small and easily crossed stream had become a torrential waterfall. The ice-crusted rocks on either side of the rushing water made Tracy shiver.

She held her breath as Frank picked up the sturdy staff and started across, gingerly digging in his heels in an effort to maintain traction. Carefully picking his way through the narrow band of rapids, his foot slipped once and he dropped to one knee and landed on a rock. The load on his back shifted downhill. It looked as if at any moment he would be swept downstream.

"Oh my God!" Tracy gasped.

Somehow, he found inhuman strength and with a surge of effort pushed himself upright, swung his pack back into position, and took the last two steps off the ice and onto frozen, but solid, dirt.

When he turned, Tracy saw determination in his face alongside a hint of embarrassment. He motioned for them to wait while he walked up the trail and disappeared into the woods.

A short time later, he returned with a long, sturdy tree limb. Grabbing hold of a small sapling beside the stream, he handed Tracy one end of the branch across the creek. Holding on to the other end, he motioned to her to come on across.

Still holding her breath, she gingerly stepped onto the ice and, like Frank, slipped and fell to one knee. Deciding that was the safer, she crawled the short distance to the water's edge, rose to her feet and hanging tightly to the branch made two steps across the tumbling water where she dropped back onto her knees to finish the journey.

"Good job," he exclaimed as he helped her to her feet. "I think your laced shoes kept your feet dry, too."

She nodded and helped him hold the stick for Emma to cross, which she did uneventfully as they all held their breaths.

Then it was Bertie's turn. With her face grim, she carefully made her way across the slick, frozen area. As she started across the rushing water, she slipped on an icy rock in the middle of the creek, lost her balance and fell, water rushing in over the top of one of her shoes. Her pant leg soaked, she struggled to get upright.

"My ankle!" she sobbed.

"Hang on, Bertie," Frank hollered over the wind. He left Tracy and Emma holding the branch, crawled out on the ice, grabbed Bertie's free hand, and pulled her up and out of the water. Finally, she too was back on solid ground.

"My ankle," Bertie cried, pointing at her soaked foot. "It's so cold."

Frank brushed the snow off a nearby downed log, sat her on it and began carefully removing her shoe.

"That ankle is swollen," he said. "We'll see if she can walk. Get me a dry sock out of one of the grips." But Tracy was already digging in the closest bag and handed him a long, woolen stocking.

They had to put Bertie's wet shoe back on but at least she had the dry sock next to her skin. Tracy's admiration grew as she watched Frank. His confidence gave her strength she had not known since she was a little girl and Papa was there to manage unforeseen circumstances.

Yet the temperature was below freezing, and the wind was howling. She worried that poor Bertie with her wet shoe and pant-leg and injured ankle would have trouble the rest of the way. The closest place was Seidls' on top of the bluff, still a long way across a pasture and out of the shelter of the hillside.

They made it to the top where the trail veered slightly northeast through more trees. Bertie gamely limped along with Tracy hanging onto one hand and Emma to the other. Snow started falling again, beating their faces with every gust.

They came to the clearing, where normally Seidls' cabin was in plain view, but the only thing visible was the white veil of snow. Tracy had heard stories of people walking in circles in a blizzard. *Oh God, help us,* she prayed.

She saw Frank take something out of his pocket and look at it. Why in the world does he need to know the time? she wondered.

As they pushed their way through the furious wind, she noticed that he kept his eyes on the watch. They walked for what seemed like an eternity when she heard a cry above the wind and looked down to see tears streaming down Bertie's face disappearing under her scarf.

"Frank!" she hollered, but the wind blew her voice away.

"Frank!" she called again as loudly as she could. It was snowing so hard she could just make out his back even though he was only a few of feet ahead of her.

Emma made her way up to him. Tracy watched as she saw Frank stop, lean down to listen, and then they both turned and came back.

Frank leaned down and said something to Bertie, but the wind was so noisy it blew away the words before Tracy could catch them.

He slipped out of the rope that held the grips, untied one, and handed it to Emma. He tied the two remaining lines back into place and picked up the slight fourteen-year-old as if she were a small child. He gently lifted her over his shoulder and motioned for them to follow.

Emma and Tracy hung on to each other, each now hauling a load, with the snow blinding them. *I wonder if we'll even be able to see the Seidls' house*, Tracy worried.

She heard a noise and saw Frank point to the left. There almost beside him was a corner fencepost. They followed the fence for what seemed like a long way and finally came to the barn. Tracy went ahead, feeling the wall until she found the door, pushed it open, and ducked into shelter. She thought she had never smelled anything quite as wonderful in that moment as the odor of hay and manure wafted her way. She had never before found it a bit pleasant.

Frank put Bertie down and pulled the door shut to keep the worst of the storm at bay. The cattle milled in a small enclosure, steamy breath surrounding them. They too were safe from the arctic temperatures; their bodies helping to heat the building.

Shivering in the cold, their scarves frozen with saliva and tears, the group knew they still had to find the house for Bertie's safety.

"Are you all right?" Tracy managed to croak, anxious about her younger sister.

Bertie groaned as Tracy took off her sister's mittens and felt her hands. Icy cold. *Help us get her to Mrs. Seidl*, she prayed.

"What door do they use when they come out to milk?" Frank asked.

"I think that one over there," Emma answered, pointing to a small door near the opposite corner. "I came over here once with Ferd and Arnold, and we came out to the barn."

Frank went over, opened it and came back. "We're in luck," he said. "He's got a rope stretched and tied to the doorjamb. I'm betting it will take us to the house. Come on, let's give it a try."

Frank held the door open for them, picked Bertie up again, and they followed the rope, startling the Seidl family as they knocked on the back door of the one-room cabin.

"Bring me some warm water," Maria Seidl said to her daughter, Lizzie, as she put a blanket around Bertie's shivering shoulders. Emma and Tracy unhooked and pulled off her boots and socks. Then they removed their own shoes, as Jacob handed them dry knitted woolen socks. Frank sat by the fire, his face mirroring Tracy's feeling of gratitude and relief.

With her arm around Bertie's shoulders, Maria gently led the young girl to a bed with a curtain around it.

"Put both irons on the warming shelf," she called out as Tracy followed to help.

Maria worked fast, stripping clothes off Bertie, then pulling a large, flannel nightgown over the shivering girl and wrapping the excess around her tightly.

"Don't rub her foot, Tracy. It could do more harm than good."

Tracy stopped immediately, holding the white toes gently in her hand, willing warmth into her sister's feet.

Shortly, Jacob brought in a tub of water. Maria tested it and then gently submerged the frozen foot. Bertie began to sob as feeling started to come back to her toes.

"What's the matter?" Emma asked, her head poking through the curtains.

"It hurts really bad," Bertie replied. "I think I'd rather just let it be frozen."

"I know," Maria said, "but if we do this right, you probably won't have any lasting effects. I don't want you to have chilblains for the rest of your life."

"Chilblains?" Bertie asked.

"They cause pain and sometimes your toes get red and ooze. In the old country, my father's friend had them after frostbite, and he lost most of his toes on one foot."

Bertie sobbed louder. "I don't want to lose my toes," she sniffed.

When Emma, wrapped in a blanket, brought in the warmed irons, Maria placed them in towels, then put one of them behind Bertie's legs and handed her the other to clutch to her chest.

"There now, that should make you feel better," Maria told her.

Bertie nodded, the warmth calming her.

Now that Bertie looked better, Tracy realized that she was shivering herself and looked down to see both pant legs sopping wet.

"Take those pants off and wrap yourself in this," Maria said, handing her a large heavy towel.

Maria left and came back with a bowl of hot soup from the black kettle on the stove. "Come. Tracy, I have your supper in the other room."

She pulled up a small bedside table for Bertie to use.

Tracy, shrouded in the dingy white towel, followed her out from behind the protection of the curtain. She could feel the heat in her face and was unable to look at Frank, who, was sitting near Emma; both had their feet in basins of tepid water and looked tired and hungry.

Later, Maria made beds for the girls on the floor of the living room next to the fireplace. Frank went up to the loft with Henry. They listened all night as the wind howled around the corners and the snow pinged against the windows.

Tracy shivered, snuggling down in her blanket and quietly saying her rosary, giving thanks they were safe and wondering how long the storm would last.

"Mama, where are the sisters?" Arnold asked.

Julianna sighed and glanced once again out the window. The family woke this morning to bright sunshine and high drifts of snow covering the east windows. Frank had left three days ago to walk the girls up the hill. She hadn't heard from him or her daughters since. She prayed the girls either had not tried to come home or had found shelter at one of the neighbors.

"They'll be home soon now that the snow has stopped," she said with a confidence she did not feel. Something told her they would be all right, but she could not keep the worry at bay. The not knowing was silent agony.

She remembered the two young sisters in Illinois when she and Alex were first married. The girls were found frozen to death in a snowdrift. On their way home from school, a blizzard caught them by surprise, and they had become disoriented in the swirling blasts of snow—not a hundred yards from their home.

Julianna had not slept much the last few nights, between keeping the fire stoked and fearing for her children. As the morning dragged on her anxiety tripled, and she found herself impatient with the youngsters.

"I must not be cross," she scolded herself. "The children have done nothing wrong."

Sometime later, she heard a squeal and ran to the other room to see the children gathered at the window.

"There they are, Mama!" Josie cried pointing toward

the gate.

They watched as four figures picked their way through the drifts, seeking bare frozen ground as they made their way toward the house. The east wind was just a breeze.

Ferd and Josie ran outdoors to greet them, with Arnold close behind. Julianna kept Jackie and Little Alex inside despite their complaints.

"I'll not have you catching your death out in that freezing weather," she said to them, her knees wobbly with relief. She noticed Bertie walked with a slight limp, holding on to Tracy, and she wondered.

Chapter 32

JANUARY 1900

"This isn't a watch," Frank said, pulling the round instrument out of his pocket. "If I hadn't had this," he continued, placing it and his pocket watch on the table to compare, "we would never have found Seidls' house in that blizzard."

"The teacher showed us once in school," Ferd said, turning the compass slowly. "Look, the needle always points one way."

"That's right. The reason this works is because we have a known fact. It always points toward magnetic north, and that gives you all the other directions," Frank continued. Taking the compass from Ferd and laying it on the table so they all could see, he slowly turned it to match the needle with the N painted on the face.

"We learned about magnets in school," Arnold exclaimed.

"The needle must be made of iron." Josie's eyes sparkled.

Frank nodded. "You're right."

"So you knew which way to walk," Jackie chimed in. "You're pretty smart."

"Not as smart as I was scared. The sky just didn't look right to me, so I took readings on the way down the trail. I've been in some pretty bad storms back east and didn't want to take any chances."

Frank noticed Tracy looking at him from the sink and felt himself flush. Her dark hair, pulled back in a loose bun, framed her face and highlighted her hazel eyes and delicate nose. He liked the way she held her hands, feminine, yet strong and determined. He promptly forgot what he was saying.

"So if that's the case, then Frommelts' place is west of us," Ferd's voice brought him back to the moment.

"And Seidls' too," Bertie spoke up.

"Yes, it is," he said, impressed with their eagerness to learn.

As each child took their turn trying to read the compass, Frank coached them and again realized how difficult it must be for them without their father.

He noticed Julianna, busy tidying up after supper, and wondered how she had survived these past couple of years. Sheer grit and determination more than likely. She finally sat down across the table and seemed interested, so he passed the compass her way.

"My father had one of these," she said, peering into the crystal. "He was very proud of it." He noticed the faraway look in her eyes. "*Vor langer Zeit*—in the distant past."

"I understand his pride. I'm very happy I have a compass."

"So are we," Julianna murmured. "So are we."

Tracy's eyes met Frank's as she nodded in agreement and, flushing again, he realized how happy he was that the girls had delayed their leaving, even though Christmas and the storm were over. They brought cheer to this often cheerless house.

Julianna had told him once, in a rare showing of her soul, how much she yearned to have her girls home with the family. Now he could see how the younger children missed them, too.

When Frank and the boys walked part of the Seidl trail earlier in the day, they found the sticky mud of a thaw and decided it was far too slippery and dangerous to take the steep path to Troutdale. Tracy and the girls were overjoyed with the news.

"We'll get to stay extra time," Bertie had said. "It's hard to leave. I get so lonesome for everyone."

"Me, too," Emma agreed. "Everyone asks me why I miss being out in the wilderness when I can enjoy the culture and excitement of Portland."

"What do you tell them?" Josie joined the conversation.

"I tell them that my family is out here and my friends, and sometimes I just want to be home."

Frank, touched, noticed Tracy hadn't joined in the chatter. He pondered that the rest of the day. Either she didn't miss the family and was content to be in Troutdale, which he doubted, or it was too painful to discuss.

On their trip down the trail earlier the boys revealed to him that Tracy had had a suitor who drowned in the Columbia. Maybe she was still grieving? This was something he could understand.

That night, comfortable in his warm bed in the straw, he thought about the last few days. How he had slept on the floor in the living room during the storm to keep the fire burning and how he sneaked a peek at Tracy and the girls when they walked by him to go upstairs to bed.

She's only sixteen, and I have nothing to offer her, he thought. *I believe I'll just wait and see what happens.* Relieved that he had finally decided on a plan, he drifted off to sleep.

Chapter 33

SPRING 1900

Julianna

"Where in the world did you get her?" Julianna asked, taking a step back from the strangest horse with the longest ears she'd ever seen.

"Meet Molly the mule." Frank laughed. "I bought her from Robert Graham for fifteen dollars."

Molly's brown coat shone in the spring sunshine, with a black mane, tail, and four stockings, as she stood patiently while they visited.

"*Oh mein Gott!* Where did you get the money?"

"Don't worry, Julianna," he said. "I gave him five dollars of my own money and told him I would pay him at least two dollars every week that I have vegetable deliveries this season until I get her all paid for." He reached up, patted Molly on the neck, and stuck a handful of oats under her nose.

"I hope you don't mind, ma'am. I guess I should've come and talked with you first," he added as if the thought had just occurred to him. "We'll still have to borrow the implements from Joseph and Franz, but at least we have a draft animal. I've been worried about wearing out the neighbors' horses."

Julianna agreed that tasking their friends' animals with working in her fields and pulling the produce wagons once a week was too much. She had worried about that for some time.

"Mr. Graham threw in the collar and the harness and even a bag of oats," Frank said proudly, as if to convince her. "I'll build a cupboard in the barn to hang the rigging, and I'll teach the children how to care for her."

"They will be so excited when they get home," Julianna said, beginning to feel better after discussing it with the quiet young man. "Arnold has asked and asked for a horse."

"When I had to wait for a horse to get the early plowing done and then it rained, I knew we had to do something. I stopped in to visit Mr. Graham the other day and mentioned needing a draft animal. He said I could have this 'darned old mule' cheap, 'cause she wouldn't do anything he wanted her to do. He said he would never have anything on the place but a horse from now on."

"If he can't do anything with her, why do you think you can?" Julianna asked, curious about his ability.

"I don't know as I can, but Papa and my uncles always said I had a way with animals, so I thought this was a good time to find out. So far I haven't had any trouble with her."

He seemed confident enough, and he certainly had fulfilled his part of the bargain on the farm, so Julianna let him have his way, hoping against hope it would work. It was difficult to farm relying as they had on neighbors the past few years. The young man seemed to have a flair for farming and carpentry, so why not animals? *So much like Alex*, she thought, with a familiar pang.

"What about feed?"

"I thought we could turn her in with the goats for now, if it's all right with you, and I'll build some more fences as soon as I have time," he said. "We can leave that upper field in grass this summer and cut it for extra hay. She will need a lot more feed over the winter than the goats."

"I wonder if that will be enough?"

"No, we will have to spend some of our produce money on grain. If I had a way to harvest it, I'd raise a crop of oats this season."

Julianna wondered silently about another mouth to feed, but nodded.

"I'm gonna see if I can round up some wheels. It sure would be helpful to have a wagon during haying time."

Julianna noticed then that he looked excited, and she thought of the children. Maybe this could help bring the family back from the misery they had shared since the loss their father and baby brother. Just maybe this young man, a de facto older brother, could do what she had been unable to do.

"When do you think you can get started working up the ground for our early planting?" Julianna asked, her practical side again in command.

"Joseph said I could come get the disk on Monday, and the plow would be ready a few days after that," he said in his quiet voice. "I'll get started on the lower field, if it doesn't rain."

Molly brayed as soon as Frank mentioned "plow," and stepped back, shaking her head, almost like she knew what was being said. Julianna suspected she might.

JULIANNA GLANCED OUT THE WINDOW AND NOTICED

Frank had the mule with the disk down on the lower field. *Looks like they are doing all right*, she thought. *Maybe he does know a bit about animals.* She wondered for a moment why she had been so skeptical of everyone and everything lately. She hadn't been that way growing up, certainly not with Alex.

Life's journey has a way of changing things. A picture popped into her mind, and once again she was sitting on a bench back in another time, waiting for Alex to disembark from the ship to join her. She remembered that day in New York City as being bright and full of hope, and for an instant she marveled at where his dream—perhaps hers, too—had taken them. From then to now. How excited they had been to see the world and explore the city.

Later, they arrived in Freeport, Illinois, and met all the wonderful German people who had immigrated previously. Then she was introduced to Alex's friends, Franz and Katherine, who also shared their dream. It seemed that things could not be better.

But Alex and Franz had wanted land of their own. She smiled as she remembered how excited the four of them had been to make the passage on the train from St. Paul to their new life in Oregon. And how sad she and Katherine were when the men told them they had lost what they believed was their land in Bethany west of Portland.

"*Mutter*," Jackie said, interrupting her thoughts. "Frank asked if he can have some carrots for Molly."

"Of course, we have plenty left in the pit," she answered. "Why? Didn't he feed her this morning?"

"Oh yeah, he did, but she does not want to go up the row very much."

Julianna looked out the window and saw them in the middle of the field, halfway up the furrow, with Frank standing near Molly, whispering something in her ear.

"Yes, go take him a handful, Jackie," she said, her curiosity piqued.

She watched as the boy, followed closely by Little Alex, ran back and handed the young man a bunch of large carrots. Instead of giving them to the mule, Frank seemed to make a point of showing them to her, even letting her smell them. Then he put some in each of his pants pockets and walked ahead, leading the animal down the row. Molly shook her head, brayed, and slowly followed him; the disk, with several large rocks on top to push it into the soil, rolled easily behind.

When they reached the end, Frank pulled a carrot out of his pocket, broke off a piece, and let her savor it. Then they turned around and repeated the process. Watching, Julianna hoped they wouldn't run out of carrots before the spring work was finished and made a mental note to plant extra rows next season.

By the end of April, with most of the spring planting done and the next winter's wood split and piled, Julianna asked Frank to start cleaning up the forest trees they had lost during the winter storms.

"If you will cut and split the blow-downs and make cord wood, we can sell it to the steamships," Julianna said to Frank and the children at the dinner table one evening. "Franz said they're paying as high as $7 a cord. With money like that, I can pay you part of it."

He shook his head, "*Nein*, put it toward my land," he said. "If I run short of cash, I'll take the tools and do some carpentry for the neighbors or wait until the produce run."

The arrangement seemed to suit Frank just fine. She noticed he spent much of his time in the woods until harvest began that year.

On a Friday in mid-May, Pleasant View School hosted the end-of-the-year picnic. The whole neighborhood took the day off to see the children perform and visit with friends.

Julianna overheard Arnold telling Josie, "I wanna see Harley Bates. It's been a long time since I've seen him, and he's my friend." She realized the children were as lonesome as she was. She felt bad having to pull the children out of school earlier in the spring, but she had no choice. Spring planting was later than she would have liked, and she needed them to help catch up in the fields.

The day of the picnic was cloudy and overcast, but the crowd expressed gratitude for a dry day and reminisced about the terrible weather they had for last year's picnic, forcing them to the school play shed.

Then the conversation turned to the storms of the past winter. A shudder went through Julianna, thinking of the girls and Frank and their harrowing walk from Troutdale, uphill in the blizzard. Thank God they are all safe. And Bertie's foot had no ill effects as near as she could tell.

Some time after they finished their picnic dinner and were visiting, Julianna noticed Frank leaning against a fir tree talking to Lucy Mershon. It wasn't very long before young Bob Larson joined them. She smiled to herself, thinking about young love and her memories of a dance in Baden long ago.

Chapter 34

SEPTEMBER 1902

Frank

Frank straightened his back and faced east, letting the harsh hot wind brush his face. It had blown steadily since the first of September, discouraging much-needed rain. The region had not seen moisture since the first of August and then only a trace. The carrots he was pulling were still damp to the roots, surprising him. Good, rich soil, he thought, plenty of mulch to hold the moisture.

Still, the lack of rain was a concern. *There's a lot of timber on this place, and the woods are dry,* he thought. *It could go up like kerosene on a fire.* He couldn't get his mind off a story he'd heard. The last time he stopped in at Louie Helming's saloon in Troutdale, Louie told him about a family up the Gorge who had tried to outrun a fire with a horse and wagon and didn't make it.

He shook his head and thought of something much sweeter: Tracy. She was never far from his mind these days and was much more pleasant to think about than lack of rain or outrunning fires. She was coming home Saturday to help her mother and sisters can applesauce. He had never canned anything but decided he should learn.

He had seen her every Sunday since the Fourth of July picnic. On those days, after the family rosary in the morning, he took the lantern, walked to Troutdale, and spent the day. He usually left for home just before dark. He had walked the trail a couple of times in the blackness of the night without a lantern, but never on purpose. Too many steep drop-offs to suit him.

Once he went down to Troutdale on Saturday, and they attended a party at one of the Foxes' neighbors' on Dora Street. And once Tracy came home on a Saturday afternoon. That Sunday they had all attended church at the Seidls' place, where Father Wachter, a new priest from Mount Angel, said Mass. Afterward they had a potluck picnic celebrating little Joseph Frommelt's First Communion.

Thinking about it, Frank decided to take the opportunity to talk to the priest, since he figured it might be some time before he would have another chance. He knew he wanted to marry Tracy and hoped she cared enough about him to agree. After all, she worked at a store and saw many eligible men. It seemed to him that she didn't show interest in any of them, and she always seemed happy to see him.

It took him some time before he mustered up the courage, and then he had to wait for the priest to have a moment alone. When he saw his chance, he hurried over to him.

"I'm thinking of asking that young lady over there to become my bride," Frank motioned discreetly toward Tracy. "I need to know how to go about the formalities of the engagement, like posting the banns. I'm not sure how to do that out here so far from a parish."

At that moment, his knees weakened, and doubt washed over him. He wondered if he had assumed too much. What if Tracy refused his offer? Then what?

"The best thing you can do when you are ready is to go into Portland and talk to the priest at St. Joseph's. He can post them in his parish." The priest spoke kindly, putting Frank more at ease. "That Portland parish is where most of your friends and acquaintances attend Mass."

Startled back to the present by a whiff of smoke, Frank jerked his head up. He saw nothing and wondered if he were imagining things. His eye caught the charred tree bark on the hill where Julianna had spoken of a fire that raced through the farm several years before they arrived.

Finishing the last of the carrots, he loaded the two bushel baskets on the wagon along with Julianna's other vegetables. There was still enough daylight left to load Joseph's and Franz's produce. Then he would be ready to start his run up to the logging camps before daylight the next morning. The sooner he got started, the sooner he would be back, hopefully in time to walk to the bottom of the trail and surprise Tracy on her way home.

Early the next day before dawn, he had the team hitched and on their way. The sun was just peeking over the horizon as he passed Pleasant View School situated north of the Wire Trail.

About three miles farther up the trail, he doffed his cap to the Taylor School teacher, who had just arrived and was opening the door.

He passed the Columbian Grange Hall and soon the road forked. Urging the mules toward the right, he followed the well-traveled Larch Mountain Road and noticed pupils in the Mountain School yard waiting for the bell.

There, he smelled smoke again. He felt his eyes tear up. Winding his way up the mountain, he arrived at the Brower Road junction and headed north toward the little logging town. Skittish, Molly shook her head and gave a nervous bray. She was teamed with Franz's mule, Jack, who plodded along, undeterred.

"Where ya bound?" a logger walking toward him asked, looking curiously at his load. His stagged trousers revealed the high-laced caulked boots, signs of his trade.

"I deliver vegetables to the folks in Brower and Palmer."

"Well, we've been smelling smoke for the last couple of days, and it seems to be gettin' worse." The man continued up the road. "I'd get those vegetables delivered and get out of here," he hollered back over his shoulder. "I don't trust it with this wind, it bein' so dry."

Frank took the advice seriously and hurried the animals along, noting how many trees had been logged and how steep and bare the hills looked. *This is the place to be if a fire comes tearing through*, he thought, looking down the steep canyon wall to Latourell Creek below. *Except for the slash piles, this is the perfect fire moat.* He remembered the pictures in his schoolbooks of castles with water surrounding them. He wondered if the moat had been dug specifically for fire protection.

"Don't worry, Molly, we'll be all right," he said. A place to run helped him feel more confident, if, God forbid, they got caught in a fire.

He quickly off-loaded his order for Murphy's store in Brower and, in the interest of time, decided not to check with the few other residents who occasionally bought something. Heading back the way he'd come, he turned east on the short, wooded road toward Palmer.

The odor of smoke grew stronger with each gust of wind. Molly seemed more reluctant than ever to continue, and Jack, following her lead, hesitated and needed urging. Just before they arrived in town, they had to cross the railroad track.

Though normally reluctant but eventually compliant, both mules stopped and wouldn't budge in the face of the obstacle.

"Come on, you two," Frank said, trying his best to be patient. Jumping off the wagon, he grabbed Molly's harness and softly cajoled, "Come, Molly, we have to cross this." He tried to keep the urgency out of his voice, silently cursing the obstruction.

"That blame little engine might be a big help to them; it's a darned a hindrance to me," he muttered. Molly slowly followed Frank's lead, stepping gingerly into the middle of the narrow gauge tracks, Jack reluctantly going along.

"Good girl!" Frank spoke softly. "That's the way." Molly stepped over the second rail as he continued to coax both of them. Jack had no choice but to follow.

Glad he'd secured his load, Frank watched the wagon bounce high, as it rode over both the rails and the large planks nailed on the inside of each rail. The small locomotive, nicknamed Peggy, had proven she wasn't up to the task of pulling loaded flat cars up the steep hills. No matter how much they stoked her boiler, the logs were just too heavy. Someone with ingenuity had come up with the idea of the planks. When they were greased, the crew could chain the logs together end to end, and Peggy was able to skid the logs to the mill over any terrain.

Frank led the mules down the hill past L.C. Palmer's house, which sported a new coat of white paint. As the president of the logging company, he had the largest and grandest residence in the small town.

Although smoke filled the air, the mules followed obediently. The dusty main road led them past the school and the boardinghouse. Behind these were family dwellings that nestled into the hill and were scattered in nonsensical patterns. Men stood in small groups, looking tense. *Must not be logging up at the camps,* Frank thought, happy that they were closed down. It was far too dry to be operating any machinery right now.

He found the logging industry interesting and the size of the trees remarkable. He had walked most of the town when he had first started the produce run, talking with locals and gleaning information.

"We have Douglas fir up here that the first limbs start at 185 feet off the ground," one bearded fellow had told him several months ago. "A lot of these trees are over 300 years old. That's a lot of board feet of lumber."

Frank remembered how astonished he was with those figures, and as a carpenter, how inspired.

A woman waved and ran up to him. "I need a few potatoes," she said. "You know my husband doesn't think he can have a meal without them."

Catching her breath, she continued, "I won't take many, because there's a possibility of an evacuation notice at any minute. Word has it the fire is not being controlled upriver."

Frank obligingly handed her a half dozen of his nicest Burbanks. She gave him a nickel and continued, "I hear there's a wagon coming up from Bridal Veil in a couple of hours to pick up men and take them to try to head off the fire."

Growing more concerned, he urged the mules on. He wanted to get done and start for home before the fire spread farther west.

Looking at the back of the mill, he saw the lower of the two Palmer holding ponds. He wondered if all that water could stop the fire. His eye caught the flume that took the rough-cut lumber down the hill into the mill pond at Bridal Veil. Once he had watched two men standing on the walkway as they guided the rough-cut lumber into the mouth of the structure and watched it disappear down the water-filled trough.

"The bosses at the Bridal Veil mill start the shift down there fifteen minutes after the shift starts up here," Val Gebhardt, one of the independent timber suppliers, had told him. "If they had to, maybe people could evacuate by riding the flume down the hill?" *Good idea,* he thought.

He ran into Val every once in a while on his delivery route and had learned much about lumber harvesting from the soft-spoken German man, who, besides his timber business, raised hay, potatoes, and cattle on his eighty-acre farm a short way away.

A strong whiff of smoke and his destination, Willet's store, brought Frank back to the task at hand. The store stood close to the upper large pond, across from the planing mill, strangely silent in midday.

He stopped at the watering trough beside the store and wiped the dust and sweat from his face with water from the pump while the mules drank their fill.

"Hello, Frank," Mrs. Woods, the pretty widow woman who ran the store, called out. "I'm glad to see you. I'm low on vegetables, what with the upper logging camps both shut down now 'cause of the dry woods. Some of those men are congregating down here."

"Yes, I'm glad to be here," Frank said as he hastily untied his load. "Where's the smoke comin' from anyway?"

"There was a fire at Wind Mountain over in Washington a couple of days ago, and the wind blew the sparks across the Columbia onto the Oregon shore near Indian Point. With this terrible wind, everyone's worried it'll blow this way if they can't get it under control."

Frank's face must have registered as much amazement as he felt. Clear across the Columbia? How could that be? The Columbia was a wide river. Not as wide as the Mississippi, but one of the biggest he had ever seen. *Maybe that mill pond didn't have enough water in it?* Frank thought.

"Yes, sir!" Mrs. Wood responded to his surprise. "I was shocked, but you can't underestimate this east wind. It's a powerful force of nature we have to deal with up here." She began to haul in a basket of carrots. "A man from O.R. & N. came up yesterday morning asking for volunteers to go fight it, but the men were all still up in the woods. Finally, last night they shut the operations down in the Donahue and Kelly logging camp. I heard the Apex camp is supposed to be shutting down this morning. They tell me they're still yarding out the rest of the logs."

"I wonder how smart that is," Frank said, quietly almost to himself.

"I wonder that myself," she replied, her forehead wrinkled with worry.

They just finished unloading all of the produce the store needed when Val hailed him, saying he was on his way home.

"Hey, Frank, my wife said to tell you if I saw you that she could use some of those nice cabbages for kraut, if you got some extra. We used all the heads we had, and she's sure we'll run out before winter's end."

"*Ja*, I think Mrs. Wood has all she needs." Frank indicated for him to climb on the wagon, as he tied down the mostly empty baskets. "Hop on. I'll take you and deliver whatever you folks need."

"Fire! Fire!" A man's voice hollered.

Startled, they looked up to see a stocky middle-aged fellow, his shirttail flying as he stumbled toward them screaming, "A spark from Peggy's wheels caught the woods on fire."

He drew closer, his face red and eyes full of fear. "There are five guys up there fighting it right now. I need more men to go help." He managed to spit out the words between gulps of air.

Frank glanced at Val, sorry now he'd offered him a ride. He needed to head for home.

"No. I can't go fight, I've got to go take care of my family." Val shook his head, his face showing the urgency that Frank felt. "There are plenty of Palmer's men here to help save the mill."

Mrs. Wood brought Frank's money, which he grabbed and stuffed in his pocket. She was trying to tell him something, but he couldn't understand the words and didn't care. His mind was on getting home to Pleasant View and Tracy.

"Let's go!" he said as he released the wagon brake, nodded a goodbye to her and urged the mules forward. It was three miles up to Val's place on Razor Back Ridge, and the mules were reluctant to hurry. When they got to the railroad tracks, Frank had to get off the wagon once again and lead them over.

Val jumped down and without breaking stride, began running. "I gotta get home! Follow me," he hollered over his shoulder and sped off up the road.

Frank couldn't hear or see any fire, but that was small comfort because now smoke thick enough to burn his eyes came between gusts of wind. He urged the mules on, leading them as rapidly as possible. When he came to Larch Mountain Road, he desperately wanted to turn right and head home. Tracy would be arriving soon, and the last thing he wanted to do was worry her. "*Verdammt!*" he swore in his native tongue.

Arguing with himself about it didn't change the fact that his friend needed help; something about Val's plea pulled him left toward his farm. Frank knew how desperate he would feel if it were his place in danger. He guided the mules up the hill toward the Gebhardt place, whispering a prayer that the fire would burn itself out long before the Lamperts' farm, and that Tracy would not worry.

He picked up the pace, the wagon bouncing over the ruts as the smoke grew even thicker. The mules sensed his urgency and broke into a trot.

Finally they pulled up in front of Val's homestead. A young woman, hair uncombed and apron flying, was gathering the children and hollered to him. She pointed west of the house. "Val's out in the potato field."

Frank saw that he had the horse and was disking down any combustible objects in the large acreage. In part of the field it looked like many of the potatoes had been harvested and there were mostly just weeds and other small plant growth. Thank goodness he's got acres of logged-off land around the place, Frank thought.

It didn't appear that there was another disk or piece of equipment that Frank could use to help, so he unhitched his mules, led them to the trough, and tied them near the barn. He coughed, the smoke scratching his throat. It seemed to him the wind gusts were stronger.

"What's the plan?" he asked the woman. "By the way, my name's Frank."

"I'm Barbara," she answered. Barely taking a breath, she continued, "Val asked me to get the burlap sacks out of the barn and soak them in the trough."

"I'll do that."

"Good, the children and I'll get the chickens rounded up and put in their coop."

Frank nodded and headed to the barn, where he found the pile of empty bags and put them in the trough to soak after he pumped water to the brim.

"Get the cows from the outer pasture and bring them in," Barbara yelled at him pointing to the fenced holding pen near the barn. Whistling for the collie, Frank trotted out to the pasture. The dog worked the cattle easily into a tight herd following the lead cow back to the barn. He figured if the fire got close enough they may have to let them fend for themselves, but at least for now all livestock was close by and accounted for.

"We better wet down the roofs," he hollered at Barbara. "Fill some buckets for me." He found the ladder and climbed onto the barn roof. Grabbing the pails of water that Barbara and the older boys handed up, he emptied them over the shingles to soak the dry cedar.

A gust of wind knocked him to his knees, and he almost lost his balance, just managing to right himself. When he regained his footing, his mind flitted back to the accident with the hay wagon when he was younger. Sometimes his hip still hurt from that fall. He sure didn't want to fall off a roof. With nothing to grab onto and the wind gusting fiercely, he had to be cautious. The peak was slicker and more treacherous as it absorbed the dousing. To gain traction, he kicked off his boots and walked in his stocking feet.

As soon as they finished wetting down the barn, he climbed onto the house and began to douse it. Late in the day, Val finished the field in smoke so thick between wind gusts that it hampered his vision.

Frank and Val retrieved mattresses off the beds and carried them out into the middle of the disked field. Together, they locked the dog, the horses, and Frank's mules in the barn and made sure the nervous pigs were safe in their pen. Barbara covered the chicken coop with a wet sheet.

Just before dark, their neighbors to the northeast, Albin Floss and his wife and three children, appeared. "We're safe! Our house was spared! The wind blew the flames north of the place," was about all that Albin could say.

"We want to help save your farm now," his wife, Mae, said, her shoulders bent with exhaustion. "Albin's brother Louie is on his way, too." Barbara took Mae by the arm and led her into the kitchen, where together they fixed some bread and cheese for the group along with coffee and slices of a leftover applesauce cake.

Frank admired Barbara's courage and character, and couldn't help but compare her to Tracy. He knew Tracy had that kind of grit, and it made him proud. *I wish I could get word to her*, he thought. "*Verdammt*," he muttered again.

At dusk, the Loudon and the Rayburn families joined the group. They arrived just minutes ahead of the flames which suddenly appeared on the horizon to the east in great tongues, leaping high above the trees with each gust, lighting the area like a morning sunrise.

The men grabbed the younger children from all the families and hurried them out to the mattresses, just as a herd of elk thundered out of the woods and across the pasture.

"You children stay here and don't move off these, whatever happens. And take care of the baby," Val told them. He handed, Mary, his daughter, a couple of wet sacks. "If any embers come close to you and the children, your job is to put them out with these," he said. "If the fire gets too hot, get everybody under there." He pointed under the mattresses.

Wetting his handkerchief and tying it around his nose and mouth, Frank distributed buckets to everyone. The crew divided themselves around the three water pumps that fed the house and the barn. Frank climbed back onto the barn roof, and Albin settled himself on top of the house. The two of them poured water from the bucket brigade onto the buildings as fast as they could, smoke gagging them even with the masks.

The wind whipped the flames into a frenzy. The buildings had plenty of open land around them, so the group was mostly dealing with hot cinders from the trees at the edge of the east field. Barbara and Mae beat out flames that fell close to the buildings or the children, while everyone else worked the two bucket lines.

"It's crowning," Louie shouted over the roar.

Oh God! What the heck does that mean? Frank thought, with a quick glance through the haze at the leaping flames. Seeing the fire burning rapidly over the treetops, he muttered, "All right, now I know. It's movin' so fast it's not even touchin' the ground!"

Another quick glance at the children told him they were still safe. The mattresses were situated far from the fire, on the other side of the buildings—small comfort with the wind so strong. The oldest daughter, about seven, had the baby on her lap with a wet towel over him.

Frank felt the searing heat from the intense flames as gusts blew them closer. He had almost decided to let the animals out so they could make a break for it, when he noticed that the flames seemed to be changing direction. Was it his imagination? He took his dry handkerchief off and dunked it in the bucket of water. His cheeks burning, he quickly retied it around his face, wondering if the flames were heading more toward the northwest, or if it was his imagination. Oh God! Let it be so, he prayed.

As he poured the next bucket of water, he noticed the children crawling under the mattress to avoid the intense heat and rain of burning debris. As the flames lit the night sky, he saw one of the mothers race toward them to beat out the burning embers that continued to fall. A burning cinder fell in her hair. *Oh my God*, Frank thought.

She hesitated, then wrapped her head in one of the wet sacks, putting out the flames, and continued beating out the glowing cinders on the ground. Another woman raced to help her.

After a time, Frank's lungs began to hurt, the smoke all but strangling him. He knew he was near exhaustion as he struggled with another full pail. Rayburns' oldest son climbed the ladder and grabbed the next bucket being hoisted up. He and Frank worked silently, communicating with grunting sounds.

"Look!" Val shouted from the house roof, his voice raspy. "The wind shifted!"

Frank squinted in the light of the fire, the smoke intolerable. Could it be possible? His eyes burned so badly he could barely keep them open long enough to assess the situation.

Sure enough! The flames were heading north. *I hope they skip over Palmer.* The thought crossed Frank's fatigued mind. The heat seemed to be losing its intensity. It looked like Val's homestead would be spared. Maybe Palmer would be lucky, too?

Now I have to get home to Tracy, he thought as he climbed down the ladder, letting the other fellow take over on the roof. Through the haze, he could see a hint of morning light just beginning to peek over the horizon to the east.

Frank splashed water on his face and drank his fill from the tin cup hanging on the pump. Exhausted, he leaned against his wagon. When he'd regained some strength, he slid through the side barn door, calling to Molly and Jack, who brayed back. Val's horse nickered a greeting as he weakly threw handfuls of hay to the animals.

"Looks like you're all doing well," he said, patting Molly. He stooped to pet Jessie the dog, who barked frantically. "It's fine, ol' fellow. Just don't go out and walk in it." He coughed, his throat so sore that it was almost too raw to talk.

"Frank! Frank! Palmer's gone." Val ran into the barn, along with the smell of smoke through the open door.

"Palmer?" Frank stood with the bridle in his hand, his mouth open.

"Yeah, Red, one of the loggers, ran up here a minute ago to spread the word. The whole town burned in less than an hour." Val's face was smudged with soot, and his eyes were red and swollen. "The mill! Everything! Gone!"

"Gone? The whole town?" Frank shook his head, trying to comprehend. "Where did everyone go? Are they safe? What about Mrs. Wood?"

"He didn't say. He just said he wanted to spread the word."

"Palmer burned? The mill gone, too?" Frank said, still trying to make sense of things.

"Yup, all that water in the pond didn't help at all." Val stared into space.

"I gotta get on the road," Frank said. The mental picture of Tracy's face slammed him into the present. "Maybe I can help someone along the way." He walked to the door and looked out across the field. Scorch marks blackened spots here and there, and enough smoke still curled in those areas to make it uncomfortable for anything that breathed.

I know Tracy's worried, he thought. *God, I hope she's all right*. Uncertainty boiled, making his stomach churn.

"I doubt you'll make it yet." Val's voice sounded hoarse and raspy. "The logger's boots were burnt almost clear through from runnin' through the fire. I tried to get him to stay, but he refused."

"Where's the fire now? Did he know?"

"He ran into some guy coming out of Brower who told him the fire was pretty well stopped when it got to the logged-off area south of there. No more fuel."

Frank nodded. "I noticed that area going in yesterday. I thought it might be a good safe place to run to if there was a fire."

"Come, Frank, you can't do anything without eating a bite and resting awhile."

Reluctantly, he followed his friend into the house, glad they saved his farm, but anxious to be on his way.

Chapter 35

SEPTEMBER 1902

Tracy

Tracy started at the sound of the evening train whistle. *Oh my,* she thought, glancing at the clock over the door. *It's almost seven, and I haven't finished my chores.* She snatched the dust mop and began cleaning the aisle between the shelves. Everything must be spotless because early tomorrow morning she was going home. Her heart did a little thump at the thought of seeing Frank.

True, he wasn't as jovial as Logan, nor as outgoing, but his gentle, soft-spoken ways had endeared him to her over the past summer. At any rate, when she thought about seeing him this weekend, she flushed a little, which was certainly different than the way she felt about some of the other men who paid her attention when they came into the store. Besides, as far as she was concerned, Frank was the nicest, most handsome man in town.

She knew that Billie from down at the distillery found excuses to come in to see her. At least that's what Mr. Fox told her. Of course, he was glad to see Billie because he always bought expensive items. Mr. Fox told her that's how he knew Billie was sweet on her. He was trying to impress her, and Mr. Fox said he was glad Billie's father didn't catch wind of it because he would have a fit if he found out about Billie's spending habits.

After stopping to wait on another customer, Tracy counted the till. She had just begun to add up the receipts when the bell rang, the door opened, and a bearded stranger, dressed in mountain clothes, rushed in.

"You heard about the fire up at Palmer?" he blurted.

"No, we've no word of it," she replied.

"Well, I caught the train at Hood River to go into Portland, but decided I better stop off here and spread the word. The train stopped at Bridal Veil and let some firefighters off." He caught his breath and his eyes flashed. "I suspect they'll need more help up there right away."

Her mind immediately went to Frank. *Oh God, please don't let it be all the way up to Palmer*, she worried. *I'm sure Frank's home by now anyway. He's always home by dark.*

"I think you should go down to the tavern. There'll be a lot of men down there," she said. "I'm sure some of them will go back to Bridal Veil with you."

"That's a good idea. Thank you, miss!"

As soon as he left, Tracy closed and locked the door and finished her books. With Frank on her mind, she made several silly mistakes that took her too much time to correct. *For heaven's sake*, she scolded herself. *If I don't keep my mind on my work, I'll never get out of here.*

When she finally finished and walked out into the late evening sun, a strong gust of wind almost blew her bonnet off. Worse, with it came the smell of smoke. Her glance automatically went to the east, but the Sandy River bluff loomed tall, keeping her from seeing any farther up the Columbia. *I guess I'll have to wait until I climb the hill tomorrow to see if there's any smoke close by*, she thought.

She remembered the tales her parents told of how their place had burned a few years before they'd arrived. A shiver ran up her spine.

She watched several men exit the tavern and head toward the depot. The stranger waved to her, indicating he had found a crew. She waved back. *I do live in a very special place.* Her thoughts went to her mother, who had relied so heavily on the neighbors before Frank came into their lives.

Oh, I do hope he's home by now.

At dawn the next morning she silently closed the door so as to avoid waking the Fox family and, with her heavy packboard on her back, started walking toward the footbridge. She packed an extra twenty pounds of sugar that Mr. Fox had generously donated to their canning project. He was a special man, and she was grateful to be in his employment.

That cheerful thought surprised her. As did the gradual waning of grief and anger—of Papa dying and her being forced to leave home to be the main support for her family. Logan's death had stifled her life, the way a broken track causes a train wreck. She smiled wryly. How sad to compare her life to a terrible disaster like that when now she felt so happy and free.

"Frank has done this for me," she said to herself, remembering a specific conversation. They had walked to the river one afternoon and had sat together on a log. They'd chattered about this and that before they fell into a comfortable silence. He had taken her hand in his and after a time, said in his gentle way, "It's nice to see you smile. When I first met you, you seemed blue most of the time."

"No such thing," she'd said. She had laughed it off but later reflected on his words. She had come to realize he was right. The melancholy that had settled over her had been reluctant to leave, resting far too comfortably around her shoulders.

Crossing the bridge, she peered into the Sandy. She thought how little water ran now and how dry it was. She had come to love the river almost as much as she loved the sight of the Columbia River from the homestead.

The Sandy fed the people salmon, steelhead, and smelt. Besides watering farms upstream, it provided beaches for picnics and quiet talks. But it had dangerous whirlpools and currents, and every once in a while, it took a life almost as if it were charging a fee for its bounty. The locals knew this and were careful, warning their children and visitors to be aware. Some of the shopkeepers posted warnings in their businesses. Even then, people forgot or were careless or young and daring and paid the river's price.

She breathed deeply and hurried on, hoping to spot Frank leisurely waiting for her at the bottom of the trail, as he had done so often in past months. Her smile disappeared when she arrived to find his leaning tree without any sign of him. *Perhaps he's on his way down, and I'll run into him. This pack is heavy.*

When she reached the top of the bluff out of breath and tired from the climb, he was nowhere in sight, and the smell of smoke hung heavy in the air. She felt a twinge of panic. With a renewed purpose, she shifted the weight on her back, picked up her pace, and hurried toward home.

A BARKING COLLIE MET TRACY AT THE GATE, HER younger brothers following close behind.

"Don't be afraid of him, Tracy," Jackie hollered to her. "His name is Shep. *Mutter* said we could keep him."

"Yeh, she said he was an outdoor dog and that we could only feed him table scraps, but he's ours," Little Alex said, out of breath, as he threw his arms around his sister's waist. "Besides we needed another dog, since Max died."

"Yes, I miss Max, too," Tracy said, hugging him back before she stooped to pet the dog.

"Tracy! Frank didn't come home yesterday," Jackie blurted out, as he gave her a quick hug, concern written on his face.

"Yeh! We don't know where he is," Alex said. "There's a terrible fire up at Palmer. Joseph is down talking to Ma now."

Tracy's heart plunged. As terror ripped through her, her knees buckled, and she leaned against the gatepost. She realized then how important Frank had become to her.

"Are you all right?" Jackie took her hand.

"Yes, yes, I'm all right," Tracy said, fighting to regain her composure. "Come quickly! Let's see what Joseph has to say." She untied her pack and handed it to Jackie.

The three of them ran down the dusty path to the house where Mama and Joseph stood talking. He had borrowed Franz's Spanish mustang, which grazed nearby.

"I'll leave right now and see if I can locate him," Joseph was saying.

"Yes, I think that's a good idea," Julianna agreed.

"Can I go, too, Ma?" Ferd asked. He was standing a way off but had been listening intently.

"Me too? I want to go with Ferd." Arnold, almost as tall as his brother, showed the fear that Tracy felt. It was plain to her how much Frank meant to the family and the neighborhood.

"No! You have no horse. Besides, I need you here. Joseph can take care of this," Julianna said almost harshly. Then, in a visible attempt to calm herself, she continued, "I understand how important Frank is to you boys. He's important to all of us, but I need you to do our chores and then to do Joseph's this afternoon. We have no idea how long he'll be gone."

JULIANNA WALKED OVER TO TRACY AND PUT HER ARMS around her; and for the first time in a long while, Tracy felt her mother's love. "My poor child! My poor girl," she murmured in her ear. "Joseph will find him."

Julianna's heart went out to her firstborn daughter. First Papa and Bernard, then Logan, and now Frank. Dread followed her throughout the past evening and into the night. She sensed the danger before it struck, even before Frank had left the morning before. She had thought of rising before dawn to discuss the possibility of his not going.

She wondered if he should stay home in case she needed him, but as she lay there arguing with herself, she'd thought better of it. The family needed the money the vegetables would bring in. She decided she was being a nervous old lady.

As she held Tracy, she noticed the smoke wasn't as thick as earlier. Had this fire burned itself out? *Oh, God! I pray it is so.*

"There, there," she murmured patting Tracy's back, remembering what a beautiful bright-eyed little child she had been not so long ago. "Joseph will find him," she repeated. "If Frank's in trouble, Joseph will help."

"I know, Mama," Tracy sniffed. She stood back and, looking at her mother, said, "I'm sure he will."

Joseph grabbed the horn and easily swung his leg over the saddle. With a quick wave, he headed the mustang up the narrow footpath that served as a shortcut to the Pleasant View School and the Wire Trail.

"Godspeed, Joseph," Julianna said.

Chapter 36

HOME

Tracy

The minutes clicked by, marked by the ticking of the Becker pendulum clock that the girls had purchased for the family last Christmas. Two hours passed, then three.

Tracy and the boys peeled apples furiously while Mama and Josie packed the jars, poured sugar water over them, screwed the lids tightly, and put them in the boiler in the yard. Ferd kept the fire going and the water boiling while they cooked.

"I'm certainly glad you girls gave us the clock. I was lost after our old clock broke," Julianna said as she glanced at the time. "The recipe says these apples must boil for twenty minutes. I'd never know when the time was up without it."

How can she talk about such mundane things when Frank is missing? Tracy thought, a bit of the old resentment bubbling inside her chest. The clock's ticking only increased her unease.

"Thank you, Mama. I'm glad you like it," she said, her voice flat and hollow. Josie and their mother continued to chatter, but Tracy found herself unable to converse. She consumed herself with the task at hand. She knew they were worried about her and about Frank, which kept her from acting impatient with them.

Arnold flinched, jumped from the bench, and ran toward the front door. "I hear a horse," he hollered over his shoulder as he ran outside.

Tracy didn't know how she arrived at the front steps, but there she was, looking at the man coming in on horseback over the rise on the school path. Panicked at the sight of only one horse, she watched, her feet glued to the ground. The figure came down the hill, closer, then she lost sight of him in the trees. When he reappeared, she recognized the hunched figure.

"Frank!" she yelled and ran down the stairs and out onto the trail to meet him.

When he got to her, he slid out of the saddle and into her arms. His face was smudged and burnt, his eyes red, his clothes in disarray, and he reeked of smoke, but she was sure she had never known anyone could look quite so wonderful.

"I'm sorry to have worried you," he murmured. "I wanted to come home. I did, but Val needed me. We saved his place."

She reluctantly pulled away from his arms to examine him and assess the damage. Her heart sank, seeing the blisters on his face.

"Come now," she said. Giving the reins to Arnold so he could care for the horse, she led Frank toward the house. "We've left the coffee on the stove and some breakfast. You can tell us what happened while you're eating."

"Where are the mules and Joseph?" Ferd asked as he followed them into the house.

"The school path is too narrow, he's bringing them around by the road," Frank answered as he took the cup of coffee Julianna handed him. His hand shook as he sipped, and he frowned as a drop hit the floor. "Joseph insisted that I take the path. Said I looked too weary to take the long way, and that everyone back here was worried about me." He smiled then and gave Tracy another hug.

At the moment Tracy had flown into his arms, he knew she loved him. Tired and sore as he was, the knowledge that she would be in his future brought a kind of peace he had never known. He sat in silence, breathing in the joy of being home.

"Palmer's gone," he finally said.

"Gone?" Julianna questioned. Tracy gasped.

"Yeah, the whole town burned in an hour. The wind was terrible. I never saw it blow that hard." He shook his head, poured some hot coffee into the saucer to cool, and lapsed into thought. "Except maybe some bad tornadoes back home."

"*Oh mein Gott,*" Julianna cried, remembering the tornado in Illinois that had almost killed Alex. "How could anyone survive?"

"Where are the people?" Tracy shivered.

Frank shook his head. "They evacuated the town, but no one knows for sure. I doubt we'll know the full extent of the damage for several days." He frowned as he felt his burned face and wondered if there were blisters. "Or the death toll."

"We did save Val's place." He brightened a little. "All the animals and people are safe. We had to fight all night, but nothing was touched. The flames were terrible. I stayed on top of the barn, pouring buckets of water folks handed up to keep the roof soaked." Once the words came, they came in a torrent, as he related the horrifying experience.

"I wish I could have been there to help," Arnold said, returning from the chores. His eyes shone with excitement and admiration.

Frank shook his head as he took the plate of food that Tracy handed him. Suddenly overcome by fatigue, his words began to fail him. "I don't think you would have liked it much," he said. "The smoke was suffocating." He ate the oatmeal more because it was in front of him than because he was hungry. More than anything, he wanted a bath and a soft bed.

"Those poor people." Julianna shook her head. "Where will they go?" Quiet for a moment, she said, "Ferd, you boys take the jars out of the boiler, pull it off the fire, and pour in some cool water from the spring. Frank, the boys will hold some blankets around the boiler, and you can wash up," Julianna commanded. The woman had read his mind.

"Tracy and Josie, get the boys' bed ready for him upstairs. Bertie, run out to the barn and bring him some fresh clothes," she shouted orders rapidly, very much like a crow calls a warning to its murder. "Emma, let's take care of those finished jars."

When Julianna took command, things happened. Frank admired that about her. That spunk and quick thinking is probably what saved her and the family.

After Frank's bath, Tracy spread an ointment made with butter and egg whites on his face and arms. "This is supposed to be the latest treatment for burns," she told him. "I heard about it from someone who came into the store not long ago."

He wasn't sure if it made his face feel any better, but Tracy's kind touch certainly did.

"It looks to me like you need someone to take care of you," Tracy said in a teasing voice as she applied more of the gooey ointment.

"Yes, I believe I do," Frank agreed in a sober voice. *Now is as good a time as any to ask her*, he thought. *Then maybe not. It certainly isn't a very romantic place.* He felt himself break out in a sweat as his thoughts raced. When would there be a better time?

"I can go into Portland and have the banns posted next week. We could get married in January after the third month posting in December," he heard himself say.

After a moment, Tracy stepped back, her face solemn. "No."

He panicked. *Did I misread the signs? Verdammt!*

"No, you can't go by yourself into town to post the banns," she said, grinning wryly. "I'm going with you."

Stunned for a second, he gathered his wits, stood up, and took her in his arms, ointment and all.

Chapter 37

NOVEMBER 1902

Julianna

Julianna smiled as she thought of Tracy and how much more relaxed she appeared since her engagement. The angst lines around her eyes that had begun with Alex's death had now all but disappeared. Her daughter's contentment spread through the family like the last ripple of a rock landing in a still pond. Julianna held that calm to her heart and allowed herself a sigh of satisfaction.

Having already seen to the younger children's bedtime, Julianna sat by the stove in her rocking chair. Her thoughts could wander as she busied herself sewing. This was such a large part of her life, she used it as a time to reflect. Her needle nearly flew. Tonight she hoped to finish sewing the modified gigot sleeves onto the bodice of her new dress.

Julianna remembered how Tracy had come home from the trip to Portland with lovely blue dress material for Josie and a light azure, almost-white piece of cloth for her own wedding dress.

How excited Julianna had been when Tracy handed her a package containing mauve satin brocade fabric with a swath of pale pink lace. Julianna couldn't remember the last time she'd had a new dress, certainly nothing this elegant. Not even for her own wedding long ago in Freeport.

"But *Mutter,* I want you to look beautiful for my wedding. After all, you get to give me away," Tracy said when she showed her the pattern.

"Oh, no," Julianna replied, taking a step back. "It has to be a man. A woman couldn't possibly give her daughter away."

Tracy, in an act so foreign to Julianna that it startled her, came over and put her arms around her. "It's my wedding, Mama, and I insist that you do the honors," she said, her voice soft. "After all, I am both your and Papa's daughter, and he is not here." She looked into Julianna's eyes and added, "Please, Mama." Julianna feeling her heart melt reluctantly agreed.

Even now, Julianna stirred uncomfortably. She was unable to refuse her eldest daughter's request, but the promise troubled her. What if the priest refused to permit her the honor of performing that duty? How embarrassing that would be for Tracy. *I am, after all, only a woman. But I own land, and I act as the functional head of this household.*

Alex and I left our families and came across an ocean and a continent to find this place. Tracy's right, I am her mother, and there really is nobody else to do it. The same argument had been raging in her head for several weeks. Keeping her own counsel, she said nothing to her excited family.

She stirred, adjusting her chair to find a warmer spot. *That's the only trouble with a stove,* she thought with a smile. *It often only warms one side at a time.* Julianna's thoughts drifted back to Tracy as her fingers moved back and forth without need of direction. She was impressed that, as much as Tracy wanted to be home readying for the occasion, she had remained at Fox's store, continuing to work and save her money. When she offered the money she had earned to the family, Julianna had refused it saying, "No, dear, Frank has helped so much this summer that we are managing. You keep your money for the two of you and for your life together."

The thought of her daughter's forthcoming marriage filled her with joy, and she wished her own mother and family were here to share in the festivities. *I know they would love Frank as much as I do. I can't thank the folks in town enough for sending him to us.*

As soon as Frank and Tracy became engaged, he had gone out to Alex's shop. Working with lumber from a piece of red cedar he'd saved from the woodcutter's saw, he spent all of his off hours sanding and fitting. The next time he went to Troutdale, he had brought back brass hinges for the lid and finished Tracy's trunk.

Julianna would never forget the thrilled look on Tracy's face the next weekend when she came home and Frank presented her with her hope chest. With Josie's help, Julianna and Tracy had gathered all of the handiwork that she had completed over the years, washed and pressed it, folded it, and placed it neatly in the chest.

Taking inventory, they determined that Tracy only had one hemmed tablecloth and two embroidered pillowcases, but had plenty of assorted towels and sheets. The next weekend when Tracy came home, she brought another finished tablecloth and a square yard of white lace to make her veil. The three women sat hunched over fabric most of the weekend, working feverishly to get ready for the big event.

Julianna remembered the pride in Frank's eyes when they showed him the partially full chest. She had noticed his face was healing nicely. She hoped he would not have deep scars from the horrendous night of the Palmer fire. *What if we had lost him?*

With a shiver, her musings on the wedding gave way to the tales of Mr. Loudon, a neighbor of Val's. A fortnight after the fire, he had told them of how much of Brower had burned and how Mrs. Woods and a logger from Apex Company had spent the night in the Palmer millpond. At one point she had nearly drowned, but they had escaped with their lives. All that was left of the town of Palmer was the misshapen saw from the mill and some of the railroad tracks.

He told about how two little boys lost their lives trying to outrun the flames and how the upper part of the flume burned while a couple of loggers barely escaped the fire. They rode logs down the watery chute to Bridal Veil, like rodeo riders on a wild mustang.

Loudon, on his way to Troutdale, had stopped to visit Frank and tell him once again how much his help had been appreciated.

"Val's getting the mess cleaned up. He's still got harvesting to do," he told them, "or he would've come himself." He took a breath and continued, "Miraculously, those poor children were the only ones who lost their lives, but their families are inconsolable." He sighed and added, "God bless their souls."

Julianna made the sign of the cross and whispered a prayer.

"Most everyone up there lost everything they had though, escaping only with the clothes they wore and what little they could carry," Loudon added. "Val and his family were some of the lucky ones."

It was with great sadness that Julianna thought of the death of the small boys. *That could have been my boys*, she thought, remembering her own baby's death. Bernard would have been eight now. She wondered if he would have looked like Alex.

Her eyes burned in the dim light. Blinking, she pulled her lap robe more tightly around her legs. She yawned and smiled as her memory briefly called up the angelic face of her lost baby.

"Mama, have you been sleeping?" Josie said, rounding the corner by the stove.

"Oh my, what time is it?" Julianna asked, groggily looking at the needle lying in her partially sewn sleeve. "I must've dozed off."

"It's late, Mama. Everyone is asleep. Look, the fire is almost out," Josie said as she stacked logs on it. "It's not like you to fall asleep." Josie helped her gather the needle and thread and fold the half-made dress. "Come now, let's go to bed. It's been a long day."

Chapter 38

JANUARY 22, 1903

Wedding

"It's so beautiful," Bertie said, her eyes welling up.

"Yes, it is, thanks to you," Tracy replied. "Now don't you go getting all weepy. I don't want to cry on my wedding day." The sisters surveyed the blue and white crepe paper flowers and ribbons and hurried to finish the rest of the decorations.

For some reason the excitement of her younger sisters surprised her. She had told them of the engagement last September when she and Frank visited them on their trip to Portland.

"Oh yes!" Bertie had squealed. "You have to have white and blue colors like Alice."

"Alice?" Tracy asked, puzzled.

"Yes, you know, Alice Roosevelt—Teddy Roosevelt's daughter." Bertie at 17, prided herself on her knowledge of current events. "She's all everyone talks about here in town."

"You and your friends, you mean," Emma sniffed.

"She just had her debutante party, and she wore a gorgeous white gown," Bertie continued, ignoring Emma. "They say she has the most beautiful blue eyes. That's why her colors were blue and white."

"I guess I didn't know that, Bertie, but I like the idea." Tracy remembered thinking she certainly wasn't able to receive that kind of news out in Troutdale. Even if she did, it would be weeks old. "Let's buy some decorations in those colors. I'd love it if you would help me. In the meantime, certainly, you can make yourselves blue dresses."

The three of them spent the afternoon shopping. Tracy had never experienced such an elegant day. They dressed in their finest outfits. She was a bit embarrassed because hers seemed woefully inadequate, but Bertie fixed a new bow for her hat and Emma loaned her a pair of white gloves. They lunched in the Portland Hotel eatery with their packages stacked between the chairs, while Frank went off by himself muttering something about errands.

Now, her wedding day had finally arrived. Tracy worried about the weather, but the winter storm broken a week ago, and with a warm Chinook wind from the south, the snow melted in less than two days.

The Woodard family improved the trail that Hicklin built back in '88, making it wider and somewhat less steep down the bluff. Located near where the telegraph wire dropped over the bluff and across the Sandy, Woodard Road was now sticky with mud after the thaw. When Mr. Seidl tried to drive his team to Troutdale for much-needed supplies, his wagon wheels sunk to the hubs. He had to unhitch the horses, leave the wagon, and walk home to fetch help.

Tracy, who hated being away from Pleasant View and her family, finally quit her job at Christmastime and was surprised how sad she was to leave the Fox family. She promised she would come see them and said that if they ever needed her to please send word.

"That's very nice, Tracy, but you have a new life now," Mr. Fox had said. "I heard that the Peterson girl from up near Grahams, I believe her name is Victoria, needs a job. I'll send word up there to have her come down, so the missus and I can meet her."

"I don't know her," Tracy replied, "but I know of her. Her mama died when she was six, and her papa had to send her and her brother and sister to the orphanage for a while."

Mr. Fox nodded and said, "Yes, apparently later their papa went in and brought the children home. He had to wait until the Graham girls were old enough to sit with the littlest one."

Tracy thought about the conversation as she climbed the bluff toward home. Alma and Hattie Graham were her friends from school, and if they were friends with Victoria, she knew the Peterson girl would be good to the children. Having someone to take her place with the Foxes made it easier to leave their employment.

She arrived home two days before the storm hit and spent the next several days panicked that the bad weather would keep the priest from coming. What if they ended up postponing the wedding? Her concern deepened after she heard of Mr. Seidl's experience with the muddy road. He told Frank it was so sticky it almost pulled his boots off.

Now January 22, 1903, had finally arrived: a bright sunny day with a cold, dry, east wind. Reports said both the trail and the road were frozen, but passable, and it was still two hours until the noon wedding.

Katherine, with Carolina Lampert, Tracy's distant cousin recently moved from Portland, came over early with two of the Frommelt children. They brought the wedding cake and many individually wrapped German pastries for the reception.

Joining the rest of the women in the kitchen, they worked swiftly to prepare the last of the wedding feast, centered on a large kettle of beef stew, thanks to Franz's generosity after butchering last November.

Earlier in the week, Julianna and the girls had made a dozen pies out of apples they'd dried in the fall. The pies were secured in the pie saver on the back porch with warnings not to touch, disappointing the younger boys.

The girls from Portland had come home for Christmas, and the weather had not permitted them to return to their jobs. Happy for their extra time together, they finished the bridesmaids' dresses. At the last minute, Josie was busy sewing buttons on Emma's dress.

After the holiday, Tracy had lots of time and finished her bridal ensemble. Because Mr. Fox was a most generous man, he donated a new white shirt for each of her four brothers. The boys, usually averse to a bath, agreed with much grumbling. Tracy peeked at them from the bedroom and saw that beneath their scruffy exteriors were four handsome boys. She wondered at the transformation.

Frank purchased a tailor-made black suit from Roberts Brothers department store in Portland and hired a seamstress to make him a handsome white shirt to which he added cuff links and a dark blue tie. Tracy thought the new clothes looked wonderful and couldn't wait to see him dressed up in the afternoon.

WITH ANOTHER GLIMPSE FROM THE BEDROOM DOOR, Tracy gasped to see the living room nearly bulging. The Seidls, Frommelts, Moraks, and her family members sat patiently in small groups, waiting for the priest.

Noon came and went. She worried about Jackie, who had won the coin toss to be best man. She remembered how her brothers had fought over the honor of standing up for Frank. He solved the problem peacefully with the flip of a two-bit piece. She wondered if Father Wachter would let Jackie be the best man, him being so young.

"He won the toss, fair and square," Frank said, seemingly unconcerned.

She could do nothing but agree.

"I'm going out in the living room and watch for Father," Emma announced, interrupting Tracy's thoughts. "We made this date for a Thursday so he could be back in Portland to say Mass on Sunday. We were considerate of him; you'd think he'd be on time, at least."

"Emma," Bertie spoke with more patience than any of them felt. "It's so cold and icy out there. It's a miracle that he even agreed to come."

"I'm going with Emma," Josie said, her face red with nervous energy. "I think I'll go crazy if I have to stay locked in here."

After what seemed like an eternity, Tracy heard Arnold say, "I see him at the gate. There are other people with him."

Stunned, Tracy and Bertie looked at each other. Who could it be? Everyone was here. Who would come out in this weather? Forgetting the traditions of the bride staying out of sight before the wedding, the girls rushed out of the bedroom. Huddled around the living room windows, they wiped steam from the glass and watched the small group struggle against the strong gusts of icy east wind.

"There are five of them. Six, counting the priest," Franz said as he grabbed his coat and hat and headed out the door to assist them, with Joseph following close behind. Joseph grabbed the arm of a woman as she slipped, while Franz took a small child from the gentleman's arms.

Just then, Bertie squealed. "It's Sophie and Matt!" Forgetting all efforts of dignity, she shouted with delight, "They came! They came!"

The company filed in the door, breathless and shaking. "My goodness, it's like a different world out here in the Gorge." Sophie Foeller's voice shook with the chill.

"Yes, it is," Julianna agreed as she hugged her friends. "We're so very happy you could make it."

"We are, too," Matt said, dropping his packboard on the floor. He bent to help his sons, Francis, now called Slats, and Victor, with their coats and scarves.

Franz set Catherine down, and immediately the seven-year-old ran to Bertie. "Oh my dear child, you are so cold," the older girl murmured, as she gathered the girl in a big hug and moved toward the warmth of the stove.

Father Wachter followed them inside. "I've never seen the bluff so slick. There's no way we could've brought a team and wagon up here." He took off his gloves and rubbed his hands. "I'm thankful we made it at all," he said, slipping off his coat and heading toward the stove.

"We were afraid we would have to miss this glorious affair, but Matt managed to beg off his city council meeting tonight," Sophie continued, patting her hair, mussed by her woolen hat. "They weren't happy, but he told them this was an event he couldn't miss."

"I'm delighted you came," Tracy said, before she scooted back into the bedroom. Her sisters followed with little Catherine closely on their heels.

Jackie ran upstairs to tell Frank the ceremony would begin as soon as everyone warmed themselves. The other boys brought in more wood and stoked the fire. Ferd told Tracy later that he had wanted to get everyone warmed up so they could get on with the party. She was sure the assortment of desserts motivated the boys to hurry the wedding.

Julianna was too poor to have a musical instrument in the house, so the girls had practiced singing several hymns. They wanted their older sister to have a memorable wedding and picked Tracy's favorite song, "Ave Maria." Father said it would be fine for them to sing in the ceremony and that he would accompany them with his harmonica.

"It is perhaps the loveliest song ever written," he told them.

Except for the older girls, most of the children had never seen a wedding or heard music at home Masses. Tracy had attended Lucy Mershon and Mr. Larson's nuptials, but that was a Protestant ceremony. She had worried during the service if she, a Catholic, would go to hell for attending a non-Catholic wedding. Despite her doubts, she remembered it as a gala affair with lots of music, and she enjoyed it immensely.

Earlier Emma and Bertie attended a couple of their friends' weddings at St. Joseph, but none of their other siblings knew what to expect. Josie, at age 13, appeared to be the most excited, not only about the wedding, but about having seven-year-old little Catherine hanging on her every word.

Father busied himself, placing the wine and hosts on the makeshift altar, which was covered with a white cloth and placed under the decorated arch.

When he was set, he signaled Julianna to bring the men and boys from upstairs. He assured her that Jackie could indeed be Frank's witness, and that she, Julianna, was welcome to give the bride away.

Once everyone settled themselves in their respective spots, Julianna went into the bedroom and sent all the girls but Tracy out to the altar, where they began to sing.

"You are a beautiful bride, Tracy," Julianna said, taking her eldest daughter's hand. "And I am grateful for the way you care for your brothers and sisters."

"Thank you, Mama." Tracy tried to hold back the tears. In spite of blinking furiously, her mother was only a blur.

Together they walked toward the altar where Frank stood, tall and handsome and more than a little flushed. Julianna stopped for a moment and when the singing ended, she placed Tracy's hand in Frank's and walked to her waiting chair.

PART III

The Children of the Children

The Beginning of the Clan

Chapter 39

NOVEMBER 6, 1903

The wispy blond hair plastered to his head outlined his tiny face as he pursed his lips and stretched into a contented yawn. Julianna gazed at the newborn infant, her first grandchild, resting in her arms. The beginning of a new generation, he was born a few minutes before midnight the night before. She wondered how anything so small could be so beautiful.

Her mind went back to Tracy's birth, remembering the joy of her firstborn, now repeated in her grandson. She loved having Tracy back home and dreaded the day she and Frank would have to move to their own home. *I won't think of that now,* Julianna thought. *I will just enjoy this moment.*

Frank, who sat in the chair beside her, stirred as he dozed before he fell back into his deep sleep. When he had heard his newborn's first cry, Frank's excitement had mirrored Alex's so long ago in Freeport. *It has to be difficult for the men,* she thought. *They seem so helpless when babies are born.*

She remembered another young father in Freeport who'd blustered so and strutted the floor with arrogance as if he had done it all. She'd resented it at the time but now realized that he was probably covering for his inability to participate. Still, she would rather see Alex's and Frank's joy and bewilderment any day.

"He's awful small," Jackie said quietly, coming up to inspect the newest member of the family.

"Yeh, don't break him, Ma," Little Alex echoed. Having just turned 10, he could not have remembered Bernard's birth nine years ago.

"He's pretty strong," Josie said, in an effort to reassure the two boys. "When he's older you can play with him."

Julianna appreciated the delighted gaze in her children's eyes as they examined their new nephew. She knew he would be more like a brother to them. Thoughts of their lost baby leapt into her mind, and she realized that somehow the presence of her grandson here in her lap lent a solace she had not known for a long time.

"Yeh, we'll take him for walks in the woods," Jackie said, interrupting her thoughts.

"Yes, dear, when he's older you can show him your trails and teach him about plants."

She purposely didn't say animals, remembering the harrowing experience with the wild creature Alex had to kill to rescue her and Bertie so long ago. It still frightened her to have the children walk the trails, but it had to be or they wouldn't get to school. She cautioned them and told them to make lots of noise to frighten away any danger that may lurk. She tried never to let the younger children walk anywhere alone, but she could not keep the boys out of the woods. It was their way of life. Someday she would tell them, but for now she only warned them to be vigilant. She shivered and wondered why she thought of that awful time now.

The children trooped outside to help Ferd and Arnold

harvest the last of the potatoes with the hope that the weather would hold out until they were all safely stored in the pit. Frank had wanted to go out earlier to help, but Julianna discouraged him.

"Let the children work a bit without you. It will be good for them," she had told him.

He'd reluctantly agreed. Sitting on the chair close to the stove, he dozed off. Julianna knew the all-night baby session exhausted him more than a harvest ever could.

With the children outside and Tracy in bed, Josie could be heard rattling dishes in the kitchen. Julianna laid her head back on the chair and closed her eyes. Of all the years of midwifery, this was the first child of her own offspring. It had its own set of circumstances and stresses. She'd found it exhausting, though as births go, Tracy's had been relatively fast. She had only started her labor the morning before.

The sound of the baby stirring in her lap woke her with a start. Frank was already out of the chair and heading toward her. She handed the baby to him, rubbed her eyes awake, and followed him into the bedroom to the new mother. She watched as Frank gently placed his son by his sleeping wife and bent to kiss her cheek.

Tracy opened her eyes slightly and immediately closed them. Overcome with exhaustion, she burrowed deeper into the covers. *Maybe no one will notice and think I'm still asleep*, she thought, but her son's persistent cries forced her to abandon the idea.

As she moved to reach for the baby, she started when she felt the soreness from the birth. "Oh my," she said, her movements coming to an abrupt halt.

Frank took her hand, his eyes sympathetic but helpless. She managed a weak smile.

"Nursing won't hurt as badly this time," her mother reassured her as she handed Tracy a rough towel to wipe her nipples.

Tracy nodded but was skeptical. She had used the rough towel method for a couple of weeks before the birth, and it still hurt the first time the infant nursed.

Her mother was right. This time was much less painful. She gazed at her newborn in her arms as he contentedly suckled. *Maybe I can do this*, she thought. As she looked at him, she thought how this baby reminded her of her little brother.

"I want to name him Bernard." There—she'd finally said it. She had been half-afraid to mention it these last few months because Frank's father, Ignatz, had passed away back in Freeport last August. Frank, overcome with grief and unable to be there for his mother, had announced that if this baby was a boy, "He must be named after Papa."

Tracy, usually compliant, was trying to please when it came to her husband. But she did not want her baby to have that name. It was a good, solid German name, the name of an honored saint, and the masculine of the mystical St. Agnes. But try as she might over the last months, she just didn't think the name fit her child.

She had adored her baby brother. The whole family missed him, and naming her and Frank's firstborn after him might help their grief.

Frank's eyes held a flash of dismay. "I thought we had settled this question before," he said, his voice quiet.

Tracy remained silent, wondering if she had crossed a boundary by voicing her desire to go against her husband's wishes. She had been raised to believe that the menfolk were in charge and that they knew much more than she did. She frequently worried about crossing the line of what she believed was proper when she and Frank had discussions.

She had witnessed both the Harlows and the Foxes interact. The wives did have a say in those marriages, albeit not so much in the case of the Harlows. She saw a partnership in the Foxes' marriage that she admired and had hoped that her own marriage might achieve that harmony.

Julianna quietly helped and hovered a few more minutes. As silence hung in the room, she turned and left, quietly closing the door behind her.

Tracy shuddered but stood her ground, deciding to not recant her sentiment without a serious discussion. If Frank was not ready to discuss it, she would wait until he was prepared. Although she hated animosity, she stuck out her chin in defiance.

Frank sat in silent thought. The only sounds in the room were the happy feeding infant and the whistle of the November south winds roaring down the pasture and around the corner of the house. Minutes ticked by.

Finally, Tracy's arm went to sleep. Trying not to awaken the sleeping baby, she moved ever so slowly, but even that hurt. *I'm not asking for his help*, she thought. *If he wants to come to my rescue, that would be nice, but I'm not asking.* She was surprised by her own stubbornness. She wouldn't look at Frank, and she certainly wasn't going to mention it.

How dare he not come help her. She felt anger seethe through her. Not since her mother had sent her away from the hill to work for strangers in Troutdale had she felt such outrage. How dare this man saddle this beautiful little boy with such a name! Ignatz! Everyone would tease him.

Tracy laid there, her arm numb, trying to decide what to do with her anger. She had no idea how to handle this. How could she protect her baby and still remain true to her wedding vows? She had promised to love, honor, and obey this man. She'd wondered at the time if she would be able to perform that last duty. The love and honor part worked well for her, but the obedience wasn't easy. Right now none of it felt right.

She stole a glance at Frank, who sat staring at his hands. Her heart did a little flip, but she refused to give in. What did it matter anyway? Her arm probably was dead by now. Not only will he refuse to budge on his name choice, but he would end up with a one-armed wife. *That suits me just fine*, she thought. *He can just clean his own clothes and fix his own meals.*

While she pondered the fate of her son, Frank rose and without a word, walked across the room and out the door.

Chapter 40

NOVEMBER 1903

Baby's Name

"We only got two more rows, and we'll be done digging," Ferd said as he picked up his bucket of potatoes and headed for the cellar.

Frank nodded silently, his mind in a whirl. He kept his head down, feverishly forking up another hill. *Why is Tracy so contrary about the baby's name? She's never been this way before.*

He reached down, picked up the spuds, and tossed them into the basket, trying to make sense of the dilemma. He'd never had a girl actually argue with him. Well, except the time back home when he was ten. He had tried to kiss his classmate Rebecca at recess. But that wasn't a real argument. She had just slapped his face and walked away. An uninvited kiss was easy to understand. Tracy's stubborn will was another thing all together.

Then he remembered Sally. She had not argued either. She just found another beau while he was working in Eastern Oregon. No comparison there, he would rather have Tracy any day. Not only was she his wife, but she was a good friend besides. At least until now, anyway.

"Sure is a cute baby," he heard Arnold say, but he didn't respond.

"Yeh, but he's pretty small," Alex answered.

Frank listened to the boys chatter and seethed, wondering what he was going to tell his mother. She had her heart set on him bringing a new Ignatz into the family. Before she lost Papa, she begged Frank to come back home to Illinois. He wished that he wanted to. But he loved Oregon, with its snow-capped peaks and rugged hills, not to mention Tracy and her family. He had disappointed his mother once by leaving the family back in Illinois, and now this.

There was nothing wrong with the name Bernard. He had been fine with it, except for Papa's passing. "It's family tradition, Frank," he heard his mother's voice in his head. "We've always named the first-born baby after a recently deceased family member."

This disagreement with his wife was a new experience. One he had no idea how to resolve, especially now, with Tracy being impossible to reason with. Women were not supposed to be obstinate when dealing with their husbands, although he did remember his mother and father having heated discussions at times. His mother could be pretty bullheaded, especially when Papa tried to tell her how to run the household.

"You go outdoors and run your barn," he remembered his ma saying. "The house is mine, and I'll do as I please." The memory of her voice rang in his head. "I'll do as I please!" *Jesus Christus, what in the Hölle is a man to do?* He brooded, failing to keep his anger at bay.

The angrier he became, the faster he worked, and soon he was up the row and out of hearing distance of the boys. "Good, now I can swear out loud," he muttered.

Later that evening, he waited in the barn until the children finished eating, under the pretext that Molly needed attention. This, in a way, wasn't a lie. He hadn't used her much in the last week, so he knew the mule missed him. He brushed her longer than usual, carefully removing the knots on her mane and tail, and gave her an extra measure of oats. He suspected Julianna would find that frivolous and extravagant, but at the moment, he didn't care.

"I don't understand her, Molly." He spoke in a soothing tone to his mule, telling her of his dilemma. As he spoke, his anger became less encompassing, which surprised him. He found himself trying to understand Tracy's side, even though his mother's request remained firmly in the way.

Finally hunger and the evening chill drove him into the kitchen, where he found a bowl and helped himself to the stew in the kettle on the warming shelf above the stove.

When he was about done eating, Tracy shuffled into the dark kitchen and made her way to the sink. She jumped back in surprise when she caught sight of him. Recovering, she turned her back, ladled a cup of water from the bucket on the drain board and shuffled out the door without a word.

Frank, more discouraged than ever, finished his supper and went to the back bedroom, where he grabbed a blanket off the bed and headed to his old room in the shed.

Sleeping on the barn floor had seemed like a good idea at the time, but as minutes turned to hours he was reminded of how cold it got in the barn. The wind pushed the chilled air through every small crack. Finally, he got up, threw his blanket in the hay, and burrowed into it. *Better*, he thought as he drifted off to sleep.

Sometime in the night, he awoke with a start and reached for Tracy before he remembered where he was. This could be a long, cold winter, he worried. Sleep did not come easily this time. He had a beautiful new son, something he had dreamed of often and had wondered if he would ever be so blessed. And now we have this big argument over a name, for *Himmel's* sake.

He shivered and nestled deeper into the hay, all the while wondering how smart this argument really was. After all, his mother was many hundreds of miles away—what would she care anyway? Besides, he missed sleeping with Tracy next to him. The thought of her quiet breathing and the smell of her lavender water made him ache for her. Sleep finally came just before dawn.

What seemed like only minutes later, he awoke to the bleating of the nanny goats. Pulling himself out of the blanket, he shook out the hay seeds and grabbed the milk bucket. He might as well do the milk chore for Arnold since he was already out here and not in much of a hurry to go into the house.

But it was a typical cold November morning: rain along with the chilly south wind. Changing his mind about not being in a hurry, he shivered and rushed to get the job done.

"We couldn't wait to get here," Bertie said. She was out of breath when she hugged Josie and her mother. The two girls had climbed the bluff in record time, excited to meet their new nephew.

"Yes, everyone was happy when Matt brought home the news of the baby," Emma echoed. "Franz stopped in the store to tell him."

"I wondered how the folks in Portland found out so fast." Julianna mirrored her daughters' delight.

"Oh, sister, I'm so happy you could come." Josie held on to Emma's hand. "Tracy needs you."

"Where is she?"

"She's in there," Jackie said, pointing to the newlywed's bedroom.

Tracy got up from her nap when she heard the commotion and padded to the door. "I'm here," she said, tears gathering in her eyes at the sight of her sisters. "How did you know to come?"

"Franz," Bertie said as she rushed to hug her.

"What's the matter?" Emma asked, as Tracy clutched her side when reaching for Bertie.

"I just had a baby, that's all," Tracy declared. "Come see my son." She walked to the crib. "Quietly though, he's sleeping."

"Oh my," Bertie said, gazing at the tow-headed infant. "He's adorable." Her eyes aglow, she added, "I can't wait until I have children of my own."

"You'd better be patient," Emma said. "You're only seventeen, and you don't even have a steady beau."

"What's the baby's name?" Bertie asked, ignoring her sister's comment.

Tracy hesitated and after a moment said, "We haven't decided yet."

The girls chatted, admiring the infant and catching up on news as the boys and Julianna returned to their chores.

"So where's the happy new father?" Bertie asked later. The four sisters were congregated around the stove, the baby nestled in Bertie's lap.

Tracy shook her head, her lips tight. She could see the silence made them uncomfortable, but she could not think of a thing to say. Besides, at this point she could not see any way out of the predicament.

They had not spoken for three days. She worried about Frank sleeping in the barn and missed him terribly, but he did not approach her. Not once. Truthfully, she wasn't sure what she would say to him if he came to discuss the situation. Part of her wanted to let him name their child anything he wanted. But a voice in her head prevailed, warning her not to give in so easily.

"Maybe you should tell them," Josie said, breaking the silence. "They're going to find out anyway." Josie was developing into a wise and lovely young woman. She and Tracy had grown closer during this pregnancy, making up for years of separation.

"Oh, all right," Tracy reluctantly agreed. Turning to Bertie and Emma, she said, "Frank wants to name our son Ignatz after his father who passed away last August." She paused for an instant. "I want to name him Bernard." There, she had said it, but somehow it didn't make her feel any better.

"You must obey your husband," Bertie blurted. "The church says so."

"C'mon Bertie, do you want your nephew to be named *Ignatz*?" Emma's voice had an indignant ring.

"I think she should talk to Frank," Josie intervened. "I've wanted her to from the beginning."

Surprised by Josie's statement, Tracy suspected she was right. Nothing would get settled until they had a sane, adult discussion. It was obvious that her sisters were divided on the subject, which somehow helped her begin to sort out her own feelings.

"Josie, what do you think of the name?" Tracy asked.

"I don't think it's that bad," she answered. "St. Ignatz was a great saint. After all, he started the Jesuit Order. Maybe our baby will be a holy man, too."

"Then you and Bertie think I should give in."

"No, I think you and Frank should talk about it and arrive at an agreement together. Nothing will happen until you do that." Josie sounded very sure of herself. Tracy suspected her sister had pondered the question for days.

"What do you other sisters think?"

"Wouldn't hurt to talk," Emma said, "but I'd stand up for my rights. You're the child's mother. It's important that you have equal say in the process."

That reminded Tracy of a discussion she and Emma had had about the free thinker Robert Ingersoll the last time they had seen each other. His ideas of equality for women were foreign to both of them, but she had given them much thought. Apparently, so had Emma.

"And what do you say, Bertie?" Tracy asked.

"I just know the church says that the husband is the head of the family," Bertie stuck her chin out a bit as if to add an exclamation point.

That worried Tracy. She had been arguing about that point with herself. How the family saw the importance of having Papa present and how things were such chaos after he'd died. But then she saw her mother manage without Papa. And that contributed to Tracy's less-rigid outlook on women's roles.

She pondered these questions over the last few days, but the only decision that she could come to was that the argument over a child's name was much more personal and less traditional than church law. An interesting thought, but it did not bring her closer to an answer.

The sisters chatted of this and that for a few minutes, as if waiting for Tracy to make up her mind. Alex and Jackie came in from outdoors and stood quietly warming their hands by the fire. In the back of her mind, she found it odd because the boys were rarely quiet and suddenly she realized no one was saying anything.

"Would you boys go find Frank for me?" Tracy finally asked, interrupting the deafening silence. "Tell him I'd like to talk to him as soon as he is free."

"TRACY WANTS YOU TO COME SEE HER," JACKIE SAID, standing with his hands in his pockets and Alex close behind him, nodding.

Frank caught his breath, feeling his face flush. "She does?" he muttered, giving the wire on the fence one more twist around the post with more vigor than needed.

"Yes, she said to ask you to come when you finish what you are doing." Little Alex pushed his shoulders up to his ears in an effort to ward off the biting cold.

"Tell her I'll be there in a bit." Frank managed a nod.

"All right," Jackie yelled over his shoulder as the boys rushed back to the warmth of the house.

Frank listened to the wind, pulling his knit cap further down on his ears he wondered what to do. Setting his pliers on the post, he stared over the bluff to the calming waters of the Columbia. He had wanted to go to her many times, but words would not come to him. Absently, he rubbed his brow. How could he talk to her when he had no idea what to say or how to say it?

All he knew was that he missed her company and hated their uncomfortable silence. He wondered if this was the father's part of having a new baby. *Maybe I'll just go in and tell her I love her. She can name him Hercules for all I care.*

Crazy thoughts argued through his head. *But Ma wouldn't like it.* In spite of the icy cold, he found himself sweating.

Reluctantly, he continued working on the fence and finished within the hour. Again he stood staring at the river, trying to organize his thoughts. He took a deep breath and headed for the house, stopping off in the now-empty kitchen long enough to wash his face and hands in warm water from the warming shelf on the back of the stove. Having put this discussion off as long as possible, he headed toward their room, where he knew Tracy awaited him.

Hesitating at the door, he rapped lightly and held his breath, not surprised at his shaking hands. He remembered the last time he was this fearful. It was on a roof in the middle of the night during the Palmer fire.

"Come in."

He opened the door to find Tracy with the baby in her arms, sitting in her mother's rocker, the one that her father had made. Her hair, neatly combed, was held back by a yellow ribbon which he could see when she bent her head to look at the infant. The blush was beginning to creep back into her cheeks. He caught his breath, thinking he had never seen such a beautiful picture: that of mother and son.

He felt weak when he caught the odor of her lavender water and wanted to reach for her. Instead he balled his fists at his sides.

Silence filled the room, as they each pondered what to say, where to begin.

Finally Tracy broke the silence. "I've missed you," she said, her voice almost inaudible.

Frank shuffled and cleared his throat. "I've missed you, too." He had to blink back something that he feared might be tears.

After another silent moment, he continued. "I've been thinking, my family is far away. I don't mind the name Bernard at all." He shuffled his feet and stuffed his hands deeper in his pockets; wondering why this had to be so difficult.

"That is very kind, Frank," Tracy said after a short pause.

"No, I mean it. I don't like being away from you. I've waited a long time for a wife. If a name is all it takes to have you back, then so be it."

Tracy shook her head. "No, Frank, we have to do what is right, and what is right is to name our son after his grandfather. His middle name will be Bernard."

Surprised and speechless, Frank met her gaze and saw what he thought was a deep sense of resignation.

"Our second son," she continued, "if we are so blessed, will be named Alexander."

Relief washed over him. He walked over and took her hand.

She smiled at him, but her eyes were stern. "Our son's name will be pronounced *Ignatius*. He is an American. He will not be called Ignatz."

Lampert Homestead Cira 1905 with Columbia River and the hills of Washington in Background

Bertha (Bertie) and Gabriel (Gabe) Riehl Wedding

Josephine (Josie) and Frank Fehrenbacher Wedding
Left to right: Ferd Lampert, Josephine Lampert,
Frank Fehrenbacher, and Catherine Foeller

Lampert Children Cira 1897 Children of the Hill
From left: Emma, Ferd, Theresa (Tracy), Alexander (Little Alex)
on Tracy's lap, Julius (Jackie), Josephine (Josie),
Bertha (Bertie), Arnold Lampert

Frank Wand Family circa 1912 From Left: Frank holding Alexander (Alec), Ignatius (Ig), Theresa (Tracy)

Frank and Theresa (Tracy) Wand

Pleasant View School circa 1912

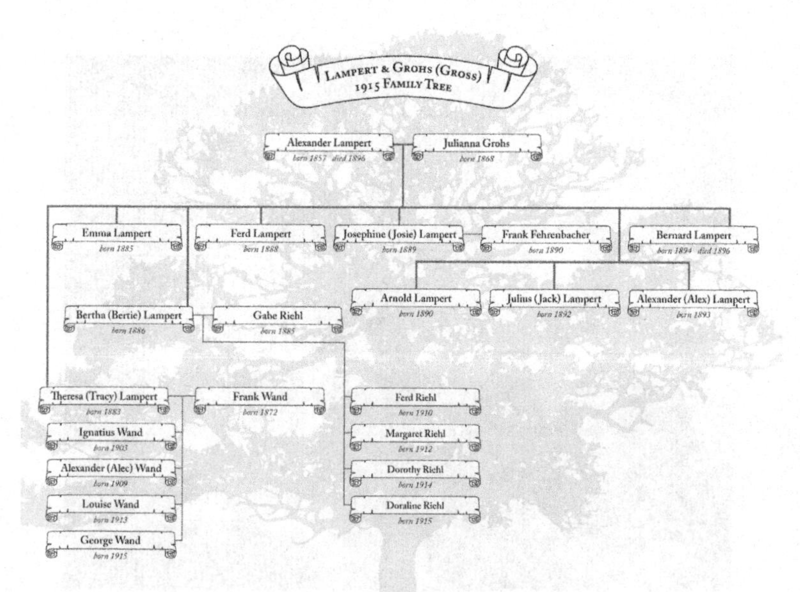

Chapter 41

SPRING 1904

Emma and Bertie

"I think you'll find what she has to say interesting," Emma said, hoping to encourage some enthusiasm in her sister.

"But she's not Catholic. How can you believe her?" Bertie said, staring at the sign on the marquee outside the First Congregational Church. Emma had walked to Sophie's, hoping to convince Bertie to accompany her to see Abigail Scott Duniway speak on women's rights, a subject about which Emma was becoming ever more passionate.

Even Sophie Foeller, a devout Catholic, was enthusiastic about Mrs. Duniway's ideas, which helped convince Bertie to attend the presentation. However, Emma suspected a large part of it was Bertie's desire to be seen in public in the fashionable new peach shirtwaist she had recently bought at Meier & Frank. She envied her sister's taste in clothes, but those words would never leave her lips. Whatever her private thoughts, Emma was delighted to have Bertie's company.

Speakers like Mrs. Duniway were one of the main reasons that Emma could bear to tear herself away from little Iggy and the farm. In spite of the grueling work it brought with it, she loved "the place on the hill," as it was now referred to by friends and relatives in Portland. When she thought about it, she had come to realize that part of her homesickness was the peaceful view of the river from the hills of home.

And of course, Frank was there. He was the most handsome man she had ever laid eyes on, and she had made a study of good-looking men ever since she was uprooted and sent away to town to work. *And I am an expert on handsome men*, she thought. *If I can't have him, I'm glad Tracy won his heart.*

Portland offered wonderful books and lectures and so, after Christmas, when it had come time to return to her duties at the Scherhauser household, she had gone back willingly, hungry to learn more.

Mrs. Duniway was scheduled to speak in less than twenty minutes, and Emma couldn't wait. She was an avid follower of the activist's writings, always eager for the latest editions of Duniway's *New Northwest* weekly newspaper and *The Pacific Empire*, a newer magazine. Both were made available for free last year by the Library Association of Portland.

The library moved into its new two-story building, and Emma often found herself in the reading room when she had a free moment. The lady in charge of the reading area had given Emma a card for two bits that gave her the privilege of checking out novels, many of them Duniway's stories of women in hardship situations.

Occasionally Emma could entice Bertie to come with her to visit the library. Mostly it was a matter of reminding her that the latest edition of her favorite magazine, *The Delineator*, had probably arrived. If the truth be known,

Emma took pleasure in her sister's excitement as Bertie absorbed the lavish descriptions of fashions and her thrill over news of romances of various celebrities. In fact, watching her sister was almost as enjoyable as reading Duniway's news magazines.

"Why do they call it 'suffrage'?" Bertie asked, reading the advertisement and jolting Emma back to the present.

"It's a political term," Emma replied. "It means protesting to give women the right to vote." And after a moment she asked, "Don't you think women are equal to men?"

She heard Bertie sigh.

Emma flashed anger, but before she could respond, Bertie said, "The church won't even let us in the sacristy unless we bring flowers to decorate the altar."

"But Bertie, those rules were made by men," Emma hissed. "Humans like us."

"I know. It's really hard to understand, because Mama took over for Papa without knowing if she even owned the land. I remember how worried she was that she might lose it. That land is all we had. She's kept the family alive. She's so brave and strong."

Emma shook her head. "Yes, she works as hard as any man, and she's still worried that someone might come and take our farm away. Women don't have many property rights."

It was Emma's turn to sigh. What in the world must she do to help her sister understand? Bertie was very much the proper young lady. If she believed for a second that something was against church teachings, she would have nothing to do with it.

Emma's religion was important to her, too. The difference between Bertie and her, as far as she could tell, was that she did not believe suffrage had anything at all to do with the church.

"Come, let's get a seat before they are all gone," she said, starting up the stairs. Perhaps Mrs. Duniway's lecture would help them come to an understanding.

THE ROOM WAS ABUZZ WITH GROUPS OF PEOPLE MILLING around, visiting with friends. Emma, pleased to see that a number of men had accompanied their wives, waved to Maddy Schmitz, a friend from church, who was making her way through the crowd toward them. *This might help Bertie see that other women of the church agree with me*, Emma thought.

The friends found three seats together near the back, a perfect place for people-watching. The sign on the wall near the pulpit blared, "*Alis Volat Propriis!*" Under it was the translation: "*She flies with her own wings!*" Emma recognized it as the slogan of the masthead of *The Pacific Empire. I like it*, she thought. *It's perfect.*

"May I have your attention."

A young lady dressed in a simple but pressed spotless skirt and shirtwaist shouted through a megaphone.

"Thank you," she continued as the crowd quieted. "This evening, we are honored to have a nationally renowned speaker join us. She has traveled and lectured all over the United States, but is from our own state of Oregon. We are very proud of her." Heads nodded in agreement. "I would like to ask you to please stay as quiet as possible. This is a large room with many people, and we want to hear every word."

Emma felt a surge of excitement as the audience clapped and somewhere behind her a man whistled. She had read many articles by this celebrity, and now she was going to see her in person. *Oh, how I wish Tracy could be here*, she thought, remembering one of their last conversations, in which they had discussed some of Mrs. Duniway's ideas. Tracy had made Emma promise to bring one of Duniway's novels home for her to read.

"May I present Abigail Scott Duniway!" She heard the announcer through her thoughts.

A rather plain-looking, slightly overweight, gray-haired woman stepped to the pulpit amid cheers. *This can't be the woman who wrote all those fiery articles*, Emma thought.

"When I was a child, I saw my mother sitting in her rocker with tears streaming down her cheeks as she held her newborn infant to her breast." Mrs. Duniway's voice roared through the crowd, changing Emma's mind about her heroine being old and dowdy.

"Worried, I asked whatever was the matter?" she thundered on. "'Poor baby, she'll grow up to be a woman someday,' my mother answered. I didn't know what she meant then, but as I grew to adulthood, I came to understand. When I was sixteen, my father, struck with Oregon fever, sold everything and announced his plans to my mother. He told her to pack the wagon because we were leaving for the West as soon as the spring thaw came to Illinois." Mrs. Duniway hesitated and looked out over the audience.

"That was the second time I saw my mother cry." She paused, weighing her words. "But she did as she was told, even though she was still weak from the birth of her twelfth child."

Audible groans were heard around the room, most from women but, surprising to Emma, also from more than a few men. No one spoke, letting the words fill spaces in their minds.

"There were fifty-two people on our wagon train. Six of them perished on the trail from cholera. Sadly, my mother, Anne Roelofson Scott, and my little brother, Willie, age three, were among them."

Emma heard Bertie utter a barely audible cry and glanced to see tears in her eyes. She knew she was thinking of Papa and Bernard and had to blink to keep from weeping herself. She remembered Papa's last words to her, "Emma, your mother will need you more than you know. Please help her." She had nodded a promise and tried to obey him. She fervently hoped that somehow she had kept her word.

"...the mass migration from East to West changed people's thinking." Mrs. Duniway's voice interrupted her thoughts. "How could that be? you ask yourselves." People nodded— some with a look of understanding, some bewildered.

"Because women's roles changed with that move," she answered her own question. "We lived up to the task. We passed the test." Again she paused, letting her words form questions in the audience's minds.

"For example, I married at the age of seventeen. My husband, Benjamin, tried his hand at farming in Clackamas County. I toiled by his side in this endeavor. It was grueling work, which I willingly did even though I hated it. I birthed my first three children during that time."

Emma shook her head, remembering the many births she had seen her mother endure.

"Our first farm was unsuccessful, so we moved to better land near Lafayette. I had two more babies and took the cradles to the fields so I could watch my newborns while I worked." Her voice rose in pitch and volume, filling the room as she continued. "After a short time, against my wishes and advice, my husband, a poor businessman, mortgaged the farm to help a friend, who soon thereafter defaulted on the note." She paused and with great force said, "We lost everything."

The audience rustled, and hushed voices of sympathy could be heard throughout the room. Mrs. Duniway waited until things quieted and said, "Benjamin, fraught with guilt, hastily obtained work with a freight company driving a team and wagon. One day, a cougar in the road spooked the horses. As he tried to control them, he was pulled from the seat and dragged some distance before he fell under the wagon. This permanently disabled him."

Can this get any worse? Emma wondered. She turned to Bertie, caught her eye, and saw the same concern from her sister.

"My point is, with five young children, I then was forced to go back to teaching, as I now was the sole support of our family. After a year or so, we realized that teaching could not support us, so I and my eleven-year-old daughter, Clara, opened a millinery shop in Albany. We ran it for five years, and in that time I birthed my sixth and final child." The audience made no sound as Mrs. Duniway took a breath and gazed at the crowd.

"While running the shop," she continued, "I met many women and learned of their plights. Women who had NO rights, not even the right to keep their children in case of a divorce, let alone their homes and possessions. Everything was solely owned by their husbands."

Mrs. Duniway's voice quieted. "Ladies and gentleman, this is NOT right." She emphasized the words, speaking slowly. Heads in the audience nodded. Emma saw the man sitting down the row take the hand of the woman who was sitting beside him. She saw the gesture as one of love and understanding, and it warmed her heart.

"Ladies and gentlemen, because of this, we moved to Portland so I could begin to publish the *New Northwest* and later *The Pacific Empire.* It is why I have continued to be active in the Oregon State Equal Suffrage Association that I founded in 1870."

Mrs. Duniway's lecture continued, pointing out that Wyoming women were the first in the nation to win the vote in 1869, Colorado in 1893, Idaho in 1896, and Oregon women failed to gain the right in 1900 by only 200 votes. She reminded the audience that it would be on the ballot again in 1906.

But how could obtaining the vote change the suffering of women, Emma pondered. *Wouldn't it take more than that?*

As if reading her thoughts, Mrs. Duniway said in conclusion, "Ladies and gentlemen, many years ago, when I worried to my husband about the women's plight, his answer was, 'Women must get the vote, before anything else can be done.' He said it slowly with deliberation, as if he'd thought about it a very long time. I know now, he was right."

The great lady paused once again before continuing. "I also know that women getting the vote won't end the suffering. It will be a beginning, not an end, but it will start the process toward the road to equal rights and autonomy for women. Everyone's life will be better and happier when men and women form partnerships in their marriages, beyond that of master and slave."

The applause was deafening as the audience stood and cheered this courageous lady. She had made many enemies throughout her crusade, including the editor of the *Morning Oregonian*, who happened to be her younger brother, Harvey Scott. In spite of that, she continued her fight. Thankfully, her ideas were growing in popularity and with them, the hope that Oregon's women would win the vote the next time it was on the ballot.

"I'll never marry until I have the right to vote," Emma hissed through her teeth to her sister and Maddy. If she knew anything at all, she knew that she was positive she was making the right choice.

Bertie nodded, her eyes wide. Emma couldn't tell if it was disbelief or an epiphany, so chose to believe the latter.

"I won't either," Maddy said, but the conviction in her voice was not strong. Emma glanced at Maddy's engagement ring and wondered if her fiancé, Robert, would vote for the measure.

Many people remained after the speech, discussing in groups, eager to chat with the speaker about individual concerns.

The girls walked home, chattering about the rousing speech and its validity. Emma, even more cemented in her belief in the suffragette movement, found herself frustrated with Bertie's reluctance to show enthusiasm.

"I don't find anything about this suffrage movement that is contrary to God's teachings," Maddy said, mirroring Emma's beliefs.

"I can't either," Emma agreed. "And I've spent many hours reading her works and comparing them to the teachings of the Bible and the church."

"I'm closer to believing now," Bertie said, "but I haven't read much of her writing." To Emma's relief, she continued, "I will now, though. She was a brilliant speaker."

As Maddy parted from the sisters in front of her house, they agreed to meet the following Saturday afternoon at the reading room. "I'll help you find her best works," Emma promised, "and we'll pick out one of Mrs. Duniway's novels to take to Tracy."

Chapter 42

SUMMER 1904

Julianna

"Mother, if you'll hold the baby, Josie and I'll finish up in the kitchen," Tracy said as she pushed back from the supper table.

"That's fine." Julianna picked up the fussy seven-month-old and headed for her favorite rocker, now in the living room. As she sat down, the chair wrapped around her and somehow projected her back to when they had settled on the hill. Alex had built the rocker with his own hands as a surprise when they moved into the house. The chair had always been a quiet refuge, and today was no exception.

Tired from pulling weeds with Josie and the younger boys, she was grateful for a moment's rest. The minute she picked up the baby, he settled down. With as many babies as she had birthed and raised, she was surprised at how much she enjoyed this first grandchild. He reminded her of Alex, with his delicate features. His hair, almost blond, was so fine it swirled in little patches. She laughed as she tried to smooth it.

"Ferd and I got the slash pile almost burned," Frank said as he walked in and sat in the chair beside her. "We'll have it cleared in time to put in the wheat this fall."

Julianna nodded but didn't respond.

"I'd like to get started on the house for Tracy and me after we finish planting," he continued.

"That's probably a good idea."

"It'll take quite awhile to build, with the farm to take care of."

"That's fine with me. You're welcome to stay here as long as it takes," she said, looking down at the now sleeping baby. "I'll miss you and your family when you have to leave."

"Yeh, it's home to me too. It's hard to believe I've been here almost four years." Frank got up to leave. "The boys and I are going over to talk to Joseph about buying the wheat seed," he called over his shoulder.

Julianna put her head back on the chair and moved to a more comfortable position. Her back, often sore, seemed to be especially troublesome this evening.

Her mind went to Frank and how much he helped not only on the farm, but as a role model for her boys. Especially Ferd, who outwardly expressed his father's loss less than the others. Nine years old when his papa died, Ferd had tried to shoulder the burden of the farm and did his best, but had little guidance.

She sighed as she remembered that although she had helped Alex in the fields in the early days, she had little knowledge of many of the outdoor chores that were necessary and had less time to learn while she was busy trying to raise the children. Truly, the neighbors had saved her by taking time from their workdays to till her fields and help her plant and harvest. So, too, had the older girls who were compelled to leave Pleasant View, take jobs, and send home money. Julianna thanked God for all of their help.

It was Frank, however, who helped her progress from barely surviving to having the farm show enough of a profit that the children were able to attend school more days. She was no longer frantic with worry about feeding the family through the winter.

Now Frank wanted to plant grain. He and Arnold had brought home the news on one of their produce runs to Palmer last fall. They'd run into Val, who told them about a fellow named Willis Hicks. "Yes, he bought the place near Corbett, where the Wire Trail comes up the bluff from Rooster Rock," Val had said.

Later as he related the story to Julianna, his enthusiasm escalated.

"Mr. Hicks is an engineer, and he's got a line on a thresher."

"Is he willing to travel to farms to help with harvest?" Julianna wondered.

"He told me he'd be willing to come up to this area, but several farms have to be ready to harvest at the same time for him to make the trip."

Frank continued, enthusiasm in his voice. As he spoke she began to feel his excitement. The Hicks' farm was right near their route, so they had stopped to talk to him. Frank said he'd found him straightforward and, in his opinion, an honest man. Willis told him that he would indeed come to Pleasant View if there were four or more farmers who needed to harvest at the same time.

Frank said that sounded like solid advice to him, but it would entail an upfront investment for the bags—something he would have to look into.

Julianna mulled the possibilities. A new cash crop was excellent news. According to Mr. Hicks, the mill would trade grains, a sack of wheat for a sack of oats for horse feed, or a sack of barley for soup. They would grind some into flour for home use as well.

"Willis says they'll buy whatever we don't need," Frank had told her.

Her arm was asleep now, and the tingling brought her back to the present. She moved it carefully so as not to wake Iggy. She turned her thoughts to Tracy, who seemed to be enjoying motherhood. *The fact that she has all her siblings ready and willing to take care of the baby hasn't hurt either.* She smiled.

She found it interesting that Tracy was beginning to discuss the political issues of the day. In that respect she took after her father. *And my Papa too*, she thought, remembering rousing conversations at the supper table when she was a young girl in Baden.

Tracy and Emma's long discussions about women's rights interested her. She was painfully aware of the laws that would not let her have as much freedom as Alex. When he was alive, it worked well for them, but those same laws had caused her much difficulty after he died.

Certainly she would never have the privilege of voting. It had not even occurred to her that perhaps she should ask for that right, but it comforted her somehow that her girls wanted the vote and were actively seeking it. She put her head back on her chair and, with her grandbaby sound asleep in her lap, closed her eyes. Just for a moment.

Chapter 43

NOVEMBER 1904

Frank

Frank sloshed through the rain, making his way over the hill toward his twenty acres. Inspecting the field they had sown in wheat in late September, he smiled, noting the tiny plants pushing their way out of the ground like a green rug. They seemed to anticipate the warmer weather of February. It appeared that the seed was evenly planted and had a good germination rate, as there were no large bare spots in the field. Satisfied with a job well done, he eagerly awaited the outcome of this new crop experiment.

A germ of fear remained in the back of his mind, remembering the time a hailstorm leveled the oats back home in Illinois. The weather here in western Oregon was even less predictable than it had been in Illinois and, being a temperate rain area, much wetter. If rain hit wheat at its ripest, it would sprout in the head and destroy the entire crop.

His father grew grain in Illinois, which Frank had enjoyed raising and harvesting. There was something almost mystical about running the newly harvested golden grain buds through his fingers. He remembered thinking that wheat fed the soul as well as the body.

The rain started just about the time he had hauled the

last wheelbarrow of dirt out of what would be the cellar for their home. It was on the land he was working so hard to buy from Julianna. He hoped to get some kind of a cover over the hole before it rained too hard, but he doubted he could make that happen this late in the season. He had dug a twenty-foot-by-twenty-four-foot hole about nine feet deep, and he was almost sure that building the cover would take more time than he had left before winter set in.

Tomorrow he and the boys planned to get ready for the delivery to Palmer. Ferd and Arnold had been asking if they could make the run by themselves, and he thought it would be a good idea. It would give him an extra day to work on the house, but Julianna wasn't happy with the thought of the boys making that long run. Frank silently disagreed, believing she was too protective. They knew the route, and over the summer they had grown used to working with the teams.

The rain fell furiously, as November storms often do, driving sideways and pelting his face. He picked up his pace, and slid once on the slick, mucky path as a gust of cold south wind almost knocked him down.

It was nearly dark when he arrived at the Lampert house, his clothes soaked, and his hands so numb he had difficulty opening the woodshed door. He stripped off his coat and boots, and by the time he arrived in the kitchen he was down to his socks, pants, and undershirt.

The smell of Tracy's fried potatoes and the warmth of the hearth bolstered his heart and comforted his chilled body. She tended the stove with the baby on one hip, while the two younger boys busied themselves setting the table. Josie looked up from the bread she was slicing and smiled at him.

Julianna came around the corner and took the baby

from Tracy as Frank went to his wife and kissed her cheek. He was pretty sure that no man could ever be as happy as this. Tracy was perfect for him. She had a sweet, kindly way, not as stern as her mother, not as funny as Josie, just even-tempered and beautiful.

"My goodness, Frank!" Tracy exclaimed when he put his arm around her. "You're soaking. Get those wet clothes off this minute."

He nodded his head and turned toward their room near the back of the house. It didn't take long for him to strip, dress, pour himself a glass of homemade apple wine, and find a place near the woodstove in the living room. The fire felt good, but warmth was slow to come.

He heard the older boys come in from the barn, but his thoughts were still with Tracy. He had grown to love the place that Alex and Julianna had built, even though he was eager to have their own home. He knew their home would be as comfortable as this. Tracy would see to it.

His thoughts turned to Tracy's passion when she talked about the women's suffrage movement. Many times on his trips down the bluff to Troutdale, she would have a book to go back to the library, or she would ask him to check for a new one by Duniway or one of the other women's movement writers. Deep in thought, he rubbed his cold hands together above the stove, trying to get rid of the shivering.

It wasn't that he wasn't sympathetic; in fact, he was downright proud to have a wife so interested in current events. The women he knew were more than capable of voting intelligently. When he was called to supper, he was still pondering why their vote was so slow to come.

Later at the supper table when the subject of the produce

run to Palmer inevitably came up, Ferd protested, "We can do it."

"I agree—the boys are old enough to make the run," Tracy said with a firmness he hadn't heard since the naming of the baby incident. Frank knew she thought her mother was too protective of her sons. Earlier, Tracy had spoken of it to him, and he had agreed.

He waited to join the conversation, listening to where it led. Although he was never made to feel like an outsider, he felt that in some respects this was a family matter. A rite of passage perhaps, which belonged to the people it affected most. He quietly shoveled in the food and reached for another piece of bread.

Julianna frowned but did not speak.

"Frank said I can handle the mules almost as good as he does," said Arnold, who rarely joined conversations, finally speaking up for himself. He seemed more content with goats and other farm animals than with people, except when he was alone with his brothers.

Frank nodded as he took a swallow of coffee. "Yes, I did."

"I understand Mama's concern," Josie joined in. "With the weather turning bad and all."

Ferd shot her a nasty look. "If the weather gets too bad, we'll turn around and come back."

"Yes, both of us have slickers, and the horses know the way," Arnold pressed on.

"Promise me that if the weather is as bad as it is tonight, no one will go," Julianna said, beginning to relent. "And if the weather is better and you do go, you'll turn around and come home right away if it gets stormy, even if you're not done with your route."

"We promise, Ma."

A DRIVING RELENTLESS RAIN BATTERED THEM THE NEXT day while the family worked in the mud, cutting and packing cabbage heads. They shivered, water running down their cheeks in little rivulets. They were happy to get under cover of the barn when the chore was completed.

The boys hauled a boiler full of water from the spring, while the other children helped Frank and Julianna retrieve carrots and potatoes from the small pit that had been dug to store them over winter.

Frank had covered the storage pit with a heavy log lid so nothing would freeze when the weather dropped into the teens and twenties. He struggled to open it, sliding in the muck until the log lid finally broke free. They hauled buckets of the produce to the barn, where they washed and packed it in bushel baskets for the trip. All were thankful for the dry place to work and grateful the onions had been bagged at harvest and were ready to go.

Finished, they packed the wagon, carefully arranging the load with things in easy reach for each stop. Julianna placed a large basket filled with produce and two loaves of carefully wrapped, fresh bread just behind the seat, reminding them "to be sure and stop by the Widow Deverell's and drop this off."

Frank caught the look between Ferd and Arnold and grinned to himself, thinking of Grace, the youngest Deverell girl. No matter she was a few years older than Ferd; older women could have a lot of appeal. He knew the boys wouldn't need much urging to make that stop.

"Boys, let's see how many points you can get tomorrow," Frank said, changing the subject. "Each time you have guessed the right amount and kind of produce for the customer, you get a point."

"*Ja*, that's a fun game," Arnold exclaimed. Frank remembered how good the boy had been at the game. When he complimented him, Arnold had told him he liked numbers.

Ferd, covered in mud, nodded. "What's the most points we can get?" he muttered pragmatically.

"Let's see…fourteen, I think. That was the most customers I have ever delivered to, counting the rooming houses and the stores. But that was in the summer." Frank hesitated, thinking of the foul weather and knowing they would never have enough time to get to all those places now with the short winter days. He continued, "Let's say ten would be a logical number. Even if the weather is perfect tomorrow, you'll run out of daylight before you can get to fourteen places."

"Yes, I want you on the road toward home well before dark," Julianna spoke up. "Those mountain roads are nothing more than narrow paths with steep banks."

Ferd scowled, but turned to his mother and nodded. "We'll be off the mountain at least to the Hicks' place before dark," he promised.

The rain stopped by the time they finished loading, and the temperature was dropping. Frank noticed just before sunset last night that the wind had shifted and was coming out of the east. *Maybe that's a good sign*, he thought; *it might be able to dry things out*.

The next morning the ground was not frozen, but there was a skiff of ice on the trough when Frank went to water the stock. The east wind, blowing loudly now, whipped the fir limbs and made the river sparkle in the early morning sunlight. Frank pulled his scarf tighter around his neck and thought of the boys on the road. They had left before daylight, laughing and jostling and shushing each other. They grabbed the tin buckets of cheese and bread that Tracy packed for them the evening before as they headed out the door, but not before they had awakened most of the family.

As soon as Frank finished the chores and a cup of coffee with his breakfast, he headed over to work on their new house, anxious to get the cellar covered.

"How long do you think it'll take us to get to Deverells'?" Arnold asked before they had even gotten out of the gate.

"*Gott in Himmel,*" Ferd replied, slapping the reins, realizing what Arnold had on his mind. "Can't you think of anything else?" Sometimes his little brother really annoyed him. "You should find your own girl and leave mine alone."

"She's not your girl."

Now he really was angry.

"I'll bet she doesn't even know you like her." Arnold wouldn't let it go.

"When have I had the chance to tell her?" Ferd fervently wished he could change the subject.

"I guess that's true." Arnold finally relented. "Are you going to tell her today?"

"I don't know. I really hadn't thought about it." He hoped it was all right to tell a small fib.

They rode in silence, with Ferd's mind on Grace. He had only seen her a few times when he went on deliveries with Frank. He remembered the first time he had seen her. They had driven in the long driveway, because earlier Mrs. Hicks had told Frank not to forget to check on Jane Deverell.

"Her husband died last year, and she and her half-grown children are trying to keep the farm together," she had told him.

No one seemed to be about as they approached the house, except a noisy dog that worried the mules. About the time he and Frank were ready to turn around and leave, they heard a girl's voice.

When Ferd turned toward the house, there on the porch stood the prettiest girl he had ever seen. He didn't quite know why, but the sight of her caused him to lose his breath. She wore a faded blue dress that swirled around her ankles as she walked. Her head tilted a little to the side, showing off her long, sensuous neck. He had never seen anything more stunning. He had dreamed of her several nights since.

She walked toward them then, her golden hair blowing in the early September breeze, and as she approached, her brown eyes questioned them. A hint of worry shone in her face, and he noticed she had kept the dog between her and them.

"What can I do for you fellows?" she politely asked, and then she introduced herself as Grace. The way the words came out of her mouth seemed like music to Ferd. He hadn't heard much singing, except the few times they'd attended St. Joseph in Portland and, of course, school plays, but he thought her voice was the most melodic he had ever heard. He wondered if maybe that was what heaven sounded like, but then he was afraid that thought might have been sacrilegious.

Ferd was happy that Frank had done the talking, because he doubted that he could have uttered a word.

"Boy, this wind is sure cold." Arnold's voice brought him back to the present.

Ferd shivered and slapped the reins.

“Well, boys, tell your mother thank you very much,” Jane Deverell said with a tired smile as she accepted the basket Arnold handed her.

“We will,” Arnold replied, looking around. “Where’s Grace?”

Ferd sucked in his breath, thanking his little brother silently for posing the question that he lacked the courage to ask. Leave it to Arnold, he thought. He might be the quiet one, but he’s not afraid to say anything to anyone.

“She’s in Portland, staying with her brother Herb for the next couple of months,” Mrs. Deverell answered. “He works long hours on the docks, and he is paying her to cook for him. We need the money, but I miss her terribly.”

Ferd turned toward the wagon to hide his disappointment, leaving Arnold to say the goodbyes. Now he would have to wait until next season to see Grace again.

Dejected, he remained quiet on the way down to Brower, ignoring Arnold’s attempts at conversation until finally his brother, too, dropped off into silence.

The east wind, not even a breeze up at Deverells’, blew hard in the little town of Brower, whipping up the trees and bringing the cold back with a vengeance. It penetrated their marrow.

They quickly made the rounds, selling produce to five of the usual eight customers. They took turns handling the reins, so one could warm his hands by sitting on them, gloves and all, while the other drove the mules.

“I don’t like the looks of the sky,” Arnold said as they left Brower.

Ferd nodded, thinking the same thing. The clouds had

turned darker and more menacing, and the temperature seemed to be dropping. Concern took away some of the sting of not seeing Grace.

"I'm cold to the bone," Arnold continued. "I think we should head for home." He shivered, his hands under his legs. "I don't care if we only got five points today; I just want to get the mules back to their stalls."

Remembering that the rebuilt town of Palmer was farther up the mountain than the one that burned and despite wanting to make more sales, Ferd agreed. "We may take a razzing from Frank for only gettin' five points, but we did promise Ma," he muttered.

What a disappointing day, no Palmer customers and no Grace, he thought as he turned the mules west at the intersection of Larch Mountain Road and Deverells' road, urging them the five miles down the mountain to the Hicks' place. The last thing Frank had told them the night before was to be sure and stop and see Willis if they had any trouble.

They arrived at Hicks' at half past two, teeth chattering. The sky appeared dark blue now and the clouds even lower than when they'd left Brower. The wind blew so hard it took their breath and left them gasping.

"Here boys, let me tend the mules," Mr. Hicks offered, putting on his coat as he came out of the house. "You c'mon in and have some of the missus's hot soup and warm yourselves a spell."

Thick with vegetables, the *goulash*, as Mrs. Hicks called it, was close to the best Ferd had ever tasted. The cheese and bread Tracy packed for them was long gone. That, along with the now freezing temperatures, made them appreciate the hearty chunks of potatoes and carrots bathed in beef broth.

Before they ate, they'd hung their gloves and coats near the stove. As soon as they finished their bowls, they quickly shrugged into the now-warm coats. Mrs. Hicks brought them a heavy lap blanket and two clean kerchiefs to tie on their faces.

"You can bring these back next time you're up this way," she said as she handed them to Arnold. "Wrap the blanket tight around both of you. It's big enough."

Her Big-Ben clock read five minutes to three as they thanked her and headed to the barn to get the team and wagon.

It'll be dark by four o'clock, Ferd thought. *We promised Ma that we'd at least be on the way home by now.* They left two bushels of carrots and a bag of onions. When Mr. Hicks handed them money, Ferd brushed it away.

"No, we appreciate your kindness. I know Ma would want you to have them," he said.

"You sure I can't talk you boys in to staying over?" Mr. Hicks asked after thanking them. "It's going to be a bitter night."

Ferd shook his head, knowing his mother would worry herself half to death. The first flake of snow hit his forehead before they left Hicks' driveway, making him wonder whether they should have accepted the offer.

They would follow the Wire Trail most of the more than three miles home, which was a great improvement over the logging town roads up on Larch Mountain. It had been widened enough that two wagons could pass, and the ruts were beginning to freeze, so there was less chance of getting stuck. He comforted himself with the thought that the road was more easily traveled as he handed the reins to Arnold and sat on his hands again.

By the time they passed Taylor School and the road down to Taylor's Landing, the snow swirled in front of them, blocking their view.

"Stop!" Arnold hollered above the sounds of the storm. "I want to make sure the mules are all right." Ferd grabbed the reins and watched as he clambered out from under the blanket, jumped off the wagon, and headed up toward the animals.

"I'll walk with them awhile," he shouted over his shoulder. He grabbed Molly's bridle and patted her head. Reaching over, he cleared both mules' nostrils of ice. Then Ferd saw him whisper something in Molly's ear.

The mule lifted her head higher and picked up her pace as twilight and the blowing snow began to make it more difficult for the boys to see the trail.

Chapter 44

JULIANNA

Julianna glanced once again at the beloved clock hanging on the living room wall and sighed. It was visible from the kitchen as well as the living room, which she found extraordinarily handy. Tonight, however, it screamed at her. The ticking, louder than usual, filled the room, resonating from wall to wall. She fought the temptation to cover her ears and yell to muffle its sound.

Eight minutes after seven. Only three minutes had passed since last time she had peeked at it. Arnold's socks, holes in both heels, lay forgotten in her lap. A length of darning thread dangled from the needle she held in the hand resting on the arm of her rocker.

She frowned as she beat back growing anxiety. In her mind she caught a glimpse of Alex's pained face as he came home that fateful summer day in Illinois after being caught in the tornado. She shuddered, remembering how frightened she had been, half-crazed with worry as the storm growled and rumbled. It seemed to be mocking her as she silently pleaded and prayed for him to come home.

Now, another storm. The boys had promised they would turn around at the first sign of problems. They were overdue by an hour. She noticed Frank pacing by the door and knew he was as concerned as she was.

The sounds of the younger boys practicing their letters broke the silence. Their voices softly recited to each other, back and forth. Instead of the usual quiet peace that children's voices usually brought her, they joined the clock as it grated on her ears.

As she listened now to the blowing snow pinging against the windows, she took a sock and slowly began to darn, picking up the rhythm of the evening. Thread in one end of the worn spot, pulling it across the tear to the other end, and then back again, her fingers skillfully weaving, repairing. It was mindless work, and it comforted her. She could see her progress, knowing she was managing this herself. She had no control over the boys or the storm. She could only hope they were all right, and pray they had sought shelter in a neighbor's home.

Behind the closed bedroom door, the baby began to cry. The muffled sounds added to the cacophony in her mind and brought back memories of her own babies and how much work it was to take care of so many infants. So many diapers to wash.

Her jumbled thoughts kept looping back to her sons. Were they out in this terrible storm? And for what? A few dollars. Never again would there be deliveries from this farm when the weather looked the least bit threatening.

"I'm going after them!" Frank said as he came into the kitchen, his eyes ablaze with a strange mix of anger and concern.

Julianna looked up, startled, and nodded.

"I'll go with you." Jackie said jumping up.

"Me, too." Little Alex never wanted to be left behind.

"No, you two have to stay here and keep the stove going," Frank said firmly before Julianna could weigh in. "I'll take the lantern and stop at Joseph's to see if they made it that far. If not, he and I can use his horses. I'll take Shep with me." He uttered a curse under his breath, which surprised Julianna. She rarely heard a word like that coming from him. He walked into the bedroom, and she heard muffled voices as Frank told Tracy of his plans.

After several minutes he returned, padded with layers of clothes and the cap Tracy knitted for his birthday last year. His heavy overcoat hung over his arm. Tracy hurried to the kitchen. She and Josie put together some cold meat and biscuits for him while he packed his packboard with extra kerosene for the lamp, extra scarves, and a blanket. Julianna listened as Tracy told him to please be careful. Then a silent moment as they said their goodbye.

Alex came to her mind again. Julianna remembered the times he had had to leave to work in Portland. How she had hated the frightening nights here on the hill alone with the small children. She felt sorry for Tracy and worried for Frank.

As if he had read her mind, Frank hesitated before he opened the back door and said, "Don't worry about me, Mrs. L. I'll be fine. Remember, I grew up in Illinois. I'm used to these storms."

Damn, I wish we would have stayed at Hicks' place, Ferd thought, straining to see the road through the curtain of blowing snow. It stung his eyes and burned his cheeks in spite of the large blue handkerchief he had tied across his nose and mouth.

The road, mostly frozen now, blew clear except in places where trees or a bend in the trail caught the swirling white mass and laid it into a gentle drift. So far they'd managed to drive around the piles of snow, but light was fading fast. To make matters worse, the drifts continued to pile higher, and the wind kept blowing out the lantern.

They left the level trail, turned right, and headed up the hill toward the Mershon place. *Maybe we can make it that far*, Ferd thought, tossing a worried look at Arnold as he stumbled. Arnold caught himself without missing a step, his hand still on Molly's bridle, and he continued to lead her.

Darkness fell the minute they entered the timbered road. The drifts continued to climb, some a foot high. Now it was too dark to safely go around them, but they had no choice.

They were almost up to the brow of the hill where the trail turned left and ran along the ridge. Less than a mile from Mershons' place. Then, less than two miles from home. Ferd hoped the straighter road would have fewer drifts.

The mules pushed on at Arnold's urging, but Ferd could see they were tiring. Almost to the turn, they ran into a drift that went well over the right wagon wheels. Arnold, suddenly up to his knees in snow, guided the mules left, apparently planning to go around the shallow edge. *Dammit*, Ferd thought, *don't get off the road.* Before he could holler, the wagon lurched right. Ferd grabbed the seat with his free hand.

"Oh, *Scheisse*!" he hollered, hanging on while still trying to control the mules. His hands were numb with cold. He felt them slipping as the wagon seesawed one way, then the other. Dropping the reins, he grabbed the seat with both hands, clinging with all his strength. Helplessness overwhelmed him.

The wagon tilted left and slowly—ever so slowly—he felt himself somersault into a foot of snow, his leg pinned under him. When he opened his eyes, he found that he had cleared the wagon in the fall. It wasn't on top of him, but the wheel was stuck on a stump. Through the blizzard he saw Arnold pulling on the mules' harness, his lips moving, but the wind blew away the words. He watched his brother struggle to settle the team.

Could he move his leg? Gritting his teeth, Ferd gingerly lifted himself up with his arms and with all his might, pushed his leg out from under him. He groaned as a sudden twang shot through his lower leg and ankle. He stopped to rest and waited for the pain to subside. Finally with all the strength he could muster, he pulled himself to a standing position and gingerly put weight on his injured ankle.

The cold numbed the pain for the moment, as he grabbed the sloping wagon. He hobbled forward a few steps and reached for the reins as the ankle now began to scream through the cold.

"You all right?" Arnold yelled as he came around the front of the team after the animals settled down.

"My ankle," Ferd answered, now hanging on to Jack's bridle for support. "Don't think it's broke, though."

"Probably not, if you can walk on it."

"Just barely." Ferd began to feel dizzy and reached for the mule's back with his other hand to steady himself.

"Maybe we should see how bad it is?"

They shouted, straining to hear over the high-pitched wind.

"No, I'm not taking my boot off," Ferd said through gritted teeth. "I may never get it back on, and it's too damn cold for bare feet."

"Grab hold of me then, and we'll check the wagon for damage."

Ferd, grateful for his little brother's shoulder, held on as they inched their way through the snow to the back of the wagon. They found three of the wooden spokes in the rear left wheel broken and the iron rim bent where it had hooked onto the buried stump.

"This isn't going any place tonight," Ferd said, turning his back to the wind to be heard.

"What do you think we should do?"

Ferd shook his head and murmured, "I sure can't walk anywhere."

Thoughts jumbled, his ankle throbbing through the cold, he thought things through. "Maybe we should unhitch the mules and ride them as far as Mershons'."

"Yeh, we could do that," Arnold said, eyeing the remaining carrots, now frozen, that had spilled off the wagon. "Give them some carrots first. You do that while I get 'em out of the harness."

"I'll take some with us, to bribe them if necessary," Ferd hollered as he painfully gathered a handful. He walked gingerly, trying to stay out of Arnold's way, and fed both mules. Molly brayed a thank-you.

After the second handful, Ferd's ankle—the pain beyond tolerable now—gave out, and he felt himself falling. He grabbed for the wagon but couldn't reach it. Unable to stop himself, he landed face down before the blackness made the pain go away.

"Ferd! Ferd!" The voice, first a long way off, was now in his ear. Someone was shaking his shoulder and hollering. He tried to move away from the sound. He was sleepy and much too comfortable to move.

Consciousness reluctantly came to him. He realized Arnold was tugging at his sleeve and yelling in his ear. "C'mon Ferd! You gotta get on Molly."

Ferd stirred and tried to use his good leg to get off the ground. Leaning heavily on his brother, he eventually got to his feet.

More aware now, Ferd grabbed the side of the wagon. Arnold helped him rise to a wobbly standing position. Ferd leaned back on the mule, clutching the edge of the wagon. *How in the heck am I going to get on that animal?* His ankle flared again.

"Maybe I can climb on the wagon and mount from behind?"

"Yeh, let's get you up there," Arnold urged.

THE COLD SLOWED ARNOLD'S PACE AS HE CLIMBED UP on the tilted wagon and extended his hand. Grabbing Ferd's wrist, he pulled with his last bit of strength. Ferd dangled, feet barely off the ground. With his free hand, Ferd grabbed the side of the wagon and threw his good leg up. Arnold continued to pull.

Molly, as if she could sense the danger, moved closer to the wagon just as Ferd made a final lunge onto the tilted wagon bed.

"Hang on!" Arnold hollered.

He jumped off the wagon. "Whatever you do, don't let go until I have your hand," he commanded loudly over his shoulder.

Oh God! Help! Arnold prayed to himself as he came around by Molly's side, patting her back along the way. He was almost as worried about the animals as he was his brother.

"Grab my hand!" he yelled, moving Molly as close to the wagon as possible. The wind, more relentless than before, shuddered through him. For the first time he worried that they might not make it out. They were so close, but everything was turning against them. *Ferd's supposed to take care of me*, he thought in protest. *He's the oldest.*

"Hurry," Ferd hollered, searching for Arnold's gloved hand in the dark. "I can't hang on much longer."

Arnold pulled on his brother's arm with all his strength. He could feel Ferd pushing off with his foot as his body inched slowly toward Molly. He saw Ferd find her collar with his free hand and pull himself over onto the mule. He lay on his stomach across her back, unable to bring himself to a sitting position.

"I can't help you. Just stay like that and hang on," Arnold shouted. "I'll lead the mules and get us out of here." He hoped he sounded braver than he felt. He waited for an answer but heard nothing. He grabbed the reins of both mules and started walking in what he hoped was the right direction.

Chapter 45

INTO THE BLIZZARD

1904

"No, I haven't seen them." Joseph's face skewed with worry.

Frank's heart sank. Somehow, he had believed he would find the boys safe with Joseph and Elma. He'd even pictured Molly and Jack munching hay in the Maroks' barn.

Joseph put his hand on Frank's shoulder. "Listen, we can ride my horses and follow the trail." He turned and reached for his heavy coat. "We'll let Shep lead the way."

Frank turned on his heel, headed for the barn, and began bridling the horses. He had just finished attaching the blinders when he felt a rush of cold wind and Joseph slipped in the side door. He came over and put empty feed bags over each horse's face. "These should protect their noses in the wind," Joseph said quietly.

They worked hurriedly in silence, barely noticing Elma, in a heavy coat with her head wrapped in a wool scarf. She brought out a packboard with bread and cold meat and handed each of them a second scarf long enough to wrap around their faces, cover their ears, and tie around their hats.

In fifteen minutes they were ready to ride. Shep, after smelling one of Ferd's shirts, was anxious for the hunt. He barked at the door when Joseph urged him to find Ferd and Arnold. Even the horses sensed their urgency and appeared eager to go.

Snow pelted their faces when they left the barn. Shep didn't seem to mind, running ahead and then back, nose to the ground. Frank prayed now, his heart heavy. *Why did I not stop them from going this morning?*

After a half hour out, the snow let up some, but Frank knew the only way they could stay on the road, blown bare in several places, was to follow the dog's lead. The men let the horses have their heads, and they followed Shep without urging.

Would the boys still be on the road? Worried, Frank muttered, "No, they must be at the Bates' or the Mershons'. They would not be out in this cold. They may have even stayed over at the Hicks' place."

"FRANK WILL FIND THEM, MOTHER. YOU KNOW HE WILL." Tracy patted her mother's arm to get her attention, but Julianna's mind seemed to have left her body. This happened every once in a while, and it never ceased to raise concern in Tracy. Almost as much as having Frank and the boys out in this terrible weather, the clouding of her mother's mind was terrifying.

Julianna stirred slightly, mumbling something. Tracy heard only the word "Ferd."

"What, Mother?" she leaned closer, relieved to see signs of life in that poor, overworked body.

"I almost lost him you know, just before he was born."

Her mother's words were plain and strong. "You must remember? I asked you to help milk Nanny, and you tried."

Tracy's thoughts raced back. She had watched her pregnant mother crawl toward the house from the barn half-carrying, half-dragging the partially full milk pail. She remembered tears rolling down her cheeks and yelling for Emma to help. Papa was away working in Portland, and no adult was there for Mama. She did remember.

"I didn't go through all that for him to die in a blizzard." Julianna's voice was firm now, strengthened by the same courage that had saved them all during that time; courage that Tracy now recognized after having a child of her own.

"He and Arnold are not going to die, Mama," Tracy said. "Frank will find them. He's from the Midwest. He knows about blizzards and snowstorms." She wished she felt as confident as she was trying to sound. It wasn't only her brothers, but her husband. She had already lost too many of the men in her life. She silently begged God to spare Frank and the boys.

All the while the snow pelted the window. Tracy shivered as the strong gusts squeezed into the house through unseen cracks.

Frank and Joseph passed Pleasant View School and continued east into the wind, following Shep's lead. The horses maintained their pace. Frank felt sorry for them, glad they had the feed bags and blinders on. Heading into the wind would have been a killer for them otherwise. One gust blew so hard he had to lean forward for fear of being blown off backward. But the snow had let up some, helping their visibility.

Occasionally he or Joseph called out, only to have the words blow back in their faces. After what seemed like an eternity, they saw a light in the window of the Mershon place near where the trail intersected with the road to the Chamberlains. Shep barked and ran ahead, sensing the destination.

Alfred Mershon, his dogs having alerted him, opened the door, and peered out into the night.

"Have you seen the Lampert boys?" Joseph called as loudly as he could, but they were too far away to be heard.

They spurred the horses to the porch. Frank repeated the question, and the answer put a knot in his stomach.

"No sir, not seen a soul," Alfred hollered back and turned to say something to his wife. "Sarah's fetching a cup of hot coffee for you, boys. Wait a minute."

He brought out two warm tin cups and handed them over while his sons Leroy and Louis carried buckets of water for the animals.

"Glad the snow's let up a bit," Alfred said, shivering in his light coat.

Frank nodded. "Yup, it seems to be," he said. He was happy for the warmth of the coffee.

"*Ja*, it should be easier to see the boys now if they're still on the road," Joseph said.

"I know they will be at the Bates'. Surely, they have gotten that far." Frank tried to sound positive. "We'd best be on our way," he said, handing back the half-empty cup and turning his horse toward the road.

They went eastward again. The snow had all but stopped falling, but the wind continued in its fury as it blew snow with every gust. Heading up a slight grade, they caught sight of a nearly full moon between the parting clouds. The storm was passing. Frank thanked God silently.

On the other side of the hill, the Bates' trail veered right through the trees, toward their house, but the dog ran ahead up the road, seeming reluctant to leave the path.

"I don't think Shep smells their scent on the Bates' trail," Frank hollered.

"Doesn't appear to," Joseph yelled back. "Let's follow her."

With a heavy heart, Frank agreed, keeping their weary horses on the normally well-traveled route, happy that the trail was mostly bare. They ran into a large drift after a few yards, but Shep nose to the ground stayed on his trail. The wind was blowing the scent toward them.

The moon showed its face again, clearer and more pronounced. In the moonlight, Frank was shocked to see the amount of snow and how high the drifted piles had grown.

"Ferd! Arnold!" he shouted.

Suddenly, Shep veered off his path and down a small embankment. At first, Frank thought she was skirting a drift, but hearing sharp excited barks, he urged his horse to the edge.

He thought he heard something. Frank halted his horse, listening. Yes, a faint sound, then nothing but Shep's yips. Wait. Again.

"Help! Help!" The voice was more distinct now. He peered into the darkness.

"Ferd! Arnold!" he hollered.

Not waiting for an answer, he slid off his horse and followed the sound. Stiff with the penetrating cold, he worked his way down the bank, almost running straight into Molly. She snorted a weak welcome, and Frank patted her side, then ran toward the voices.

"Here we are, Frank," Arnold's voice sounded strong. "We couldn't go any farther. Ferd couldn't hold on."

Frank fell to his knees. Hot tears streaked down his cheeks as he grabbed the boy in a bear hug. "Where is he?" he asked when he could get the words out.

"Here I am!" Ferd called out weakly. He lay on the ground a few feet away. "We came down here 'cause it's out of the wind."

"I'm pretty sure his ankle's broke. He doesn't think so, but I do," Arnold said, clinging to Frank as if there were a possibility he might disappear.

Chapter 46

SPRING AND SUMMER 1905

Emma

Emma let the book slip to her lap as she turned her gaze out of the window. She watched the fence posts and landscapes as they passed, searching for her first view of the Columbia River. She always enjoyed the train ride home, but this time more than ever. Tracy's last letter, full of news, had stirred Emma's heart and urged her to take time to visit the family. Besides, she couldn't wait to see little Iggy.

She had visited home at Christmas to find everyone jubilant with the recent rescue of the boys. Ferd was hobbling around on a crutch that Frank had whittled out of a limb, but other than that, both boys and the mules were safe and appeared to be healthy. Dr. Volp from Troutdale had assured them that while Ferd's ankle was badly sprained, it more than likely would heal fine as long as he didn't put any weight on it for a few weeks.

Tracy's last letter had confirmed that Ferd was making an excellent recovery and was, indeed, his old self. He needed a walking stick only if he were going long distances. Emma had read the words with relief.

The story around the Christmas table was that after Frank and Joseph found them on that fateful night, the four made their way back to the Bates place, where they left the boys in Orilla Bates's care. The men took the livestock and returned home to assure the family the boys were safe. Two days later, with the mules rested and the temperature moderated, Frank returned and brought the boys home before the ground thawed and turned to mud.

Returning to the present, Emma sighed and picked up her book, wishing that Bertie could have come home with her. But two of the Foeller children had the croup. Sophie had given Bertie permission to go, but Bertie was not comfortable leaving them.

Emma's eyes found the paragraph where she'd left off. The story, *From the West to the West,* written by her idol, Abigail Scott Duniway, was one of the most compelling she had ever read. She had been thrilled to find a copy of the newly published novel available to check out before leaving town. She so admired Mrs. Duniway's strength and spirit, and shared her determination to win the women's right to vote.

Many of Emma's and Bertie's female friends at church shared her enthusiasm for suffrage, but most were not vocal about it. She was disappointed that Bertie did not share her passion, although they had many discussions. Tracy did, however, and Emma wished she was in Portland to help with the fight. But Tracy now had a family and was unable to devote her time to outside issues. It was both surprising and reassuring that Frank shared Tracy's enthusiasm about women suffrage.

Emma knew Tracy would be thrilled to read Duniway's thinly veiled autobiography. Out of the corner of her eye,

them nodded, without exchanging words, agreeing they would try to attend.

After the ceremony the little group explored the buildings on Willamette Heights that overlooked Guild's Lake. They soon came upon the Forestry Building, which was described as the "World's Largest Log Cabin."

"It certainly is the biggest log building I've ever seen," Tracy observed.

Frank smiled and nodded. The immensity of the timber in the mountains of the Oregon country never failed to strike awe in the young man from thc plains. Emma and Bertie marveled at the immensity of the building's façade. Inside, the seventy-two-foot-tall Douglas fir logs that lined the giant hall filled it with the sweet smell of fresh-cut lumber. The group wandered through the building, admiring exhibits that showcased animals in their natural habitat and many of Oregon's natural resources.

They came to the Native American section, which showed exhibits of Indian life and culture. "This reminds me of when Papa took us on the steamboat up to Celilo Falls," Tracy said.

"Yes, remember the Indians fished off planks that extended over the water, just as they show here," Emma said. She shivered as she remembered the roar of the water falling over the rocks, how slippery the platforms looked, and how high they were above the river.

Bertie nodded. "That was a fun time. Mama and Papa were happy."

As they visited, they lost track of Frank and then found him talking to a group of men near a tall stack of thin, wide lumber. Walking closer, they heard one of them say, "This'll change the lumber business as we know it."

"I wonder what he's talking about," Bertie pondered.

"A typical salesman," Emma snorted.

"Well, whatever it is, Frank is certainly interested," Tracy said, then hurried to his side, while the display of a magnificent buck with a huge rack of antlers and sad eyes distracted her two sisters.

"Do you think it's real?" Bertie asked, her eyes wide with disbelief.

"'Course it is," Emma replied, wondering what was wrong with her younger sister. Sometimes she just seemed so naive. "Someone just stuffed it!"

Emma tugged on her arm but, inquisitive, Bertie remained, her feet planted firmly on the ground.

"I wonder why we never see any deer at the farm," she pondered.

"That is strange," Emma agreed. *Don't know why I never thought of that.* The thought flitted through her mind as they turned to follow Tracy.

"Come on! Let's see what Frank is so excited about."

"This is a new way to use lumber," Frank was saying as they approached. Emma sighed. *He's so handsome when he's happy about something,* she thought. A pang of envy surged through her. *Shame on you,* she scolded herself. *He's your sister's husband.*

Frank pointed to a man at the front of a group of ten who all stood on a flat piece of wood that bridged between two short pillars. "Mr. Carlson," Frank identified the man in front, "tells us that piece of lumber they are standing on is what he calls 'plywood.' It's composed of many thin layers of lumber laminated together, to give it strength and flexibility. They believe it will have many uses."

"What's 'laminated'?" Bertie asked.

"Glued," the man talking to Frank answered her. "The pieces of wood are stuck together with glue by a special process. See, it can hold ten men without breaking."

A sign over Mr. Carlson's head read "3-ply veneer, Portland Manufacturing Company, St. John's, Oregon."

"How will they use it?" Emma wondered.

"Mr. Carlson says they are experimenting with using it for door panels right now." Frank seemed lost in thought for a moment, and then said, "I'll bet they'll use it to make furniture someday."

Although it was difficult to lure Frank from the lumber conversation, the girls tempted him with the thought of a glass of cool Weinhard beer. That and the heat seemed to convince him to follow the women out of the building and down the steep stairs toward Guild's Lake and the carnival.

"Here's a sign that says they serve sausage in a bun," Frank said, pointing to a small stand near the foot of the steps.

"I've heard of them," Emma said. "They call them wieners."

"Yes, Annie, my friend at church, says they're delicious," Bertie said, hurrying toward the delectable smell. "Let's get one!"

They found some shade and enjoyed the rare treat. The girls cooled themselves with bottles of Hires Root Beer, and Frank, enjoying his Weinhard, went back for a second and then a third "hot dog."

After they had rested, they crossed Guild's Lake on the "Bridge of Nations" and visited the United States Government Building. It stood proudly, the spires on either side rising well above the roof line, each displaying a U.S. flag that flapped in the hot easterly breeze.

"This reminds me of the Chicago World's Fair," Frank murmured, gazing at the vast array of structures. "The buildings looked like this."

"You're probably the only one here who had the opportunity to see them both," Emma said, thinking how lucky that would be.

The Government Building, full of interesting exhibits, sat on a peninsula in the middle of the sparkling, shallow lake. The group wandered around and came upon an array of strange, fierce-looking animals. One huge creature's skeleton stood out among the rest. Beside it, the same beast had been built with an outer skin so visitors could compare the two and see what the beast looked like in the wild.

"My Lord, would you look at that thing!" Bertie exclaimed.

"What a monster," Tracy replied.

Overwhelmed, Emma couldn't speak. It resembled a picture of a dinosaur she had seen in the newspaper once, but much larger than she would have guessed. She wondered if it was real. The sign said it had probably lived millions of years ago, and scientists found its remains in Montana. Maybe it really had lived back then, before Christ walked the earth. She wondered what the church would say about that.

"It's half past eight," Frank declared, looking at his watch. Fascination and astonishment had kept them glued to the exhibits, causing them to lose track of time.

"We'd better start back," Tracy said. "It's a long walk to the trolley station."

Darkness was beginning to descend as they exited the building and started the return trek across the bridge. Suddenly and without warning, everything lit up, bright as day. Stunned at the brilliant spectacle, they heard excited comments from the crowd.

"Electric lights," Emma explained. "They say the fairgrounds are beautiful from the heights above the lake after dark."

"I read in one of the exhibits today that Portland was the first city in the country to have electricity transported by wire," Tracy said, awed at the sparkle of the bright lights. "The article said that Willamette Falls has an electrical generation plant."

"Yeah," a gentleman behind them joined the conversation. "That's how they have run the streetcars since 1890. There will be more electrical plants. Several of them will be built on the Clackamas River."

Frank dropped back to visit with him. Emma overheard the man tell Frank that this was intended as a demonstration of what electricity could do, and that attendees of the fair had reacted enthusiastically. When Frank asked him what he did for a living, he answered that he worked for the Willamette Falls Electric Company.

The small party climbed the wide staircase to the top of the heights and turned to see the bridge and the peninsula's buildings bathed in hundreds of lights. Emma caught her breath. True, Portland had a few streetlights, but this looked like nothing she had ever seen. She glanced at Tracy and understood the astonishment on her face. She, after all, lived in the country with only kerosene lanterns and candles to light the way. They stared for what seemed like an eternity.

"It's close to time for the last streetcar to leave," Emma felt obligated to remind the group—although she hated to do it. "I'm certainly not willing to walk any farther in these shoes." They had walked all day and were much too tired to walk the mile back to the Foellers'.

"I'M SURE THE LAST COUPLE OF DAYS WERE JUST A DREAM," Tracy said to Frank. "And my new shirtwaist was the perfect ending to our trip." They'd arrived home two days before, and Tracy held the exhilaration of the Lewis and Clark Exposition close, savoring it like a licorice ball in her mouth when she was a child. She remembered trying not to suck on the candy for fear it would melt away.

Her heart skipped a beat when Frank put his arms around her and nuzzled her neck. "You look beautiful in it," he said quietly.

They had not returned to the Foellers' the night of the exposition until after eleven o'clock, and they slept late the next day, a luxury that Tracy had never experienced. At breakfast, Frank suggested they spend one more day in Portland and see the town.

They had said goodbye to Emma the night before, and she had gone off to her nanny job down the street. Bertie was busy with the Foeller children, so Tracy and Frank enjoyed the day by themselves.

They had walked downtown, explored Southwest Broadway, and caught the streetcar to the top of Council Crest. They rode a carnival ride and shared a thick beef sandwich while sitting on a bench that overlooked a stunning view of Mount Hood, Mount St. Helens, and Mount Adams. Larch Mountain appeared to sit next to Mount Hood, but they knew it was much closer to Portland and wondered where Brower and Palmer were exactly located. Looking east and down, they saw the sprawling cities of Portland and East Portland spanning the Willamette River with Albina to the north.

At the end of the day, they found themselves at Fifth and Morrison Street in the five-story Meier & Frank Department Store, where Frank had insisted they each buy something new to wear.

"You're too busy with the baby and the house to sew shirts," he said, when he picked out a new one for himself.

She readily agreed. She loved to see Frank looking spiffy when he had the rare occasion to get dressed up.

Somewhere in her soul, she knew the trip and the experience had changed her life. Not that she ever wanted to move to town. She loved the hill and was more than excited that Frank was building their new home. She couldn't wait to move in. But something in her soul would never be the same. Perhaps it was an overwhelming desire to learn. She glanced at the book lying on the table, *Captain Gray's Company* by Abigail Scott Duniway. "Yes, that must be it," she murmured to herself as she pulled out the iron skillet to begin preparing supper.

Chapter 47

APRIL 1907

April 17, 1907
Woodbine, Illinois
Dear Annie,

I welcomed your fine letter written March 5. I'm glad things are going well for you and that you did not have as severe a winter as you have in past years.

Frank has our new home almost finished. He says we can move in about three weeks. We will both be happy to be in our own home. We rarely have any time to ourselves, since we have been living with my family. He still feels that he's not worked off the whole twenty acres, and will not take the deed yet.

I wish you could see Iggy. He is growing so fast. At almost three-and-a-half he is trying to keep up with his young uncles, Jackie and Alex. I'm glad to send them off to school so he can have some playtime by himself. I am afraid he will miss them terribly when we move. He's like a little brother to them. They and Josie all spoil him, but he is a good boy and I don't think it will hurt him.

The fall grain crop is coming up well. Frank seeded

an acre of oats and one of wheat for us and triple that for Mother's farm. There is a neighbor man who comes around and threshes it in the summer. He charges a third of the crop, so if all goes well, there will be plenty for our own use and some money besides.

Fortunately, they have rebuilt Palmer farther south in standing timber after the fire, so we still have customers in both Brower and Palmer.

Frank will begin planting the rest of the vegetables for the deliveries soon. He has the seed, but is waiting for the rains to let up. He had already planted early carrots and beets when we had a warm spell in February. He also has cabbage, spinach, and kale seeded in a small bed near the barn. He will transplant those into the field in May and June.

My brothers Ferd and Arnold are helping him cut half of the potatoes we saved for seed last fall. They can get three or four hills from each potato if they cut them correctly by leaving at least one eye in each piece. Frank is getting anxious to get the early crop in.

Tracy put her pen down and gazing at the rain coursing down the window, she wondered when it would ever quit. She understood Frank's anxiety; it seemed as though it was a farmer's lot. Then she remembered Frank talking about the often-terrible weather in Illinois and decided that rain might not be such a bad alternative except, of course, where planting the crops was concerned.

Iggy was playing on the floor with blocks that Frank had made for him out of scrap lumber. He was a quiet, thoughtful child and could play for hours by himself.

Tracy had finished the morning chores quickly and retreated to her room to finish writing the letter to Frank's sister, Annie. Frank didn't have the time to write, and she didn't mind. In fact, she and Annie had become friends since the correspondence had begun, and Tracy looked forward to Annie's chatty, lighthearted letters.

The two of them shared similar feelings about the suffragette movement, and Annie was a great fan of Alice Roosevelt, which endeared her to Tracy. She hoped the two of them could meet; perhaps she could persuade her sister-in-law to come west for a visit one day.

Chapter 48

EARLY FALL 1907

Pear Syrup

"The boys just brought in another bucket of pears, Mama," Josie hollered from the porch.

"All right." Julianna sighed and pushed aside the pesky strand of hair that persistently stuck to her cheek. *Thank goodness the children are big enough now to take over some of the chores*, she thought, remembering how seemingly impossible the smallest things had been after she'd lost Alex. The old sense of dread bubbled up as she ran the back of her hand over her forehead.

"Let's get what syrup is left from this batch into jars." Tracy said interrupting her thoughts while pulling the hot containers out of the kettle of boiling water on the stove.

Sweat poured down Julianna's face as she carefully ladled the boiling syrup into the warm Mason jars. When they were filled, she placed the rubber rings on the mouth of the jars, put the glass lids on, and pulled the wire bales over the top to seal them down. As each cooled, it formed a vacuum, preserving the syrup.

Julianna admired her eldest daughter. Glancing in her direction, Julianna saw the intensity in her face. Tracy had matured into a responsible young woman who cared deeply, not only her own child and husband, but for her siblings as well. Tracy's disappointment in the loss of the suffrage vote last year had worried Julianna, but true to her character, Tracy put her frustrations to work and, with Josie, started a monthly women's meeting over at the school. Julianna noticed that the worry lines in Tracy's face had eased since many of the younger women in the area began following Tracy and Josie's lead.

Josie tended the fire in the pit outside and kept the next batch of fruit boiling. Julianna decided earlier that morning that some of the kitchen work must be moved outside. The stove was not able to hold both ten quart kettles, plus the early autumn heat seemed relentless.

Several years ago, Frank had asked Joseph to haul the kettles up from Troutdale with his wagon and mules when they arrived from Montgomery Ward & Company. Julianna ordered them through the catalog because she needed to make larger batches. She put them to good use immediately, making apple butter from the Yellow Transparent tree in the orchard.

Now she had a bumper crop of Bartlett pears and was not going to see them go to waste, even though it was a big job that would require the whole family. She knew that pears do not keep well, so when they are ripe they have to be preserved immediately.

Julianna experimented that first year, trying many ways to make and preserve the sticky liquid. The best method she could come up with was to cook the whole pear, minus the stem and flower, until there was a lot of juice and then skim that off, add sugar, and boil it some more. Now they had perfected the method with bigger kettles and a routine that made the process go much more smoothly. They had also gathered a hearty collection of canning jars and equipment.

Frank took one whole month's worth of money from his earnings on vegetable deliveries and offered it to Julianna to buy whatever equipment she needed for the kitchen. *It's a good thing Frank likes to eat.* She smiled to herself. His kindness often made her think of Alex, and she remembered how Alex had enjoyed the new treat. He had used the pear syrup on everything: bread, beans, in his coffee—whenever he took a notion. She had chided him gently about being a bad example to the children, but he had just laughed.

The children now used it in place of sugar, which pleased her, as sugar was one of the most expensive things they had to buy. One of the difficulties of "syrup making" was to have enough sugar on hand at one time.

Little Iggy, face and hands grimy, wandered over to Tracy and tugged on his mother's hem. Julianna, in an effort to help her daughter, scooped the child into her arms and wiped his nose with the bottom of her apron. She smoothed his sweaty hair, pumped him a cup of cold water, and set him on the bench beside her. She kept one eye on him while she helped Little Alex clean and stem the fruit. Whenever the child fidgeted, she slipped him a small slice of pear to keep him quiet.

She glanced around at her family and proudly noted how well they worked together. She realized that in some ways, their father's death had brought the family closer. It was interesting how such a tragedy could have at least one good thing come of it. And Frank—perhaps they would never have known him if her plight had not been news in town.

Julianna smiled at her small grandson and thought he resembled his father in so many ways. But he had the small wiry build of his grandfather. She wished that Alex could have seen his grandson, remembering how much he had enjoyed his own children. *Iggy won't ever know him*, she thought sadly.

It was past dark when the last batch came off the stove. Tracy and Josie stayed in the kitchen and bottled it, finishing with fifty-four quarts of golden syrup. Only seven of them did not seal.

"That's not bad," Tracy said. "Last year we had at least twelve that we had to redo."

"I remember." Josie shook her hands after rinsing them for the umpteenth time.

"I'm afraid that's not enough for both our families," Julianna said as she rounded the corner from the living room. "I wonder if Joseph or Franz would share some of their crop."

"Let's walk over and talk to Elma and Katherine tomorrow," Tracy suggested. "I haven't seen either of them for a while, and now that Katherine is feeling better, I bet she would like some company."

"I'm sure she would. She said she was almost like her old self last week when I checked on her," Julianna said, smiling with relief.

Chapter 49

LATE FALL 1907

"I'm sorry, I must leave for town tomorrow," Emma announced emphatically, trying not to sound conflicted. She opened her grip and began to pack. The last thing everyone needed was a weepy goodbye. She missed the family terribly when she was away. Now it would be even worse with Mama so worried about Katherine.

Katherine Frommelt had taken to her sickbed late last spring. True, she had been ailing for several months, but she had rallied in early September. She'd seemed to be doing so well that everyone's fears were momentarily alleviated. Franz's face wore a permanent grin as he catered to her every wish.

Then, in mid-October she came down with a woman's ailment. Julianna, being one of her best friends and a midwife, had spent several days a week helping the family nurse their mother.

And then there was Ig, as he now insisted on being called. Such an alluring child, just the thought of leaving him brought a well of tears that Emma had to hurriedly blink away.

On the other hand, she longed for the culture and excitement of Portland. Ever since the 1905 fair, the city had bulged with the energy of youth and dreams. Once in a while, when they had managed to save a bit of money, Bertie and a group of friends from church would join Emma on a Saturday evening to attend a live play at the Pantages Family Theatre or a presentation at the Baker Stock Company. And she missed the excitement of the women's suffragette meetings and the hope that came with the young ladies and some men who longed to pursue a better future for themselves and their daughters. Emma doubted that she would ever have children, as she had never had a beau and suspected she never would. In fact, she was convinced that she was the ugly duckling of the family. Having just turned twenty-two, she was beginning to believe she would probably be an old maid.

"I hate that you have to leave," Tracy said, folding another towel from the pile of clean laundry on the bed.

"Me too, especially with Katherine so sick. I hate to leave Mama," Emma admitted with a sigh. "I feel like I'm needed here, but the Scherhausers have another baby on the way and are desperate for help. And besides Mama needs the money."

"I have to admit, the money you and Bertie send home does help. Now that Frank is busy with the finishing touches on our house, most of the work here on the farm will be falling on Ferd and Arnold. Although Frank promised he would help them after the house is done, but that won't be for a bit."

"I'm glad for that, even though poor Josie won't have any sisters here for company," Emma said, catching a glimpse of herself in the mirror as she carefully placed her clean underclothes in the suitcase. *Oh my, I forgot to tie up my hair. It's a terrible mess*, she thought as she reached for a ribbon.

"I'll be close by for Josie. She'll be fine." Tracy sounded resigned. "I am worried about Mama, though. Katherine's illness is very hard on her, and if something should happen and we lose her, it is just one more loss Mama will have to endure. I fear for her health as well as Katherine's."

Emma agreed that their mother seemed to be sliding into a deeper abyss each time she visited. Julianna's eyes had sunk deeper into her cheeks, and it seemed to Emma there was little joy in her face these days. She shuddered as doubts crowded her mind about leaving her mother.

THE NEXT MORNING EMMA BID EVERYONE GOODBYE. Little Ig climbed up her body and hugged her neck so tightly she almost changed her mind and stayed home. *He is the most exquisite child I've ever seen,* she thought, even though Tracy said he could be a handful.

Jackie and Alex walked her to Joseph's place, fighting over who got to carry her grip. They listened to Ig's cries of, "I want to go, too," until they heard Tracy's voice loudly insist, "Be still."

Emma caught a ride with Joseph, who was delivering milk to customers in Troutdale, though most of the cans would be loaded on the train headed for the dairy co-op in Portland. When she arrived, Joseph was just scrambling into the wagon. He indicated the boys should put her suitcase in the back and asked them to wedge it in tightly between the last of the load and the tailgate. Emma took Joseph's outstretched hand, stepped on a spoke of the wheel, and clambered up to the seat. This was a farm wagon, not a carriage with convenient steps. They headed out as soon as she was settled.

When they turned onto Woodard's road, she held on with both hands as Joseph pulled back hard on the wagon brakes. Halfway down the hill the steep road curved sharply to the right.

"Whoa! Whoa!" Joseph shouted. Pulling the brake handle with one hand and holding onto the reins with the other, he skillfully guided the team as he yelled, "Whoa, I say!"

Emma clung to the seat. She felt herself being pushed forward. Terrified, she pressed her feet hard against the front board of the wagon. If Joseph couldn't slow the rig down enough to make the curve, she knew the heavy load would tip over the wagon. *Oh God! Help us!* she prayed silently so as not to spook the team.

"Whoa!" Joseph continued to command. Still pulling on the brake lever, he managed to slow the heavy load just before the curve. As they made the turn, the rear end of the wagon slid in the mud. She prayed Joseph had tied the cans securely. If not and they bunched together on the downhill side, they could pull the whole wagon over the bluff, perhaps even into the river below.

With the horses braced for the turn, Joseph's steady hand pulled the reins to the right. Emma maintained her grip on the seat as the left wheels slid briefly before digging into the mud. The wagon lifted from the right. Momentarily it seemed the wagon was tipping. Then they were around the turn and everything miraculously righted.

Emma, badly shaken, breathed a sigh of relief and promised herself that no matter how nasty the walk on the trail or how bad the weather, she would never again ride down on this horrible road in a wagon.

"Well that was some ride, wasn't it?" Joseph said as he

turned to see if she was all right. His face was pale, and his eyes belied his confident smile.

She managed a nod but could not come up with a smile.

Once they arrived at the bottom of the road, the ride was quite pleasant. They followed the wide trail along the river, caught the ferry, and arrived in Troutdale, where they proceeded to the depot. By then Emma had almost quit shaking.

They made it with a few minutes to spare for the nine o'clock westbound train. Joseph unloaded the heavy milk cans, handing them to the train crew members who stood in an ice-filled boxcar. They threw down empty cans, which he loaded onto the wagon and secured with the rope.

Emma came out of the ticket office and looked wistfully back at the hill where she had left her family. Clambering up the stairs onto the railroad passenger car, she hurriedly looked away.

"You've been seeing Gabe?" Emma questioned. "I thought you and he had too many differences."

"I know, but he came over with yellow roses and a box of chocolates," Bertie said, fingers tracing the appliqued sunflower design on one of Sophie's throw pillows.

They were sitting on the porch swing catching up on the family and Katherine's illness. The fact that Bertie went to the church card party with Gabe Riehl caught Emma by surprise. She had wiped away so many of Bertie's tears over him and thought she had convinced her sister not to see him again. Though she had to admit that he was a dashing fellow.

"It wouldn't be the first time a girl's head is turned by flowers and candy."

"I told him we would just be friends. I told him that until he was ready to settle down and quit carousing with the fellows, that I would see other men."

"Have you?"

After a long hesitation, Bertie said, "Well, not really."

"Has anyone else asked you to accompany them anywhere?"

"Yes," Bertie answered indignantly.

"And you told them no?" Emma, trying hard not to lose her patience, gazed helplessly at her younger sister. Here was a beautiful young woman, kind and gentle, who would make anyone a lovely wife, and she couldn't even look at another man. Emma had to admit that Gabe was charming, but she was afraid he didn't have enough ambition. How could he take care of her sister and the inevitable children? Emma had her doubts about him, but it seemed that Bertie had already made up her mind.

"Yes, I promised Gabe that I'd wait for him to get a good job and save some money," Bertie admitted.

"And what did he say?" Emma demanded.

"He said he loved me and that he would be back and let me know when he found work. He's a farmhand. He needs to get a trade so he can make better money." Bertie blushed and added, "I am twenty years old, you know. Time is running out for me."

Emma sighed and shook her head. She understood the feeling. "Please make him stick to his promise, Bertie. Once you're married, you're married for a long time." She prayed her sister would take her advice, but they were after all sisters, and sometimes did not heed each other's words.

Thank God I haven't met anyone that I cared for that much, Emma thought. *Maybe being an old maid isn't half bad. At least I can see whom I like when I like, and I don't have to make promises to anyone but myself.*

Chapter 50

MARCH 1908

Julianna and Katherine

Julianna wiped her friend's face, knowing there was nothing more she could do. For weeks Katherine's illness progressed slowly with intermittent pain, followed now with uncontrolled bleeding. Julianna, with her years of experience as a midwife, feared the worst. She and Alex's distant cousin, Caroline, took turns using all the methods known to them to stanch the flow.

Two days ago the bleeding had quit as abruptly as it had started, and once again everyone breathed a sigh of relief. Franz hovered and when it was over strutted around like a man freed from original sin. To Julianna, it seemed as if most of his soul funneled back into his body, but a small part of it stayed with his wife. Now her condition again appeared to worsen.

Julianna got along splendidly with Caroline through Katherine's illness, but Julianna knew that Caroline disapproved of her. She was not, after all, a member of the Lamperts' Walscher tribe, as she had been born in Baden instead of Treisenberg or Balzer. She had heard rumblings here and there of Caroline decrying her displeasure with Alex for having gone outside of Lichtenstein to obtain a bride—someone who didn't even speak the same Alemannic German dialect.

But Julianna had learned to let such things slide off her shoulders. With a family to feed and crops to grow, her sensibilities would not let her harbor hard feelings. True, her boys sometimes ran about freely, but Julianna was of a mind that there was not too much they could hurt. They worked so hard they were too tired to do much damage.

Together the two women and Franz worked out a schedule that included Julianna, Elma Marok, Maria Seidl, and Caroline Lampert so each would spend time with Katherine, both to tend to her and see to her family. Each day for the next two and a half months, except when the weather would not permit, one of them arrived at the Frommelts' door with a meal and stayed most of the day, allowing Katherine time to heal.

But Katherine did not thrive. Most days she made every effort to do her share of chores, but was unable to stay up for more than an hour before exhaustion forced her back to bed or into a chair. Although she rarely complained, Julianna noticed that she rubbed her abdomen often. Once when she inquired, Katherine nodded and showed her how distended her abdomen had grown.

Excitement had run through the small group. Franz stayed close by, remarking how well Katherine looked. He told everyone she was just with child and although it promised to be a difficult pregnancy, she was no longer in danger. Julianna prayed it was true, but she was not convinced, encouraging the small group to continue their daily vigilance.

In time, Katherine's pain became more intolerable, and her belly continued to swell. Julianna sent Franz to

Troutdale to fetch Dr. Volp, who after a brief examination, admitted that he was not sure that Katherine was pregnant. He prescribed laudanum as needed and said he would stop by again in a few days.

Two days later, Katherine began to flow again. Julianna again looked for signs of a pregnancy and found nothing. She made a silent decision to wait for Dr. Volp. He would be the one to tell the family that this was not what they had hoped.

In the meantime, the women doubled their shifts. The Frommelts' oldest children worked frantically, helping where they could, somehow knowing as close family members often do, that their mother was in grave danger.

Over the next few days the pains worsened. Laudanum began to lose its effectiveness, and Julianna doubled the dose, then doubled it again the next day. When Dr. Volp returned, he told the family to make the patient as comfortable as possible, using whatever dose was needed. He shook his head while Franz stood by his wife's bedside, helpless and frightened.

Now finally, Katherine began to slip into unconsciousness. If Julianna or Franz spoke softly to her, she would respond, though only with a whisper or a nod. The bleeding worsened that morning, and none of the remedies worked.

Julianna washed Katherine's face with warm water often, and when Caroline returned from a rest, she tried to take the cloth from her, but Julianna was reluctant to give it up. She doubted Katherine would last through another shift.

Finally, she stepped back and let Caroline take over. Joseph came in from the field to say goodbye to his sister; the only family he had in this country. Julianna shared his tears and could not bear to leave her friend's bedside, afraid of missing a rally if Katherine should have one.

While Caroline tended to Katherine, Julianna had more than she could do to comfort and support the children. Franz sat immobile by his wife's bedside as she drew her last breath.

Chapter 51

CHRISTMAS 1908

"It's been too long, Bertie," Josie exclaimed as the little group congregated on the porch under the newly built roof.

"Come in! Come in! You're drenched," Tracy said after quick, wet hugs.

"Mama, this is Gabe," Bertie introduced her beau as they walked in the door.

Even though he was soaked, Julianna couldn't help but notice his neatly trimmed beard and charming smile. "How you do?" she said in broken English.

"It's all right, Mama, he speaks German," Emma assured her mother.

"Yes, I do," Gabe reached to shake her hand. "It's German with a Russian accent." He laughed and said, "I came to this country when I was five, back in '88." His voice gently resonated, and Julianna remembered Bertie's letter proudly announcing that he had begun singing in the church choir.

Julianna accepted his damp handshake with a faint smile. "*Wie geht's*," she said kindly. The handsome young man standing in front of her evoked a twinge of envy. *Alex was handsome, too*, she thought, *and I only had him for fourteen years.*

Her envy surprised her. Guilt made her say a silent prayer that Bertie would be happy with Gabe and that they would have a long life together—if she, indeed, decided to marry him.

"Come, girls, get your wet things off," Julianna commanded as she herded them to Josie's room. "Arnold, show Gabe upstairs and take a towel," she yelled over her shoulder. "I don't want the three of you to be sick for Christmas."

"Molly and Jack had a tough time getting up the hill," Frank said as he walked in the kitchen door and stuck his head into the living room. "The mud's bad." He paused. "Another day of rain, and it'll be impassible out there." Water dripped off his hat. Instead of getting out of his wet clothes, he grabbed some rags and hurried back to the barn.

"I'm going to help him." Ferd snatched his hat off the nail by the back door. "He's too soaked to be out there rubbing down those mules." He hesitated a moment, then nodded toward Gabe and said, "Nice to meet you," and headed out into the downpour.

"*Ja*, I'm working with the boys at the Baker Stock Company," Gabe said, reaching for another piece of chicken.

"What kind of work do they do?" Frank helped himself to more potatoes, enjoying the family and the conversation.

He and Ferd had lengthened the table and built two new benches to fit everyone around it for Christmas dinner. He thought Julianna looked unusually happy, probably because her whole family was present.

"We're remodeling the Tabernacle on Twelfth and Morrison. Rumor has it they're going to rename it the Empire Theatre," Gabe answered.

Frank nodded and passed the gravy to Jackie who, at fourteen, was impossible to fill up. "How much they payin' you?" Ferd was always on the lookout for a good paying job.

"Six bits a day." Gabe frowned. "They say I'm still apprenticing."

Bertie smiled proudly and patted his arm.

"That's very good money, Gabe," Julianna said.

"*Ja*, well, everyone says it's good training."

Frank fell silent, remembering his discussion with Alfred Mershon. Alfred had asked him to build a barn. *I could use some help*, he thought, pondering the cost. *Six bits a day would sure be a stretch for us.* Frank noticed how Bertie's beau was enjoying the meal, and wondered if Tracy's cooking might make up for his lack of funds.

"How long is that job going to last?" he finally asked over the chatter of the rest of the young people, now mostly grown-ups.

Gabe shrugged. "I'm not sure. At least through spring, probably."

"See any horseless carriages in Portland?" Jackie asked, bored with a conversation loaded with work and money.

"Oh yeah! My boss's son owns a 1904 Ransom Eli Olds with a curved dash. Rumor has it that he paid $650 for it," Gabe answered, his face lighting up. He took a swallow of coffee and eyed the apple pie.

"What's it look like?" Arnold asked, immediately engaged in the conversation.

"It's very pretty," Bertie said, her face beaming.

Gabe nodded. "The only way I can describe it is that it looks like a regular buggy except it doesn't have a tongue or a hitch." He paused, waiting his turn for dessert.

Frank shook his head in disbelief. No place to hitch the horses? He wanted nothing to do with something that upstaged and probably would scare the mules. He had seen a few automobiles in the city and hated them. They were noisy and unreliable as far as he was concerned; and they smelled bad.

"You steer it with a tiller and that turns the front wheels, much like a rudder steers a boat. And there's a small area behind the seat where someone could ride," Gabe continued.

"Have you ever ridden in one?" Josie wanted to know.

"As a matter of fact, I did ride in it once. It's real pretty and goes fast, but it's not good in the rain."

"Would you be interested in helping me build a neighbor's barn in the spring?" Frank blurted out. He had pondered the automobile question through most of his pie. As far as he was concerned, the conversation about a horseless carriage was over. "I could only pay you four bits a day, but we could fix up a bunk for you in the woodshed," he continued.

Gabe's quizzical look made Frank add hurriedly, "Tracy's a good cook and makes wonderful pie."

A grin broke over Gabe's face, and Frank was pretty sure he had a helper.

"I'M HAPPY THAT GABE IS DOING SO WELL OUT HERE IN the country," Bertie confided to her sisters on a beautiful day in late May. She had come home for the Decoration Day holiday to visit the family, but Tracy was quite sure it had less to do with family and the holiday and more to do with Frank's helper. She decided to stay a few extra days and was reluctant to say when she was returning to Portland.

She and Gabe were inseparable now that they were both out at the homestead. Bertie walked the three-mile round trip to the Mershons', bringing the men's lunch to the job site almost every day.

Tracy thought Bertie looked particularly happy and told Emma as much when they were alone. Emma said she suspected love did that and changed the conversation immediately. Emma's attitude worried Tracy. She adored her sisters and was thrilled that Bertie had a nice beau, but she had never seen Emma act enthusiastically toward the young man.

Tracy knew it was no use trying to discuss anything of importance with Josie. She was just too happy-go-lucky. Bertie had invited Catherine Foeller out with her, at Josie's request. She and Catherine had become pen pals and rapidly became fast friends. Tracy was sure that at this young stage of their lives, neither of the girls ever had a serious thought. And that was more than likely not a bad thing.

Chapter 52

JUNE 1909

Tracy wiped her brow with her apron and moved with effort as she pinned damp laundry on the line. *I can't believe how tired I am*, she thought, rubbing her extended belly. "I know you're in a hurry, little one," she murmured. "So am I."

Frank was down in the lower field planting the late corn. She had urged him earlier not to forget to plant extra popcorn. Now that Ig was going to school, she used it for snacks when he came home.

The family had settled into their new house a few months before, and although Tracy loved having her own home, the adjustment of leaving the female companionship of her mother's homestead was even more difficult than she anticipated. In a way, she wished they could have stayed until this child was born, but Frank was eager to be in his own place. She remembered watching him and her mother sign the papers deeding them the twenty acres. He beamed as he talked, and later that night, after everyone was asleep, he held her tight and told her that he had everything he'd ever dreamed of: a beautiful wife, a son, and his farm.

Now he was about to have another child, and he grinned every time he spoke of it. But right now she couldn't think of much to smile about. As perspiration ran down her forehead, she grabbed another clothespin from her apron pocket and finished hanging one of Ig's school shirts. She noticed it was frayed around the cuff and made a mental note to mend it when it dried. *He goes through clothes so fast*, she thought. *Two shirts are not enough for this active little boy.* She promised herself to make another one for him soon. *I think there's enough good material in that old blue apron of mine.*

The baby kicked again, harder, and again she grabbed her abdomen. She wondered if it were positioning itself for birth. She had often thought how much babies in the womb do for themselves, yet how helpless they are after birth. It was one of life's mysteries.

"My tobacco crop looks fine," Frank said as he rounded the corner of the house.

"Good." She shook a pair of Frank's trousers absentmindedly, remembering how disappointed he had been the year before when he couldn't get the seeds to sprout. This year, he'd started the tobacco seeds in a cold frame back in February. Using fresh cow manure for heat, he had been delighted to find the plants had sprouted, grown, and then survived the transplant.

"Yeh, I'm glad old man Bates told me about that coyote tobacco," Frank said as he came over and gave Tracy a peck on the cheek. "We got plenty of wood ashes to help the seeds sprout." He laughed then, and she couldn't resist returning the kiss on his stubbly face. When he held her and looked into her face, his eyes turned solemn. "Are you not feeling well?" he asked, his voice uneasy.

"I'm not sure." She grimaced, wondering this time if the baby kicked or if it was the beginning of her labor pains. "I'm trying to decide."

She insisted he go back to what he was doing and assured him that she would call him if necessary. The next couple hours found her increasingly uncomfortable. She tried to finish her chores, but pain and exhaustion consumed her. When she sat down, there was no comfortable position.

FRANK FOUND HER SITTING ON THE BENCH ON THE BACK porch when he came to check, and just about that time, Ig came down the trail from school. "Go get your grandmother," he commanded as soon as the boy was in voice range. Frank glanced at Tracy, and she nodded. He took her arm, helped her to the bedroom, and sat by her. Her pains came closer together, which he knew meant the baby was probably coming.

"But no one can tell how soon," she assured him.

Julianna and Josie found Frank looking baffled as he tried to help Tracy change the bed.

"It's perfectly natural, Frank," Tracy was saying. "I'm fine."

"Here, let us do that, Frank," Julianna said. "The best thing you can do now is get Ig some supper. He's a hungry little boy."

Reluctantly, he kissed Tracy and left the room, looking quite powerless.

"What's happening, Papa?" Ig asked. "Is Ma all right?" He looked like he might cry.

How do I answer that question? Frank pondered. *The boy needs to be told, but what can I say?* He sighed. *I've never been good with words. Now I wish I hadn't sent him to the house when Bossie's calf was born.*

After a moment, he motioned for him to come sit by him at the table. “Mama’s going to be all right,” he said, whispering a prayer that he was right. He put his arm around his son and continued, “She thinks that sometime tonight, you’ll have a baby sister or brother.”

“Oh, what fun,” he said, his eyes shining. “He can go to school with me.”

“What if you get a sister? Will you take her to school?”

“Yes,” he said thoughtfully. “But she’ll have to grow a bit first.”

Frank laughed at the logic or lack of it and nodded. “Now let’s get something to eat before we both starve.”

After supper, when Ig was in bed, Frank went out on the back porch and sat on the bench. With shaking hands, he succeeded in getting his pipe lit. He got up and paced, sat down and worried, got back up and paced some more. His pipe, now cold, was absently clenched between his teeth. He lit a lantern and walked to the barn, scolding himself that he had not yet milked. *Some farmer I am*, he admonished as he threw oats to the cow. He went through the motions, filling the milk pail as Bossie gave him grateful nudges. Everything seemed to be in slow motion.

He found himself hoping that neither he nor Tracy would have to go through anything like this again, and wondered how they could keep it from happening. The only answer he could come up with did not please him, so he continued to fret.

He found himself back in the kitchen, the fresh milk in the sink in cold water. He went back out on the porch and lit his pipe as he waited for the milk to cool. Later, he realized that he felt better having something to do, even if it was just separating the cream and taking it and the milk to the basement to continue cooling. Tomorrow, maybe Josie would help out and make butter. He was pretty sure she would.

He went to the bedroom door and peeked in. Tracy, in tears, shooed him away, but not before he saw a lot of activity, much of which baffled and unnerved him. Josie followed him out.

"The baby's coming Frank. Mother said to tell you that Tracy is doing well and not to worry that she's crying," Josie said, heading to the kitchen. She came back seconds later in a rush with a stack of clean muslin towels. "Mother says Tracy's very brave, and you should be proud of her."

Funny, he didn't feel that good about it. Anything that made her cry did not make Frank one bit happy. He grabbed his pipe and headed once again to the comfort of the porch and wooden bench.

He sat with his head in his hands, having given up on lighting his pipe. After what seemed like an eternity, in the wee hours of June 12, a second son was born. Tracy had her Alexander.

Chapter 53

JULY 1909

In 1909 the Fourth of July picnic was celebrated a day early because the fourth fell on a Sunday that year. People started to arrive at the school early while the day was still cool. Since it was a Saturday, remarks were made about the joy of having two days off from work. Picnic baskets were unpacked, and children played tag among the grown-ups.

The men carried out the school benches where the grown-ups sat in groups engaged in jovial conversation. Some of the women took charge of the food that was arriving, while the older ones and the ones with infants and toddlers visited while they kept an eye on the children at play.

Tracy sighed when she sat down and signaled to Frank to set the baby basket in the grass beside her.

"Bobby is growing so fast," Tracy said, falling into conversation with Lucy, her old school chum.

Lucy nodded and gazed fondly at her child. "Yes, he is," she agreed, "but I'm having a hard time with his father. He keeps calling the poor child 'Tood.'"

When Tracy questioned her with a look, she said, "I have no idea why." She made a face and then leaning over the basket remarked, "And your newest one looks like a fine young man?"

"Oh, he is. I rarely hear a peep out of him. Only when he is hungry."

"And where is little Ig?"

"He's over with my brothers playing Andy-Over-the-Play-Shed." Tracy pointed to a group of older boys, who had taken some of the younger children under their wings and were instructing them on the rules of the game.

"Your brothers are so good with the youngsters," Lucy said with a hint of envy. "I wish Bobby had some older children to play with." She watched Jackie help young Cab Seidl attempt to throw the baseball over the roof.

"Don't worry. Bobby will have lots of children to play with when he starts school," Tracy assured her. She glanced over to where Emma chatted with a group of young women, including the Chamberlain girl. Just for an instant, Sue's brother Logan came to mind. With a glance at Frank, who was visiting with a gathering of neighbors, she suddenly realized she was filled with so much joy that the pain of Logan's death had been moved to a smaller corner of her heart. She was pretty sure that's where it would remain, but she knew it would never completely leave.

As the day warmed, older people sought shady areas, while the younger men and boys began a casual game of baseball, which rapidly turned competitive. Many of the women gathered to watch. To some of the older women's astonishment, Josie and Catherine demanded to play. After some discussion, Ferd said that it was all right with him, and most of the other fellows agreed.

"*Ja!* We need more players anyway," Jum Mershon chimed in.

There were only a couple of frowns as the girls pinned up their skirts and headed onto the field. Tracy noticed Emma wore one of those frowns and thought it strange because she was such an avid suffragette. *The poor girl—life must be hard for her*, she thought.

"What's wrong?" she asked her sister when Emma wandered over.

Emma shook her head. "I just think it's wrong for Josie and Catherine to go out there and act like men," she said firmly. "Mama won't do anything about it. I asked her, but she just laughed."

"They're having such a good time, Emma, and most people don't seem concerned," Tracy answered as gently as possible.

They sat in silence for a while. Ig came over and crawled into Emma's lap. She snuggled him while he rested. When he got up to play again, Emma straightened her dress and watched him lovingly as he ran to join the Seidl brothers. "I adore that boy," she said.

"I know you do, Emma." Tracy nodded. "I'm glad you're able to come home more often so you can spend time with him."

They sat together until Bertie and Gabe came over. Emma excused herself and went to join her friend, Lena, who sat under the large maple tree.

The ball game lasted until suppertime. Catherine had several good hits and even brought in a run.

"Where'd you learn to hit like that?" Arnold yelled from the sidelines.

"She plays with her brothers and the neighbor boys in the street in front of her house," Josie answered for her, since Catherine was on second base and couldn't hear.

Poor Josie couldn't get a solid hit but did hit a lot of foul balls. That made her smile and stick out her chin with a look that said, "See? I told you so."

After supper, Mr. Henkle brought out his accordion, and sounds of "Sweet Genevieve" filled the air. The men hurriedly cleared the floor of the play shed, and the women cleaned up the food as a few couples began waltzing.

Tracy felt Frank's arm slip around her and hesitated only briefly before her feet found the rhythm, and soon they were lost in music. Everyone joined in whirling and twirling to the well-known tunes. Even the very young tried the steps at first, but then sat on benches and chairs at the edge of the floor. Exhausted from play, many were soon asleep.

"Mama," little Ig woke suddenly and called to Tracy.

"Please dance with Emma," Tracy asked Frank as she left his arms to tend their son and check on the baby. She was ready to rest anyway.

Frank nodded, and when Tracy glanced their way, she was relieved to see Emma smiling.

The party broke up late. With sleepy children and men carrying lanterns, the Wands and the Lamperts walked up the path and over the hill to their respective houses. Bertie and Gabe stayed well behind the rest of the group. Tracy smiled to herself when she heard him say that he would walk her home.

The morning after the picnic, the baby awoke early in need of food and a change, but Tracy let Ig sleep as long as possible. There had been word that a priest might be at Seidls' to say Mass, but she learned at yesterday's picnic that it had been postponed to the following Sunday. After Frank and she had taken care of the morning chores and with the baby sleeping in the crook of Frank's arm, they enjoyed a leisurely cup of coffee in the cool of the morning.

Later, they carried a pot of beans across the hill to the homestead for the weekly Sunday dinner. Tracy was hoping to have a chance to visit with Emma alone. She felt Emma's unease, almost as if they were womb mates. They had suffered through so much together. Emma was due to return to Portland on Monday, and that always made Tracy sad.

When they entered the house, Josie and Catherine were in the kitchen, giggling as they prepared dinner.

"Isn't that Gabe handsome?" Tracy heard Josie say.

"Not as good-looking as that brother of yours," Catherine had replied.

"Which brother? I have four, you know."

"Ferd, of course." Catherine sounded indignant, but then peals of laughter came from the kitchen.

"Are you upset about Bertie and Gabe?" Tracy asked when she and Emma found time to talk.

Emma, quiet for a moment, nodded and said softly, "He often doesn't go to church."

"I thought he sang in the choir?"

"When he goes to church, he does."

"Emma, they're a couple. I wouldn't be surprised if they married someday." Tracy tried to be patient.

"I know," Emma relented. "I just want the best for her. She's a good person."

"I do, too," Tracy agreed, "but if she chooses him, all we can do is wish her happiness." Silent for a moment, she added, "He's a bit of a rogue, but underneath he does seem like a nice fellow."

Chapter 54

SEPTEMBER 1909

Ferd and Arnold

"I told you: she likes you," Arnold said, his voice filled with annoyance.

"But I'm going to ask Grace to go to the Box Social with me. I can't go with two girls at the same time," Ferd said. He had waited for a long time for Grace to return to Brower country, and he wasn't going to pass up a chance to spend time with her.

"In the first place, you don't even know if Grace remembers you, let alone likes you." Arnold took the straw out of his mouth, looked straight at his brother, and continued, "You gotta ask her, and you got no way to get up to her place to even do that."

"I can walk."

"Well you better get started—the Box Social is Saturday night."

The boys stood in silence. Arnold leaned against the barn door and Ferd, his arm over the fence rail, stared out toward the pasture.

Arnold broke the silence. "Look, why don't we ask Franz if we can borrow his team and wagon. We can ask Josie and Catherine each to bake a pie and go with us." Arnold spoke slowly, choosing his words. "That way we can all go to the Grange, and you can see if Grace will even dance with you."

Ferd studied his younger brother, who amazed him with his insight. He slowly nodded his head and said, "Not a bad idea. Not a bad idea at all." Silent for a moment, he continued, "The girls will get a kick out of it. Maybe we should go ask them now."

"I'll go ask them. I don't want Catherine to get her hopes up, as long as you have eyes for another girl."

Arnold turned and headed toward the house. His nonchalant gait made Ferd wonder if he had an ulterior motive. His brother had been finding more excuses than usual to make his way into the kitchen.

"THIS IS SO EXCITING," CATHERINE EXCLAIMED, AS SHE took Arnold's hand and climbed down from the wagon. "You country folks have such fun!"

"We don't get to do this often." Josie handed Ferd the carefully wrapped pies and two boxes of fried chicken. "We were lucky Franz wasn't planning on using the horses on Monday."

"Yeah, that and needing fried chicken. We'll buy more chicks next spring. Ma wouldn't want us to kill too many of her hens." Arnold offered a hand to Josie.

"I had to convince her that it was one that wasn't laying," Ferd, quiet for most of the ride, answered his brother. "Besides, I had to promise that tomorrow I wouldn't complain if we have milk gravy and potatoes, instead of our usual Sunday dinner." He laughed, not his usual hardy guffaw, but stunted and nervous like he had something pressing on his mind.

Arnold watered the horses at the trough, tied the team to a hitching post along with a dozen other teams, and gave them each a handful of oats with a promise of the feed bag later. He climbed the stairs to the Grange Hall, and once inside, searched the crowd as he walked toward his group. After a quick glance, he saw there wasn't another girl in the place any prettier than Josie and her friend Catherine. By golly, if Ferd wasn't going to bid on Catherine's basket, he would.

FERD LEFT ARNOLD WITH THE GIRLS AT THE CHECK-IN and wandered nonchalantly toward a group of Pleasant View men visiting in one corner. His eyes scanned the growing group as he navigated the crowd, but he did not see a sign of Grace.

About the time he gathered enough courage to ask a fellow from the mill at Palmer if he knew of her whereabouts, he spotted someone helping a young woman climb off a wagon near the front door. He murmured an excuse and moved closer. He didn't recognize the man with her, but the girl was Grace. Another couple accompanied her inside, while the gentleman paid a couple of young boys to tend to the horses.

Ferd wasn't sure why, but she looked different. Her dress was stylish, with a smooth white shirtwaist, lace decorating the front, and she wore a large floppy sun hat. It looked like the country had been polished away, leaving something shiny and extraordinary. Something he had seen before, but perhaps she had not; probably didn't even see it now. Whatever it was, she must've found it in the city. He wondered how it happened and suddenly felt awkward in his bib overalls. Even if he did have on a clean white shirt, he began to doubt whether he should bid on her dinner.

He didn't recognize the other couple, except something was familiar about the man with the other woman. He heard someone holler a big hello and call him "Oscar." Then he recognized him as Grace's brother, whom he had seen once when he delivered packages from Julianna to his mother.

Walking back to where his family stood, his eyes met Arnold's. Arnold tilted his head ever so slightly in an effort to indicate that he had caught the entire scene and understood. Brothers have a way of doing that for each other. In that moment in spite of his confusion and doubt, Ferd was grateful for the support.

"They're going to start the bidding pretty soon," Josie said and giggled. Catherine joined in, irritating him. He wondered if it had been wise to include them in this outing before he remembered that Arnold had been the one that wanted to bring them.

"We're about to begin," a gray-haired, mature-looking woman named Clara, who had introduced herself as one of the chaperones, called from the food area. "Please! Let's have the gentlemen to my right and ladies to my left. And, ladies, please stay here until your dinner has been bid on and paid for."

After a few more instructions, Clara turned the party over to Val, who started bidding on a beautiful basket tied with a red bow. After much ruckus, it finally sold for $2.15 to a gentleman who outbid the girl's beau for the honor of having dinner with her.

The man who lost, obviously not happy, aggressively bid on the next box, which happened to be Josie's. George

Neilson, one of the Pleasant View fellows who knew it was Josie's box, began bidding with bold determination. He won the dinner for $2.25, much to Josie's excitement. "At least I know him," she exclaimed.

The bidding continued. One basket went for as low as 75 cents but most averaged around $1.50. Finally, after much anxiety from Ferd, Grace's basket came up and the man who helped her off the wagon bid 50 cents with much authority. Ferd raised his hand and bid 65, and the race was on. Finally, Ferd bid $2.65, including the absolute last penny he had, and the gentleman named John outbid him by a nickel. Nodding and smiling, the winner went to pay and pick up the meal. Ferd felt worse than he could remember, maybe even as bad as when the wagon turned over in the snow. He caught Catherine's eye but could not read the message.

Disappointed, Ferd bid on the next basket and won it handily at $1.10, ruefully aware of how much money he saved. It turned out to belong to Geneva Johnson, a lovely young woman who lived in the Hurlburt district. They sat under a large tree on the Grange Hall grounds and visited while they ate.

"I'm one of seven brothers and sisters," she told him. "My brother, Art, brought me." She pointed to a tall, slender fellow, eating with a young lady across the lawn.

As they chatted, Ferd began to forget why he came and started to enjoy himself. Geneva was fine company and made a delicious apple pie.

Catherine's box came up next to the last, and Arnold had bid $1.00, winning it handily. When they headed outside, they joined Ferd and Geneva. Ferd thought Arnold looked happier than he had seen him in a long time. Maybe ever.

As they were finishing supper, they heard the fiddle and accordion warming up. The understanding was that the gentleman danced the first set with the lady whose box he'd won. It wasn't long after the first dance that Ferd gathered enough courage to approach Grace and ask her for a dance.

She agreed, excused herself from her friends, and the two of them danced to the soft refrain of the *Missouri Waltz*. "You are the one who bid against John." It was a statement rather than a question.

"Yes, ma'am, I was."

"Why?" She gave him a quizzical glance.

Ferd groped for an answer that wouldn't make him look stupid. After all, he had only spoken to her once, and that was several years back. "Ah, I, ah …" he stuttered.

She giggled and looked at him straight on. "Thank you for doing that," she said. "It's good for John not to take me for granted, especially as we are engaged."

"You're welcome," he muttered, doing his best not to look devastated.

"I don't think any man should take a woman for granted, do you?"

"Ah, no," he said, not having the slightest idea what she meant.

Chapter 55

OCTOBER 9, 1909

Bertie's Wedding

"What is that awful noise?" Julianna stepped down from the porch as she saw a cloud of dust coming through the gate. "What in the world?"

The wedding party rushed out of the house and stood gaping as a screaming black monster turned the corner and headed toward the astonished group. A cloud of smoke followed close behind it.

"Gabe said he had a surprise for me!" Bertie squealed.

Julianna stood in awe. Fear's ugly fingers wrapped themselves around her throat. Speechless, she could only watch the thing as it drew nearer. She tried to pick up her feet and run, but they were nailed to the ground.

It pulled up close to the group in whirling dust and stopped, dirt settling around it and on the wide-eyed audience. With one ear-shattering bang, the monster quieted and disgorged two laughing, grimy-faced men dressed in wedding suits and ties.

"Horseless carriage!" Jackie hollered and bolted toward it, almost running headlong into Gabe.

"Oh my," Julianna uttered. So this was the famous automobile. *It's no wonder Frank's not enchanted with it. It's ugly and loud! And smells terrible*, she thought as she caught an acrid odor of gasoline on the breeze.

"The groom's not supposed to see you until the wedding," Josie yelled as Bertie ran to greet them.

"Nonsense," Bertie hollered back over her shoulder as she leapt into Gabe's arms.

I guess she's not afraid of the monster, Julianna thought. She began to relax a little at the sight of the boys' excitement, but certainly not enough to move any closer.

Ig, who hid behind his father's legs, peeked around. Before Tracy could grab his hand, he raced to the car and scrambled aboard with an impish grin. Frank rolled his eyes, went over, whispered something to him, and lifted him out of the vehicle. Undaunted, the child walked a few steps back, and eyes wide with excitement, stood transfixed.

"Whatever have you done, Gabe?" Emma demanded, eyeing his rumpled suit.

"Well, I haven't bought an automobile, if that's what you think."

"Then whose is it?" Emma stood, hands on her hips.

"Oh, I'm sorry," he said and, ignoring Emma, he looked at Bertie. "I forgot my manners. This is a fellow from work, Henry Mann. He's going to stand up for me and then loan me his automobile so I can drive my bride into Portland." His eyes twinkled.

"Oh my," Bertie said, catching her breath and looking a bit overwhelmed.

Julianna shook her head. *I'm not sure I want Bertie to ride in that contraption.*

"It's too dangerous to ride all that way," Emma interjected, obviously defending her sister, before Julianna could say anything.

Both Gabe and Henry assured the family that it was safer than horses. Frank frowned and shook his head, but Bertie's brothers all wanted to go for a ride.

"Is this a Ford?" Ferd wanted to know, running his hand over the front fender.

"Yup, it's a 1905 Model N Ford," Henry proudly declared. "See, it has a top that comes over the passengers if it starts to rain." He tugged at the cloth and metal in back of the seat as he demonstrated how it worked. The young men crowded around and watched in rapt attention.

"How much did it cost?" Arnold asked.

"They sell new for five hundred dollars, but I bought this from a woman whose husband is too sick to drive it. She sold it to me for half that." Henry, tall and awkward, uncomfortably fingered his necktie and looked for all the world like he felt overdressed.

"He got it for a good price," Gabe chimed in. "I'm gonna have one just like it someday." Hair ruffled, he grinned his intention to Bertie.

"It's only fifteen minutes to wedding time," Josie interrupted her excited brothers. "Bertie and I have to finish getting ready. In the meantime, you fellows make yourselves useful and get the broom. Both Gabe and Henry need their suits brushed off."

The three younger brothers did as they were bid, but Julianna noticed Ferd staring at the machine. She saw him put his foot on the lone step, climb up, and lean over the door. He touched the wheel that Gabe had held onto when he turned the car as he drove up. *The boy loves that machine*, she thought as she turned toward the house.

At precisely 11:00 a.m., Father Turner took his place at the altar under the decorated latticework arch in the corner of the living room—the same one that Tracy and Frank had stood under not too long ago. Gabe's sister and her friend, who had come out by train the night before, stood near the stairs and began singing "Ein neues Lieben" as friends and relatives filed in, followed by Gabe and Henry, who took their places in front and to the right of family and friends.

Julianna, standing by her seat in the front row, suddenly lost her place. She couldn't remember what was happening. For a moment she was back in church in Malch. Her schoolmate Frieda was to come down the aisle. She remembered Frieda's lovely white dress and glanced down at her own dress, startled to see it was slightly faded. Oh yes, she remembered, that was the dress she had worn six years ago at Tracy's wedding. Today was not Tracy's or Frieda's wedding day, but Bertie's.

Relieved to be back in the present, she soaked in the comfort of her family as they gathered together. If only Alex were standing by her side.

The girls began to sing "Ave Maria," and Josie, the maid of honor, dressed in the brand new blue dress that Emma and Bertie had sewn for her, came slowly down the stairs and walked gracefully to the altar. Julianna stared at her youngest daughter and wondered when she had become a grown woman.

Choosing to walk alone, Bertie, wore a white silk dress with a long skirt and a veil, and followed Josie. She smiled widely as she took her place beside her sister and next to her betrothed.

Father said Mass and, in place of the homily, led the happy couple in the recitation of the marriage vows. After Mass was over, the priest blessed the two of them and introduced the married couple to the group. Julianna felt the length of the bride and groom's kiss lingered much too long for common decency. She hoped the younger boys and her grandson had not noticed.

As soon as she went through the receiving line, Julianna hurried to the kitchen where she joined Tracy and Emma in putting together the final preparations for the wedding feast. Luckily, it had not rained for several days, and the sun poked its head out early in the afternoon, making it warm enough for the majority of people to eat outside. Everyone soon gathered around the large wooden table that Frank and the boys had fashioned under the prune tree.

"The diocese has plans to build a church in Gresham," Father Turner announced as he scooped a helping of mashed potatoes.

"Gresham—where is that?" one of Gabe's sisters wanted to know.

"It's about nine miles southwest of here," Joseph, sitting next to his wife, answered before the priest could respond.

"That would be wonderful," Julianna spoke up. "Alex so wanted a church nearby."

"Yes, Masses, marriages, and other church issues will all be taken care of there," the priest said enthusiastically, and as if an afterthought, continued, "You folks are aware of the little mission Catholic church a few miles farther west on Powell Road, aren't you?"

Several people shook their head. "Yes, St. Joseph Kronenberg. Although it's farther away, it might be a chance to attend Mass until your new church is built."

People exchanged glances, and a few nodded.

"A church in Gresham would be most welcome," Frank said. "In the meantime, I'm going to take a day and investigate how much of a trip it would be for us to attend this St. Joseph Church. We just may be able to take advantage of it."

Father nodded encouragement and continued, "The bishop told us they have a priest for the church in Gresham in mind, a Father Brunagle. He's a German carpenter and is building a church somewhere down in the Willamette Valley right now. He is much in demand, so it may be several years before he gets to Gresham."

"The bishop told us the other day that it's getting harder to get to the more remote areas these days." The priest took another swallow of coffee. "Portland is growing so fast it's all the church can do to manage the congregations in town. We are very short of priests, you know."

Julianna didn't know how she felt about all the news. Change seemed to create chaos in her mind. *I guess I'll just have to trust Frank and Tracy to decide*, she thought.

By midafternoon, with dinner over, Bertie went upstairs to change into more serviceable clothes. The group drank a toast with Frank's year-old applejack, after which Gabe loaded Bertie's grip behind the seat of the sporty black car. He then gallantly helped Bertie into the carriage and climbed into the driver's seat as Henry, standing in front of the vehicle, cranked the engine.

Instinctively, Julianna put her hands over her ears. The motor coughed and sputtered as Henry continued turning the crank. The car finally roared to life, clanked noisily, then sputtered, and almost died. She noticed Gabe pushing down a lever by the wheel that steered the machine, which seemed to help it continue running. Finally the engine smoothed out, and he slowly backed the automobile around.

Henry grinned proudly as he watched his car carry the happy couple. He'd said earlier that he was going to escort the ladies to the train and back into Portland, to which Emma had almost choked, whispering to Josie her concerns about someone that skinny being able to protect even himself. Later, the group had realized that he had eyes for Gabe's sister.

Everyone waved and shouted as the newlyweds headed up the driveway toward the gate. Julianna watched with worried eyes and prayed they would survive the trip down the steep, rutted road to Troutdale, let alone all the way into Portland.

Chapter 56

LATE FALL 1909

1904 Model C Ford

"I found what we've been lookin' for," Ferd announced as he pulled the team to a halt.

"What's that?" Alex walked out of the barn, a harness in one hand and a screwdriver in the other.

"The perfect auto and the perfect price." Ferd stepped off the wagon, his words coming fast with excitement. "It needs some work, but you and Jack are good with that sort of thing, and Arnold and I can straighten out the body."

"What's all the racket out here?" Eighteen-year-old Jack stuck his head out the door with a curious look.

"Oh, nothing." Ferd grinned.

"Ja, nothing at all," Alex chimed in. "He just may have found us an automobile."

"Where is it? Does it run?"

"Well, that's why it's so cheap. It hasn't been run for a couple of years." Ferd paused as he bent to unhook the horses. "We cranked on it but weren't able to get much of a pop out of it."

"Where is it, and how much is it?" Arnold asked as he came around the corner of the barn, the empty feed bucket in his hand.

"I saw it behind Metzger's store over in Gresham. When I asked, the storekeeper told me that it belonged to Harvey Metzger." Ferd handed the reins to Arnold and began gathering the harness. "I went out back to take a look, and noticed it had a bad dent in the front fender; looked like it was rubbin' on the tire. The light's busted out, too."

"Is that all? That can be easily fixed," Alex said, his voice eager as Jack nodded.

"So I decided to look up this Harvey fellow. I found him in the Kidder's hardware store, which worked out well 'cause I needed to pick up those harness rings anyway."

"For cryin' out loud, get on with it!" Arnold, rarely impatient, began to lose his composure.

"Yeah, well, it seems as though Metzger was speeding along Powell Road after one of his buddies challenged him to a race, and the car spooked a team of horses." Ferd lifted his cap and scratched his head.

Alex shuffled his feet. "Geez," he murmured under his breath, knowing full well that if he made any kind of a fuss, Ferd would just slow down even more.

"Holy smokes!" he heard Jack mutter.

"Well, anyway, I asked Harvey how much he wanted for it, since it hadn't been run for quite a while, and it was pretty well beat up."

"So," Arnold asked, his voice held an edge of irritation. He could get away with it since he was almost as old as Ferd, but one of the younger fellows wouldn't have been that lucky. He was as big as Ferd and had beat him several times when they got to wrestling.

"So anyway, he wanted a hundred dollars for it."

Arnold whistled. "A hundred dollars?"

"Yeah, so I started to walk away, and I hollered back over my shoulder and told him he'd never get that price for the shape it's in." Ferd shook his head and continued, "Heck, he didn't even know if the darn thing would run."

The men stood, Jack with his arms through the bib in his overalls and Alex leaning against the fence, waiting for the next sentence. Arnold looked like he might strangle his brother, but Ferd was blissfully mulling the story over in his mind.

"So Metzger changed his tune a little and said we should go see if it would start before we settled on a price. I told him that was a fine idea, and we did. 'Course it was out of gas, so we had to find some, and then we took turns crankin' on it. The thought ran through my mind about the tenth crank that maybe horses might just be the better bargain." He laughed and continued, "We got it to cough once or twice, so I thought maybe with some tinkering we could get it running."

"Yeah, I'm sure we can." Alex's face showed he was eager to try.

"I told the Metzger fellow that I wouldn't pay more than twenty-five dollars for something that wouldn't even start," Ferd continued. "So he says, 'It's worth fifty if it's worth a nickel,' and I says, 'Not so.' I let him simmer a bit, and then I said, 'I'll give you thirty dollars and not a penny more,' and he says, 'Sold.'"

The three brothers let out a collective sigh of relief.

"So I guess we tow it home with the horses?" Arnold said, happy they had been able to finally buy a team after last season's crops left them with some extra money. "We'll have to rig up some kind of a hitch."

The following Monday, Ferd and Arnold left, each leading a horse. The harnesses were secured over the back of Arnold's horse, and Ferd's horse carried the chain and cleaves, which they planned on wrapping around the frame of the automobile to act as a hitch.

After they arrived and paid Metzger the thirty dollars, they led the horses around back to their brand new, slightly used, automobile. Before they hooked it up, they had to straighten the fender so they could steer freely, but the roads were dry and the auto was lightweight, so towing wasn't much of a chore.

On the way home they decided to take turns; one rode and steered the auto while the other led the horses. They switched places about halfway and decided that the machine was pretty tricky to maneuver, not at all like horses and a wagon.

"It's gonna take some practice," Arnold observed, as he hurried to steer away from the bluff while climbing the road that passed the Neilson place.

WHEN THEY PULLED IN BY THE BARN, JACK AND ALEX rushed over with Josie close behind. There hadn't been that much excitement on the place since Christmases when they were children.

Josie was ready for some fun. She climbed in and sat on the leather front seat, amazed at the comfort, having never ridden in anything but a wagon. "It's got a top on it, so we won't get wet." Her eyes sparkled. "And it can take at least six of us at a time. I can't wait to show everyone."

"Let's not tell anyone until we get it running," Alex suggested, gazing at the engine. The last time he and Jack had gone to Portland, he had bought a magazine that explained how the gasoline engine worked. He and Jack had poured over it until they both knew it by heart.

WITH FURTHER INSPECTION, THEY FOUND THEY NEEDED at least one larger screwdriver and a couple of smaller monkey wrenches. "It wouldn't hurt to have another pair of pliers either," Jack observed as they inspected the engine.

"Did any of you men even look at that top?" Josie pointed at the tonneau cover over the two seats. "The fringe is mostly gone, it's got rips everywhere; for heaven sakes it's not going to keep anyone dry."

"Hum, I guess you're right," Arnold muttered as he made a careful inspection. "It's made of canvas." He fingered one of the larger holes.

"Next time we make a run up to Palmer, we can pick up a piece at the mercantile store. Maybe they would trade produce for it?" Ferd mulled.

"What about the fringe?" Josie wanted to know. "After all, if it started out with fringe, it should continue to have fringe."

Arnold nodded with an expression of something close to understanding, while Ferd answered his sister with a scoff. "No need of that, we just want a cover to keep the rain off." He frowned and added, "How about working on the cover is your job?"

Josie badly wanted to be a part of this exciting project, but no way was she about to throw away a perfectly good bargaining chip. She waited as she thought over the prospect.

"If I work on it, I'm in for a fifth," she finally said. "I will own a fifth."

"What the heck?" Jack looked disgusted; he felt he already had to share it too many ways.

Josie held her ground. "I cook and wash and clean for you boys. That's not a lot of fun, you know." She stopped, folded her arms, and let that piece of information settle. "Now there is something fun to do, and I want to do it." She paused again before continuing, "And I want my share for the work I put in. I can do other things, too. As far as I can see, I know just about as much about this as you fellows do."

Arnold nodded. "She's right, you know. If we had to survive on our own cooking, we'd be in bad shape, and we know darn little about making this auto work."

"She's always been capable," Ferd agreed. "I don't see why not. We need that top."

"And reliable," Arnold added.

Josie took a deep breath and said, "And there's one more thing."

"What's that?"

"You will teach me to drive it. If you men can do it, I can do it."

Chapter 57

LATE FALL 1909

"Wonderful! A letter from Annie," Tracy exclaimed as Frank handed her the opened envelope. Frank's sisters had made friends through their correspondence with his young family. He seemed delighted that Tracy had become close to his family even though she may never meet them.

"Yeah, and here's the Elizabeth newspaper, too." He laid it on the counter and pumped himself a cup of water. "I'm dry as a bone," he added.

Twice a week Frank walked down to where the school path met the Wire Trail and picked up the family's mail from the empty powder box on which he had painted "Wand" and nailed to a tree at the crossroads. Bill Wright, a man in his early twenties, traveled from the Troutdale post office to Pleasant View on horseback and deposited people's mail in their respective receptacles.

Tracy read the letter and then reread it. It told of a hot summer on the Illinois farm and a late-July tornado that had missed them, but had come close enough that they'd had to run to the storm cellar.

"They had a bad storm back there," she said, remembering how Mama had related the story of Papa getting caught in one when they lived back there. "I'm glad we live here."

"I miss my family, but I sure don't miss those storms," said Frank, adding after a moment, "They don't get the ice storms like we have, though."

"True." Tracy shivered and thought of the one they'd had last winter that lasted five days. Frank had crawled to the barn four times a day to break the ice on the water tank. He told her he'd had to feed twice the rations to the livestock to keep them from freezing. The east wind blew so hard that the cold seeped in around the windows of the house and the furnace couldn't keep them warm.

Tracy shivered at the memory and hugged her husband just as the baby woke with a cry. Before Tracy could turn to go pick him up, Frank gave her another quick squeeze and left, murmuring something about packing the rest of the produce for Palmer.

Tracy loved having her brothers make the deliveries. Rarely now did Frank or Joseph have to take the run. She had been surprised at their enthusiasm after nearly losing their lives during that snowstorm a few years back.

She laughed to herself for thinking of them as boys. Ferd just turned twenty-one, and Arnold was now nineteen. She suspected there were enough pretty young women up in the logging towns to make the trip interesting for her brothers.

Mostly, though, I just want Frank nearby. I guess I'm selfish that way, she thought, as she sat down to nurse the baby and read the next installment of *A Pirate's Tales*, a novel written by a Freeport, Illinois, author. She wondered if the author had ever even been to the Caribbean.

FRANK PACKED THE LAST CRATE OF CABBAGE AND

stacked it at the edge of the field. While he waited for one of the brothers to bring the wagon by for loading, he walked to the edge of the woods and studied the tall Douglas firs with a familiar sense of wonder. He had managed to clear almost five acres, and now he needed more farmable land. Since fall was the time to make more firewood, he could do both. With the Lampert brothers help, he had cut close to fifteen cords last fall. It was now well seasoned for use this winter.

Each family was asked to annually donate a cord of wood, cut and split, for the stove in the school. Surprisingly, they usually used almost all that was donated. Whatever he had left after family use and the school donation, he sold at Taylor's Landing for the steamboats.

He had picked out a tall fir last year, about eighty feet high with a four-foot-or-so diameter. The first limbs were well over twenty feet above the ground by his estimate. Counting the bottom limbs, he figured it probably contained somewhere near thirty-five cords of firewood. *As soon as the fall rains come, I'll take this one out and the one over there*, he thought, looking at a companion fir that was not quite as tall. Either way, the firs were interfering with his plans for more cleared land and had to go. He loved to work in the woods, so it was no hardship.

He heard the team and turned to see Ferd in the wagon pulling up by the stack of packed boxes. Frank hurried up the hill to help him.

BY MID-OCTOBER, THE FALL RAINS WERE UPON THEM, and by All Hallows Eve the temperate rainforest began its usual dripping. Frank knew fire danger was over and now was the time to take down the first tree. He had already decided he wanted to deal with only one tree at a time. Frank whistled for his collie, King, and headed down to the woods with his short ladder in tow. He carried a hand auger with a four-foot-long bit and chose a spot on the south side of the tree about chest high. If it burned the way he planned, the tree would fall uphill, making it easier to buck and split—but there was no guarantee where it would end up when a fellow used fire rather than an axe to notch it.

It took him most of the morning to drill as far as the auger would go straight into the tree, through at least four inches of bark. He noticed with satisfaction that pitch oozed out the two-inch diameter hole and ran down the tree as he wound out the bit. Pitch burns hot and fast.

He wondered if he should collect it. Several men in the area sold pitch for ship caulking. He had thought about it often, but decided the time it would take to collect this product was better served by selling cord wood to Taylor for the steamboats.

He burrowed another hole about twenty inches above the first one, drilling it at a downward angle in hopes that it would connect with the previous opening. He drilled both places twice more to increase each hole's diameter, giving him a better chance of joining the two interior openings.

By noon he figured the two holes were as close as possible to meeting and forming something similar to a sideways V inside the tree. As long as part of it met, the fire, spurred by the pitch, would eventually burn out the rest. The top angled hole acted as a chimney and, once it was burned through, would have a powerful draft.

He went to the house for a bite to eat and a short rest. Then, grabbing his small hand axe, a can of kerosene, a couple of rags, and a handful of matches, he went back down and began the next stage under the threat of yet another shower.

Using the axe, he cut a small ledge in front of the bottom hole. He pulled a long piece of wire out of his pocket, straightened it, and wrapped one of the rags around the end. He dipped the rag in the kerosene, lit it on fire, and shoved it in the bottom hole as far as it would go and waited with anticipation for smoke to come from the top hole.

After a couple of minutes, a small curl made its way out of the chimney hole. Satisfied that he had drilled a good connection between them, he pulled out the wire. Using what was left of the kerosene rag, he took his stash of dry kindling, rubbed the pieces in pitch, and built a fire on the back part of the ledge. Then relaxing, Frank pulled his pipe out of his pocket and lit it. Leaning against a nearby stump, he folded his arms and watched, tending the fire until he was satisfied that it would continue burning. After fifteen minutes or so, he tapped his pipe to empty it, whistled for the dog, and headed back up to the barn to mend a piece of mule harness for the boys.

He tended the fire daily and several nights later, a loud crash pierced the dark quiet. He woke with a start as the tree, having burned through, hit the ground with a giant rumble. Hoping none of the rest of the family had awakened, he grabbed his pants and, making his way to the stove, threw a couple of logs on the fire. Once the fire was bright with flame, he lit the lantern with a piece of kindling to save matches, buttoned his jacket over his night shirt, and made his way down to the fallen tree.

He pulled his crosscut saw from the shelter of a nearby stump and spent the rest of the night and into the morning sawing the burnt end of the log. He didn't want to lose any more cord wood. It took him the better part of the day to remove the end and bury it in the soft dirt to put out the fire completely.

He didn't care about the stump. That could burn down as far as possible, as he would have to clear it anyway. The less dynamite he needed to use the better.

Chapter 58

EARLY SPRING 1910

Queenie

"She cost me $55," Frank exclaimed. "Look at her. She's got good lines." He patted the mare's nose and ran his hand down her neck.

"She's a beauty," Tracy agreed. "Where did you get her?"

"Bill Mershon sold her to me. He calls her Queenie and said she's got a good disposition, but most Percherons do." He ran his fingers through her ruffled mane. "She's small enough to ride, but she can pull a plow or a new wagon just as well."

"New wagon?" Tracy wasn't quite sure they could afford all this new equipment.

"That's the one I made. Remember when I bought wheels from Mr. Seidl?" he said as he stood back, admiring his handiwork.

"That's what you've been working on out in the barn." *He's full of surprises.*

"Yes, it was Ig's and my little secret." He smiled at his son.

"Well, you certainly succeeded in keeping it," she laughed. "And a beautiful black horse to pull it."

"Yup! Bill has several black ones and says they are even smarter than the gray ones. I find that hard to believe, though. Papa had a team of gray geldings back home, and they were smart animals." He brushed a hunk of mud off the mare's withers.

"I thought we could take the new rig to St. Joseph Kronenberg on Sunday for the eleven o'clock Mass." Frank paused thoughtfully before he continued. "We'll get up before dawn and should make it in plenty of time."

"That would be nice. It's been a long time since we've been to Mass on Easter Sunday." Tracy glowed. "I thought last week's Mass at Seidls' would have to do."

FRANK WAS UP AND DRESSED BY FOUR O'CLOCK SUNDAY morning and went out to feed the stock while Tracy fixed a cold breakfast and dressed the baby. She smiled at Ig as he came out of his room wearing his best knickers with a coat and tie.

"You'll have to wear your long coat over that. It might rain."

"Yes, Mother," he said and went to find it while she finished with the baby.

Frank came in from the outside, shivering. "It's chilly out there. Let's bring the lap robe and a couple of other blankets."

They were on the road before five. Frank, holding the lantern, led Queenie up the muddy trail to the equally sloppy road. *Thank goodness Frank put on his knee boots,* Tracy thought, wishing she could do something to help him. Ig sat quietly on the seat beside her, and soon she felt his head leaning on her arm. Alec, always a good baby, rested quietly in her arms. *If he's awake, you would never know it,* she thought as the buggy bounced along the muddy ruts.

Frank stayed with Queenie, leading her down past the Woodard farm where Ed and Olla lived. About two-thirds of the way down the road, they turned right onto the Neilson Cutoff, as the route to the Sandy River was commonly known.

Dawn was just beginning to break as Queenie's shod feet clomped noisily across the rickety wooden bridge over the Sandy River. The baby stirred but settled down. Ig awoke with a start, rubbing his eyes, too sleepy to say anything. Tracy noticed him stare in awe at the full, rushing river below. When they arrived on the other side, Frank blew out the lantern and climbed aboard.

Tracy had never been this way before and noticed many waterfalls along the bluff on the south side of the Sandy. Someone had put culverts under the road and graded it, making it much less muddy than the trails they had just come over.

"That's because this is part of the Baseline Road," Frank explained when she commented about it.

"Baseline?"

"Yeah, it's the main survey line for the northwestern U.S." He squinted into the morning light, moving Queenie to the left, away from the steep bluff down to the river. "They put the road on it. In Portland they call it 'Stark Street' now."

"No wonder they take such good care of it."

"There's gravel on it at the top of the hill." He pulled Queenie to a stop on the side of the road and let her drink out of a large pool. She shook her head at the spray from the falls and drank her fill.

They stopped again to water the horse after they had crossed the Beaver Creek Bridge. It started to rain softly. They rested in the canvas shelter of the wagon while each took a turn heading into the woods. Tracy tried not to get wet, but by the time she returned to the buggy, her shoes were soaked, and she wondered why she had ever thought this would be an elegant trip.

"Are your feet wet?" she asked Ig when he returned. He shook his head no as she dried his face and hair, glad she thought to bring some towels. Wrapping him back in his blanket, she planted a kiss on his forehead, thankful for the canvas top.

She enjoyed the smoother ride on the graveled road and was sorry to leave it when they turned south onto Fairview Road, which was full of ruts and mud, slowing them down once again.

It seemed to Tracy that it took forever before they had gone the mile where they crossed Section Line road. Her feet, still damp, were turning numb. She gave the baby to Ig, pulled off her shoes, and wrapped her feet in a dry towel. A shiver went through her as she pulled the blanket firmly around her shoulders and took little Alec back.

It was another mile before they arrived at Powell's Valley Road, where they turned west and headed toward the church. *Thank God, this is smooth. Some dear soul must have graded this road,* too, she thought. Queenie picked up her pace, following another wagon that headed in the same direction.

They heard the bell before they saw the church. By the time they arrived at the small, white building nestled in the trees, people were gathering. Horses, single and teams, were tied to the fence in front, and several more were scattered nearby, tied to trees and posts.

"I figure we just came about eleven miles, and we have ten minutes to spare," Frank said as he checked his pocket watch. He wrapped the reins around a tree, grabbed the water bag from the back of the buggy, and gave the mare another drink. He instructed Ig to give her a couple of handfuls of oats.

Tracy pulled on her wet shoes. Once that was done, she handed the baby to Frank and took his hand, eager to get her feet on solid ground. She had a fleeting thought, as they hurried to the vestibule, dodging the mud puddles dotting the churchyard: perhaps this trip wasn't the best idea so early in the season. She wondered if she'd ever feel her feet again.

"Why don't you folks come by the house for dinner before you head home?" said Antone Schantine, brushing his hair back and slipping his cap over his brown curls. "We just live five miles north of here on Sandy Road. It would be a nice break for you." He pointed toward the Columbia. "Mary's got a big kettle of stew on the fire, and she's always happy to meet new folks, especially ones from church." His handsome face showed his eagerness to visit over a meal.

"That's real neighborly of you, Antone," Frank said, shaking his hand. "Tracy's got wet shoes. That'll give her a chance to dry 'em, and it's always good to rest the horse." He paused and thought a minute. "Besides, we can go home through Troutdale when we leave your place. I think it may be closer."

The Schantines sat in front of them during church, and Mary admired the baby on her way back from communion. Frank thought she seemed like a nice lady, someone Tracy would like to know.

The Schantines had several children. Frank shook hands with the oldest boy, George, who was scrambling to get the team and wagon ready to leave. There was a young girl about ten who was talking to Ig. Yes, these people could become good friends.

"The priest was very nice, wasn't he?" Tracy said, as they settled into the wagon and started to follow the Schantines north on Jenny Road. "It seemed like he liked us and was pleased that we had driven so far, especially in such muddy conditions."

"Yeah, that's what I thought, too." Frank held the reins firmly as the mare trudged through the soft ruts. He was beginning to have second thoughts about having Queenie pull such a heavy load with mud slowing her down. He would have to rest her for a few days when they got home.

"I'm happy to have new friends," Ig said, barely containing his excitement.

"I noticed you talking to Antone's young daughter. What's her name?" Tracy patted her son's hand.

"They call her Mazie. Her real name is Margaret Katherine." He grinned up at his mother. "I think Mazie is a fun name. She's ten. She's really nice."

"I'm glad you like her, son," Frank said as he steered Queenie to the left to avoid a particularly deep rut. He noticed Antone drove mostly on the side of the road and decided to do the same.

They pulled up at the Schantine place about a quarter past two. The children jumped off the family's wagon, and Mazie and a brother came running over to meet the new family.

"Hello, I'm Joseph," said a laughing tow-headed boy as he stuck his hand out for Frank to shake.

"I'm Frank Wand, and this is my wife, Tracy."

"I'm so pleased to meet you, Joseph," Tracy said as she shifted the weight of the baby to the other arm and took his hand.

"This is my sister, Mazie," Joseph continued, "and that older girl over by Mother is Mary, but we call her Mamie." The boy spit out his words, sounding like the engine in Henry's Model N. He pointed to a small boy probably a couple of years younger than Ig and said, "That's my little brother, Tony. They named him after Papa."

Ig jumped down from the buggy and ran off to play with Antone's energetic children. "We may not see him again until we get ready to leave," Frank said, watching him run.

"Don't worry about him," Tracy replied. "I've never known that boy to miss a meal. He may be particular about what he likes, but he always comes to the supper table."

"I CAN'T THANK YOU ENOUGH, MARY," TRACY SAID, SITting in her stocking feet in front of the stove; the baby asleep on a blanket beside her. "My feet are dry and warm, and my family is fed. I'm very grateful for all you've done for us."

"Well, I'm happy to do it. When else can we have company for Sunday dinner? Neither Antone nor I have any family out West. We miss their good cheer."

Tracy smiled, enjoying the warmth of her newfound friend. They visited another few minutes before Frank came in to tell them Queenie was hitched up and ready to go. Mary's clock said half past four, urging Tracy not to dally. It would be another three hours, well after dark, before they would get home.

"You folks just plan on having Sunday dinner with us

whenever you get a chance to come to church," Mary said, walking her out to the buggy. Tracy could tell she was reluctant to say goodbye. She felt like they were squeezing the last drop of juice from ripe summer fruit.

"It's been such a lovely day." Smiling, Tracy added, "This visit made all the mud and rain worth it."

The sun peeked out as they waved goodbye to their new friends and headed east on Sandy Road toward Troutdale and their hill.

Chapter 59

FALL 1910

Julianna

"Here's the money, Ma." Ferd put coins and two paper bills on the desk.

"Money?"

"Yes, Mama, the money from the deliveries," Ferd said, sounding surprised at his mother's reaction. "This was a good day. We sold all but a bag of onions and two bags of potatoes."

Julianna picked up a handful of coins and looked at them. Oh yes, I must count these, she thought. Here's a two-bit piece. She hesitated and stumbled over the next coin.

"Here, you count it for me." She shoved the pile toward Ferd.

Puzzled, he took the coins and began to separate them. Julianna, too tired to watch him, closed her eyes. She thought of Alex. He was often with her these days.

Sometimes at night, when everything was still, she talked to him, and he would answer in his soft, gentle way. His voice calmed her when she worried about the crops, or when she heard the cry of the coyotes and feared for her chickens. Then she would reach for him, but could not find him.

Much of the time, she looked for him everywhere, sometimes frantically, but mostly with a quiet desperation. It aggravated her when her mind wouldn't work. Frustrated, she quietly screamed for him.

She woke with a start wondering why Ferd was counting the money. "What are you doing?" she demanded.

"I'm counting the take from the delivery, Ma. Like you asked me to do."

"I did no such thing. I'm the one who counts it. Don't you forget that." She tried not to be cross, but the children knew better than to keep any money from her.

"I'm only counting, Ma. I'll give it to you when I'm done, and you can give Arnold and me what you think is fair, just like always." Ferd looked perplexed and continued to count.

"What's the matter?" Josie came into the room in the middle of the strained conversation, wiping her hands on her well-used apron. Her hair had been tied neatly in a bun, but now much of it flew in spidery wisps.

"Ferd's counting the money, and he knows I always do that." Julianna pursed her lips as anxiety welled up.

"I'm just helping Ma out. She said she was too tired to do it and asked me if I would."

"I did no such thing. That money is the only thing between us and starvation." She would never ask someone else to take care of it. "How will I feed my children if someone takes it? What if we lose it?" Her hands shook, and her voice rose as she groped for words.

"Mama, Mama, please listen to me, Mama. We aren't children anymore," Josie pleaded softly. She took her mother's hand and said, "I'm almost twenty-one. If we have any money problems, I'll go to Troutdale and get work." She patted her mother's stooped shoulder. "We'll be all right." The younger woman's face was haggard beyond her years.

"We have twelve dollars and thirteen cents here," Ferd said, pushing the pile toward his mother. "What would you like me to do with it?" He spoke plainly, seemingly without concern, but his hand shook.

"What's the matter, Josie?" Julianna wondered why she seemed so upset. "Is everything all right in the kitchen?" Her voice was now strong and firm. She worried about Josie. Maybe she should take a holiday. Go to Portland and visit Catherine Foeller. Yes, I should go with her. It's been a long time since I've seen Sophie.

The deliveries had been good. Maybe a trip to Portland would be just the ticket. Everyone would feel better. After all, even the Bible says that we have to rest sometimes, she thought as she picked up the money and headed to the cupboard to find the money jar.

Chapter 60

CHRISTMAS 1910

"It's not such a merry Christmas for we women." Emma frowned at Josie's greeting. "We lost the suffragette vote again."

"I know." Josie sighed as she gave her sister a hug. "Tracy and I followed the election. Both Ferd and Frank said they voted for it."

"Well, thank goodness for that."

Emma had spent several days volunteering at her precinct counting ballots. Mrs. Scherhauser had been supportive and actually encouraged her in her work, but when Mr. Scherhauser found out, there was hell to pay. He had scolded Emma soundly and told her women had no business in politics.

She stomped her foot and told him that was a lie. Women needed the protection of the laws, just like men.

They had gotten in a huge screaming row, and his wife had to intervene. In the end, he had allowed her to keep her job, but docked her wages for every day she spent working the precinct. That didn't bother Emma; she knew it was the right thing to do.

The argument had helped, though, because it soothed her anger about her father's death, of all things. She had never been able to forgive him for leaving the family in such a terrible state. Yelling at Mr. Scherhauser had changed something, and in the fiasco she began to feel like she was screaming at Papa. She threw the book she had been reading across the room and shrieked until she had collapsed sobbing into Mrs. Scherhauser's arms.

She was embarrassed when she thought of it later. Even now she blushed when it came to mind. She wasn't given to losing control and had no patience for emotional women.

And then, after all that, suffragettes lost the election once again. How many times was that now? At least five resounding losses, the first one way back in 1884 before she was born.

"Don't worry, Emma. Tracy says the pro-votes are getting closer." Josie patted Emma's arm and in a reaffirming voice said, "She's sure we'll get it next time. She says if Washington state can pass it, so can we."

Emma didn't feel encouraged but nodded in agreement anyway. She bent to hug her mother, wincing as she caught the fleeting sign of puzzlement in Julianna's eyes. Josie's last letter had said her mother was forgetting things, but that she had pretty much decided it was not a serious issue.

"Mama! It's good to see you." Putting her arms around her mother, Emma was surprised to feel how frail and bony she was. "You must not be eating your mashed potatoes," she said with a smile she did not feel.

"Oh! Don't be such a worrier," Julianna replied, patting Emma's hand.

Emma smiled at Julianna, relieved to hear her mother sound like her old self, and put to rest the concern she had felt since she had received Josie's letter.

"Emma, Merry Christmas!" Ferd exclaimed, coming in from the barn, where he had been working. It seemed to Emma there was always something to do out here on the farm. She had gotten used to curling up with a book in her favorite window nook for at least an hour or so when the children were napping. She marveled at Tracy with two children and a house to run, yet able to keep up with the newspapers Frank brought home.

Arnold and she had a good conversation while he drove her home in the wagon. The weather was clear, although the east wind blew cold. She was glad he had thought to bring extra blankets. They chatted about the harvest and about Arnold's desire to have a car like Gabe's.

"Do you think Santa will bring you one of those fancy machines?" Emma said with a snicker.

"Oh, *ja*." Arnold grinned back at her. "I expect those boys'll deliver it any day now."

"Well, I certainly hope so, and in the meantime Santa did bring you a little something." She nodded toward her grip and the two large bags sitting behind the seat.

"That's mighty nice of you, sis."

"It's the least I can do," she told him as the buggy hit a frozen bump and she grabbed for the seat. "But if I get thrown off this thing, I'm returning all those gifts," she warned with a chuckle.

"I'll be careful. Besides it's these gol-darn mules. If I had that car, there wouldn't be these problems."

"I thought you boys bought a car?"

"Yeah, we did, but it's broke down again. Jack says he and Alex can get it running as soon as they can get a part." He smiled and said, "It's a good thing we kept the mules."

His smile warmed her. She admired the man her brother

had become. The thought crossed her mind that they had made it in spite of Papa's demise.

Now, just for an instant, the look in her mother's eyes made her wonder at the high price that had been paid. Thinking of the family's sacrifices made her happy to bring a few small gifts for them.

Being home with the pungent smell of the fir tree in the corner and the crackling fire in the stove brought a kind of comfort to Emma that she hadn't felt for a long time. I'm here now and can help Josie, she thought. We'll let Mother sleep every morning until she wakes up. All she needs is a little rest.

"I can do it myself." Ig took the coat from his mother. He'd just turned eight, and his independent streak continued to grow.

"I know, dear. Sometimes I just forget how big you are."

"Do you think Santa brought our presents to Grandmother's already? It's pretty cold out."

"Santa lives at the North Pole. It's much colder up there. I doubt he had any trouble."

"That's right! Now I remember. Mrs. Gable brought a compass to school and showed us how to find the North Pole. Maude Henkle asked her how we really knew where Santa lived if there is difference between that and magnetic north."

He went on to tell Tracy that Mrs. Gable told the class that no one knows exactly where Santa really lives. "She said that was part of the magic of Christmas." He paused with a thoughtful look and asked, "Do you think that's part of the magic, Ma?"

"Yes dear, I think Santa represents the goodness and enchantment of Christmas."

"What about the Baby Jesus?"

"There would be no Christmas without the Baby Jesus. Remember, it's his birthday. In fact, look at the first part of the word."

Ig thought for a moment, and said, "Oh, *ja*, that's 'Christ.'" He seemed satisfied with the explanation and, turning, announced that he was going out to the barn to help his father finish feeding the stock.

Tracy nodded and smiled in wonder at the inquisitive mind of a child. She didn't remember that with her siblings. Probably because we were too busy. With that thought, she realized she had spent most of her brothers' and sisters' growing-up years working in Troutdale and had missed much of that part of their lives.

Excitement grew as it came closer to the time to see Emma and Bertie and spend Christmas with them. She hadn't seen Bertie since last summer, before she had the baby. Must have been in July because Bertie had little Ferd in early August. Oh, I hope they make it in time for dinner.

And Emma! Tracy couldn't wait to compare notes with her. Emma had sent her a letter a couple of weeks before, telling her how she helped at her Portland precinct and had gotten in trouble with her employer's husband. Tracy often worried about her sister. Emma had such a distinct sense of right and wrong it sometimes got her in trouble. I wonder if she is at Mother's yet? The thought made Tracy want to leave right away, and she wished Frank would hurry with his morning chores.

Finally on their way, they walked west, with their backs to the wind. Tracy was glad it had eased from the harsh earlier gales. Frank carried Alec, and she tried to hold Ig's hand. It wasn't until she asked her son to help her walk on the frozen ground that he put his hand on her arm as if to protect her.

When they arrived at the Lampert homestead, they removed their gloves and overcoats, hustled into the attached woodshed, through the back door, and made their way to the roaring fire in the cookstove. Emma rushed in from the living room and gathered Ig in her arms, kissed both his ruddy cheeks, turned to Tracy's hug, then nabbed Alec out of her brother-in-law's arms.

Tracy's brothers soon joined the kitchen festivities and stayed until an exasperated Josie herded them back into the living room to join their mother. Julianna sat in her favorite chair, the rocker that her Alex had so lovingly made. The look of joy on her mother's face when she first saw it sitting by the living room stove came to Tracy's memory, a pang of grief at Papa's death followed, tearing at her heart. Just as quickly, she pushed the thoughts away.

"Where's Bertie?" she asked Emma as they made their way back to the kitchen to help Josie.

"I met her downtown two weeks ago, and she said she and Gabe planned on coming out today." Emma shook her head. "But Bertie did tell me that Gabe's car was giving them a lot of trouble. Actually, what she said was that she rarely saw him these days because his head is under the hood working on the motor."

"They say automobiles are more trouble than they are worth, but I sure think it's fun to have one," Josie said with a gleeful look in her eye.

"That's beginning to be my thinking as well. Frank says he wouldn't have one on the place anyway, so I guess I don't have to worry." Tracy brushed the hair out of her face and started peeling potatoes. "At least not until Ig gets older."

Bertie and Gabe had not arrived by the time they were ready to sit down to dinner. Since no way had been found to keep a houseful of young men from the table, they decided to start without them.

For the first time since the Christmas of '96, there was a family member missing for this most important event. After saying grace, there were murmurings around the table, but mostly everyone kept silent. Tracy knew that their sister's absence was on everyone's mind as they raised Frank's strawberry wine in a toast.

After dinner was finished and the Grace of Thanksgiving had been said, the women adjourned to the kitchen while Ferd and Arnold headed for the barn and the evening chores. Frank, with Jack insisting on accompanying him, took the lantern and walked back to the Wand barn to milk. When they'd finished, they brought back another bottle of wine.

It was well after dark, with all chores finished, and everybody reluctantly held out hope that Bertie would somehow appear. Finally, just as they decided they couldn't make the children wait any longer to open their presents, Alex jerked to a start, looking out the window.

"There's lights coming down the road by the gate, Mother," Alex exclaimed. He now demanded to be called "Alex." At seventeen, Tracy knew he hated being called "Little Alex." And besides, there was now a younger little Alec, who lay sleeping beside her.

"By golly, there is," Frank confirmed, peering out the living room window. He grabbed his coat and rushed out the door, followed by the Lampert boys. Tracy suspected part of her brothers' excitement was the car.

As soon as Bertie and Gabe's new son, Ferd, was introduced to his aunts, uncles, and cousins, everyone settled down to let the newcomers feast on leftovers. Bertie explained that the car had been packed before nine o'clock this morning, but it had taken Gabe until one o'clock to get it started.

Gabe mumbled something about ice in the carburetor. "*Ja*, once it started, though, it made it all the way out here without so much as a cough." He folded his arms over his chest in a gesture more of thanksgiving than arrogance. "I finally figured out to put a little whiskey in the gas line to get rid of the water. Then it started right up."

Tracy, happy to see her sisters after all this time, not to mention a new nephew, sat close to Emma and Bertie for the rest of the Christmas celebration. The clock struck midnight before they settled down for the night. The Lampert brothers generously gave up their beds for the families, because no one wanted to leave. Besides, Josie had announced she had biscuits rising "for breakfast in the morning."

Chapter 61

EARLY SPRING 1912

Julianna rose from her chair, rubbing her arms. "So cold!" she muttered while searching for paper to start a fire.

"Can't find!" she exclaimed. "Out of newspaper?" Grumbling, she went to the kitchen and came back with paper she found in the cupboard. "This'll burn," she muttered, crumpling it up in small pieces.

"Freezing." She shivered, looking for the matches. "Here they are," and grabbing one, she struck it on the stove door. "Oh, the kindling. Forgot the wood. Where did the boys put that?" Again searching, she murmured, "Alex forgot to bring it in." Just then she spied the finely split wood in the bucket by the stove.

Shoving a small stick in on top of the paper, she tried again to light it, but the match went out. More paper, she thought and went back to the kitchen. Now where was that? I can't remember! Frustration took over, followed by seething anger as she searched the cupboards.

"Here it is," she screamed, but words came out jumbled and incoherent. "Why would anyone put newspaper in a jar in the cupboard?" Bewildered, she shook her head and took another handful into the living room. Placing it on the simmering log, she watched, fascinated by the tiny flames that licked around the wood and grabbed at the paper.

"Mother, what are you doing?" Josie demanded as she came in the front door. "Oh my God! Mama, are you burning money?"

Startled, her mother shivered. "Freezing! So cold!"

"Mama! You can't burn that!" Josie grabbed the bills out of the flames. The ones she could hang on to were saved. Some, she had to drop back into the flames when they burned her hands and singed the hairs on her arm.

"Ouch!" She dropped one that burned rapidly, sending flames to her thumb. It fell to the rag rug on the floor.

"We have so little money. You can't burn it!" she exclaimed, stomping out the fire. Then Josie tried to grab another one in the stove where only the edge had been burned. In the end, Josie could rescue only nine one-dollar bills. She didn't know how many they had lost. She made a mental note to count the money every day. Her mother was no longer capable of handling their finances.

Later that evening Julianna walked in on the boys, who were talking in hushed tones at the kitchen table.

"...and when I caught Mama, she was almost to the bluff. My God that's dangerous!" Jackie was saying. "Another few steps, and there was an eighty-foot drop-off."

What's he talking about? she wondered. *I never leave this house.* She tried to tell them, but again her words made no sense. Why can't I talk? Her mind swirled and her hands shook. There's something wrong in my head!

"I think the time has come to never leave Ma alone," Ferd spoke slowly, as if feeling the words one at a time.

"That's gonna be difficult." Josie turned from the sink and joined the conversation, wiping the last of the dishes.

"You know, I've got outside chores to do."

"Yes, we will just have to take turns being with Mama. She can help you outside for one thing and when you need some time, one of us men'll watch her."

"*Ja*, we can't expect you to handle the whole burden." Arnold looked at Josie as he talked, but his tone sounded like it was aimed at his brothers.

Julianna couldn't follow who said what. All their words jumbled together, but she heard the word "burden" and that made her anxious and angry. Were they calling her a burden? How dare they! She screamed at them in words she couldn't understand, tears flowing freely down her cheeks. Some dripped off her chin. Josie hurried to her side, talking softly.

Her voice soothed Julianna's anxiety, but her hands still shook. Josie took her by the arm and led her to her bedroom. Julianna knew it was no use to try to talk to her children. They couldn't understand, and somehow she knew she wasn't able to, either.

"MA! MA!" TRACY HEARD IG YELLING FROM THE BARN. What in the world? It's not even midmorning. What is he doing home from school? She hurried out to the porch and peered up the path, watching him run toward her.

"Ma! Cab said Grandma Julianna is sittin' on the Seidls' porch!" His breath came in gulps, and his eyes were bright with fear. His usually perfectly combed hair flew in every direction.

"Wait! Stop! Stop!" Tracy held him at arms' length. "Slow down now. What about Grandma?"

"Cab and John both said it."

"Said what, honey?"

Exasperated, he started over, "Grandmother is sitting on the Seidls' porch. She was there when they got up this morning." The words tumbled out. "Cab's mother told him to tell me right away!"

"Oh my goodness!" Tracy had a lump in her throat as she untied her apron.

"You'd better go back to school. I don't want you to miss any more." Her mind raced. "Tell Cab I'm on my way over there right now."

She fetched her coat and hailed Frank, who came hurrying up the hill, hoe in hand. She repeated what Ig said about Julianna.

"I'm going over right now."

"I'll go with you," Frank said with no hesitation. He rushed to the outdoor pump to wash his hands. Then he grabbed a clean jacket, while Tracy put a wrap on Alec.

They hurried over the hill to the Lampert home and found Josie in the kitchen, her arms in dishwater up to her elbows.

"Josie, Mama's over on the Seidls' front porch."

"No she's not—she hasn't come out of her room yet."

Tracy ran to her mother's room and opened the door. No one was there, but the bed had been slept in.

"Oh my goodness!" Josie's jaw dropped. "I can't believe I didn't check on her."

Chapter 62

EARLY SUMMER 1912

"Tracy said Mama's really sick." Emma sighed as she handed Sophie the letter. "I'm afraid I'm going to have to quit my job and move home to help out." She put her head in her hands, remembering how badly she hated leaving home to work in Portland. Now, leaving the city was unthinkable.

"What about my work with the suffragettes?"

Sophie sat silently reading:

Josie found Mama burning money a few weeks ago. We think she burned almost $10. An amount we desperately need to get us through until harvest. When Josie asked her why she was doing it, she was unable to give a reason. In fact, she often is incapable of speaking in clear sentences.

A few weeks ago, Seidls found her on their front porch when they got up one morning. She's wandering away often. It's hard for the family to watch her constantly. Everyone has been agonizing over how to help her. Ferd thinks that perhaps Father Durrer at St. Joseph might have some answers. I also suggest that you discuss this with Sophie. Perhaps she has a doctor you could see and talk to about Mother...

It was Sophie's turn to shake her head. "Maybe it would be a good idea to walk down to the church." She grimaced and blinked back tears. "How very sad. Your mother is one of my dearest friends." She laid the letter on the end table and studied her folded hands. "I think of her so often."

"She loves you, too." Emma rubbed her forehead and wondered what to do. She wanted to fix it, but some things had no fixes. "Yes," she finally said, "perhaps we should seek Father's counsel. I don't know what else to do."

They had a bit of lunch though Emma wasn't hungry. The rain had stopped by then. Taking their umbrellas, they walked to the church, hoping the priest would be in his office.

Sophie, a member of the Altar Society, had remarked that sometimes the priest visited parishioners and shut-ins on Saturdays. When they arrived, the housekeeper answered their knock and confirmed their fears. "Yes, Father Durrer is out until at least suppertime."

"Maybe Doctor Bell will have a moment to talk to us," Sophie suggested, as they turned to leave the rectory. "He'll probably tell me it's all in her head," she said, a hint of disgust in her voice.

"Frankly, I am afraid that Mama has lost her mind," Emma confirmed. "Remember what Tracy wrote. Mother herself said, '*Something is wrong in my head.*'"

They walked in silence, trying to understand the terrible news. This strong capable woman who now, according to Tracy, was losing her ability to even darn socks, one of the simplest of duties and one she had done scores of times. Emma thought her heart would break. Tears welled several times, but she clenched her fists and would not allow them to erupt.

She gasped as another thought crossed her mind. What will the neighbors think? People thought this kind of affliction was a terrible disgrace. How can we keep this to ourselves? Emma mulled the dilemma, adding it to the stack of sorrow she already carried.

When they arrived at the clinic, they took seats between a man who coughed into a soiled handkerchief and a mother with a sick child on her lap. I hope we don't catch anything bad, Emma thought with a shiver. His breathing reminds me of Papa's and baby Bernard's before they died.

"Sophie, what are you doing here?" Doctor Bell exclaimed when he came out to call in the hacking gentleman. "Are you sick?"

"No, thank goodness, but Emma's mother, who is one of my dearest friends, is very ill. Emma received a letter from home. It said her mother was becoming forgetful. We need your advice."

"If you can wait until I finish with these two people I'll be available. Why don't you go next door to the café and relax. Just come back in thirty minutes." He gave them a sympathetic smile.

"That's a fine idea," Sophie said and rose to leave. Emma followed her with a sigh of exasperation.

"It's only a few minutes. I would enjoy a cup of coffee." Sophie's voice soothed some of Emma's anxiety.

The doctor was just finishing with the child when they returned to the waiting room. They visited quietly to pass the time.

"Now, what can I do to help you?" Dr. Bell asked Emma when they were seated in his sparsely furnished office.

"I don't know what to do, and neither does my family," Emma said, blinking back the tears. "My papa died back in '96, along with my baby brother. Mama raised eight children by herself out in the wilderness, and now this."

He took the envelope she handed him and sat down behind his desk. He pulled out the letter and, putting on the glasses he retrieved from his breast pocket, leaned back and began to read.

Emma strained to hear any tidbit he might have to say, but all she heard was, "Oh my, my..." and "Sad...sad..." She felt her heart being torn out by the roots and was positive she would see a pumping bloody mass spring from her chest at any moment.

Dr. Bell cleared his throat and leaned back in his chair still clutching the letter. "Your mother bore eight children in how many years?" he questioned in a voice gentle.

"Nine children," Emma corrected, wondering why he would ask such a question. "In fourteen years," she added.

He nodded and rubbed his eyes.

"Yes, that might be the cause." He hesitated and continued, "There is some literature suggesting that women who have many babies close in age sometimes lose their mind in later years."

He looked solemn. Emma thought she might have seen a doubt in his eye, but then dismissed it as her imagination.

"Unfortunately, at this time there is no cure for this affliction," he said after what seemed like an eternity. "There is only one suggestion that I can give you." His voice sounded dull and far away.

"What?" Emma held her breath. Her heart lodged firmly in her throat.

Sophie reached for her hand, anticipating the terrible

news that she suspected may be forthcoming.

"Your family is likely going to have to commit your mother to the Oregon State Mental Hospital in Salem."

Emma gasped. She clasped her hand over her mouth, stifling her groans. State Mental Hospital! *Oh mein Gott!*

Sophie's hand tightened. Emma glanced at her mother's friend and saw tears running down her cheeks.

Dr. Bell cleared his throat again and continued. "I would take her to a local doctor if you are unable to bring her in to see me. Maybe there is a physical ailment that is causing her brain to not work correctly. A slight hope, but one we must consider."

Emma nodded, relieved that there may be another answer. Dr. Volp would surely help them find one. She remembered how Mama had told her that he came to the homestead to help her after Ferd was born back in '88. Emma had been three years old at the time, but the incident was on the edge of her memory.

She admired the good doctor since she had heard the story. He had a kindly face and a beautiful black trotter to pull his buggy. She often saw him on the streets of Troutdale when she came home for a visit. He always tipped his hat and waved, but mostly she knew him by reputation. Surely he would know of some cure.

She thought of Mae, the lovely Indian woman who had saved Mama's life during that time, and wondered if Tracy knew of her whereabouts. Perhaps she would have a tribal remedy? Something? Anything? She had been such a wonderful friend to Mama over the years.

Sophie stood, handkerchief in hand, dabbing her eyes, and turned toward the door without speaking. Emma, her brain numb, followed.

"I truly hope someone can help you," Dr. Bell said, looking perplexed.

LATER THAT AFTERNOON, EMMA TOLD HER EMPLOYER, Mrs. Scherhauser, that her mother was very ill and that she was obligated to go home. She had no idea when she would be back.

"I'm so sorry about your mother's illness," Mrs. Scherhauser exclaimed.

"Thank you," Emma answered, unable to explain further. "I guess you will have to find a new nanny for now." She had resigned herself that when she came back she would have to seek other employment.

The next morning she took two valises full of her belongings over to Sophie's for storage, returned, retrieved her last suitcase, and left for the train depot. The brief walk to Sixth and Hoyt took longer than she'd anticipated. Out of breath, she hurried to the ticket booth, hoping there was still room on the next train.

Portland had grown in the last ten years. The population now numbered over 200,000 people. The newcomers increased the crowds in the downtown area and had not gone unnoticed by the locals. Emma felt fortunate that the railroad had added more cars to accommodate the passenger demand. She was able to get a ticket.

Thank God, she thought to herself. That would've been a pretty pickle, if I hadn't been able to get on the early train. I would never have gotten up the hill in the dark, especially with my suitcase and no light.

She left on the 11:35 eastbound train and arrived in Troutdale in early afternoon, then made a beeline to

Dr. Volp's office. She could see him through the window, hunched over at his desk, thin gray hair fringing the bald spot on top of his head. He seemed to be concentrating on paperwork.

Startled by her knock, he responded immediately and invited her in.

"Dr. Volp, I need your help," Emma blurted.

"Are you ill? Please sit down. You do look a little pale."

"No, no! It's not me. It's my mother."

"Mrs. Lampert? Oh my, I didn't realize."

"Yes! She's becoming very forgetful. My family wrote me—she's wandering away from home at night." She felt her eyes filling. "I went to see Dr. Bell in Portland, and he thinks we may have to commit her. He said to have you examine her. Perhaps you would find something else wrong, and you could treat her."

"I'm sorry to hear that, Emma. You are Emma, aren't you?"

She nodded.

"Can you bring her here?" He spoke softly.

"I don't know. I'll find out. I haven't been home yet."

"If she is not able to come to my office, send word, and I'll go up there." He folded his hands around his abdomen and leaned back in his chair. He thought for a moment and said, "Maybe we can find some help for her." He hesitated, then added, "But don't get your hopes up."

She thanked him and left, feeling some better. A little hope is better than none, she thought as she walked down the street to Foxes' store.

Although her heart wasn't in it, she bought a few sundries, hesitating to buy much because her suitcase was already heavy. She paid for the purchases and turned to leave, nearly running headlong into Joseph Marok, who had just come in the door.

"Well, well, who do we have here?" he asked, a smile lighting his face. "I believe I have a passenger riding up the hill with me," he said, eyeing her packages and suitcase.

"Oh! Yes, that would be most helpful." She set her packages down, happy for the offer to lighten her load. She had worried about lugging everything up the hill. Even though Woodard Road was much better and not as steep as the Seidl trail, it was still difficult to climb and muddy this time of year.

Emma celebrated the good fortune of meeting Joseph in Troutdale just at the right time. She bought a large sack of horehound candies for her family and one for Joseph's, two sticks of licorice for Ig and Alec, and a fifty-pound sack of flour that she knew the family could use.

Chapter 63

JULY 1912

"I'm not sure what to do," Tracy said, looking at her hands while reaching for strength. The family's courage, mirrored by Julianna's strength under adversity, had carried them through thus far, and it wouldn't do to break down now.

"Ma, do you know who I am?" Ferd rested his hand on Julianna's arm. After a long moment, he repeated the question.

"Ferd," Julianna said slowly, nodding her head but looking straight ahead, her stare vacant.

"Mama, do you know what Dr. Volp said about your condition?" Emma walked across the room and put her arm around her mother's shoulders.

Julianna showed no reaction, even as the question echoed around the room.

Mein Gott, what are we to do? How can we take Mama off this hill away from her farm? Tracy remembered how fiercely Julianna had protected the homestead, always saying that was what Papa wanted. She told Tracy once that she made a promise to Papa to guard the homestead and had sold bits and pieces of it only when in dire need.

Tracy watched Josie's tears flow freely. She was the one

daughter, after all, who had traveled this journey with their mother. The other three were married or away working in the city.

"Bertie's unable to come home because she's going to have a baby sometime in August," Emma delivered the message when she had arrived. "Apparently it's a difficult pregnancy. Gabe said she isn't able to travel." Excepting Bertie, everyone gathered, speaking with strained faces and soft voices as they discussed their mother's impairment.

As the conversation continued, Jack, saying nothing, rose and walked away. Surprised at first, Tracy remembered that he was a sensitive boy when he was younger. She doubted that he was able to discuss his mother's illness. Never mind, she thought, let him go. I know he'll agree with whatever decision we have to make.

Ig, who idolized his uncle, followed Jack. Little Alec, always in Ig's shadow, toddled after them. Best they go with Jack, Tracy thought. They don't need to hear this.

"You know what both doctors told us," Arnold said, interrupting her thoughts. His voice filled with resignation. "And the letter from Sophie said Father Durrer would give her a blessing, but he agreed with 'whatever the doctors decided.'"

"Mama, what do you think about going to the hospital?" Tracy asked, without much hope of a reply.

The air was thick with anxiety stifling the room. Perspiration ran down Tracy's back. She wondered if it was the heat or this horrible dilemma. Everyone held their breath.

Frank, who had been standing back, now moved closer and stood behind Tracy with his hands on her shoulders. Her hand reached up to find his as they waited.

"Julianna, you can make up your own mind about going to the hospital," Frank said, his voice gentle and caring. "As always, we'll abide by what you decide."

Silence filled the sticky room, punctuated by Josie's sniffs. Julianna, head bowed, moved as if to get up from the chair, reacting to some unseen stimuli. Her vacant stare turned to a look of abject fear. Suddenly she grabbed Emma's arm and jerked hard causing her daughter to lose her balance; although she had done nothing to provoke her mother. Fear turned to fury. She gritted her teeth and slapped at Ferd as he stepped in to help his sister.

"Now, Ma!" he said. "That's no way to treat Emma. She's only trying to make you comfortable." He held her firmly, and his gentle way found its mark.

Hearing his voice settled her down. She always said his voice reminded her of Alex's. Her right hand shook as she set it back in her lap.

"I'll go," Julianna answered. Her voice was plain and clear for an instant, and then she said, "Alex will be there."

A collective sigh filled the room. Hearing her mother's answer, Tracy knew then what she had suspected the last few weeks. Her mother, unable to express herself most of the time, was still here with them for a moment or two at other times.

"Are you sure, Ma?" Arnold asked.

But Julianna's mind was gone again, as quickly as it had returned. Always amazed at the bizarre behavior, they exchanged concerned glances.

"I guess Ma's settled it for us." Ferd mirrored Arnold's resignation. After a moment he said, "I don't think the farm can spare us right now, though. It's the height of the growing season. Maybe we can wait until after harvest."

Silence again dropped on the group as each mulled over their own thoughts and waited for the others' responses. Julianna got up and headed toward the kitchen. Josie pulled her back.

"Yes," Tracy finally agreed. "It would be nice to give her one more summer here on her farm."

"How can we do that?" Josie said, her tone fearful as she finally found her voice and added to the conversation. "Someone has to be with her at all times. It's just too dangerous to leave her alone." She blew her nose and dabbed her eyes as she rose to follow her mother.

"I'll stay home this summer," Emma said. It was obvious that she was trying to look courageous. "We can take turns being with her, and when we need a break, we'll take a turn in the fields so one of the boys can help."

"I think that will work," Tracy said, relieved the decision was finally made. "If Mama's having a good day, she can help with the chores."

"Yes! She can do some simple tasks, but you have to tell her exactly what to do and then work with her," Josie agreed.

"I'll come over and take a turn," Tracy said. "In fact, I'll bring her home with me one day a week, so you can get a day of rest." Worried about Josie, she was anxious to take away some of her burden.

There was one thing Tracy was not going to share right now. Something she hadn't even shared with Frank. She was almost positive that she was again with child and that she would probably be having it sometime in February.

Two weeks later, Bertie sent her regrets in a long letter, telling of her discussion about Julianna with the priest from St. Anthony church. He, too, had said that he would pray for the family, but doubted there was anything the doctors could do for their mother.

Bertie's letter contained serious information about her own condition, too:

> *"I have been flat on my back for three weeks. It is so difficult with a husband and small child to pamper myself like this, but the doctor said it must be done for the good of the baby as well as for myself. I don't know what to do. We have no money to hire help. The baby is not due until August..."*

Tracy read the letter again, folded it, and held it in her lap. "Who's going to help her?" she said after a few moments.

"I think we should send Josie," Emma said without hesitation, glancing over her shoulder at Tracy. "She has not been in the city much, and the change would do her good. I have been worried about her since I've come back." She wiped the drain board as she talked. "She's shouldered most of the burden with Mama."

Tracy nodded. Josie did seem a bit peaked lately. "How are we going to make that work?"

"You and I can take turns."

"I guess we could try," Tracy said, but thought the job was too immense for the plan to work without more help. Especially now that she was fairly certain she was with child.

Emma went to find Josie, and when they returned they found Julianna sitting on the edge of her bed attempting to fold the wash. Tracy sat beside her, carefully redoing each item of clothing and stacking them in separate piles.

"Do you think I really should go help Bertie? I don't

know one thing about childbirth." Josie's face shone with excitement, but her voice sounded unsure.

"That's not what you need to know, Josie. Bertie has a doctor; she just doesn't have a nurse."

"I can do that."

"Of course you can," Emma chimed in. "You've done it for Mama for a long time. This should be easier."

"It'll be good for you to get off the farm for a while," Tracy added, picking up Josie's pile of clothes and handing it to her. "And Bertie will love having you there."

"It seems to me that she gets lonely for her family." Emma paused, then added, "I've seen it in her face when I go visit her."

The sisters spoke in hushed tones, the two older ones sharing advice with the younger. Suddenly, Julianna stood and started for the bedroom door. "No, Mama," Josie said and reached for her arm, but missed.

Tracy moved to block the door, while Emma took Julianna's other arm. "Where are you going, Mama?" Emma asked.

Her answer was incoherent, but when asked again, Julianna indicated that she was going to the kitchen.

"Mama, we can't let you in the kitchen by yourself," Tracy said, taking her hand—the one that had been covered in blisters a few weeks before. For some reason Julianna had opened the door of the cook stove and reached in the fire. No one had the least idea why.

Josie had seen her do it, grabbed her mother, and pulled her back before more damage was done. Josie said she had pumped water over her mother's hand for several minutes. Afterward she had applied lard and wrapped her hand in bandages made from one of the boys' worn-out shirts.

She sent Arnold and the two younger boys to Troutdale to get medicine from Dr. Volp. He told them they were doing the right things and sent home a small bottle of laudanum. He instructed them to give her two drops at a time if she seemed to be in pain.

Julianna rarely complained of discomfort, but once in a while she would jump or say "Ouch!" if someone bumped her hand.

"This," Josie told the family, "proves she can feel pain, but is unable to express it in words." Her voice turned firm when she said, "I decided to give Mother two drops of the medicine three times a day."

"That medicine helps her settle down," Josie added. Both Tracy and Josie were grateful for it, as Julianna would usually nap after a dose and they could get their chores done. "Besides, before I started giving her the medicine, Mama had continually tried to take off the bandages," Josie added.

"The menfolk will have to help when Josie leaves," Emma said, bringing Tracy back to the present dilemma.

"Will they do that?" Josie sounded doubtful.

"Every day one of them will have to find work near the house." Emma obviously had thought this through. "That one will come in and take Mama for a walk so we can cook dinner and then again when we fix supper." Emma thought for a minute and added, "On wash day they will have her most of the day. That way I can get it done. It's been awfully difficult lately."

"I'll have Frank bring our laundry over here. Then we can do it together. That should make it easier," Tracy said.

Josie seemed satisfied with the arrangement, especially when the men agreed. They discussed it at the supper table that evening over a cup of coffee. Ferd's encouraging words, led the rest of them to follow.

Tracy and Frank stayed for the family meeting but worried that this arrangement would be hardest on Emma, who had cultivated friends in the city. She could tell by Emma's face what a sacrifice she had made by encouraging Josie to go to the city.

The next day Jack and Alex, carrying valises, walked Josie to the train while Arnold hitched the team to the cultivator and began to clean out the weeds between the cabbage rows. Ferd took the first turn with his mother. He built the fire under the washtub so Emma and Tracy could wash the clothes.

Chapter 64

AUGUST 1912

Tracy, excited to hear from Josie, tore open the letter that Frank handed her. Reading it slowly while Frank readied the horses, she savored every word.

August 17, 1912
Dear Family

Bertie had a little girl on August 8. You were right. The doctor came to the house and helped her. He was very kind and took good care of her. She had a hard time with the birth. She is quite weak, but says she feels stronger every day.

A shiver ran through Tracy as she read about the birth. Memories of Mama's troubles with her brother Ferd's birth, and tales that she had been told or seen as a midwife, were burned into her mind. Now that she was carrying another child, the familiar fear bubbled up. Tasting it, she swallowed hard.

Then, pushing it to the back recesses of her mind, Tracy continued reading Josie's letter:

The baby's name is Margaret. Most of the time when she was first born she was a good baby, but sometimes she cried very hard. Bertie said she thought her fussiness was because she had a difficult birth, and besides her milk was slow in coming in. The baby is much better now and sleeps a lot.

Gabe is happy I am here. He says I can cook almost as well as Bertie. Little Ferd is such a dear boy. He's got thin, golden hair and the sweetest smile. Sometimes I have to make myself put him down so I can do my chores. Bertie tells me she idolizes our brother Ferd. That's why she named her first son after him. She says not to tell him because pride is not a good thing, especially when it is in her brothers. Then she laughed.

Now that Bertie is recuperating, I think she'll be able to go to Mass with us tomorrow. I am happy that St. Anthony is so close. It's just kitty-corner from where Bertie lives, across Holgate Street. Bertie would never be able to attend so soon if the church were farther away. I could not have imagined living so near a church.

I worry about Mama and everyone out on the hill, but Bertie is begging me to stay awhile longer. She says I'm a godsend when it comes to helping with Ferd and the baby. I must say, I am enjoying them.

The other day Gabe took us all for a ride in his automobile. I thought it was great fun, but Bertie thinks he drives too fast. She says it scares her. I'm sure it's because she's still not strong.

When Tracy finished reading the letter to herself, she read

it aloud to Frank. He finished watering the horses and was sitting beside her, reins in hand as they rode in their wagon up the hill toward home. They had left little Alec and Ig with Emma and traveled to Troutdale for supplies for both households and picked up a load of rough-cut lumber from the mill. Frank needed it to fence in a lane up to the new pasture.

"Josie writes a fine letter," Frank commented when she was done. "It sounds like you girls were right: the change is good for her."

Tracy nodded and thought for a moment. "She seems fond of the children. Perhaps when they get a little older they can come out to the country and spend some time. Maybe if I write to Josie about that, she'll feel better about leaving them."

Comfortable in each other's company, they could discuss what might be called the mundane things of life. Tracy purposely didn't bring up her mother's plight. It seemed over the past few months they had talked it to death and had nothing left to say.

Still, she dreaded the inevitable, and Frank shared her feelings. There was no need to go into the situation again. The fact is, she thought, Mama is getting worse by the moment. She could hurt herself badly or could hurt someone else.

Frank had promised to travel with her to take her mother to the asylum. Still, she couldn't help feeling terrible about it. She wondered if there were anywhere else at all they could take her. A place that would care for her, yet not force her to be around insane people. Mama's not crazy, she thought. It's just that she had so many babies so close together and she had to work so hard.

Word somehow got to Mae, the Indian woman who had saved Julianna when Ferd was born, and she stopped to see the family. She was older now, with more wise lines in her face and more silver in her hair.

Seeing Julianna made tears come to her eyes, and she told them that she knew of no herb or medicine that would bring their mother back to them. When she left, she held Julianna and said foreign words in her ear. They knew, somehow, that it was a native blessing, and it made them all feel better.

Chapter 65

EARLY SEPTEMBER 1912

Josie grabbed the side of the passenger door and, pulling up her skirt, stepped gingerly off the train. She reached for the two valises, now even heavier than when she'd left home two months ago.

"Need help with that?" a deep baritone voice came from behind her. Startled, she dropped the heavy valise she was trying to pull off the train and whipped around, almost falling headfirst into a white shirt. The sleeves, rolled up to the elbow, displayed sinewy strong arms. Her eyes moved up to the open collar and still farther to the face of the tallest, most handsome man she had ever seen. Even in Portland in church she had not seen anyone like him. His square jaw and intelligent green eyes left her speechless.

"Here, let me get that," he said. His voice resonated, reminding her of the deep mellow tones of a cello solo she had heard long ago when visiting Emma in Portland.

She stood, trying to find words, while he busied himself gathering her things. When he handed her the purse she had laid down while wrestling her suitcases, she saw that he had larger hands than most men; he easily picked up her belongings and turned to walk off the loading dock. Then he hesitated.

"I'm sorry, I didn't introduce myself. I'm Frank Fehrenbacher." He stopped and looked at her as he spoke. "I'm thinking you are Josie Lampert, since you were the only young woman to get off the train."

She managed a nod and, taking a deep breath, asked, "How do you know my name?"

"My family moved up on the hill about a quarter of a mile from your people. Your brother-in-law, Frank Wand, is helping us build our house. When he found out I was coming to Troutdale today, he asked me to meet your train and bring you home." He paused and readjusted his grip, moving the heaviest suitcase to help balance his load. "We have to get that house up before the snow flies."

She nodded again, wishing something would come out of her mouth and hoping that if something did, it would make sense.

"We just moved here a month back. We lived in Portland for a while, but we all missed the country. Guess we just don't like city life." With his long stride, she found herself running to keep up.

"Where did you come from before that?" Josie asked, relieved to hear her voice. He looked at her again and grinned. She wasn't sure whether he was teasing or just proud of himself for getting her to talk.

"Up east. A place called Early, Oregon, on the John Day River south of Rufus."

"I don't know where that is."

"It's southeast of The Dalles about thirty miles as the crow flies." He smiled and added, "It's up in the hot, dry country."

Josie remembered Mama telling the story of the family trip with the Frommelts up the Columbia on a steamboat, and how they had stayed at that beautiful hotel in The Dalles. She thought about the description Mama gave about the crazy riverboat captain and how he had taken the steamboat Harvest Queen over Celilo Falls.

"Yes, I've heard of that town." She brushed a sweaty piece of hair from her eyes, wishing she'd brushed it before she got off the train. "Have you ever heard of Celilo Falls?"

"Oh yes!" he exclaimed. "It's a magnificent place. The river's so loud it sounds like thunder. You can hear it before you see it."

"I've wanted to see it ever since I can remember."

As they walked to the waiting wagon, she told him about the boat trip her family had taken when she was an infant. And that she'd heard about the amazing fishing grounds all her life. When she finally found her voice, her words tumbled out, like a steamboat whistle when the captain pulls on the rope multiple times.

Frank, his muscles bulging, easily threw the valises up into the loaded wagon. When he reached to help her onto the seat, Josie had already scrambled aboard. She could see that impressed him. Besides, she needed to send the message that she and her sisters were suffragettes and were able to do for themselves—except, of course, when it came to hauling those heavy suitcases up that steep hill.

"Well, here we are," Frank said, as he pulled the horses to a stop.

Excited to be home, Josie had mixed feelings when Frank turned the horses through the gate into the homestead. She enjoyed his warmth and humor.

"Yes! Thank you!" she said, but didn't have another moment to dwell on her thoughts, as Jack and Alex hustled out to the wagon.

"Come, sis! We'll get your bags." Jack's face mirrored her joy to see them.

"Yeah, we've missed you," Alex said, his usual deep voice sounding even deeper.

She allowed them to help her down while Frank unloaded the suitcases and the supplies that Emma had on her list.

"Thank you for bringing these," Emma said, appearing from inside the house. She had left Julianna sitting on the front porch in bewilderment.

It only took one glance for Josie to see the deterioration in her mother as she ran to greet her. Julianna lowered her head when Josie reached to embrace her; not a sign of recognition flickered across her countenance.

"Mama! It's Josie! I've come home with news of Bertie and her baby." Tears rushed to Josie's eyes, but she tried to speak without the frustration and sadness she felt.

"Josie?" Julianna murmured, her voice confused and disoriented.

"Yes, Mama! A nice young man drove me up from the train."

A second of awareness flashed in Julianna's eyes. "Josie, *du bist zu Hause*."

"*Ja, Ja, Mutter*! I'm home!" She hugged her mother, gasping with disbelief at the fragile thin body in her arms. Over Julianna's shoulder, her eyes met Emma's, and Josie knew the time to take her mother away was nearing.

Then, just as quickly, Julianna's mind left again. She turned toward the house muttering unintelligible phrases in her own language. Wringing her hands, she stood and paced the floor. Josie watched in disbelief, until she could stand no more and turned to see Mr. Fehrenbacher climbing onto his wagon.

"Thank you!" Josie waved to Frank as he clucked the reins and headed over the hill past the Wand place.

He lifted his hand in a wave, tipped his hat, and was on his way.

"Handsome, isn't he?" Emma spoke quietly. Neither of them dared to alert their brothers to that fact or the teasing would never stop.

"Oh, my! Yes," Josie whispered. "Very!"

Chapter 66

LATE SEPTEMBER 1912

Tracy

"I'm not sure how we should do this." Tracy arose and brought the coffeepot to the table. Frank and she always enjoyed a quiet midday meal together in the rare times they found themselves alone. Emma had come over earlier and taken Alec home with her for a few hours, declaring, "I need some child time. It's Jackie's turn to see to Mother."

With Ig at school, Tracy and Frank found themselves together in the silence. She wished they didn't have this terrible decision hanging in the air and resented the intrusion. Yet somehow she was glad to have a time for discussion when neither of them was so tired that it was an effort just to find their way to bed.

"How should we do what?" Frank poured a bloop of hot coffee into the saucer and blew gently on it to cool it down.

"Mama." She spoke matter-of-factly, but feeling anything but nonchalant. "I guess we will just take her to Salem by train."

"That sounds like the most obvious way." He carefully lifted the saucer to his mouth and took a gulp.

"But it's so hard to do."

This was one of the times she found his quiet ways annoying. She needed his input. Somewhere in her core she wanted him to tell her everything was going to be all right. That Mama would soon be well. She sighed, knowing that was something he could not do.

Julianna, now nonfunctional, had many of the neighbors not only thinking she was crazy, but that the whole family was teetering on the edge. The worst offender seemed to be Caroline, Alex's distant cousin who had never approved of Julianna, and whom Frank continued to visit. He insisted it wasn't Caroline he talked with, but her son, Julius, who was his good friend. He often took Ig and Alec when he visited because he knew Caroline was fond of the boys.

Tracy brushed away the negative feelings, silently scolding herself. I'm being terrible! Caroline isn't so bad; she just doesn't understand. It's probably a good thing that Frank talks to her. Someone has to keep the lines of communication open. It struck Tracy that her husband, a man of very few words, was the family ambassador.

"What are the neighbors going to say when they find out Mama's insane?" she spoke after another pause.

"Losing her mind doesn't make her insane."

"I know that, but the neighbors don't seem to realize it."

He was silent, while she sat staring out of the window, trying to make sense of the feelings roiling inside her. How should one proceed? How does someone put their mother in an asylum? Who can help sort out the answers?

She reread the postcard that Emma had brought over earlier. When she handed it to Tracy, Emma said, "I wanted to get this to you this morning so Ig can tell the children at school today. I swear that's the easiest way to get the word out about church."

Tracy reread it again. It was addressed to Julianna Lampert, and the postmark read September 26, 1912. The new priest wrote that he would be at the Lampert home for Mass and confession the following Sunday. Maybe, just maybe, he was the one with some answers. She could only hope.

"I will discuss this with Father Martin next Sunday." She seemed to blurt the words, but she hadn't meant to.

Frank took a last swallow from his cup and set it back into the now empty saucer.

"That's a good idea." He reached for another gingersnap.

"I'm going to discuss it with him while he's hearing my confession," she announced. "I don't know if that is immoral or not, but I'm not going to have the neighbors listening in on the conversation."

She clamped her lips tightly shut, took in a deep breath and, as an afterthought, said, "I'm annoyed that some of the children already try to hear what the adults say to the priest."

"I've seen that, too." Frank sounded indignant. "I'll go over there before next weekend and fix a quiet place in the barn for confessions." He gave her a sympathetic look, and after a moment added, "I'll stand outside while people are in with Father."

Rising from the table, he bent over and kissed her on the cheek as he reached for his cap. Her concerns left momentarily as she patted his arm and thanked him for his help.

Frank hurried his pace on his way to help Ferd and Arnold. Earlier he had found his yearling heifer caught in the barbed wire fence and freed her. He had dabbed some kerosene on her wounds, fed her, and left her in the loafing shed near the water trough.

Now, much later than he wanted to leave, he headed over the hill to Julianna's home. They had a small leak in the barn roof that he'd promised to patch, and then he planned to build that confessional.

He found it amusing to have something as holy as a confessional in the barn and laughed out loud, startling a gray digger that had been hiding in the branch of a vine maple along the trail. The little squirrel reminded him of home and how much he missed his family.

But he had his own family now, and in many ways, that was even better. Still, he wanted to go back to Illinois someday, at least for a visit. He worried about his own mother, now that Papa was gone.

Listening to the little varmint chatter, he remembered Christ was born in a stable. Not much difference, he mused as he planned the makeshift confessional for the following Sunday. Well, maybe it is.

The priest usually got to the house before ten o'clock on the Sunday mornings when he visited the small enclave of Catholics on the hill and heard confessions until eleven. Then he closed up and said Mass in the living room, or if it wasn't raining, outside under the shade of the cherry tree in the front yard.

Frank remembered how excited Julianna always was to hear the news that Mass would be at the Lamperts'. Having the priest in her home was a great honor. She and the girls cleaned and cooked for days. He doubted there would be much change in that routine now with Julianna's illness, because both Josie and Emma kept a nice house.

He stopped and switched the strap on his toolbox from his right to his left shoulder. Even though the Lamperts had a nice array of tools, he was more comfortable working with his own. Something about the balance of his hammer and the true of his saw.

His thoughts went back to the conversation he and Tracy had yesterday about Julianna's fate. His stomach curled and knotted with the thought of her sickness. For some reason he was unable to confide in Tracy about how difficult it was for him to see Julianna like this, and how hard to see Tracy in such pain with the decisions about her mother.

Although he was loath to admit it, he knew Caroline and the newer neighbors talked among themselves, clucking their tongues and shaking their heads over the fate of the Widow Lampert. He did his best to tell them, whenever the chance came up, how well she was doing. "Much better than expected!" Then he would try to smile reassuringly.

But he could see they didn't believe him, and at some level he did not care. They had no business disparaging Julianna. He knew her to be a bright, witty woman who had run the farm and raised her family as best as any widow could. While he lived and worked on the place he'd come to know her and to rely on her knowledge of the weather and her experience in the farming practices of the area.

Deep in thought, he heard a soft cry and turned to see who was on the trail behind him. When he saw no one there, he realized the sound had come from him. *Why would God do this to the family he had come to love and admire?*

"I'm sorry, my dear," said Father Martin, his voice soft. Tracy felt she could speak to him about this matter because of his gentle kindness. "I see that your Mother is very ill." The look in his eyes told of the unspoken pain he had seen over the years; perhaps his own? Tracy wondered but couldn't be sure.

"Yes, she is very bad now. We can't leave her alone for a moment. Josie caught her burning money some time ago." She paused, studying the shaft of light coming through the crack in the barn door. Watching the dust particles swirl, she added, "And you can understand what a problem the lack of money has been for us over the years."

He nodded, showing his thinning gray hair and the grime from the trail on his collar. For an instant she felt sorry for him; his was a lonely life in many ways, yet he shepherded many souls.

"Whatever are we to do?" she asked, fearing the answer, yet a part of her welcoming the weight that she hoped would be lifted from her heart.

"You told me you were going to speak to Dr. Volp last time I saw you. Did you do that?"

Tracy sat transfixed, hardly daring to answer the question.

"Well?" he asked again after a few moments, his voice calm and gentle.

"He said she needed to be in the asylum." She shuddered. "How can we do that to our own mother?" Her words were barely audible.

Taking her hand in both of his, he leaned forward and softly said, "Just last month my friend Father Wolfgang had to help his family put his mother in the Salem hospital."

Father shook his head as if he couldn't believe what he had just said. "She was the mother of thirteen children. That is the cause Dr. Steiner gave him when he talked to the head of the hospital down there."

Tracy shivered. "I have heard that, too. Do you believe it?"

"Too many children and too much work is usually the cause of dementia in women. That is the belief of the medical community." He straightened up and looked out at some unseen thing and added, "Lots of men are committed because of excessive alcohol and mania." He paused again and added, "Some women have those problems, too, but I doubt your mother is one of them."

"No, she rarely has a glass of wine, even when the rest of us are enjoying a drink. She often said she wished wine tasted more like the beer her father brewed in Germany when she was a girl."

Just then the life in her moved, and she touched her extended belly before she realized what she was doing.

They sat in silence, listening to the neighbors' children play on the grass by the house. Tracy wondered what else to ask. Her mind ran down the list she had prepared and thought she had memorized. For the life of her she couldn't think of anything. She chastised herself for forgetting something as important as this. Her family depended on her to get answers from the priest.

"We don't know how to do this, Father," she finally said. "I had several things I wanted to ask you, and now I have forgotten." She fought back the tears.

He took her hand once again and said, "I would like to stay after everyone leaves and talk to your whole family. I think we need to have every adult present, including your mother."

Tracy nodded, thankful once again for his kindness and worried about her own forgetfulness.

MASS WAS FINISHED JUST AFTER NOON, AND WITH THE

neighbors help, dinner was ready shortly thereafter. Earlier, the men had put boards on sawhorses to create the outside table, and soon everyone was seated on the benches that surrounded it.

"In the name of the Father, the Son, and the Holy Ghost," Father said, sitting at the head of the table and making the sign of the cross. "Bless us our Lord, for these thy gifts..."

Soon everyone was chatting amid the passing of the food, trying to keep it all going one way, while dishing their own and their children's plates.

It was a time Tracy usually enjoyed, catching up with local news and renewing friendships, but now it was different. The weight of her mother's illness, as well as the memory of Katherine's ailing and death, tugged at her. She feigned lightheartedness.

Best friends, her mother and Katherine had gone through so much together. She remembered the last time Katherine sat like this with her family after Mass. She and Julianna sat together visiting quietly, reminiscing. Katherine, with worry lines and deep sunken eyes, seemed to thrive under Julianna's quiet laughter. The thought came to Tracy that these two knew, at some level, that it was the last time they would be able to share in health.

After they'd bid the neighbors goodbye, Father sat down with the family surrounding him and told them the story of Father Wolfgang and his mother. His kindly words and the fact they were not alone with this problem brought a kind of peace to Julianna's family.

"These are nothing but rags." Emma held up a dingy chemise with one loose strap and a hole ripped in the back.

"I know," Tracy said, shaking her head. "I've been worried about Mama's clothes for a long time. I am glad you're home to help us."

"That's mine." Julianna reached toward Emma while trying to grab the undergarment with her other hand.

Emma pulled it away and shook her head. "Yes, Mama, it's yours. We just want to fix it."

Josie came through the door just in time to hear them. "There's nothing I can do about the mending. I just don't have time to do it, let alone sew, with all the housework," Josie said, her face pouty and her voice on edge.

"Yes, we understand, Josie. It's no one's fault. Everyone's busy," Tracy said as she reached to distract her mother, "and the truth is, none of us wanted to admit anything was wrong with Mother." Tracy drew a deep breath. She had rarely seen Josie so dejected and was surprised at how down-in-the-dumps it made her feel. Josie was the one who always laughed. She's the one who made everyone feel better.

"Josie, it's all right. We know how much you do, and everyone appreciates it, especially your cooking, even if nobody says much. If you notice, they all eat it and ask for more," Emma said, quietly slipping into the conversation. "Why don't you take Mama out to the kitchen and find a chore for her? Tracy and I'll go through her things and see what needs to be done. We can spend some time this evening discussing Mother's clothes once we look them over."

"Well, we don't even know if Mama has to go away," Josie sniffed and took her mother's hand.

"I'm afraid it's inevitable." Emma, the pragmatic one, uttered with resignation. Her ability to cut through layers and get to the heart of the matter amazed Tracy.

"Tomorrow I'll have Frank take us down to visit Dr. Volp," Tracy said. "He would have done it today, but he had to get the vegetables ready for Joseph to take up to Palmer."

"I'll stay home with Mama and do some housework. Josie, you go with Tracy. I think it will do you good. Besides, I can see you have questions," Emma said, her voice steeped in resolve.

Tracy knew Emma had made up her mind and was waiting for the rest of the family to catch up. She was almost there herself, after watching her mother as she seemed to dissolve before her very eyes. It was obvious she would need skilled care.

But Tracy kept the thoughts to herself. Josie was upset enough. Instead she held up what was once her mother's Sunday white bonnet, now stained, with part of the front torn and only one tie string attached. "Huh," she muttered. "Unrepairable."

The next morning Tracy hauled the last of the sliced apples up to the attic and spread them on a clean sheet to dry while Frank milked and did the chores. *When these dry, we should have just over a bushel*, she thought, satisfied that would be enough to see them through the winter.

Just as she came down the stairs, Frank entered the kitchen and announced that Queenie was hooked up and ready. He hurriedly changed his shirt, and soon they were on the trail to pick up Josie.

By 8:30 they were making their way down the road to Troutdale. Tracy thought about how many times they had walked down the steep trail, and she thanked the Lord they now had a wagon, a strong horse, and in the summer a decent road. She thought about how difficult it was to walk that far when she had been carrying Ig—and her time hadn't been as near then as it was now. Her hand automatically went to her abdomen.

Quickly she grabbed the front of the seat as they came to the steepest part of the road. She watched as Frank held the brake handle with one hand and pulled back on the reins with the other. The baby kicked furiously, not liking the bumpy ride one bit.

They came to the first platform, where the horse rested and the baby calmed. There were three platforms the neighbors built a year or so ago after deciding that the horses needed a place to rest when climbing the steep hill. The platforms actually helped going both ways—especially the middle one, where there was a spring-fed watering trough.

Tracy was frightened of the steep, windy road and was happy when they reached the bottom of the bluff, where it flattened out and followed the Sandy River as it meandered toward the end of its journey into the Columbia. Fresh air filled her nostrils with pungent fragrances of river, with smells of buckbrush, and salmonberry bush here and there. The dew on the bright orange berries sparkled when the sun hit them just the right way.

She relaxed and, glancing back at Josie, smiled as she saw her sitting in the wagon bed holding Alec. Josie pointed at the river and whispered a secret into the toddler's ear. He giggled and jabbered something inaudible. Child and aunt were content in each other's company as they turned and crossed the new bridge.

Near ten o'clock they pulled up in front of Dr. Volp's office. "It doesn't look like he is in there," Frank murmured as he climbed down from the wagon. "I'll check." Walking over to the door, he hollered back, "The note says he'll be back by noon."

"It's a good time to pick up the supplies we need," Josie said. The relief in her voice reminded Tracy of how a convict must feel when he's just been granted a stay of execution. The realization of how much dread hung over this moment hit Tracy like an icy shower on a cold day.

"I HAVE A LETTER HERE FROM THE SUPERINTENDENT'S office at the Oregon State Insane Asylum. It's a form letter really. I saw one like it several years ago."

Dr. Volp paused and met Josie's eyes. She hoped they didn't betray her. She couldn't bear to break down in front of him.

"How did they know?" A flash of anger flew across Tracy's face. "We haven't authorized anything."

"I'm sorry, but your mother's confinement is inevitable. There is no way you can keep her safe where she is now." The doctor spoke softly with conviction, but his face belied his tone. After a moment he said, "You know, I never get used to this. It's exceedingly hard—maybe harder than death." Again he paused, and with eyes narrowing, said, "At least in death, you know it's final." And with that he clenched his jaw and, blinking his eyes, turned his face away.

"Thank you for your kind sympathy, Doctor," Josie said, fighting successfully to keep her tears at bay.

"Yes, it does help," Tracy agreed.

"So tell us, Doc, what does the letter say?" Frank asked, taking Tracy's hand.

Chapter 67

THE LETTER

28 August, 1912
Dr. Heinrich Volp
Physician & Surgeon
Troutdale, Oregon

Dear Dr. Volp,

In regards to your letter dated 03 August 1912, which discussed Mrs. Julianna Lampert's mental condition, I am happy to relate to you that we will have room to place her in Ward 44 of Building J by the third week of October.

As to your question of facility overcrowding, the near completion of the Dome building on the hospital grounds will relieve some of that. The state is also building the new Eastern Oregon State Hospital in Pendleton which should be open later next year. We will be transferring some patients up to that facility. There is a possibility that Mrs. Lampert will be one of those transferred. In that case, the family would be notified.

Please advise, do we need the sheriff to escort Mrs.

Lampert from her home to Salem?

Yours very truly,
Dr. R.E. Lee Steiner
Superintendent
Oregon State Insane Asylum

Dr. Volp read the letter, his voice quiet, deliberate. He didn't hesitate, even when he read about the sheriff escorting her mother and heard the soft cry that escaped Josie's lips.

"No need to worry," he said when he finished reading. "It's perfectly fine for family members to take their loved ones down to the hospital."

"Yes, we can do that." Tracy unconsciously clenched her fists and glanced at Frank, who nodded. She noticed the doctor had carefully chosen the word *hospital* in place of *asylum*.

"I know how hard this is for you, but please remember that the hospital has a policy of kindness toward the patients. Dr. Steiner's goal is to cure everyone in his care, and from what I have heard, he does his best to make that happen."

Dr. Volp took a breath, looked at his hands, and said, "I don't want to give you false hope, but every year some of the patients do get well and are released."

"Do you suppose Mama could get well?" Josie spoke up.

Tracy noticed Frank running his finger around his collar. He had little beads of perspiration on his forehead, relaying the message that he doubted her mother would ever recover. She knew it to be true and was pretty sure most of the rest of the family did, too.

"They have lots of activities for both patients and staff," the doctor continued. "I hear they have dances regularly, for one thing."

"Dances! Mother once told me she loves to dance!" Josie exclaimed, her voice excited.

"I'm not sure she could do it anymore," Tracy remarked quietly. "But I know she might like to watch."

"Yes, I believe she would," Frank finally spoke up. "I believe she would at that." He smiled softly and met Tracy's eyes.

THE WAGON HIT ANOTHER RUT AND BOUNCED WILDLY. Arnold pulled back on the reins, his face dripping sweat. Julianna hung on tightly and frowned. Why had they put her in the wagon? She had heard one of the children say they were going to the hospital. Was somebody sick? And for heaven sake, why were they taking her rocking chair?

"Sick?" she asked, and tried to ask who, but the sounds came out jumbled.

Unable to form words, her anger seethed, and she felt the tears come.

No one answered her. Everyone looked solemn, even Arnold who was usually lively and funny. She remembered Josie crying when they left, and she vaguely wondered why. Jackie and Alex had kissed her—something neither had done for years.

Her agitation rose as she tried to talk and no one seemed to pay any attention. It was as if she were imprisoned in a glass room, screaming, scratching at the enclosure, and couldn't make herself heard.

When they arrived at the Troutdale depot, Ferd helped

her down, guided her to the ticket office, and sat her on the bench outside the window facing the tracks.

"Stay here, Mama," he commanded. "We need to get tickets and check your rocker through."

How dare he tell me to stay put when everyone else has left? But her thoughts made no sense. She started to get up to find her children, but a lady appeared out of nowhere, came over, and sat down beside her.

"Mama, we are going to take you to a hospital where they can help you with your mind."

Julianna briefly wondered why the lady looked and sounded like Tracy, but seemed upset. Mind? Julianna, struggled to get the words out, but they didn't sound right. Angry, she tried with all her might, one last time, and the entire sentence spewed out, words coherent: "There's something bad in my head."

"Yes, Mama, there is something wrong with your mind. We hope they can help you." The way the lady who looked like her daughter said it told Julianna she should believe it, but she didn't.

When Julianna tried to answer her this time, her tongue twisted and would not let her. But then something told her this person was indeed Tracy and that calmed her.

As Tracy watched her mother struggle, resentment crept around the edges of her soul. Why? Why must Mama battle daily just to keep her dignity? Guilt often washed over her when she wondered why her mother couldn't just pass away and join Papa.

Out of the corner of her eye, she noticed a couple at the west end of the platform waiting for the train. The woman, dressed in a stylish bonnet and a light brown jacket, whispered something to the gentleman, and they both turned and stared.

Tracy felt her face burn and, holding her head higher, tilted her chin. How dare they look down on us? I try to keep Mama looking nice, but it seems I cannot hide her uncomely demeanor. She glanced at Julianna, who was pointing at something in the distance, while jabbering incoherently. She can't help it, Tracy thought. Why should she be shamed? Why should any of us be shamed? She patted her mother's hair down and straightened her collar.

"There now, Mama, you look beautiful," she said, wishing it so, as she watched her mother's vacant stare and heard gibberish coming from her lips.

She instinctively put her arm around her mother's waist and realized how much she had shrunk over the last couple of years. She seemed to be getting smaller in front of their eyes. Tracy didn't know why, because she still had a good appetite, but Frank's hand could encircle Mama's upper arm almost completely, his thumb and forefinger almost touching. Maybe it was because she had taken to pacing the floor and moving constantly. Even now, Mama's fingers worked the edge of her jacket, as if touch was the only sense not foreign to her, or perhaps the only one left.

Soon a second couple joined the pair at the end of the platform, and once again they turned to look in their direction. She glanced at her mother's glazed eyes engulfed in a sense of helplessness. Suddenly she had an overwhelming desire to give those haughty passengers a piece of her mind. Just as she began to rise from the bench, Ferd appeared in front of them, as if on cue, with tickets in hand.

"Arnold's going to stay here until we're safely on the train," he said, oblivious to the scene playing out in front of him. "He just put the chair on the baggage car."

"What's going on, Tracy?" Frank asked, as he and Arnold came from watering the horses.

He can always see right into my soul, she thought, a bit irritated. Why can't I keep any thoughts to myself? There are some things that even a husband shouldn't know, but God help me, that man always does.

"Those people over there," she said, deliberately pointing to the small group waiting. "They remind me of Caroline and the other neighbors that say Mother is to blame for her illness. She would never ask for anything like this."

"They are not worth worrying over, Sis," Arnold said in a curiously somber tone. "They have no idea about what Ma or any of us have been through. Everyone gets something, someday. One day they'll have something bad too. I know we've had our trying moments, but all in all, I think our family has handled this as well as we possibly could."

Surprised, Tracy looked at her brother as if she had never seen him. His usual laughing eyes had a new kindness in them, much different than the happy-go-lucky lad he always seemed to be. She wondered if this sadness had changed them all. She knew her little brother was right. Still, she had to push down the impulse to go over and slap those people right off the platform.

As she tried to settle her emotions, she realized her feelings bubbled up rapidly and were so raw that she was surprised she could keep them repressed. She thanked God that when one family member seemed likely to lose all control, the other siblings' love was there to give them strength and guidance. For the first time in several months, she was genuinely happy about the coming birth of her third baby. This was the gift of family she was giving her children.

Julianna moved, mumbling something inaudible, and Tracy instinctively knew she was about to get up and pace. How much did her mother understand of the conversation? Where was she? Sometimes she knew her mother was in there, and sometimes she had no idea where her mind had wandered. Was she smelling the wild currant blooms in the May woods or walking along the bluff looking down at the Columbia as she used to love to do? Tracy didn't know what her mother was thinking. She wished with all her heart she did.

Frank sat with his arm around Julianna as the train wended its way south through the broad expanse of the Willamette Valley.

"Why don't you two stretch your legs?" he said to Tracy and Ferd. "You've been tending to your mother all morning."

"Yes, I would like to move a bit," Tracy said, tossing him a grateful look.

"Come on, Sis." Tracy's pregnancy was evident now, so Ferd took her arm, helping her from the seat. "We can go to the diner car. I could use a cup of coffee." As they started to leave, he turned and asked Frank, "Want us to bring you one?"

"No, when you get back, I'll get one." Looking at his mother-in law, he added, "Why don't you bring Ma back a cup? She may like it." Although it was difficult to tell what she wanted, he remembered the many times they shared ideas and coffee as they sat at the kitchen table: When to seed? Was it time to plant the second crop? Should they buy another cow or just breed ol' Bossy for this year?

They discussed most of the farm management while sharing leftover *Kuchen* and sipping the thick black liquid they called coffee. She liked it as strong as he did. He remembered her once, in a rare moment, thanking him for introducing her to coffee and saying how much it helped her get through the long days. She had laughed then, remembering how badly she hated it growing up.

The memory somehow lightened his load as he watched the brother and sister disappear behind the closed coach door. Habit compelled him to glance at Julianna. She was still fussing with her buttons and mumbling incoherently, but for the moment seemed comfortable enough.

He watched the countryside fly by admiring the flat ground and a well-kept farm that came into view and quickly left. Although he could see the Cascades in the distance, the wide, level expanse of the Willamette Valley made him think of places back home in Illinois, where the flat lay of the land made it perfect to turn a furrow.

The memory brought to mind his family and how different it must be back home without Papa. He thought about the difficulties Julianna faced when she lost Alex, and he was grateful his siblings were grown by the time his own mother found herself widowed.

In her last letter, his sister Lizzy told him the family was considering selling the farm and moving into nearby Elizabeth. He was happy to hear the news and hoped the sale would be soon. He felt some guilt about not being there. Mostly he was worried about how his brothers were managing the land without either him or Papa.

Julianna stirred. Her attempt to rise off the bench startled him back to the present and, with it, the pain of this trip. "Where're you heading, Julianna?" he asked as he gently pulled her back down on the seat.

Her words were incoherent, as she pointed anxiously toward the door.

He shook his head and assured her that Ferd and Tracy would return soon. In an effort to distract her, he pointed out the window to a farmhouse nestled in a grove of large oak trees with a wide swath of productive fields surrounding it.

"Look," he said. "There's a nice farm."

"No, Alex," Julianna said, the words clear and crisp, followed by intonations, but nothing more she said made sense. She continued anxiously trying to rise out of her seat and head toward the door. Frank, startled to hear her mistake him for her dead husband, tried to soothe her while keeping her beside him. After a moment she ceased struggling, but her anxiety became more uncontrollable as tears streamed down her cheeks.

Her shoulders shook as she blurted, *"Alex, bring mir das Baby!"* The command was clear and distinct, leaving no doubt that at times she was coherent, though confused.

Instinctively he put his arm around her. "No, Julianna, the baby's fine." He gentled his voice, and the softness seemed to calm her. His heart raced when Julianna once again called him Alex. *Mein Gott,* he thought, this poor woman is in a private hell.

As soon as Tracy and Ferd returned, Frank, shaken, headed for the smoker car and lit his pipe. He quieted himself and began to enjoy the peace. He now realized again what an impossibly exhausting job it had been for the family to care for their mother in her illness.

After some calming moments, he returned to the family

just as the train entered the Salem city limits. Frank briefly related what had happened and what her mother had said.

"I was very small when Mama and Papa brought me to Portland by train," Tracy said and wiped a tear.

"That explains it." Frank took her hand. "There's a certain sense to it now. Julianna remembers when the three of you came West on the train," he said, marveling at finding a speck of lucidity in the mass of discord.

In a short time, the train pulled into the depot. Grabbing Julianna's two grips, the men stepped off as soon as the train came to a stop. Frank reached to help Tracy, who had one hand on her swollen belly, while Ferd took his mother's arm, guiding her down the steps. Leaving Tracy with her mother, Frank retrieved the rocking chair.

"Where do we catch the city trolley to the insane asylum?" Frank asked the conductor.

The official directed him to the sign indicating the depot office. "There's where you buy your tickets," he said. "They will tell you where to go."

SOON THE TROLLEY, CARRYING SEVERAL PASSENGERS—and the rocking chair and other luggage secured on the roof—crossed Mill Creek and made its way out of Salem to flat open country. In less than an hour, they stopped in front of a grassy park-like area with a grove of tall, bronze-leafed native oak trees.

A few benches scattered here and there across the greenway looked like they were flung out by some giant hand. Most were empty, save for one near the gate. A lone man sat smoking a long curved pipe, his collar pulled up around his ears to ward off the autumn chill. He ignored the trolley and stared into space.

The people disembarked in front of a gate under a tall white trellis. It stood nobly, a weak attempt at cordially welcoming the inmates. Frank smiled to himself and mused about the irony of it all.

An orderly in a horse-drawn cart pulled up and loaded all the suitcases and Julianna's chair onto the wagon, then headed toward the back of the building while the trolley driver indicated the passengers should enter the gate.

The trail led under the arched arbor to a large, stately three-story brick building on the other side of the park. The foursome, along with a dozen other people, walked the shaded path. Ferd went first with his arm around his mother's shoulders. Frank and Tracy, her arm linked in his, followed silently. *Interesting*, Frank thought. *All these people, and the only sound is the quiet padding of feet and the occasional crackle of a kicked dried leaf.*

When they came closer to the building, they saw it had a front porch with three white arches separated by four posts, giving it a kind of strange festive feel. As they approached and began to climb the stairs to the portico, Frank felt Tracy's arm stiffen. He glanced down and saw a tear run freely down her cheek.

Chapter 68

FALL 1912

Emma

Emma stayed home while the others took Mama to the state asylum, but as soon as they returned, she left for Portland.

Fearing that Josie might be close to a breakdown after months as her invalid mother's sole caregiver, Emma sent her back to Portland to help Bertie with her children.

The brothers had done their best to help Josie, but the farm and, now, the harvest demanded most of their attention. These last few weeks on the farm had enabled Emma to understand the difficulties her family faced with their mother's illness.

A few days after Josie left for town, and just before Tracy and Ferd left to take Mama to the hospital, Arnold brought home a letter addressed to Emma from Sophie. It stated that her heroine, Abigail Scott Duniway, was going to sponsor a rally downtown for the suffragettes on October 8 and needed volunteers. The suffragette vote was due to occur on November 30.

"I wish I could go to the rally," Tracy lamented after reading the letter. "Maybe I can, if we get Mama settled without too much trouble." Her voice didn't hold much hope.

"I wish you could, too," Emma said, knowing that she might not be able to get there herself.

As it turned out, after just spending five days helping her mother settle into her hospital routine, Tracy decided she must stay home. Frank needed help with the last of the harvest.

"Besides, this pregnancy is wearing," she confided to Emma.

So Emma hugged her young nephews and scrambled aboard the waiting wagon, while Tracy and the boys waved goodbye. Arnold drove her up the driveway and on to Troutdale to meet the train.

Her train was delayed, so Emma arrived at Sophie's house just in time for them to hurry off to the rally. On the way, Sophie told her the Sunday before Mrs. Scherhauser had ask her to have Emma come back to work for her as soon as she returned to Portland much to Emma's relief.

"I'M CERTAINLY HAPPY TO SEE ALL THESE MEN TURNING out to support our cause," Emma said to Sophie after they pushed through the throng of people and arrived at the gathering place.

"I just hope we can get through the crowd in time to help," Sophie said, lifting her skirts and stepping over a mud puddle.

Emma had received a letter from Mrs. Duniway's personal secretary, saying they would be glad to have two more volunteers. The pair made their way to the side door as the letter instructed.

As Emma's eyes adjusted to the inside light, she spotted Mrs. Duniway across the hall. Grabbing Sophie's arm, they eased through the crowd toward her. Mrs. Duniway's eye caught Emma's, and she pointed to the entrance, mouthing, "Take tickets." Then the elderly woman was on to something else, leaving them to elbow their way back through the people to relieve the two harried volunteers at the gate, who seemed delighted to see them.

As the time for the program drew near, they inched their way to the auditorium doors where they could keep their eyes out for latecomers at the entrance and still see the program. Glancing inside, Emma was surprised to see the large room fairly bulging with people of all types and colors from all walks of life.

Promptly at seven o'clock, Mrs. Duniway, frail and slow, came forward to the stage and signaled the small band to strike up the *Star-Spangled Banner.* When the rousing song was finished and with the audience still standing, she led them in the flag salute. Afterward the crowd erupted in cheers and applause. When the audience showed no signs of settling down, Abigail signaled the band leader to blow his trumpet, bringing the meeting to order.

Armed with a megaphone, Mrs. Duniway, in spite of her obvious ill health, gave a short, rousing speech on how it was "women's turn this time." Emma noticed the pallor in her face and worried that she seemed weaker than she had last summer. In spite of her fragile state, her voice held a strength that could only come from the depths of her soul. Her dedication to the suffragette cause consumed her, belying her obviously delicate condition.

Mrs. Duniway reminded the people that Washington state had won the vote for women's rights in 1910 and California in 1911, leading to more whistles and clapping.

It pleased Emma to see men standing up beside their sisters, wives, and sweethearts.

Mrs. Duniway attempted to calm the crowd, but failing, again signaled for the musician to blast on the trumpet. When everyone quieted, she introduced the main speaker for the evening. A lovely middle-aged woman, with determined eyes and copper skin, rose from her chair on the stage when her name was called. Hattie Redmond, who represented the Colored Women's Equal Suffrage Association, appeared to be filled with as much enthusiasm and excitement as Mrs. Duniway.

"Ladies and gentlemen! If you think being a white woman without a voting voice is difficult, try being a Negro woman without it." Her young voice rang true and clear without the megaphone.

Throughout her impressive speech, Mrs. Redmond stoked the crowd's enthusiasm as she described the plight of all women and how only the vote could improve their children's lives.

Feeling reinvigorated after Mrs. Redmond finished her speech, Sophie and Emma presented themselves to the Portland Women's Club's Suffrage Committee Campaign table. They suspected that Mrs. Duniway was not in good enough health to continue her work, and this committee appeared to have taken over many of her duties.

"We want to help in any way we can," Emma told the young lady whose name tag identified her as Grace Watt Ross.

"Please fill out this card," she said, handing each of them a small piece of heavy paper and a pencil.

When they were done, she took the cards and, noticing they were members of Portland's St. Joseph parish, said, "Please check in at the precinct near your parish on Wednesday of next week. We will be leaving word of the duties you are assigned." She handed them a flyer with the name and address, then jotted a note on each card, filed them, and smiled a thank-you.

On Wednesday, they picked up their informational packet, and their first duty was to canvass house to house in a ten-block radius around the precinct. For the next week and a half, as soon as the children were off to school, Emma and Sophie took up where they had left off the previous day, talking to everyone they met. On days without rain, Emma brought the littlest Scherhauser toddler in a buggy. When the baby became tired and fussy, they quit and finished the route the next day.

October merged into November, and Emma, despite blisters on her feet and the stresses of her job, was determined not to let anything stop her. She felt fortunate that her employer had rehired her immediately and had convinced her husband that the work they were doing was important. In fact, happy with her nanny's suffragette work, Mrs. Scherhauser occasionally even insisted the baby stay home with her. Those were Emma and Sophie's most productive days.

Most of the electorate was at least polite. The ones who patronized them were more than annoying. After one of her few days canvassing alone, Emma stopped by Sophie's house to complain about the simpleminded ruffians who had no idea about the importance of this legislation.

"You should be ashamed," said the proprietor of a cigar shop they visited the next canvassing day. The fifty-something-year-old fellow with a handlebar mustache and suspenders over his ample belly peered over his glasses at them.

"Number one, this is a cigar shop, and I would thank you women not to come in here." He took a breath, reeking of stale breakfast and recent cigars, and continued, "And secondly, you are doing the devil's work. Women have no place in politics."

"See here, mister," Emma sputtered, about to lose her temper. How dare he! Who did he think he was?

Before she could finish, Sophie grabbed her arm and steered her toward the door, saying to the uncouth gentleman, "I'm sorry you feel that way. You are very wrong, you know." Her voice calm, but firm.

Emma continued to spout as they walked along the street. "That's so unfair!"

"Yes, it is," her older friend agreed. "But we're wasting our time with him. Let's talk to men and women who will listen." Although Sophie's hands shook, she caught her breath and said, "We only have to win by a few votes. If we can just persuade fifty percent of the people we talk with, that's all we need."

Emma noticed that Sophie's lips were pinched tight, and her eyes held a stubbornness Emma had never seen there before. Somehow, her gracious agony gave Emma courage to continue.

On the November 5, 1912, election day, the women started early in the morning at the precinct assisting the throngs of men who came to vote. Emma's face was frozen in a constant smile as she encouraged the men to "Vote for women"—without ever saying it. That, of course, would be illegal.

After the polls closed at eight o'clock that night, the women sealed the ballot boxes and readied them for pickup and delivery to the county office. None of the precinct crew was allowed to leave until the boxes were safely shipped. Finally at a quarter after eleven, the exhausted workers hailed the delivery wagon and helped haul out almost two dozen boxes.

After a week of counting, the verdict came in. *Thank God!* Emma thought, as she read in the *Morning Oregonian* that women's suffrage had passed with 52 percent of the vote. Oregon could now take its rightful place among the most progressive states. She was elated. In the next election, they would not have to content themselves with working the precincts; they would vote as well.

In spite of her efforts to shove away thoughts of Mama, Emma thought about Julianna and how the vote might have spurred her to get her citizenship papers. Perhaps, she might have had a better life. We'll never know, she thought. We'll never know.

A week later she received a letter from Tracy, telling her that Frank had worked until four o'clock on voting day, eaten a quick supper, then taken a lantern and walked the seven miles round trip to the Grange Hall to vote. So his wife, too, could have the right to cast a ballot in the next election. He did not arrive home until after midnight.

"You know Frank," she wrote as an afterthought, "if he worked the horses the day before and plans on working the horses the following day, he will not take them out needlessly. He says, anyway, walking is good for the soul."

Chapter 69

FEBRUARY 1913

Baby

Emma hugged the basket of clean laundry she was carrying from the basement line and grabbed the letter Mr. Scherhauser handed her. The address, smudged from being in his overcoat pocket, had not completely escaped the rain. Water dripped from his cap onto the newly waxed floor. She knew he had missed the trolley again and walked the twelve blocks home in the downpour.

"Oh, thank you," she called as she hurried up the stairs. She quickly folded the laundry and as soon as the clothes were carefully put in drawers and on hangers, she sat on her bed, tore open the letter from Tracy, and began to read.

February 24, 1913
Dear Emma,

I could hardly wait to write and tell you that you have a new niece. Her name is Louise Julia Wand. She was born in the morning of February 22. We love that she shares a birthday with the Father of our Country!

A girl! she thought. *It has been a long time since we have had a baby girl in our family.* Her mind raced, trying to decide when to leave for Pleasant View. *I am sure Mrs. Scherhauser will give me some time off. Maybe just a few days over next Sunday.*

She took a deep breath and continued reading:

She looks so tiny, but I know it's because her brothers have grown now. She has wisps of blond hair and seems to be of good disposition. Frank is so pleased. Whenever he is in the house he has that baby in his arms. He tells me he misses his sisters and now he has a daughter of his own. The boys love her too. Alec calls her "my baby."

The birth wasn't as difficult this time. Josie and Caroline helped me. I was grateful for Caroline because Josie is not as experienced at bringing new life into this world. I think she has graduated now, though, because Caroline taught her many things. You know she never had the midwife training that we had. She was always the one who stayed home while we helped Mother with the neighbors' babies.

In spite of all the excitement and the persistent rain, Frank has managed to get almost an acre plowed, disked, and ready for early seeding, thanks mostly to the nice weather we had that first week this month. He wants to put in carrots and rutabagas. He says they are good early sellers. He didn't mention tobacco, but I know that needs to be planted early too.

I hope all is well with you, and you are over that nasty cold you came down with after Christmas. I think that is something that we are not as prone to out here, although Alec did come down with the grippe in late January. I wrapped him in mentholated packs and gave him buckets of ginger tea, so it didn't last long.

Josie is home now and our brothers are happy to have her back. They don't like batching it. Jackie says, "Arnold's cooking tastes like cardboard."

Josie's writing to that nice Frank Fehrenbacher. I think she is serious about him. I hope he is about her. You know he is very handsome. My fear is some other woman will catch him while he is away working. Josie doesn't seem worried though. She must know something we don't.

Have you heard from Bertie? I received a letter from her two weeks ago. She says the baby is growing fast. She said Gabe has applied for a city job, and she hopes that he gets it. It will give them a steady income which is something few of us except you have.

I wrote a letter to Mama in January and have not heard back. The nurse told us someone would write to us and keep us informed. If I don't hear something soon, Frank and I will return to Salem and make sure she is being cared for properly.

I miss you.
Tracy

Emma reread the letter, folded it, and slipped it back into the envelope. Placing it on the bedside table, she vowed to read it once more before bedtime. Hurrying downstairs to rescue more laundry, she ran headlong into Mrs. Scherhauser, who had just shooed her husband into the bedroom to get out of his wet clothes.

"There you are; I was worried when you rushed up the

stairs."

"Oh! Ma'am, I have a new niece. I'm so excited. We have had no girl babies in our family for over twenty years, and everyone is celebrating!" Emma hesitated and, drawing courage from the news, asked, "Um, ma'am, do you think I could take next Friday and, and maybe the following Monday off? I… I want to meet her."

She held her breath, remembering all the time she had taken off work helping with the election.

"Of course you can," Mrs. Scherhauser exclaimed. "I can't pay you for the time, though."

"Oh my. No, I wouldn't dream of asking for that."

Mrs. Scherhauser nodded and, thinking out loud, said, "I'll get Rachel across the street to help after school."

Early Friday morning, Emma caught the trolley to the train depot and was on her way to Troutdale before mid-morning. She wore her rubber boots in case there was no one in town who could give her a ride up the hill. If she had to walk, that was fine. She just wanted to meet that baby girl.

Chapter 70

EARLY MARCH 1913

The New Road

It was midmorning when the train pulled into the Troutdale depot. Emma smiled to herself as she looked out the window at the one-sided town. Tracy had told her that Captain Harlow had struck a bargain to let the Oregon Railway and Navigation Company keep its entire right-of-way. Because of that, no buildings had been constructed on the north side of the road, making it lopsided. It reminded Emma of a wagon with two wheels on one side and a sled runner on the other. Just picturing a wagon looking like that always made her smile.

She disembarked and hurried up the hill and across the main road to the Foxes' store in hopes of finding a small gift for her new niece. When she walked in, the bell over the door jingled, and Emma saw a man from the train standing at the counter talking to Mr. Fox. His hands were gesturing and pointing, his voice animated.

She couldn't help noticing him on the train. He sat several seats behind her. His voice boomed at times, which she found annoying. But when he said something that piqued her curiosity, he had lowered his voice, which made it impossible for her to follow the conversation. Although she doubted he realized how much attention he caught, she was sure it would not have mattered to him either way.

He was a portly, square-faced fellow with thick gray hair. He wore a fine black suit with a gold watch fob that hung stylishly across his vest. His jaw had a stubborn line, and although he had no beard, he did wear a well-manicured mustache. He clenched a stubby half-smoked cigar between his teeth. Emma thought it looked nasty and smelled worse.

When he re-lit the cigar in the train, the smoke permeated the air, forcing Emma to attempt to open her window. It promptly jammed, aggravating her. She hated cigar smoke. It choked her and, besides, she believed only unruly men or those who thought themselves important smoked cigars. She had dealt with many of them during the suffragette campaigns, and most of them were against the women's right to vote.

Now here he was again. She tried not to attract attention, hanging back, pretending to look at the overshoes and rain gear in the window, but all the while she listened intently. The man made her uncomfortable, which annoyed her even more. She was, after all, a courteous, proper young woman and to have someone make her feel less, even just by their presence, was unacceptable.

"Nice talking to you, old man," the ample fellow said, popping a fresh, unwrapped cigar into his vest pocket. Then he turned and walked out the door, brushing past her on the way.

"Well, well, it's nice to see you, Emma," Mr. Fox smiled and beckoned her to come over.

"It's nice to be here, Mr. Fox," Emma said in reply. "Have there been any hill people down today, or are you expecting any?"

"As a matter of fact, I suspect some will be down later

this afternoon for the meeting."

"Meeting?" Emma said, never missing a chance to hear about current events. Tracy always laughed and called her a politician. She loved a lively, if not contentious, gathering.

"The fellow I was just talking to is Mr. Sam Hill." He gestured toward the door. "He's the head of the Portland's Good Roads organization." Mr. Fox picked up the cigar box, closed the lid, and put it back in the display case. "From what he just told me, they are hoping to build a highway through the Gorge. He's still recruiting a crew as well as financing for the project. He tells me this should bring wealthy city people out here, and with them, a lot of revenue to our area." His face turned pink as he talked, and his voice rose in enthusiasm.

Before she could answer, he continued. "He sent out flyers about the meeting two weeks ago. It's to be held in Larsson's Saloon at four o'clock this afternoon. He wants locals to help build the road. The conversation around here tells me the whole town is turning out."

"Oh, my," Emma said, torn between wanting to attend the meeting and wanting to hold the new baby. She remembered reading about the expensive project in the paper. Something about the wives not wanting to ride in their husband's automobiles on uncivilized "cow trails."

"Apparently, they're raising money for the project from the city fathers in Portland," he said, compelled to discuss it further. "It's good roads for them anyway, so they should pay. They all have these new cars, and the roads are terrible when it rains."

"Yes, there are quite a few automobiles in Portland now."

"Mr. Hill seems hell-bent on seeing the project to the

finish. Lots of people think it's an impossible feat. The 1870s' old Sandy-Dalles wagon road was never completed because of extreme grades; even Woodard Road is steep, but they have managed to shave it down some. Besides, he just told me he has some engineer interested in the project. Some fellow named Samuel Lancaster; at least I think that's the name he told me."

"I don't think Mr. Hill will get discouraged. He looks like a gentleman who works all the angles. I doubt he will quit easily."

Mr. Fox gave her a quizzical look.

"Well, there were some people who said we women would never get the vote, either. We didn't let that stop us," Emma replied, her voice firm. "I worked with Abigail Scott Duniway. She didn't quit."

"Oh yes, that's right. Your brothers were in here bragging about you last fall."

Emma grinned at the news. Her family recognized her work!

Although she was torn by the news of a meeting and didn't have a ride up the hill, the thought of her new niece made her decision. "I'll leave my grip in the storeroom, if you don't mind," she said, not relishing the idea of carrying it up the steep trail. "I expect one or more of my family will attend the meeting this afternoon. I'll ask one of them to bring it when they come home."

"SHE'S LOVELY!" EMMA SAID, HOLDING LOUISE, A TINY, fine-boned, healthy baby. The infant pursed her lips and stretched.

"Yes, isn't she?" Tracy said, wiping the counters in the

kitchen while she visited, telling Emma for the third or fourth time how happy she was to see her. "Never a day goes by, but what I don't wonder how you and Bertie are doing, so far away in Portland. It is nice to have Josie nearby, but sometimes several days go by before we get to see each other."

The sisters' conversation turned to the new road. Frank and two Lampert brothers left for the meeting a few minutes before with orders to bring Emma's suitcase back with them. There was exuberance in the air, an excitement of a steady income—something none of them out here in the country had ever experienced. True, Emma sent money home every couple of weeks, which helped keep the family in staples, but the farm income usually didn't stretch into year-round money. Only when the harvest was good and the price was right, and it was rare that the two happened in the same year.

"We're excited about the prospects for the new road," Tracy said, taking the baby from Emma. "Frank says the pressure is off for the time being. He's hoping to build his dairy herd, but he's hesitated because it's quite costly." Carefully covering herself, she proceeded to feed the infant and continue talking. "This way he can use some of the money he earns working on the highway to get his herd in shape."

"That's a good plan," Emma agreed.

"Our brothers are going to take turns; two of them will work on the new road, while two of them stay home to tend the farm. They'll change every year."

"Who's going first?"

"I think Arnold plans on taking Jack with him to work on the road, and Alex'll stay home with Ferd. Frank will pay them to come over to our fields and help him with whatever chores he is unable to get done."

The conversation turned to the baby's christening. "I won't be bringing her to Portland for baptism," Tracy said somewhat ruefully.

"Oh my, why not?" Emma asked. She so looked forward to the family reunions in Portland around the baptisms.

"Father Brunagle is in Gresham now. He is making plans to build a church. In the meantime, he says Mass in the dance hall above the Rexall drugstore. I am hoping he will baptize Louise out here." She laughed and added, "Ig is so disappointed. He was looking forward to the train ride into Portland."

"Oh my." Emma sighed. "Things are different now, aren't they?"

"Different, but better."

Emma wondered if she heard a note of doubt in her sister's voice.

It was after eight o'clock before the men returned from the meeting. Arnold and Jack helped Frank with barn chores while the women got a late supper on the table.

"It was an interesting meeting," Arnold said between mouthfuls.

"*Ja*, we learned a lot," Jack interjected. At almost twenty, he was no longer the "little" brother. Muscles rippled under his shirt, and he usually had a tall tale to tell. Tonight, however, Emma felt something different about him. In his face she saw an earnestness that she had never seen before. *Perhaps*, she thought, *it is the maturity that accompanies a young man who has come into his own.*

"Tell us about it," Tracy urged, her voice impatient.

Emma knew what a hardship it was for her not to be included in community business. Up until Tracy had children, she'd attended every meeting, coming out with strong, valid opinions. Frank stated often, "Most of the family decisions depend on Tracy's sound advice."

"Well," Frank started slowly. "Mr. Hill wants to pay us two dollars and twenty-five cents a day." A slight smile curved the side of his mouth while he waited for their response.

"Oh my goodness, Frank!" Tracy exclaimed, "That's more money than you've ever made!"

Emma, speechless, watched the joy play out on her family's faces. Alex broke into laughter and reached for another slice of Tracy's freshly baked bread with one hand and the jar of strawberry jam in the other.

Arnold grinned and said, "Not only that, but if you have a team of horses, they're gonna pay you an extra two dollars and twenty-five cents a day to use them, too."

"That's four dollars and fifty cents a day!" Alex said, in the middle of slathering jam, looking as if he would burst with exuberance.

"When will this start?" Emma wanted to know.

"They are hoping to get started by June," Arnold said, pausing to reach for the bowl of potatoes, then continued. "They have to be sure they have the funding for this stretch of road. Mr. Hill mentioned that the papers have carried articles about the project in hopes of getting support. In fact, I guess there was a piece in the *Gresham Outlook* awhile back, but few people this far from Gresham read it."

"According to him, Multnomah County will be issuing bonds totaling a hundred thousand dollars to begin building a new span to replace the old Neilson Bridge across the Sandy. That'll hook the Baseline Road with the new Columbia River Highway," Frank added. "So things are beginning to happen."

"They're gonna make the road as scenic as possible, too," Alex said, his eyes shining. "Mr. Hill said he and Sam Lancaster went to Switzerland to study the roads and tunnels there. He even hired some Italian stonemasons to come over and build the walls along the road's edge. They fit the rock together so tight they don't even need mortar."

Chapter 71

FEBRUARY 1913

The Baptism

Frank paced the mule. It had been a week since the last rain, but he chose to ride into town rather than risk getting the wagon stuck in winter mud should the rains begin. Besides, he rarely had the opportunity to enjoy the freedom of traveling astride. *February often brings a few days of good weather,* he thought as he made his way down the steep road toward Troutdale, *but you just can't trust it.*

Tracy, not wanting to chance a winter storm with a new baby, had asked Frank to ride into town to speak to the new priest about coming to the Lampert homestead for the baptism. After all, a Mount Angel priest had baptized both Ig and Alec at the farm when they were very small. She wasn't excited about having her baby baptized in a dance hall above a drugstore.

Now Frank was on his way to Gresham, but he had noticed cracks in the old wooden Neilson Bridge over the Sandy River and was afraid it might be unsafe. With the water coming directly off the snowpack from Mount Hood, the Sandy River was too cold and too high to ford in winter, so he chose the other route over the river—the recently built Troutdale Bridge, which would soon be part of the new highway.

Gresham had grown to 540 souls in the last decade, enough to prompt Archbishop Alexander Christy to ask the Holy See for permission to start the Catholic parish in Gresham. With their permission, Father Henry Brunagle had been assigned, partly because the archdiocese recognized his carpentry talent.

Frank, happy to make the trip, was enjoying the crisp, mountain air. He noticed the pussy willows were starting to break. *A sure sign of spring,* he thought as he spotted a flowering plum bud swelling near one of the winter springs cascading off the bluff. He shivered and turned his collar up to cover his neck, glad that winter was coming to an end. As an Illinois native, where harsh winters were common, he experienced some winter storms in the Gorge that matched his childhood memories, complete with blizzards and furious winds.

He waved to Aaron Fox, who was sweeping his boardwalk, as Molly took him through Troutdale.

"Nice day!" Mr. Fox said, returning the wave. "Where you headed?"

"I have a new baby daughter!" Frank said, feeling his chest swell with pride. "I'm riding into Gresham to fetch a priest to baptize her." He wondered if Mr. Fox, a member of the Jewish faith, knew about baptism. He decided that Aaron was one of the smartest men he knew and would most assuredly be aware of Christian traditions.

"Congratulations!" Mr. Fox hailed back. "Tell Tracy hello for me."

Frank nodded, waved again, and turned up Buxton Hill toward Baseline Road. At the top of the steep hill, he stopped to use the water trough at the Baker farm. Molly took a long drink and shook her head in appreciation.

He was in Gresham before ten o'clock, checking in at the drugstore for the whereabouts of the new priest.

"He's staying with James and Marie Chiodo west of here on Powell's Road," said Art Dowsett, the proprietor, sticking his head out from behind the medicine-laden shelves of the pharmacy.

"Yeh, but he's saying Mass every Sunday upstairs in the dance hall," Mr. Dowsett's business partner, Joseph Patneaude, said as he came from the back room with an armful of aprons. He began hanging them on a display rack in the window and muttered, "We have a special on these today. Want to take one home to your wife?"

Frank shook his head and wondered how he could think of something so trivial in a time of such great importance. "I heard about Mass," Frank answered, ignoring the apron offer. "I just haven't been able to bring my family yet. My wife and I just had a baby girl."

"Well, congratulations!" Mr. Patneaude beamed. "My wife is expecting, too. We're very excited!" He jumped down from the display window and added, "This is our first."

They chatted for a few minutes before Frank left in search of the priest. Mr. Dowsett had described the Chiodo house and farm and informed him that if he got as far as St. Joseph of Kronenburg Church, he would have passed his destination.

Just after Frank left the last store in Gresham headed west, he spotted a husky man coming down the hill toward him and noticed what looked like a white collar. *Yes, by golly, it is a collar,* he thought as he got closer. *That's him.*

As Frank arrived beside the priest, he couldn't help but be amazed at his burly size. "Hello!" he hailed, as he pulled Molly to a stop and dismounted. "Are you Father Brunagle?"

"Yes, I am!" the man said and stuck out a large hand.

"I'm Frank Wand," Frank said. The priest's beefy hand made his feel small. "I'm from a homestead east of Troutdale, and my wife just had a baby girl."

"Congratulations!" the priest said, giving his hand an extra shake. His large square face beamed.

"Yes! Thank you! Do you think you could come up and baptize her in the next few days? I'll rent a horse for you at the livery stable, and we will have something for you to eat when you arrive."

"That would be kind of you." The priest nodded and continued, "Yes, I can do that."

"I appreciate it. It's a long way to our place, but I consider it a necessity." Frank hesitated. "I can't bring my wife and new daughter into town in the winter in an open wagon. Although they are both in good health, I can't risk it."

The priest agreed, and the two walked back into town, Frank leading the mule as they discussed the logistics of the trip to the hill east of Troutdale.

"I'd better get used to riding horseback to parishioners' homes," the priest said, laughing. "The boundaries of the parish are the Columbia River to the north and the Boring-Foster Road to the south."

"Sounds like you have a lot of miles to travel. Might do you well to get a buggy, at least for the dry months."

"Not only that, the east boundary is the Hood River County line, and the west is Buckley Avenue nearly to Portland," Father Brunagle said, adding, "I agree about a buggy, but for the moment I don't mind riding."

When they arrived back at Main Street, Frank tied the mule to a post, drank a cup of coffee, and ate a sandwich at the drugstore fountain while he drew the priest a map of the road to the Lampert house.

"Some maps say we live on Chamberlain Hill, but most of us just call it Pleasant View after the schoolhouse," Frank explained as he finished the last of his coffee.

"Doesn't look too difficult to find." The priest studied the map while finishing off his cheese and biscuit.

"When do you plan to start building the new church?" Frank asked, eager to have a parish in the community.

"We'd like to start around the first of June," the priest answered. "I have to get the parish house built before I can start on the church. In the meantime, we'll continue to have Mass in the dance hall."

"I know the Catholic community on the hill will help as much as we possibly can. We've wanted a closer church for a long time." Frank paused and asked, "Where will it be built?" He was curious as to how far his trip to church would be, remembering the all-day trips to St. Joseph Kronenberg, the mission church over at 160th Street and Powell's Road.

"Samuel and Ella Thompson sold us a tax lot on First Street for five hundred dollars," Father said, and added, "The archdiocese bought it for us." Then he laughed, a deep hearty sound emitting from the depths of his soul and said, "But, we are on our own to build the church."

Frank thought a minute. "I think I can get some people from the hill to donate some rough logs, if we can find a way to get them to you. That might help some."

"Indeed! It certainly would."

"When you come to our house, I can show you a pile that I cut last fall." Frank knew that Tracy would insist on them doing as much as possible for their new church, so he did not worry about making the offer.

In the end, Father Brunagle consented to come up to the Wands' on Friday, February 28, and would arrive just as close to eleven o'clock as possible. On his way out of town, Frank stopped at the livery stable and gave the man six bits for the horse rental for the priest.

As he started for home, a soft mist began to fall. By the time he arrived at the top of Buxton Hill, the temperature had dropped, and the rain had a mix of snow. He shivered and pulled his slicker tighter around his shoulders, as he peered into the black mist of the storm. *It's going to get dark early tonight with all this rain*, he thought, digging out the hood of his canvas raincoat and pulling it over his head.

The road turned muddy rapidly in the driving rain. Fortunately, Molly was as sure-footed as any animal he had ever owned and seemed to have no trouble navigating the slippery river road. However, when they turned up Woodard Road, she slowed her pace with the load and the rapid climb.

"All right, old girl," Frank said as he stiffly swung down from the saddle, his long raincoat bumping like a wet board around his legs. *Doesn't matter if I get muddy, I'm already wet and cold*, he thought ruefully.

He led the animal in the twilight, allowing her to stop and rest on the platforms and drink from the adjoining spring. His wet misery could not allow his mule to dally; he just wanted to get home.

About the time he hit the Wire Trail, the rain stopped. He pushed back his hood and listened to the wet forest drip in the coming darkness. Patting the mule's neck, he thanked her for her strength and told her he, too, would continue to walk the rest of the way home.

It was completely dark by the time he arrived at the barn, and he was surprised by the lantern burning inside. He opened the door to see Ig sitting on the three-legged stool, his head resting on Bessie's flank and a half-full milk bucket between his knees. *Looks like my nine-year-old has just about reached manhood*, he thought proudly.

ON FRIDAY, FATHER BRUNAGLE ARRIVED AT THE LAMperts' before eleven o'clock as planned to find many aunts and uncles waiting for him, as well as the Seidls and Maroks. The Frommelts were noticeably absent, as Franz had not been himself since Katherine's death. An impenetrable gloom had wrapped itself around the Frommelt house and tightened even more after Julianna left. Even their jovial Uncle Joseph Marok was unable to penetrate the shroud of melancholy.

Frank brought his family over in the wagon, as the rain stopped a few days before and most of the mud had dried. Besides, he didn't want Tracy walking in the cold, and he worried about bringing the tiny baby out in the elements.

"We are doing God's work," Tracy told him earlier. "Don't worry. He'll take care of us."

Of course, he thought. *I wonder why I was so concerned.* Once again he realized how he treasured Tracy's simple pragmatism.

Josie and Emma had a large kettle of soup on the stove, and the smell of it, along with Maria Seidl's fresh bread, permeated the house. Along with Elma Marok's apple pies sitting in the pie saver on the porch where Ig and Alec hovered, keeping an eye on them.

And so, with her godmother Emma holding the infant

and godfather Arnold standing beside them, Louise became the first baby baptized in St. Henry Parish on the twenty-eighth day of February in 1913.

Chapter 72

SUMMER 1913

Tracy

With three children to keep her busy, Tracy had little time to catch up on news and social events. She worried about Frank, who worked almost every day except Sunday since early spring on the new highway project. It seemed she saw her brothers more than she saw Frank.

She had to admit it was nice to have steady money coming in. That was something she'd not experienced had since working in Troutdale—and never for herself. Now Frank talked Father Brunagle into letting them help him build the new church a few hours every Sunday, too.

"Honey, you know we can trade work, instead of tithing right now," Frank had replied to her protest. "We need all the money we can earn to build up our milking herd."

"But you already work six days a week," Tracy persisted, "and the church says you must rest on the seventh."

"I know, Father Brunagle said the same thing. We had to persuade him, too. I'd much rather be home, but this church has to be built. I'm a carpenter by trade, so I'm obligated."

The disagreement had continued into the summer and now in early August, she noticed he was losing weight, so she began packing bigger noon meals for him.

Father Brunagle worked every day on the church, while other parish men closer to Gresham worked with him a day or two a week. Every Sunday the hill parishioners could see progress, motivating the families to trudge on. Right after Mass—still held in the dance hall on the second floor of the drugstore—the men changed their clothes, gathered their tools, and went to work. The women unpacked food, got a meal together, watched the children, and caught up on visiting.

Since the priest had already built several churches in Oregon, he assured the parishioners this was his last. The archdiocese promised him he could have his own parish this time.

Tracy liked the affable priest and felt like things were fit and right. She and her siblings had never attended their own church every Sunday. It was a new experience for her, but not for Frank. Most of his growing up years, he and his family had the opportunity to go to Mass at St. Mary's in Elizabeth, Illinois, most Sundays. Building the church was a homecoming for him, and she could understand why he wanted this so badly.

One day, while the women were cleaning up after eating, Tracy suggested that perhaps while the men worked, they could bring any extra fabric and their sewing supplies and make the altar cloths. After all, what is a church without the needed linens inside? So, after a brief discussion, they added that job to their already busy lives of feeding families and watching children.

Once they started, the sewing went faster than expected because they also worked on their projects at home in the evenings. Every Sunday the men hammered, sawed, and climbed ladders, and the older girls watched the smaller children, while the wives laughed and visited as their needles flew. Someone came up with a name: the Altar Society. When the women finished making everything they thought they might need in the church, including several tablecloths and dozens of napkins for church dinners, Tracy and Josie approached Father Brunagle and asked him if there were any vestments he might need.

"Bring some of the women, and let's see," he said. "I have a surplice and several chasubles, but I think I could use a couple more cassocks."

Later when supper was over and before they left for home, the women accompanied the priest to his quarters to inspect the church vestments in his possession. Wondering if it was a mortal sin to see inside the priest's dwelling, Tracy worried until she couldn't hold in the words.

"Father, is this proper, for us to accompany you to your house?" she blurted almost without thinking.

"Well, my goodness," the stunned priest sputtered. "I can't imagine why it wouldn't be."

Her mind at ease then, she and the others waited for him to bring out his vestments for inspection. A gasp was heard around the room when he brought out a white fiddleback chasuble with an ornate red-and-gold cross on the front and back.

"It's lovely, Father." Josie was the first to find her voice.

"Yes, isn't it though? My mother lives in Germany, and when I wrote her that I had received the sacrament of Holy Orders, she sent me this and specified that I could only use it for Christmas, Easter, and other very special Masses."

"Oh, it has a tear in it," Tracy observed, "and I noticed several of your other vestments are badly in need of cleaning and repair."

"Yes, and I need a couple of those cassocks, too. Perhaps you can take one of my old ones to make a pattern."

"We can do that." The women took them home, washed them, and Tracy chose the worst one to rip apart for the pattern. The next few Sunday afternoons, they continued to mend and sew the vestments.

Finally, by the second Sunday in September the church—framed and walled—sported a finished roof. Father Brunagle, having ordered a dozen pews and kneeling benches early in the summer, took delivery of them the first of the month. They were placed in two rows of six each, with an aisle in the middle. The men worked to complete the altar railing, but the altar itself, for the moment, was a crude rough-cut table one of the Gresham parishioners had donated until a proper altar could be constructed.

"Ladies and gentlemen," Father said to the gathering at the end of the day, "we will have our first service in St. Henry's brand new, not quite finished church. The blessing and dedication will be at Mass next Sunday morning at eleven." Murmurs of delight went through the small group, the ladies immediately planning what food to bring for the celebration meal.

So, on a warm Sunday morning in late September 1913, St. Henry parishioners were finally in their own church. There was no tower or bell, but there were beautiful new brick stairs, thanks to the Olbrick family. Father Henry Brunagle dressed in his special, newly mended white fiddle-back chasuble with its gold-and-red crosses and celebrated the first Mass in only the second Catholic church in all of east Multnomah County.

Chapter 73

APRIL 1914

The New Highway from Portland to The Dalles

With sledgehammer and shovel tied with a leather thong and slung over his shoulder, Frank carried his noonday meal in a lidded tin bucket as he walked down the Wire Trail to the Mershon Gravel Pit. The pit was gouged into the side of the hill directly below Pleasant View School and had caused quite a commotion in the community.

"I don't know why you have to mine your rock there," Tracy said, with more than a hint of anxiety. "What would happen if the dynamite failed and blew rocks up into the schoolyard?"

"I know the location is bad, but it's got a good gravel seam," Frank explained. "And I've already talked to Charlie Bramhall about it. He's the boss, and he promised to go up to the school every morning before we blast and tell the teacher to keep the children inside."

"I still don't like it." Tracy wanted a better explanation than the one he had before she would accept it.

"The trees buffer the schoolhouse." He took a swallow of coffee and continued. "Besides, the bluff itself is so tall that the school is protected." He paused, trying to think of something to put her mind at ease. "You have my word, nothing will happen to any of the children. Don't forget, I'm a school board member, and I have an obligation to protect the students."

"I trust you, Frank. I really do." That was the last she spoke of it, but as the days passed, he could see the worry lines in her face. Part of it was for the children, but he also knew she worried about him when he worked with dynamite.

"Just be glad it isn't nitroglycerin," he said once when he was teasing. "Now, that is bad stuff. At least you have to light dynamite before it explodes."

Tracy shook her head, looked him in the eye and said, "I would never agree to you using that. Dynamite is bad enough."

As the work progressed, Frank saw how dangerous it could be. The men took every precaution, with extra-long fuses and small charges. And true to his word, Charlie always climbed the hill to the school the morning of a blast and warned the schoolteacher, Mrs. Gable. As the days passed, Frank began to feel more confident.

Once they blasted, it took a day or two of pounding the larger rocks to gravel before it was ready to haul to the road site. They, along with the men at the Baker gravel pit across the Neilson Bridge, were able to keep up with the road crew, which was working between the tiny settlements of Corbett and Springdale.

"By golly, that's a rickety bridge," Charlie said of the old wooden structure over the Sandy River. "I'm sure glad they're replacing it."

"Ja, I won't take my family over it," Frank agreed.

A couple of the other men standing by shook their heads.

"The last time I took the team over it, it shook and creaked so bad, I was just plain worried about gettin' across," Arnold spoke up.

"Keep your fingers crossed that the Baker gravel pit plays out before the bridge does," said Frank Fehrenbacher, standing with his arms through his overall bib. He had laughed as he said it, but it didn't sound like much of a joke to Frank.

"Yes, it better," Charlie said.

Charlie had a large Model T truck that could haul twice as much rock as a wagon, but was much heavier, almost a ton, when loaded. He and his crew used the truck to bring the Baker gravel while the Bates, Lamperts, Mershons, and two other families each had a team and wagon hauling from the Mershon site. With so many wagons available, they could trade off and give the horses a rest.

Each vehicle had to be loaded and unloaded by hand. Manning sledges and shovels was exhausting work, so the men traded jobs—sometimes driving the wagon and crew, sometimes remaining at the pits pounding rocks.

April 25, 1913, Good Roads Day, turned out to be warm and dry. It had been a cool week and, up until the day before, there had been several days of the good soaking April rains, moisture that local farmers had come to rely on. Frank, along with several crew members, spent the morning using their sledgehammers pulverizing the rocks. They had just finishing loading the Mershon wagon, when a man roared up on a motorcycle, stopped on a dime, and yelled, "A Model T truck loaded with gravel just broke through Neilson's bridge. The truck's in the river!"

"Oh my God!" Arnold blurted out.

"We gotta get to them," Frank hollered. "Grab the ropes. Two of us can ride down on the horses."

"*Ja*!" Jack exclaimed. "Maybe I can ride down with this fellow?"

The helmeted man on the motorcycle nodded and started the cycle. With Jack hanging on to his back in what looked like a death grip, he turned the motorcycle around and sped off in a cloud of dust.

"You other fellows head down toward Springdale and alert the Mershon crew and the guys at the blacksmith shop," Frank ordered. "We don't know what we're gonna find when we get there, but I know we're gonna need a lot of manpower to get that truck out." He paused as he led the mule to a rock and mounted bareback. "And we don't know what kind of shape the crew is in," he hollered as he followed Arnold down the path, a rope coiled around his arm.

It seemed to take a long time to get down the hill to the Sandy River, but it was hot and the horses had been worked hard the last few days so they couldn't be pushed. Frank and Arnold knew it would take time, and they were confident that Jack and the man on the motorcycle could take care of immediate problems. Some of the Baker crew had to be safe, in order to tell the fellow on the motorcycle where to go to find the crew and give the news.

When they arrived at the bridge, the truck was up to the top of its tires in the water, too heavy to float. Thankfully, the rain earlier in the week here in the valley had brought more snow to Mount Hood. The temperature on the mountain was still was too cold for a spring thaw, so the river, still low could be forded.

Frank counted all of the crew on their side of the bank, along with Jack and Harry, the fellow on the motorcycle.

The fellows from the truck were dripping wet, and Charlie Bramhall was sitting on the bank holding his arm.

"Looks like the only one hurt is Charlie," Jack said as he hurried over to meet them. "He's got a broken arm, probably from holding on to the steering when it landed. He said the wheel wrenched his arm." He paused, looking at the destroyed bridge, and said, "That's a heck of a long way to drop."

"Yeah, it sure is," Arnold said as he dismounted.

"Rest of you fellows all right?" Frank asked as he walked over to survey the damage, while Arnold went to tend to Charlie. The Baker crew looked stunned and were mostly quiet, but a couple of them nodded.

"Somebody's got to set this thing," Charlie said through gritted teeth. "It hurts like hell."

"Anybody got any whiskey?" Arnold asked the rest of the crew. No one spoke up, and a couple of the fellows shook their heads.

Just about the time Frank and Arnold were deciding they would have to set the arm without anything for pain, the Mershon crew arrived. They were followed from Springdale by the most god-awful sound: Ferd Smith driving up in his one-cylinder Cadillac.

Ferd surveyed the scene. "Put Charlie in my car, fellows. The river is pretty shallow. Hook the horses to the bumper. Just get me across the river, and I can get him to Gresham. With any luck Doc Hughes is in his office."

The men tied ropes to the Cadillac and soon, with Frank and Arnold leading the horses and others pulling on ropes or pushing, the Cadillac slid down the bank and into the fast-flowing shallow river. The engine died, but they crossed without incident, the horses doing most of the work.

It was another story at the other side. Everyone stopped, while Ferd got out to start the car. He cranked for several minutes with not even a pop. Arnold took over the crank while Ferd returned to the driver's seat and adjusted the spark lever on the steering wheel column.

"I think we'd better just pull the car up the bank and work on it on the flat ground," Ferd said after many more unsuccessful cranks. "I'll check the carburetor. Maybe it got wet."

"Yeah, we probably will have to dry it out," Charlie agreed through gritted teeth; his blanched face contorted in pain.

The men once again took their stations, leading the horses or pulling on ropes, and this time with several of the crew members pushing from behind, the car began to creep up the steep embankment. Suddenly halfway up, the car began to hesitate.

"Pull! Pull!" Jack yelled from the back. Others took up the cry as the crew in the back pushed, using all of their strength to hold the auto in place. The horses strained, and the men in front heaved with all their might. Ferd jumped out of the car and helped. Charlie grabbed the wheel with his good arm and sticking his leg over the brake, prepared to hit it if the car began to roll backward.

The Cadillac inched slowly up toward the top of the hill and then, once at the top, bounced over the brow. The men breathed a collective sigh. Many leaned on their knees to catch their breath, unable to believe any car could be so heavy. The horses, now unhitched, headed back to the water for a long drink.

With Charlie's instructions and Arnold's help, Ferd pulled out his screwdriver, removed the carburetor, and inspected it. He reached into the toolbox, pulled out a vial of wood alcohol, and poured some into the body of the carburetor to clean and dry it.

While Ferd was replacing the carburetor, he asked Arnold to take the wrench and remove the spark plug. Once that was out, Ferd poured the remaining alcohol into the cylinder, and Arnold quickly dried and replaced the plug.

"Charlie, give us some spark," he commanded, as he replaced the plug wire. Once his hands were out from under the hood, he said, "Now crank it, someone!"

It only took one crank for Arnold to get a pop, and the second one started the engine. Charlie let up on the spark, and the engine coughed. He gave it more gas and, though rough, the motor continued to run. Once Ferd was sure it was going to continue running, he dropped the spark, and the engine roared and smoothed. He pushed the gas lever on the steering column back to idle.

"I'll ride the brakes a bit up the hill," Ferd hollered over the noise of the engine. "That'll dry 'em out." And off they went, a look of relief on Charlie's face.

Arnold looked at Frank, shook his head, and said, "What the heck just happened?"

"I'll be a son-of-a-gun if I know."

"I just know we all got a good cold dip in the water," said George Mershon, one of the Baker crew, who shook his head with a rueful grin.

Frank Fehrenbacher nodded in agreement. "I'll be darned if I want to do that again." He hesitated and took a breath. "I guess we won't have to for a while, anyway. At least until they finish the new bridge."

Getting the gravel truck out of the water was another thing again. It took all four horses and half the crew pulling while the other half pushed to get the truck upstream several hundred feet and out of the water. But try as they might, they could not get the loaded truck up the short steep bank. After a long conference, they decided to leave it until morning, when, with fresh horses, they would bring the wagons and transfer the gravel.

"God knows, we don't want to lose perfectly good gravel," Frank said to the crew.

Two days later, after transferring the gravel, they finally got the empty truck up the bank and back on the road. Charlie's crew, stiff and sore, were given a pass for the next few days as the rest of the men cleaned up the mess and got the truck running before Charlie came back to the job, his arm in a sling.

Ed Neilson inspected his father's wrecked bridge with John Yeon, the Multnomah County roadmaster. They immediately had a crew working: first to dynamite what was left of the old bridge, and then to speed up construction of the new steel bridge.

Even though activity increased in the quarry beneath the bluff south of Pleasant View School, there was not one blast-related problem with the students, much to the community's relief.

Chapter 74

SUMMER 1914

"Here's a letter from your mother's nurse," Frank said, handing the mail to Tracy as he came in the door.

"Oh, thank you!" Tracy said. She tore open the envelope from Pendleton, where Julianna had been moved, and began to read out loud:

July 2, 1914
Dear Theresa and family,

I know it has been a long time since I received your letter inquiring about your mother, so today I am making a point to catch up on my letter writing.

Your mother is sitting beside me. When I told her that I was writing to her children, she smiled. That is a good sign, as sometimes she does not respond.

She is not on any medicine except laudanum for sleeping, as she often wanders at night if we do not give it to her. As I recall, that was one of the worries you had when she was still living at home. She eats well, but it takes her a long time to finish. Otherwise, she seems healthy and content, unlike some of the other residents who are often anxious.

Please know that we take good care of her and that you are welcome to come and visit anytime. Our Sunday visiting hours are from 10:00 a.m. to noon. Just remember that sometimes she may not know your names, but she will know you are someone she loves.

When you come to visit, please bring her a new skirt, top, and some undergarments. She will need a size smaller now.

Sincerely,
Mary Jones, Nurse
Dr. Wilson D. McNary, Superintendent
Eastern Oregon State Hospital
Pendleton, Oregon

"Some of us have got to visit her, Frank," Tracy said, blinking back tears. Feeling his arm around her shoulders brought her that familiar, soothing comfort. Once again Frank knew just what to do at just the right time.

"When we go over to the homestead next Sunday, we'll decide." He spoke in his usual quiet tone. "Maybe the family can split and some go this time, and later in the fall before cold weather some of the others can make the trip."

The following Sunday, the discussion centered on the letter and the plan to visit their mother. The only one who really didn't want to go was Arnold.

"I want to remember her back before she got sick," he said repeatedly when asked. "I can stay here and take care of things."

So it was decided that Josie and Ferd would stay at the Wands' place and tend the livestock and the children, while

Frank, Tracy, Jack and Alex would take the train east the next Saturday, visit their mother on Sunday, and catch the late train home that evening. Tracy wrote both Emma and Bertie a long letter explaining what was happening, and suggested they go in the fall to visit their mother along with Josie and Ferd.

HERE AND THERE ALONG THE WAY, ESPECIALLY BEFORE The Dalles, they saw signs of progress on the new highway. Horses pulled wagons full of gravel and Fresno scrapers to level the road, while men swung sledges, picks, and shovels, all hard at work. One tall hill, looking like a perpetual rock slide, was being used as a gravel pit. A ladder by the pit led up to what appeared to be the beginnings of a tunnel. Someone on the train said they were passing Mitchell Point.

It had been a long time since Frank had been to Pendleton, but he remembered the vast wheat fields and the spectacular view of the Umatilla River from the top of the hill before they descended to the valley; the town nestled below.

Frank spent the afternoon on the train describing the summer he had spent as a ranch hand in the Eastern Oregon steppe country as Tracy and her brothers listened intently. Then Tracy told the story of when Papa and Mama took them to The Dalles and on to Celilo Falls, where they watched the crazy steamboat captain deliberately run the sternwheeler over the falls.

"Papa told us later that "the foolish man went on to pilot the boat through the Narrows and the Cascades, finally ending up at the shipyards in Portland to be repaired and used on the lower part of the Columbia."

Tracy remembered her parents commenting on the

crowds of people who had come to watch this historic but frightening feat. She wondered if her mother had seen the falls from the train on her way to Pendleton two years ago, and if she remembered that gala holiday trip. Sadly, she doubted it.

The train car windows were open to cool the passengers, so when they stepped off at the Pendleton depot, the 102-degree heat of wheat country hit them squarely in the face. Temperatures in Troutdale had been climbing toward another eighty degree July day earlier when they boarded. They were surprised at the vast difference of the effect of those extra degrees. Tracy was always uncomfortable anytime the thermometer rose above ninety.

They went immediately to the hotel, a large five-story, brilliant white building—the tallest in town—and checked in. Frank inquired about traveling accommodations to the state hospital.

"We can have a buggy here tomorrow morning whenever you would like," the clerk said.

"I understand it's only a mile out of town, but since we'd like to go to Mass first, we probably do need a ride in order to get the hospital when it opens at ten. We'll walk back to town in the afternoon."

"The ride will be here at 9:30 tomorrow morning to be certain you'll get there in time."

"That'll work just fine." Then Frank inquired about the nearest Catholic church and learned it was St. Mary's on Barnard Street and the first Mass was at 7:30 the next morning.

They spent the rest of the day exploring some nearby businesses. The town was quiet for a Saturday, as most of the farmers were deep into the grain harvest. Only the townspeople were out and about.

The next morning they arrived at the hospital at ten minutes before ten o'clock and waited outside. They commented on the immensity of the building and how nice it was to feel the cool air blowing off the river. There were a few people sitting on benches here and there, and a nurse walking with a couple on the path leading to the water.

When the door opened, they were led inside. Tracy was grateful for the thick brick walls, which kept some of the heat at bay. They were brought into a sitting room and invited to take a chair.

"I'll go and fetch your mother," a cordial young lady said to the family.

Soon Julianna appeared in front of them, a confused look on her face.

"Mama, it's Tracy," she said, more calmly than she felt.

"Tracy?" Julianna's murmur was barely audible.

"Yes, my dear," Tracy said, putting her arms around her mother, realizing how thin she had become. "With Frank, Jackie, and Alex. The rest of us will come in the fall to see you."

Her mother had a puzzled look, and then her face lit up as recognition slowly formed. These people were her children. She spoke only in garbled words but with familiar intonations. The sounds gave the children some notion of what she was trying to say.

"She loves to walk outside," said the nurse, who introduced herself as Genevieve, as she took the bundle of clothes from Tracy. "Why don't you all go out there. Maybe it'll be easier for her to talk to you."

They spent the next two hours with their mother, visiting mostly among themselves, with an occasional comment or question directed toward Julianna. Tracy's heart bled silently as she realized this was all that was left of their mother. Only a shell with her soul clinging mightily to her inner strength, not yet wanting to let loose and fly away.

Tracy could see her brothers' distress and admired their courage and gentleness when they held their mother's hand or kissed her forehead. She saw that even Frank, her rock, was having a difficult time keeping his composure.

From somewhere in the depths of her spirit, Tracy found the courage not to break down in front of her family. No tears, no despair. She came to the stark realization that her role as the eldest among her brothers and sisters held certain obligations. Now the matriarch, she must mirror to her family the kind of strength their mother had worked so diligently to accomplish after the death of their father and brother.

In the shade of the hospital, they sat on the grass with their mother on a bench, reciting the prayers of all fifteen mysteries of the rosary: the Joyful, the Sorrowful, and the Glorious. Julianna sat, her face a mask of contentment and a faraway look in her eyes. Tracy wondered where her mother's mind had taken her.

Chapter 75

LATE SUMMER 1914

The Men and the Truck

"We need a real truck," Ferd said, staring out over the river. They stood beside the barn, where the view of the Columbia River was especially scenic now that they had cleared more trees from the lower field. They used the new field the first year for pasture and planted cabbage the next. The following year they seeded alfalfa, pastured it early, and, with the May rains, let it grow and cut it for hay in July.

"*Ja*, I been thinking that too," Alex replied as they headed for the hay field. They had rigged the back of the car with a large box that could be removed when not in use, but they had outgrown it and needed more room for their produce.

"Josie would never let us sell the Model C," Ferd said with a grin.

"No, she'd turn Fehrenbacher on us, and he's a pretty big fellow."

They worked quietly side-by-side while they mulled over the problem. Ferd had no idea how to find a good used Model T Ford coupe they could convert into a truck.

"We'll see what the other fellows think," Ferd said after a long silence as Alex climbed onto the wagon and urged the horses toward the barn. Once in the barn, Ferd scrambled to the top of the haystack and began throwing forkfuls of hay into the mow while Alex stood on the pile in the barn and spread the hay into the corners.

Heading out to the field for another load, Alex raised the subject once again. "It would be easier to haul hay with a truck." He sounded like he had made up his mind.

The next Sunday, as they were sitting around the picnic table after church, the subject of the truck came up again. Everyone agreed that a truck would be a great asset to the farm. No one wanted to get rid of the car, but they couldn't justify two vehicles. After all, a truck could haul them all to church just as well as the auto. Maybe not quite as comfortably, but nobody was used to much comfort anyway.

"Frank, how 'bout you buying the Model C?" Jack blurted, his face lit up with the idea.

Tracy's forehead furrowed and Frank looked stunned, as if the thought never entered his mind. He slowly shook his head and finally said, "I'm a horse man myself. I've no need or desire to drive a car."

Jack deflated, and the whole table went silent. Frank was the one with three children. They certainly couldn't ride on the back of a truck all the way to Gresham.

"Our wagon is suitable for the family," Frank continued. "We'll go to church when the horses are rested."

"My Frank will buy it," Josie said with a nod to Frank Fehrenbacher, who was sitting across the table from her. "He often speaks of buying one of those 'new-fangled automobiles.'" She glanced at him and said, "Don't you, Frank?"

"Actually, yes." He sounded somewhat surprised, but eager. "I've been saving for a car, and I would definitely be interested in buying Josie's car. It runs well and is fun to drive." He took a sip of coffee. "Besides, then we could drive Frank and Tracy to church when the horses have been worked the week before."

"That would be nice, Frank. Thank you," Tracy said with a smile as she shoved another spoonful of potatoes and gravy into Louise's eager mouth.

"Well good, that takes care of a couple of problems," Arnold said, taking a piece of bread and passing the plate. "Now all we have to do is find a suitable truck."

"I heard Charlie Bramhall say he wants to sell his," Jack said.

"Not a chance," Arnold replied. "That thing's been in the water, and we have no idea what damage has been done to the engine."

"I'll bet he'd sell it cheap." Jack wouldn't let it go.

"How cheap?" Ferd's ears perked up at the word "cheap." "What about the body? When it dropped in the river, something had to bend or break."

"Charlie's gone over the whole thing. He replaced the tie rod and all four wheels," Jack said nonchalantly. "I've driven it, and that truck handles almost as well as our car." He helped himself to a piece of pie. "I'll talk to him tomorrow, but I'll not let on we're interested."

"Good," Ferd said. "Just ask him everything about it that you can think of, especially about river damage."

By the end of the following week, Jack had made himself Charlie's right-hand man when it came to the truck. He helped change tires and spark plugs and replaced the brakes, which seemed to go out on a regular basis when hauling those heavy loads of gravel. He realized that as the road progressed and gravel had to be hauled farther distances, Charlie would need a larger truck. He was not selling the

Model T because it had been in a wreck. Surprisingly, it was still in pretty good shape. "You can't hardly 'kill' one of these goll-durn Model Ts," Charlie said with a howl of laughter.

Jack relayed this information to his brothers and the two Franks the next Sunday afternoon as they sat visiting in the shade of the apple tree.

"Did ya' ask what he wants for it?" Arnold now seemed convinced that it might be all right to buy it.

"No, I wanted to talk it over with you all first."

"I drove it the other day," Arnold interjected. "Drove pretty good."

"I'd like to drive it before we commit." Alex said trying to hide his eagerness to try it out. It was he and Ferd's turn to farm the homestead and a bigger truck would certainly lighten their workload.

"I'll talk to Charlie tomorrow before anyone else has a chance," Jack said. "I'll ask the price and tell him you two need to drive it before we agree to buy it."

When approached the next day, Charlie said, "I'd like to get at least $75 for it. Since it fell in the river, I really can't ask for any more than that."

Jack nodded and didn't say anything for a while, thinking things through. The brothers and Josie had saved up well over $300 with two of them working on the road. They could afford the $75, and besides he liked Charlie. He didn't want to dicker over what he believed was a fair price.

"The other fellows and Josie want to drive it before we buy it." Jack scratched his chin. "Would that be a possibility?"

Charlie nodded. "You bet. I'll bring it up next Sunday afternoon, and your family can all try it out." He smiled and said, "Even Josie."

"Good!" Jack grinned. "She's the best driver of the bunch. You ought to see her crank the Model C."

After they bought the truck, they left the side boards on the bed and had the blacksmith weld a steel frame to slip them into corner pockets. Josie, with Arnold and Alex's help, sewed a canvas cover to make a top and sides for the Larch Mountain produce run. The frame and cover could be removed, so they could use it as a flatbed in the fields.

They used more of their savings to order a two-pronged fork and a couple of large pulleys from the Sears & Roebuck catalog. These would allow two of them to unload the hay more efficiently in the barn. When the apparatus arrived, Frank, having used one like it in Illinois, helped them hang it in the loft. They were now using the best machinery and farm practices available, thanks to the highway job.

Chapter 76

MID-AUGUST 1914

Emma

"I brought these newspapers for you," Emma said as she hurried into the house on a bright September afternoon. "I've been saving them up." The hay was stashed in the barn, and the truck, stacked high with produce, was ready for the Palmer delivery the following morning.

"Oh, thank you," Josie replied. "We're so hungry for news." She sighed. "We were concerned when we heard the Austrian archduke was killed. I've heard several people say they're worried that Germany could get into a war over it."

"They are already at war," Emma said with a sigh. "Germany went to war on August first."

Josie's eyes widened and her face paled. "That is terrible! I'm scared!"

"It's a long ways away from us." Emma being her pragmatic self, spoke in soothing tones. "I don't think we have to worry."

"I suppose not." Josie hesitated. "But the Germans are our people." She spoke with emphasis.

"I think not, Josie," Emma's voice went up a notch. "True we have family in Germany, but we were born in the United

States. We speak English and women have the right to vote. We are Americans!"

"That is true," Josie broke into a smile, unable to stay troubled for long. "It's so good to see you," she said, changing the subject. "How long can you stay this time?"

"I've quit my job. The children have outgrown me," Emma sighed. "So I can stay at least a few days after we get home from Pendleton, and longer if you need me."

"Oh good, maybe you can stay until my birthday," Josie said. "It's high time I had a big birthday party. Catherine Foeller said she was coming out, too. Now that she's working for the phone company, she says she can afford it."

"We can practice for your party when we celebrate Ferd and Arnold's," Emma said, recalling that both celebrated birthdays on September 16, though two years apart.

"Yes, we've been planning for it. We're trying to keep it a secret, but I suspect they have figured it out."

"If Jack's in on it, I'm sure it's not a secret." Emma laughed and changed the subject. "Everything looks so good around here. The fields are well cared for. The truck is loaded."

"I can't believe the difference that truck has made on this farm," Josie said. "We can get twice the work done in half the time. Especially now that all the boys stayed home the last month for harvest." Then smiling her dimpled grin, she added, "I even get to drive it when they load in the field."

They chatted until it was time to fix supper, and then visited some more as they worked. When the men came in, laughing and jostling for the first hug from their older sister, the volume ratcheted up as they caught up on news and events.

When Frank brought Tracy and the children over after supper, there was even more visiting among a family hungry for one another's company. Emma saved every morsel of interesting happenings and shared the events, especially about the families in St. Joseph Church in Portland.

Traveling to town was a treat—one that rarely happened for farm families in outlying areas. Not so much because they couldn't afford it, but because farm was a dawn-to-dark job, especially the last couple of years as the men worked on the new highway while keeping up the chores at home. In many ways they were happy to be done with the grueling work.

Early the next morning, Arnold drove Josie, Emma, and Ferd to Troutdale, and they caught the morning train to Pendleton. Bertie, with a youngster, a toddler, and a brand new infant, had sent her regrets and asked that they take her love with them for their mother.

Chapter 77

SUMMER 1915

Josie's Frank Fehrenbacher

Josie thought of Frank often and wrote to him at least once a week between laundry and other household chores. The highway was completed up to The Dalles, except for the paving. There was talk of building a comfort station on Thor's point. Some of the highway officials, calling it "Crown Point," were opposed on the grounds that it would be too costly.

Frank Fehrenbacher, still living with his parents near the Wands, had left the car with Josie and, catching the train east, continued to work on the road as it pushed from Arlington toward the Idaho line. Before he left, they'd talked about marriage, but Josie told him that she would settle for nothing less than a proper church wedding. "And that takes time and planning," she stated firmly.

"I want to spend the rest of my life with you," Frank had replied softly, taking her hand in his. "I've already got some money saved up, and I've got a small crop of potatoes in. That should bring in a decent bit of cash."

Josie knew all of this. Arnold had told her that they were going to take care of Frank's crop in his absence, but she didn't let on that she had an inkling of the plan.

"I can get a cheap place to rent with a couple of the other fellows up there," Frank went on. "We should be home by the first of September for harvest." Frank put his arm around her then and said, "I'll leave the car here with you. That way you can take my folks and Frank and Tracy to church."

Josie said nothing for what seemed like a long moment. When she did it was just a murmur, "I will start planning." She wished he didn't have to leave.

"I should have a wad of cash when I am done with the job in late August," Frank continued with an optimistic grin.

FRANK WORKED LONG DAYS THAT SUMMER, OFTEN TEN or more hours in the blistering sun of Eastern Oregon, where there were lots of rattlesnakes but few shade trees. It brought back memories of his life on the John Day River when he was a young boy in a place near Early—a settlement that consisted of a gristmill dam in the river and a nearby school.

He and his brothers and older sister had ridden horses to school. He rode behind, hanging on to his older brother, Ben. They left from their ranch and followed the east side of the river to where their father had put up a small covered shed. "To keep the horses out of the weather," he told them. They tied the horses under the roof, crossed the wobbly cable bridge, and walked the short distance to school.

The snakes' affinity to the water was the biggest danger the children faced. They often dismounted and led the horses to keep them from bolting when startled by one. Now back in rattler country, he found himself on high alert most of the time, even while tending to his job.

The days passed slowly one into the next, interrupted only by Sundays, when the road crew found themselves at church and afterward reading their mail and answering it. Most of them spent Saturday evenings in whatever saloon they could find in whatever town they were near, but not before finding a place to bathe and wash their clothes. In this arid country, both dried within the hour.

Frank, who carefully kept his wages in his money belt, avoided the taverns except for a meal. He did allow himself one shot of whiskey a week, drinking it down after a salute to his intended bride-to-be.

One particularly blistering day, they heard a scream from down the line at the gravel pit. Dropping their shovels, they ran to see what the trouble was and found Will, one of the crew members, on the ground clutching his leg and screaming, "Snake! Snake!" Apparently it had struck from a rock and bit him just above the knee. The first man who arrived on the scene tore off his well-worn pant leg and used it to fashion a tourniquet around the upper part of Will's leg. Another fellow took out his bowie knife, grabbed Will's leg, cut a large X into the fang marks and began sucking and spitting the venom out.

After a couple of minutes, another tapped him on the shoulder and took over the job. The first man rinsed his mouth with his canteen.

Frank pulled out his canteen and held it to the victim's lips. "You gotta drink!" he said. "Help us get that poison out of you. Wash it out now," he urged.

Frank didn't really know if that would help, but it gave the patient something to do and kept him busy. He remembered when one of his schoolmates had been bitten years ago, the teacher had told one of the older students to give water to the victim, while she cut, sucked, and spit. She had sent Frank's brother riding to the wounded student's ranch to get his father, who came hurrying to the school. Some of the older boys helped load the injured boy into a dinghy. The man rowed his son the few miles down the John Day River to the confluence of the Columbia where the Twin Bridges store and garage were located. There the boy's father rushed into the garage and hollered for help. The mechanic drove them the five miles to Rufus, where there was a doctor. Frank remembered how his classmate got sick but recovered without even a limp.

The town of Arlington, about thirty miles east of Rufus, was only a mile or so west from where they were working now, so he handed the canteen to someone and ran for the tar-covered wagon. He slapped reins on the horses and brought the rig back, where four of them loaded the poor fellow into it, sticky tar and all.

They followed the road back toward town, slowly so the men riding in back with the patient could continue to perform first aid. When they pulled into the shade of the physician's office, they hollered as they tied up the horses. The doctor met them at the door, his barking dog by his side. He grabbed a kit as soon as he heard them yell "snake bite" and motioned for them to come in.

Once they had lifted the patient onto the table, they stopped briefly for a drink of water. Their only other pause was to let the horses drink from the trough before heading back toward the work site.

The sun was low in the sky by the time they got back. Most of the men had knocked off early, sullen and pensive while they waited for word.

The next day the crew boss met them at the job site with the news that the victim had survived the night, but the doc wanted to keep him one more day. He'd prescribed rest for the next couple of days.

Frank didn't write about the episode to Josie. He figured it wouldn't be a good idea, but he did tell her how much he wanted to be with her and signed his letter with "love." He had never done that before.

SEPTEMBER CAME, WITH ITS COOLER WEST WIND, AND Frank yearned to get back to Pleasant View and his life. It was fine to work, but he was not going to leave again next season. Whatever it took, he would find a way to stay close to Josie.

After one more week on the job, he left and surprised her at the Lampert supper table, where he ate his best meal of the summer. They caught Frank up on the news, and he described his own adventures, conveniently leaving out any mention of rattlers. He couldn't bring himself to worry Josie.

Later, he and Josie drove over to Frank and Tracy's, hugged the children, and caught up with the Wand family news. Then Josie drove him to his folks' place, where they inspected his potato crop. Afterward, they sat under the bigleaf maple in the front yard with his parents and visited past dark. Later when his folks said goodnight, Frank and Josie were alone for the first time in many weeks. He pulled her to him and kissed her with a sudden passion, surprising her.

"Any chance we could drive into Portland and find someone to marry us?" he blurted.

She returned his passion, her heart racing. *Oh God, this is what I want.* She held him tight with happiness, but slowly came to her senses. No way was she going to make the same mistakes her mother had made. She pulled away gently, shaking her head. "We're going to do this right," she said. "I love you so much and missed you every day, but…"

"What's right?" he asked. His green eyes danced, reflecting the light of the kerosene lamp sitting on the table. "This feels pretty darn right to me."

She laughed and the moonlight caught her face in shimmering silver. "Proper is: engagement, banns, and a church wedding." Her laughter turned sober. "And a solid nest egg." She paused, searching for words that would not hurt his feelings. "I grew up poor, Frank, and I promised myself that I would do everything in my power not to have that for my children." She rubbed her eyes and lifted her face to look at him. Continuing, her voice now strong with resolve. "I watched my mother struggle and weep and work. I saw my brothers slave in the fields before they were ten years old and my sisters leave home to earn money because we had no cash." She paused again and said softly, "I didn't even know my sisters until now. They were gone for most of my growing up years."

"I guess I can understand that," he said after a moment of quiet contemplation. "Ma always said that a promise to yourself is the most powerful pledge a person can make."

"I believe that." She took his hand then, and they sat in silence, listening to the frogs sing in the nearby woods.

Though he was disappointed, Frank wasn't surprised. Her brothers had shared with him their family's difficulties. Even though his family was never wealthy, they always had enough to eat. Most of all, he was grateful to have grown up with both parents, even if he did have to share them with eleven siblings.

Even though he ached for her, Frank drove her home. The next morning early, he cranked up the car and headed down the hill toward Gresham where he found a jeweler more than ready to sell him a ring.

"Now if that don't fit her finger, you bring her in, and we'll get it the right size for her," the jeweler told him, peering out from beneath his visor. "And congratulations, young fella."

He nodded his thanks and left, the ring in a white box in his pocket. He knew he would do whatever it took to spend his life with her. If he had to wait another year, then so be it.

Chapter 78

FALL 1915

Josie

Josie felt bad. She knew Frank was disappointed, and so was she. In fact, she often wavered, trying not to be too stern. Perhaps she should just go ahead and run away with him. She heard they could get married in Vancouver, right across the Columbia River.

But then her mother's voice came into her thoughts, almost as if she were telling her not to relent. It was always Julianna's voice saying, over and over: *Remember, I was impulsive—I left my family and ran away with your father.*

She knew her mother had loved her father deeply. It was obvious to the children at a very young age, but was love enough? Josie wasn't sure. What she really knew was that when Frank was coming over, she could not wait to see him and her heart did silly little palpations. He was always on her mind. He made her joyful, even to the point of whistling and dancing with the broom.

"Why are you so happy today?" Ferd asked as he came into the kitchen with a basket of vegetables.

"I'm always happy," Josie retorted. "Didn't you ever notice?"

But it was different now. Even if they had to wait for

marriage, she was sure that Frank felt the same way. She felt it in her very marrow.

He came over for several days in a row, helping the men harvest their potatoes in late October before the crew went to Frank and Tracy's place to clean out their potatoes. When that was done, it was on to Frank's parents place to dig his crop. The men continued to be surprised at the potato size and tonnage per acre they were harvesting.

But the price wavered from fifteen cents to twenty-five cents per hundred pounds, from low to not quite so low, though much less than last year's price of six bits per hundred pounds. The men talked quietly among themselves. Frightened, Josie picked apart their arguments, praying they had false information and the real price was much higher. She and Frank counted on the cash from this crop to put money down on a place of their own.

With her brother's potatoes stored in the Lamperts' barn and Frank's in his parents' barn, they waited for the price to jump. For several days Frank didn't come around, and Josie began to worry. Just a little, and then a bit more.

Then one day, in mid-November he finally showed up in late morning with one of his broad grins.

"And where have you been?" she asked, after she had kissed him much longer than she thought proper.

"Come with me, and I'll show you." He hesitated and said, "But you can't tell a soul."

"What?"

"No, you can't tell anyone what you are going to see."

Josie turned to get her coat. "You'd better put on some boots, too," he called after her. "It's pretty muddy where we're going."

Curious now, she hurried, and soon they were motoring up the lane past Frank and Tracy's, and then past the Fehrenbachers' place, onto a bumpy rutted trail.

"Where in the world are we going?" Josie hollered over the sound of the motor. "It's so muddy you're going to get stuck."

"No, we're fine," he replied, then asked if she was chilly. It was, after all, well into November. The rains had been upon them even before they had finished their potato harvest. Today, however, was partly cloudy with a hint of sunshine peeking here and there.

They drove into the woods, farther back than she had ever ventured as a child. They stopped at a gushing spring where the water came out of the side of the hill between the rocks and tumbled down the bluff, hurrying to taste the Columbia River. There beside the water was a platform with a large metal tank sitting inside a steel frame, much like the one the blacksmith had made for their truck bed.

"What?" Josie asked, wide-eyed. "What is that monster?"

Frank threw his head back and laughed, a hearty laugh that echoed through the trees and back to them as he shut the motor off. He put his arm around her and said, "That, my dear, is a good old-fashioned still."

"Oh my God!" Stricken, she stared at him in disbelief. "Have you lost your mind?"

He laughed. "I don't think so. But if it is gone, you have it along with my heart."

"So what in the world are you going to do with this awful thing?"

"I'm waiting to see if our potato crop is worth selling. If the price doesn't come up to last year's, I'm going to make whiskey out of my potatoes." He said it with resolve. "And if it sells, I'll buy your brothers' crop and make some more."

"No one will drink potato whiskey."

"The Russians do. They call it *vodka*."

"Who do you know that is Russian?"

"Well," he said thoughtfully. "Now that you ask, your brother-in-law Gabe is Russian. He's told me he likes it, and that it is popular with his Old World friends."

"Oh my goodness."

"Yes." He paused and said, "It should bring in some cash, and if I'm careful, I won't get caught."

"Why? Is it illegal?"

"Only if I don't pay taxes on it."

"Well then, you will pay them, of course."

"Of course!"

Chapter 79

EARLY SUMMER 1915

"Catherine Foeller is coming out tomorrow," Ferd said, head down while filing his hoe. "Gonna visit Josie."

"Yup." Arnold didn't seem too interested.

"You want to go down to the depot and meet the train?"

"Nope."

"Me neither."

There was a long pause in the conversation as both men readied to go to the lower field and hoe the corn they'd promised to grow for Frank Fehrenbacher. He had sold so much vodka over the winter that he bought what potatoes the Lamperts had left over and convinced them to raise some more. And even some corn for his still this season.

"How about Josie driving down?" Arnold asked, gathering his canteen and grabbing his sharpened hoe.

"Not a chance. Josie asked me because Tracy is so close to having this baby, she'll have to go right away to her house if the little fellow comes today or tomorrow."

"Well, she asked you. I guess you'd better go," Arnold hollered back over his shoulder.

Ferd, still smarting over Grace after all these years, had decided to be a bachelor. In fact, he and Arnold had made the pact. Neither would marry. They had Josie, and when she got married, they agreed they would pay Emma to come home and cook and clean for them. They reminded each other of that often.

But the problem was that Ferd really liked Catherine. She was pretty and smart and very funny. When she and Josie got together, you just didn't know what to expect. Often when she visited from Portland, the boys would find the two women doubled up in laughter at some crazy thing that had happened to one of them and that would get them all to laughing. Generally sober, he found he enjoyed the levity. Chortles and chuckles were things that had not filled the house often in their growing up years.

Once they had come into the kitchen to find the two girls singing "A Little Bit of Ireland" at the top of their voices.

"What the heck is that song?" Jack asked.

"It's an Irish song," Catherine answered. "It's all the rage in town now. I'm teaching it to Josie."

"Yes, and it's a beautiful song." Josie was indignant.

"But you two ain't even Irish," Alex protested.

"Doesn't matter," Josie shook her head. "It's popular this year. Besides, I like it and it's fun to sing."

"Well, then teach it to us," Ferd demanded.

And soon they all were singing the chorus, with Catherine and Josie filling in the verses. When they finished, they all laughed. Ferd tried to remember the last time he had sung, just for fun, and he couldn't.

Catherine was like that. Josie said, "She always makes me laugh." And Catherine said the same about Josie. Ferd thought she was very pretty, maybe even prettier even than Grace, but he was firm in his conviction that he remain single. Dating and marriage were just too complicated. Besides, he couldn't let Arnold down.

That evening when Jack and Alex arrived home to a cold supper, the subject came up again.

"Someone has to go down to the depot and pick up Catherine tomorrow," Arnold said before Ferd could bring it up. "She's coming out from town to help Josie and Tracy."

"Who's gonna help *us*?" Alex asked, a bit downhearted and worried that no one would be left to cook for them. He enjoyed his hot meals.

"Never mind that." Arnold was persistent. "I'll go to work for you tomorrow, Jack, and you can stay here and go down to Troutdale and meet the train."

"Why can't one of you do it?"

"Because we don't want to."

"You fellows are plain nuts," Jack said, astounded. "She's so pretty, it's a privilege to pick her up." He paused, his face lighting up. "Sure I'll go. She always smells good, says it's lavender or something."

"She says it's lavender," Arnold sing-songed, poking fun.

"Never mind him," Ferd said to Jack. "Just plan on not going off the farm to work tomorrow."

THE NEXT DAY, JACK WAS IN TROUTDALE MEETING THE 10:15 train at few minutes past ten o'clock. He figured he shouldn't dare be late for such a pretty passenger.

When Catherine stepped off the train, he grabbed her luggage, but not before she gave him a big bear hug and told him how glad she was to be out in the country again. Jack helped her into the seat of the truck, went to the front, and cranked the motor over a couple of times, holding his breath. Much to his relief, the engine started on the fourth try. *Thank God*, he thought. It was embarrassing whenever the thing flooded and wouldn't start.

They were off down the little town's main street, getting more than a few glances from local townsfolk. He proudly waved at some people he recognized, knowing some of the younger fellows would ask him later about the lady who was with him. Then again, the attention might be about the ten-mile-an-hour speed limit in downtown Troutdale, which he rarely obeyed.

Deciding not to hurry, he slowed down when he crossed the bridge. After all, he would just have to go out to the field when he got home. He caught a whiff of sweet flowers and wondered again how his brothers could pass up a chance to ride with Catherine.

"Anyone going to come over and fix us dinner tonight?" Jack asked as he walked Catherine to the door at Frank and Tracy's house. He waved to Frank who, looking apprehensive, was working, or maybe just hovering, close to the house.

"We'll cook enough here for all of us. You can either come over close to five and pick it up and take it home. Or you can come over here and eat," Josie said after greeting Catherine.

"I'll come over and eat and take some home for the others," Jack volunteered.

"That's very thoughtful of you, Jack," Josie said, in a voice that sounded like it was anything but gracious of him.

That evening when Jack brought home the dinner, he had news as well. Tracy was very close to having that baby. He lowered his voice and told them, "Catherine said she's worried because she has never attended a birthing before."

"Don't worry," Josie had told her. "I've attended several. We'll be fine and so will Tracy. She's an old hand at this by now."

In the early morning hours of August 28, 1915, George Julius joined the Wand family. His proud father named him George after his brother in Illinois and Julius after Tracy's fun-loving, lighthearted brother, Julius, who answered to the nickname of Jack.

THE NEXT MORNING, ON JOSIE'S ORDERS, TRACY STAYED in bed enjoying the tiny baby resting beside her. She lay there, half asleep, listening to Josie and Catherine giggle in the kitchen. *They are so happy-go-lucky together,* she thought with a smile. *It's no wonder Josie looks forward to Catherine's visits.*

As she dozed, her thoughts turned to Frank and how she had come to love him more than she thought possible. True, she had been attracted to the wisdom in his hazel eyes and his kind, handsome face many years ago when they first met. But no one had told her of the joy of love. It aged like a fine liquor over the years until the smoothness of it brought comfort on cold nights and joyful laughter at mundane things.

She often thought of Logan, and once in a while even wondered if the friendship they once shared would have grown like this. Perhaps not? Would they have grown apart? No one could guess. A question with no answer.

Earlier, Frank had come in after his morning chores to check on them. He'd kissed her gently on the cheek, his whiskers scratchy and comforting, thanking her for being the strong one and for giving the family another beautiful child. She patted his arm and thanked him for being a good friend and husband. Over the years of helping her mother midwife women in the community, she knew that not all husbands were as attentive or as involved in their wives' and children's lives as her Frank.

She loved that he often sat and listened to Ig or Alec recite their school lessons. Ig would soon be twelve and would be into his eighth reader this next school year. She caught herself watching her oldest son as he busied himself with a project and marveled at his attention to even the smallest of details.

Not long ago, Ig and Frank had gone over to Caroline's to visit her son, Julius. Earlier, the widow Caroline had contracted to have a telephone installed in her home. She told Frank it made it easier to check on the family rental businesses in Portland. Wide-eyed when he came home, Ig told his mother about the phone and how it worked: the crank activating a small generator, and the number of cranks equaling the number of rings.

"I can't wait until we can get one," he told her.

"Well, we probably don't need one quite yet. It would be nice to keep in closer contact with our family and the neighbors, though," his mother replied, seeing his eagerness.

She thought now about her two sons. Alec had turned six last June. She smiled when she thought of how compassionate he was. She worried about his tender heart. He loved the cows and worked with Frank every day before school and in the evening, while Ig would much rather be fixing something.

She was constantly amazed at the difference in her children, their personalities—actually their whole beings. Tracy wondered how this newest child would see the world around him and how he would react to its joys and tribulations.

Louise, with the sweetest face at almost two and a half, was developing a personality all her own. Her two older brothers spoiled and protected her. Tracy rarely worried about her, except when she was outside. Then Louise had a habit of exploring on her own.

Just this last week, when Tracy was so large she could not bend over, her daughter was out the door and down the steps before Tracy could call to her. A flurry of activity resulted with Alec finally coming to the rescue, hauling his little sister back to the safety of the back porch and his mother.

Tracy sighed, shook her head, and wondered as she drifted off for another nap how many head shakes it would take to raise their four children to adulthood.

Chapter 80

1916

Josie and Her Frank

Over the spring and summer of 1916, Frank Fehrenbacher did not have to leave the hill to work in some distant town. His still brought in good money the previous fall and winter, keeping him on the farm and not out chasing one job and then another. Josie worried about what might happen if word got out to the wrong people about his vodka enterprise. It was bad enough when he had to leave for weeks on end to find work, but to have him go to jail would be even worse. She heard enough gossip already in the neighborhood.

One late August evening, they sat on a bench on the Lamperts' front porch in the twilight. She had been trying to decide how to bring up a discussion about Frank's possibly illegal enterprise. He said he paid the taxes, but she wasn't sure he had, and it worried her. He had been acting strangely during dinner, making her wonder even more. Was he in trouble? Should she ask him? She searched his face for some hint, but got none.

"What's troubling you, Frank?" she finally blurted when she could stand it no longer.

"Ah," he said softly. "I, uh, uh—I don't know how to say

this." He looked even more perplexed. "I thought it would be easier."

Oh my, she thought, her heart leapt into her throat. *Whatever can it be?* Anger replaced her fear as it became apparent he had gotten into trouble. *I just knew it*, she thought.

"I've been carrying this around for months. I just haven't known when to ask you." He shifted his weight and turned to her, his face contorted with the recollection that she turned him down once.

Her curiosity piqued, she looked him in the eyes, speechless, not knowing whether to be upset or frightened. She just *knew* the rascal hadn't paid those taxes.

"I…I want you to have this." He pulled out the small white box. "That is, if you'll have me," he said as he opened the box and handed it to her.

Josie could only stare. There, sparkling in the evening twilight, glimmered a small, delicate diamond in a gold setting. *Oh my God, is it an engagement ring?* Neither of her married sisters had gotten an engagement ring.

Her voice left her again as she reached to touch it, mostly to see if it was real.

"D-d-don't you like it?" She heard Frank's stutter, far away and a bit panicky.

"I love it."

"Then you'll marry me?"

"You *did* pay your liquor taxes!"

"Well, yes, I told you I had." Frank's hands shook as he took her hand in both of his, and with a determined voice, asked again. "Will you marry me, Josie?" He paused and continued, "I've loved you since I met your train at the depot in Troutdale, and I thought you loved me."

"Oh my, yes!" Josie said finding her voice and squeezing his hand. "I adore you. Of course, I'll marry you."

FERD WAS THE FIRST TO HEAR THE NEWS. FOR HIM IT was not unexpected. Frank had discussed it with the brothers several times, and besides, he spent more time at their house than he did his own. Frank had already asked Ferd to be his best man, if and when Josie would ever consent. So Ferd was the first of the family to wish them happiness and the first to give his little sister a congratulatory hug. Arnold followed, and then the younger boys, and there was no privacy for the happy couple for the rest of the evening. It was well after ten o'clock when Frank finally cranked up the Model C and drove out the back way toward his parents' home.

The next Sunday after Mass, Frank left the crowd visiting outside the little church and, finding Father Brunagle standing with the Chiodos, asked politely if he could have a moment of the priest's time.

"Father, I asked Josie to marry me last week, and she finally said yes." Frank, never having been accused of being shy, found himself uncomfortably tongue-tied. It amazed him as he was one of the only parishioners who stood taller than the priest.

"Well, well," Father Brunagle said, grinning broadly. "I could see it coming, but I'm telling you, I had no idea when."

"Me either. I want to hurry up the banns before she changes her mind."

"Oh, yes, the banns." The priest thought for a moment, figuring the timing. "If I announce the first one next Sunday, that should put the wedding date about mid-November."

"Let's do that then, Father." He grinned back and said, "I think I have waited long enough."

"Yes, I would agree."

Just so there would be no quibble about someone seeing the banns and objecting to the marriage, Frank and Josie set the wedding date for November 16, a Thursday, in late afternoon. The reception immediately following the wedding would be held in the newly finished basement of St. Henry Church. Both families agreed that it was a good date because the potato harvest would be finished, and with any luck, the weather would not be too cold yet. Of course, the weather that time of year was always a concern, though no one spoke of it.

Frank vacillated between walking on air and finding the days passing more slowly than he could ever remember. Suddenly, there were twenty things to do in the short three months.

His father, now elderly, suggested they move into the house with him and his mother and sister, but the more Frank thought about that, the more it made sense for Josie to stay at the Lampert place. They depended on her to keep house, and there was already a bedroom that Frank and Tracy had shared for the first few years of their marriage. It was made to order, but he had to ask Josie.

The next Sunday morning, he suggested they take a ride up the new highway, maybe even as far as Multnomah Falls. A bright sunny September day, it was perfect to explore the road in a car instead of working on it. So after church and the noon meal, Josie packed a small supper and off they went, down past Pleasant View School. They wound around past the gravel pit and then past the Mershon homestead. The road, now graveled, was traveled enough that ruts had started to form.

When they reached the highway, it had been paved with something called Warrenite. Although it was bubbly from the hot sun, the ride was smoother with no dust. They continued east to the Taylor School and on to the Hicks' place. Right before Larch Mountain Road leading to the Brower and Palmer cutoff, they had a flat tire.

Dad-gum, Frank thought, but said, "This won't take a minute to fix."

"Yes, I know how long it takes." Josie laughed. He laughed, too, remembering how good she was at driving. She'd changed several bad tires herself over the last couple of years.

While she waited, Josie wandered back down the road to inspect the art studio. A fellow named Charles Post built it a few years back, and curiosity got the better of her. He lived up in Pleasant View across from Frank's people in a large lovely house he'd named Mae View, after his daughter. Frank had told her that Post had traveled to France to study when he was younger. She peered into the windows, seeing easels and paint cans everywhere, with a paint-stained apron hanging over a hook near the door.

The studio had a magnificent view that looked east up the Columbia River Gorge. In the foreground, Thor's Point thrust out into the Gorge. Below it, standing straight and tall, was Rooster Rock, a monolith with a fish cannery built on the west side. As she studied the open view of the Gorge, it occurred to her that the tall odd-shaped rock looked for all the world like it had broken loose and slid away from the bluff below the point.

No wonder he built his studio here, Josie thought. *This is truly one of the most beautiful places I've ever seen.* She stood admiring the scenic vista; the Washington mountains to the north and the blue hills of the river's south side peeking out from behind Angel's Rest. She stood mesmerized for several moments, saying a silent prayer in thanksgiving for this beautiful piece of God's work, and for Frank.

When she returned to the car, the tire was back on, and Frank was just tightening the last lug.

"You've got to turn around, I want you to see what I just discovered on the other side of the road," she said.

"Yes, it is beautiful isn't it?" he said, and looked at her. "That's right. This is the first time you've been up this far on the highway. I forgot about that."

Once more eastbound, they chatted as they made the twisty curves in good time in their little roadster. Once in a while they passed another car coming their way, and finally they got stuck behind a line of cars following a log truck.

"What do you think of living at your house for a while after we're married?" Frank finally said, deciding to just bring it up. If she wasn't fine with it, then he'd know and could make other arrangements. "There's Frank and Tracy's room."

"I've been thinking about that," she said. "I would agree to that for a couple of years. I don't think Emma is quite ready to leave town, and I know the boys would appreciate my being there."

He nodded.

"With two of my brothers working for neighboring farmers, I believe the ones at home could use another hand," Josie continued. "Besides you're close enough that you can see to your folks and still raise some of your crops over there."

Chapter 81

1916

Josie's Church Wedding

A church wedding was the one thing Julianna had wanted for her children. Josie was the first of the family to have one in their own parish, with their own priest officiating. Over the last few weeks she thought of her mother often, and an idea took root and grew in her mind. All she had to do was convince Frank.

As soon as Josie could get away, she took the train into town. Emma and Catherine both took the day off, and they visited the Meier & Frank department store, shopping for material for her wedding dress. Emma bought fabric for new dresses for their sisters.

Catherine bought a ready-made dress for her duty as the maid of honor, saying, "This is because I work full time for the telephone company and have no time to sew." She paused. "Besides, I'm not very good at stitching." Another few seconds of silence passed before she finally confessed that she didn't even like to do it, which sent the sisters into a fit of laughter.

They had lunch downtown, where Josie discussed her idea and asked their opinion. They asked some questions, and she had the answers, so it didn't take long for them to agree. Then they shopped and window-shopped, giggled, and visited some more. Later in the day while they rested, Emma told Catherine how happy she was to have her in the wedding party.

Silently, Josie breathed a sigh of relief. She felt guilty to not have asked one of her sisters to stand up for her. The problem was she didn't know which one to choose, so she asked that they all be bridesmaids. Now she was sure the arrangement was fine with them.

The following weekend, Emma took fabric over to Bertie, and they spent as much of the two days sewing as caring for the children allowed them. They told Gabe he would have to be happy with leftovers, and he said he was just glad to get supper. Bertie later laughed and told Emma that she thought he felt overwhelmed with both of them and all the children buzzing around.

Back at the farm, Josie and Tracy worked as often as possible on their dresses, too. It didn't take long for them to realize it was better to work at Tracy's so she could more easily care for the younger children.

One evening, Tracy's Frank came home with the mail. Later, after the children were in bed, Tracy settled down with the latest Sears & Roebuck catalog. As she flipped through the pages—lo and behold—there was a sewing machine, a Singer Model 28, three-quarter weight treadle, to be exact. After sewing dresses by hand for two weddings and now a third, plus clothes for a family of four growing children, that machine looked like pure gold. At least that was how she described it to Frank the next morning at breakfast.

She showed him the picture, which he studied for some time. She busied herself feeding little George and seeing that Louise finished her oatmeal, all the while watching for Frank's reaction. She found herself holding her breath.

"I get machinery that I need for the farm," Frank finally said. "I can see how much this would help you here in the house. I know my sisters would've liked one of these."

"Oh thank you, Frank," she exclaimed and kissed him on the cheek, taking care not to get oatmeal on his shirt.

"It looks like something I can probably fix if it breaks," he said, continuing to study the picture. "I'll take the order down to Troutdale this morning, and maybe it will get here in time to be of use to you and Josie before the wedding."

When Josie came over later that day, she too stared at the picture and planned what to continue sewing by hand and what to leave for the new machine. They had to be prepared if the machine did not arrive in time for the wedding gown.

"You're getting the best wedding present," Josie teased, and they both laughed.

Three weeks later Frank brought home Tracy's Singer sewing machine, well in time to break it in with their two wedding dresses and a dress for Louise, who proudly announced that she was Aunt Josie's flower girl.

THE WEDDING DAY, NOVEMBER 16, 1916, ARRIVED DRY and cloudy and mild. The roads, muddy from the last rain, were at least passable, according to Ferd, who left before dawn to check them.

He came back with the news and told Josie that Frank had asked him to drive the family to the wedding and bring back his parents afterward. So Josie, her trousseau packed and her wedding dress safe inside a waterproof basket, climbed into the truck between two of her brothers, while the others sat safely on the bed, leaning against the cab.

They headed over the hill to Tracy's and picked up Ig, Alec, and Bertie's son, Ferd. Bertie and Gabe had arrived at Frank and Tracy's house yesterday afternoon and would bring the rest of both families, as Gabe had sold his first car and purchased a larger two-seated 1915 Model T Touring Car large enough to carry his growing family.

Ig, dressed in a dark, long pants with a white shirt and blue tie, grumbled about sitting on the truck bed. "I don't want my new suit to get splattered," he muttered, rolling his eyes. "I can't wait to get my own car." Everyone laughed except Ig.

People started to gather at St. Henry Church around 10:30, with the wedding scheduled at 11:30. Sophie and Matt arrived with Catherine and the rest of their family shortly after Josie. Catherine joined the wedding party in the basement near the restroom, where Father Brunagle had placed a good sized mirror. The groom and groomsmen were relegated to a corner of the kitchen, well away from the food preparation for the reception.

Josie wondered how Frank was holding up, but protocol stopped her from going to him. So when Ig slipped away and came down to see what was going on, she sent him next door to check on the men.

"They look fine to me," Ig said when he came back, "but your Frank looks sweaty. I can't figure that out, 'cause it's not hot outside."

Catherine laughed and told him not to worry about it, and Josie gave him a quick hug, thanked him, and sent him scooting back upstairs to the church.

Much to Josie's relief, the wedding went off without any problems. Later she told Louise she was the best flower girl she had ever seen, and the toddler danced in a little circle. Never mind that Josie had never seen one before—in fact, she'd never been to a church wedding.

Frank looked relieved at the reception and was gracious to all the well-wishers. Josie admired the way he handled himself with the crowd. He told her later that he was surprised at the number who showed up and suggested that most of them were relatives. "What with both of us having such large families, ya gotta be careful not to criticize anyone," he said with a laugh.

"Where's the honeymoon?" someone asked as Frank and Josie were escorted to their car. Josie had finally discussed her idea with him a month before the wedding, and Frank had agreed.

"We'll tell you when we get home," Frank said with a laugh, then thanked everyone for attending. They headed out of Gresham, turned east onto the newly paved Baseline Road, crossed the bridge, and turned right onto the new highway.

THEY ARRIVED AT THE CASCADE LOCKS WELL AFTER dark and checked into the hotel on Main Street. The next morning they left late and drove to The Dalles, and on the third day they drove to Umatilla.

"It would've been a whole lot faster to take the train," Frank said with a laugh as they walked around the small cowboy town.

"Maybe, but it wouldn't have been nearly as much fun."

On Monday, the fourth day, they drove into Pendleton

and checked into the hotel. The next morning they were at the asylum at 10 a.m. when it opened. Signing in as Mr. and Mrs. Frank Fehrenbacher, Josie assured the nurse that Julianna Lampert was her mother.

They followed the nurse to the sitting room, where Julianna, seated in her rocker, stared at the floor. Her hair had grown gray and much longer, her face sallow and sunken.

"Mama," Josie said as tears streamed down her face. "Mama."

Julianna sat, unmoving.

"Mama, I'm Josie." She took her mother's hand and waited for some kind of reaction. Seeing none, she said, "I got married in a real church, Mama, just like you always wanted."

Julianna stirred and slowly turned, looking at her.

"Josie," she murmured. After a few moments, she muttered something incoherent.

Josie kissed her mother's cheek and said, "I brought my husband, Frank Fehrenbacher, to meet you."

"Frank?" Julianna's voice wavered.

"Yes, Mama, I have a Frank, too."

Julianna, with a quivering hand, slowly reached out to him.

SELECTED REFERENCES

For additional information about the 1905 Lewis and Clark Exposition, Portland, Oregon, visit these suggested websites:

https://www.oregonencyclopedia.org/articles/lewis_clark_exposition/#.YMfPwX5lBLM

https://en.wikipedia.org/wiki/Lewis_and_Clark_Centennial_Exposition

For additional information regarding the Chicago Columbian Exposition visit these suggested websites:

https://en.wikipedia.org/wiki/World%27s_Columbian_Exposition

https://www.architecture.org/news/evolving-chicago/chicagos-ferris-wheel-story/

For additional information regarding Abigail Scott Duniway visit your local library or the Multnomah County Library's collection of books about this dynamic pioneer wife and mother, author, newspaper editor, and suffragette. Listed below are a few suggestions:

Moynihan, Ruth Barnes, *Rebel For Rights, Abigail Scott Duniway*, Yale University Press, New Haven and London, 1983.

Shein, Debra, *Abigail Scott Duniway*, Boise State University, Western Writers Series, Department of English, Boise State University, Boise, Idaho, 2002.

Smith, Helen Krebs, *The Presumptuous Dreamers, A Sociological History of the Life and Times of Abigail Scott Duniway (1834-1915)*, Volume I (1834-1871), Smith, Smith and Smith Publishing Company, Lake Oswego, Oregon 97034, 1974.

As well as these suggested websites:

https://www.google.com/search?client=firefox-b-1-d&q=1893+Chicago+World%27s+fair%2Fferris+wheel

Additionally, I want to recognize local authors whose books and documents I used for background information while writing this story. I recommend these books, many which are still in print, to anyone thirsty for more information about historic Portland, Oregon, and the Columbia River Gorge country.

Dobbs, Linda and Buan, Carolyn, *Portland, Then and Now*. Thunder Bay Press, 2001.

Cowling, Tom, *Stories of Bridal Veil: A Company Mill Town, 1886–1960*, The Bridal Veil Heritage Collection. Acorn Publishing, 2001.

Cowling, Tom, *Stories of…The Ghost Towns on Bridal Veil Creek*, The Bridal Veil Heritage Collection. Acorn Publishing, 2010.

Graff, Beatrice "Bea" Faught, and her committee, *Oral and Written Pioneer Histories*. Compiled by East Multnomah County Pioneer Association, 1956-1970.

Klock, Dorothy, *Crown Point Country Schools 1874-1974*. Self-published, 1973. Revised & reprinted (including pictures) by Clarence Mershon, 2nd Edition 2002.

Mershon, Clarence E, *Living East of the Sandy, Vol. I.* Published for East Multnomah Pioneer Association by Professional Graphic Center. Inc., 1999.

Mershon, Clarence E, *Living East of the Sandy, Vol. II.* Published for East Multnomah Pioneer Association by Clarence E. Mershon, 2003.

Mershon, Clarence E, *The Columbia River Highway, From the Sea to the Wheat Fields of Eastern Oregon.* Produced and printed by Guardian Peaks Enterprises, 2006.

Nesbit, Sharon, *It Could Have Been Carpdale, Centennial History of Troutdale, Oregon 1907-2007.* Pediment Publishing, 2007, 2nd Edition 2020.

Rollins, Charles A. and Kizzar, Marie J, *The Loggers How They Saw It.* Photo restoration & published by Kizzar Publishing. Printed by Inkwater Press, 2010. 2nd Edition 2012.

Thompson, Richard, Portland's Streetcar Lines; *Images of Rail.* Arcadia Publishing, 2006.

Willis, Peg, *Building the Columbia River Highway: They Said it Couldn't be Done.* History Press (Arcadia), 2014.

Woodward, John, *Beneath the Ashes: Oxen, Axes, and China Teacups, Palmer, Oregon.* Edited by Cowling, Tom. Bridal Veil Heritage Collection, Acorn House of Publishing, 1975, Revised Edition 2006.

ACKNOWLEDGMENTS

First I thank the volunteers at the East Multnomah County Pioneer Association and the five local historical societies: Crown Point Country Historical Society, Troutdale Historical Society, Gresham Historical Society, East County Historical Organization, and Oregon Historical Society for their help researching pioneers and events. Without those organizations I would never have known the Model C Ford automobile existed or how Fairview came to be named Cleone, as well as several other delightful factual tidbits.

I am grateful to the Chrysalis Women Writer's Group at Clackamas Community College for their thoughtful and beneficial critiques, chapter by chapter, as I wrote this story. I extend heartfelt appreciation to my many beta readers: Joan Casciato, Ann and Kari Dombkowski, Carolyn Eslick, Florence MacKenzie, Jeanette Pinheiro, Jan St. John, David Wand, and Patricia Wand. As well as my editors, Pat Lichen with her introspective view, Sharon Nesbit offering informative historical editing, and lastly for Christie McClure's copy editing and formatting the early manuscript; all have my deepest appreciation for sharing their masterful skills.

Matt Leamy, Leamy Printing and Design, Troutdale, Oregon, designed the front and back book covers and created the diagram explaining the cover photo. I am grateful for his artistic ability, his helpful suggestions, and his patience.

My great-niece Ellen Coy shared her editing expertise by formatting and editing the later stages of the manuscript. The roles my sisters, Patricia Wand and Carolyn Eslick, served throughout this process are too numerous to mention. Their suggestions and support are invaluable. My brother David Wand, keeper of the Wand family records, offered many historical suggestions, provided several photos, and spent untold hours preparing the map of the Crown Point country in east Multnomah County. I thank all of the above most deeply, as well as Terri Johnsen for her help with photos; Margaret Collins Hietpas for her stories about her great-grandparents; the Schantine family; my cousin Arnold Williams, grandson of Julius (Jack) Lampert, who enhanced photos for this book; and my sister-in-law Dana Wand, an author herself, who shares my enthusiasm.

Last, and perhaps most importantly, I am eternally grateful to my grandmother Theresa "Tracy" Wand and my father, Ignatius "Ig" Bernard Wand, for their patience in answering my interminable childhood questions about the "olden days." A special thank-you goes to my mother, Alice Suhr Wand, for her infectious delight in lifelong learning.

Note: This book would never have been published if it weren't for the friendly, helpful folks at Luminare Press LLC, whose editors, proofreaders, and graphic artists were invaluable. Thank you.

ABOUT THE AUTHOR

RAISED IN THE PLEASANT VIEW DISTRICT OF OREGON'S Columbia River Gorge, Helen attended Corbett schools, square danced at the Grange hall on Saturday nights and hiked the area's forested hills and streams in her free time.

While pursuing life careers, she steadfastly persevered in her search of regional history; joining local historical societies and recording the stories of the children of early settlers. Helen published her first historical novel, *Where Eagles Nest, The Second Wave of Pioneers* in 2013. Her second novel, *Echoes of Forgotten Places,* set in the early 1900's continues the Lampert family saga as they struggle to save their land and maintain their homestead in the wild, rugged terrain above the Columbia River.

Now retired, Helen resides in Gresham, Oregon, where she writes, gardens, and volunteers for the Troutdale Historical Society, the Crown Point Country Historical Society, and the Northeast Multnomah County Pioneer Association.